DEDICATION

To all the members of my reader group, The Front Porch.

ACKNOWLEDGEMENTS

Writing this book has been hard with everything going on in the world. My tribe has been steady, though. Whether they are there in chats, calls, or in spirit, I couldn't have made it through this book without them all.

Candy, Kerstin, and Nikki – thank you for the awesome feedback. Each one of you had a hand in making this book so much better.

Jay, you are a trooper. With all you have going on in your own life, you still manage to create such beautiful artwork that is my covers.

To all the wonderful readers in my group, thank you for taking time out of your days to make me smile and let me ramble on.

To the man: Here's to another year together. I love you.

"Now hear another monstrous sight: Beware:

The sharp-beaked hounds of Zeus that never bark"

~ Aeschylus, "Prometheus Bound", 5th century BC

"Mother Earth, hear me calling
I'm your daughter, you're my home
Sister moon, hear me calling
In the night, we are not alone
Father Sun, hear me calling
Let your strong light shine in me
All my ancestors, stand by me
Teach my spirit to be free."

Pagan Chant – Origin Unknown

STARTING A RYOT

The Hounds of Zeus MC
Book 3

By Faith Gibson

Copyright © 2020 by Faith Gibson

Published by: Bramblerose Press LLC

Editors: Jagged Rose Wordsmithing, Candice Royer

First edition: August, 2020

Cover design: Jay Aheer, © Simply Defined Art

Cover photography: Golden Czermak, © FuriousFotog

Cover model: Thomas Tourville

ISBN: 978-1732864863

PROLOGUE

Rhiannon

RHIANNON WALKED OVER to the window and looked out. The house next door hadn't changed much over the last ten years. She wondered if Jimmy's parents still lived there. If they did and she saw them outside, maybe she could get them to help her. Rhi was looking for any type of movement outside when her bedroom door opened. Her captor had a plateful of pizza in one hand and a grape soda in the other, and he placed them on the dresser.

"Just in case you get hungry." He didn't say anything else before leaving her alone again.

She *was* hungry, but did she trust him not to poison her? He said he was protecting her, so that had to count for something. But it didn't mean he wouldn't drug her. He'd already proven that when he knocked her out. Rhi had already decided to bide her time, so if he did drug her and she passed out, that would make her time there in her old home go by quicker without her having to interact with him. Rhi picked up a slice of pizza and sniffed it. It didn't smell funny, and there didn't appear to be any type of powder sprinkled on it. She shrugged, then took a bite. Rhi moaned around a mouthful of extra cheese. God, how she'd missed pizza. She devoured the three slices and downed the soda.

1

Never again would she take greasy food for granted. She wiped her hands on the paper towel he had brought, then resumed staring out the window.

Movement next door on the second floor caught her eye. Was that... Jimmy? It looked like him, but she couldn't be sure. Rhi reached for the lock on the window when she felt her body getting numb. "Son of a bitch."

"Momma, what's wrong with the bunny?"

"It looks like a larger animal attacked it. That's a hard lesson nature teaches us. There are always bigger, stronger of our kind we have to watch out for."

"But I want to help it."

"You can't help it, Baby."

"But I can. Momma, please. I have to try."

Momma sighed, smiling. "Okay. And when it dies, I'll help you bury it."

Rhi sat down on the ground next to the bunny and cried for the tiny creature. She didn't understand how something could attack such an adorable animal. A breeze blew through the trees, whipping Rhi's hair around her head. Rhi concentrated on the rabbit. She closed her eyes and prayed to the goddess, the way her momma taught her. She had no idea how long she sat outside with the animal, gently rubbing it's back where it wasn't harmed. When her mother returned to take her inside for the night, she gasped.

The bunny, which had been happy in Rhi's arms, startled at the presence of someone else and wiggled until Rhi set it down. It hopped away, stopping next to a larger rabbit.

"Rhi... Honey, what did you do?"

"I fixed it."

"But how?"

"The way the goddess told me to."

"Oh, Rhi. I knew you were special, but that..." Momma sat down next to Rhi and grabbed her hands, looking at Rhi's palms. "Rhiannon, you have a gift, but it's yours and yours alone. You can never tell anyone what happened. Not even your daddy. Okay?"

"But why, Momma?"

"Because it's too special to share with anyone. Promise me you'll never tell anyone how you helped the bunny."

"I promise."

Rhiannon's back ached. When she opened her eyes, she realized why. She had fallen asleep on the floor. No, she had passed out from being drugged. Again. Stretching her legs, she noticed something strapped around her ankle. It was a piece of black plastic attached to a band. She pulled on it, but it wasn't coming off. *What have you done to me now?*

CHAPTER ONE

Rhiannon

RHIANNON IGNORED THE preacher as he droned on about the same things he had for the last ten years. One would think the man would find something different to talk about. There were sixty-six books in the Bible, but he only taught from those in the Old Testament. Rhi had been raised pagan, so she tried to tune out what he yelled about. Fist pounding, spit flying. Why he felt he had to yell to get the message across was beyond her. Ever since she and her father had come to live in their new community, Rhi had been the outcast. Whenever she found herself in trouble, she had to read the Bible as penance. What she found was Jesus of the New Testament was a kind man. One who loved everybody, much like her goddess. When she brought that up – not about the goddess, but that Jesus was kind – her preacher yelled at her for insolence.

Her father had left the punishment up to the preacher since the man was the shepherd of their little town. Rhi hated them both. Hated her father for taking her away from their home after her mother died. Hated him for allowing *his* mother to tell him how to raise Rhi. Hated the preacher for keeping Rhi from having friends. For keeping her away from the plants. Away from anything resembling normalcy. Rhi had gone from a loving home where she and her mom tended the gardens daily, laughing and enjoying life to the

4

fullest, to one where she wasn't allowed to speak to anyone other than the other girls who lived in the small community. Instead of going to public school with hundreds of kids her age, Rhi sat in a classroom with forty kids of varying ages.

"*Ow*," Rhi hissed to herself when the older woman standing next to her pinched her arm. Rhi glared daggers at her father's new wife. Well, she wasn't new; they'd been married for years.

Marion wasn't supposed to be there. This morning's sermon was for the single women. Single men had already heard their daily lesson, and couples would hear their lecture next.

"Anna, you need to pay attention," Marion scolded, using the name the preacher insisted upon because it sounded more biblical and less worldly. Rhiannon loved her name. She'd been given it by her mom who loved old rock 'n' roll music. Another thing they had shared a love for. While kids her age listened to the newest hits, Rhi had loved singing along with her mother to the older stuff.

Rhi looked around. The other single women had already left the church, which explained why Marion was there. Rhi had been lost in her head again. Without a word to her father's wife, Rhi stood and strode out of the building and over to the dining hall. Her stomach rumbled, but she wouldn't get to eat for a while. Not until the others had been fed. She hated her job of washing dishes. Another punishment for being different. For being difficult, as the preacher put it. She hated her life. Nothing about it was hers.

Martha scowled at Rhi as she did every time Rhi was even a minute late. Rhi ignored the older woman and got busy cleaning the dishes from the couples' meal. Every day was the same. Get up. Shower. Head to the dining hall for breakfast, then clean the dishes. Go to church. Go back to the dining hall. Clean more dishes. Eat quickly so she could clean even more dirty plates and utensils. Rhi's hands had long ago gone from smooth to a wrinkled mess. Hands that were no longer allowed to feel the softness of flower petals or the silkiness of leaves or the soothing richness of soil as she tended to the plants that had once filled her life with happiness.

Normally, Rhiannon rushed through her job so she could get back to the quiet of her little cabin. Once she finished with the noon meal, she had a couple hours' free time where she enjoyed her solitude. The two women who shared the cabin had jobs that kept them away all day, and for that, Rhi was thankful. Today, though, she had been summoned to the preacher's home. She spent her two hours of solitude dreading the upcoming session. Couples who came to the town already married were allowed to live together. Single men and women weren't permitted to be together without a chaperone, and that happened to be the preacher. Rhi had caught the eye of a man named James. An older man whom Rhi had no interest in. But that didn't matter. Women in their community had no say in anything. Everything was dictated by the men, overseen by the preacher. Another reason she hated him.

Instead of a smaller cabin like the rest of the residents had, the preacher's home was a three-bedroom house which sat back away from everything in their town. Rhi dragged her feet as she walked through the trees. Rhi couldn't stop and enjoy the greenery. She wasn't allowed to commune with nature, and that was the one thing that had killed her soul soon after being taken from her home. A guard was two steps behind, always accompanying Rhi so she wouldn't stray from the path.

This wasn't the first time she and James had been together for what the preacher deemed their courtship. They had been meeting three days a week for several weeks. Rhi found it ridiculous. She might have been thirteen when she was thrust into this new life, but she never forgot what it was like out in the real world. Where families sat down to

6

dinner together. Where kids were allowed to play in the streets or visit each other's homes and watch TV or play video games. Where they rode the bus together to school and ate lunch together. Where boys and girls laughed and flirted with one another. She would never forget, because one day, she would be back in that real world.

One day needed to come sooner rather than later because the preacher had promised James he could take Rhi as his wife. It didn't matter that Rhi couldn't stand James. It didn't matter that she flinched any time he tried to hold her hand. If the man tried to kiss her, she'd probably vomit from repulsion. She didn't find him attractive in the least. In fact, she found no redeeming qualities in him whatsoever. Why couldn't one of the younger men have sought her out? Oh, because she "needed a firm hand." Rhi needed a man who could keep her in line. Yes, that's what the preacher had told her the first time he'd summoned her to his home and informed her of James's intentions to marry her. Rhi had proven his point when she laughed and said she refused to marry James or anyone else in their town. It was one of the few times she had spoken in the last few years.

Sure, there were some younger men who were nice enough to look at, but even they weren't *nice* enough for Rhi to give up on her dream of one day escaping their little community. The men weren't allowed to take a wife unless they were over thirty. Rhi tried not to imagine what those younger men did to relieve their sexual tension. She couldn't imagine masturbating in a cabin with two or three other men sleeping only feet away. They probably took care of business in the shower like she did.

When she arrived at the preacher's home, he and James were waiting for her outside. She knew today would be one of those times she was allowed to accompany James into town. The first time had been a shock to her system. Rhi would never forget it.

"Anna, today you are going to accompany James to town for

7

supplies. *This will allow you both a bit of privacy. I have arranged a set of clothes for you to wear on your trip so you will blend in with the outsiders. You are not to speak to anyone other than James. You will represent our town with the same meekness I have attempted to instill in you over these last ten years. If you disobey, you won't like the consequences. Am I understood?*

Rhi nodded. The preacher sighed, but he didn't chastise her for not vocalizing her words. She hadn't spoken to anyone since the day she argued about marrying James. When the women joined the preacher in hymns, Rhi simply moved her mouth, pretending to sing along. Music, which had once been a huge part of her life, held no joy when the message was praising a god she didn't believe in.

"Go inside and get changed. The clothes are in the yellow bedroom. You have two minutes."

Rhi was excited at the prospect of leaving their little town, even if it was with James. It had been ten years since she'd been in the outside world, and she wanted to see how much it had changed. What she had missed out on. What she had to look forward to one day. She hurried inside and switched out the drab cotton pants and top for a dress that looked like something her grandmother would have worn. Did the preacher think this would make her stand out any less? When she walked back outside, both men eyed her appreciatively. As much as the man spoke against sins of the flesh, he didn't school the lust in his eyes when he raked them down her bare legs.

"Where are the pantyhose? It's too cold for you to go without them."

Rhi just stared at him, refusing to answer. Grabbing her by the arm, the preacher dragged her back inside. "Put the stockings on, Anna, or you'll find yourself in solitary for a month."

That didn't sound so bad to her. When she was confined to the square concrete room, she didn't have to clean all the dishes or have her "dates" with James. On the other hand, she wanted to go into town. She grabbed the offending garment off the bed, kicked off her shoes, and sat down on the floor with her back to the preacher. She hadn't worn stockings since she was little, and as *soon as she pulled them up her legs, she cringed at the way they clung to her. Rhi hated the way the nylon rubbed against the hair on her legs. That was another thing she hated about where she lived. Women weren't allowed to shave. The preacher was probably afraid someone would use the razor to slash their wrists.*

Rhi shoved her feet back into her shoes and pushed past the man to head back outside. He grabbed her wrist, stopping her from getting far. "I'm warning you now, Anna. You make one move while on the outside, and you'll regret it." Rhi faked a smile and nodded all while contemplating his murder. No, she wouldn't ever actually kill someone, but a girl could fantasize. In her heart, she knew what the preacher and his little community stood for was wrong, but she was one against many. She continued to stare at him innocently, and finally, he loosened his grip. When she walked back toward the front door, the preacher's wife, Nadine, was standing at the kitchen entry, arms crossed over her chest. Lines creased Nadine's forehead, making her look older than she likely was. Her gray hair was plaited, and the braid hung over her skinny shoulder.

Ignoring the scathing look, Rhi continued on outside where James was waiting. His eyes darted to Rhi's legs, then he schooled his features. Probably because the preacher was right behind her. "James, you know the rules. I expect you back within three hours."

"Yes, Brother Josiah. Thank you for this opportunity. I won't betray your trust. This way, Anna."

Rhi ignored his offered arm and walked ahead of James to the truck. He rushed to open the door for her, and when he attempted to help her climb inside, she turned and frowned at him. Polite or not, she didn't want him touching her any more than he already did. Sitting in Josiah's living room, side-by-side on the sofa while the preacher and his wife watched over them was more than she could stomach. Whenever James reached for her hand, Rhi put both of them under her legs, knowing James wouldn't dare touch her there. Not with their chaperones watching over them. Nadine never spoke during their "dates," but her eyes spoke volumes. She didn't approve of Rhi on a personal level. She had been vocal on more than one occasion regarding Rhi's insolent behavior, but that

9

was only when her husband wasn't around.

Rhi watched out the side window as James drove them off the property. "Oh, I almost forgot." He stopped the truck and held out a black cloth. "You are to be blindfolded during the drive as a precaution."

Rhi shouldn't have been surprised because she knew their little community was a secret from outsiders. She grabbed the proffered cloth and tied it around her head. It wasn't like she wanted to find her way back, but then she realized what this was about. They didn't want her able to find her way *out*. When music filled the cab of the truck, it startled Rhi. It had been so long since she'd heard secular music, and her soul mended just a fraction.

"I hope this is okay," James said. "I like making the supply runs because it gives me a little more freedom." Rhi didn't respond, but she did tap her fingers to the beat, using her thighs as drums. James made small talk, but Rhiannon ignored him so she could count the songs. When James announced they had arrived, Rhi smiled inwardly. Not counting the seconds in between when the deejay spoke, there were nineteen songs, which meant they had been gone approximately an hour. She wasn't sure how far in miles that was, but it was farther than she could walk without James or Josiah catching up with her if they figured out she'd left. She didn't think she could walk that far without giving out. Sure, she walked everywhere she went, but their community wasn't that large. She doubted she got in half a mile per day. No, she'd have to figure something else out.

"Go ahead and remove your blindfold," James instructed. Rhi slid the fabric off and blinked against the brightness of the afternoon sun, taking a look around. After a few more turns, the town came into view. It was larger than she'd expected, and there were all kinds of new stores she'd never heard of. A lot could happen in ten years, and judging by the design of cars, the marquees on the storefronts, and the updated clothing people wore, she had missed all of it. She focused on the women walking around and the way they were dressed.

Couples strolled together, holding hands, laughing about some secret only the two of them were privy to. Moms corralled *their children, smiles mixed with flustered expressions. Teenagers joked with one another, being young and enjoying their lives with no rules keeping them from speaking to one another. People went about their lives freely. This. This was what she was missing. Rhiannon almost wished she'd not made the trip with James. Seeing how others were able to go about their days the way she did when she was young was a painful reminder of the way things had been before her mother died.*

"Here's what's going to happen," James said, breaking Rhi out of her rumination. "We're going into that restaurant and have dinner. Afterwards, we'll go gather the supplies."

Rhi frowned, wondering if this was a test. Josiah hadn't said anything about them eating while they were gone. She crossed her arms over her chest and shook her head.

"Brother Josiah isn't here. You and I can't get to know one another if he and his wife are always there watching over us. Consider this our first real date. If you behave, I'll bring you to town on all my runs. And you can stop with the silent treatment. I know you can talk. You just choose not to. If you're going to be my wife, I'll expect you to address me appropriately when I speak to you. I'm also looking forward to hearing you cry my name after we have sex. Because Anna? We are going to have sex. You're as good as my wife already. Now get your ass out of the truck."

Rhi looked around, taking in all the different stores. If she played her cards right, she might be able to —

"Now, Anna." James came around to her side of the truck and opened the door. She unbuckled and slid to the ground. When James reached for her hand, Rhi cringed. James wasn't overweight, but he was slightly balding and sweaty, even in the brisk autumn air. He practically dragged her into the sandwich shop. If this was his idea of a date, he was lacking in the romance department, but she already knew that about him. When they got to the counter, he ordered for them both. Plain sandwiches, no chips, and water to drink. The least he could have done was to get her a cookie, but sweets weren't allowed. Goddess, what she wouldn't give for one of the fresh-baked, double chocolate treats.

For whatever reason, James always chose the small deli.

He never ordered anything other than the plain sandwiches. She figured it was because money was tight. Or maybe James was cheap. Although it was suppertime, Rhi wasn't hungry. She nibbled on the sandwich anyway, not wanting to give James a reason to rush through their meal. James had chosen a booth, sliding in opposite instead of sitting next to her. Her back was to the door, so all she had to look at was the hallway leading to the restrooms. And the back entrance. *Yes.* Rhi pointed to the hallway, indicating she needed to use the facilities.

"Yeah, okay. But hurry it up. We're going to be late as it is."

Rhi nodded in agreement. She rushed down the hallway, knowing he was watching. When she opened the door to the ladies' room, she glanced back. Rhi could no longer see James, which meant he couldn't see her. She ran to the back door, flung it open, and took off down the pavement behind the buildings, not caring that it was pouring rain. Rhi knew she didn't have much time before James figured out she was gone.

Chapter Two

Ryker

THE WIND PUSHING against Ryker's face was chilly. It should have been exhilarating. Should have been enough to break him out of his shitty mood. It wasn't. It had been two months since he found out his lover was using him, but he couldn't shake his anger. He needed to find a way to get over it because it was affecting everyone around him. He had been a surly bastard for the last twenty years. Ryker had chilled somewhat when he found out his baby girl was alive, but seeing the scar marring her beautiful face reminded him how he failed both Mac and her mother. Juliette had been the love of his life, and he hadn't been home when she'd been taken.

Ryker couldn't take away the scars. His daughter's face wasn't the only place damaged. Her heart had been ripped apart from having her baby sold to a strange couple. Her soul shattered when her boyfriend had been shipped off to another cult. Ryker couldn't fix Mac's face, but he'd find Elijah for her. Or die trying.

Other than Mac, the only bright spot in his life was Maveryck's twins. Major and Marshall had a rough first four years, but now Mav and Natalia were giving the boys their best life possible. The kids were so damned cute, and they never failed to make Ryker smile. The little dudes had taken to biker life naturally, and if they had their way, they'd never ride in a cage. They had their own sidecar, tricked out by their Uncle Hayden. The Hounds took a group ride a month back, and the boys had waved at every car they passed. When they stopped for gas, one couple had been so enamored they wanted photos of the twins. Maveryck, being the papa lion he was, had bristled. He was overprotective of his cubs, but Natalia had soothed the beast. Ryker wasn't jealous. Okay, maybe a little. He was glad both Mav and War had found their perfect mates, but his heart ached at not having that connection. That bond with a female who had his back.

He'd had that for a short while with Juliette, and damn if he didn't long for it again. Living hundreds of years as a Gryphon, Ryker didn't want to go the rest of his long life alone. But he had responsibilities to both the MC and his family. Responsibilities that included finding a new organization to work with, which led him to the trip he was currently making. Nexus, the underground organization of assassins he contracted with the last twenty years, had been corrupted from the inside by Ryker's lover. Cassandra had fooled Ryker into believing he meant something. What he meant to her turned out to be a means to an end.

Sutton, Ryker's father, had turned over the MC to Ryker so Sutton could focus on helping people get out of the cults the Hounds disbanded. Not all cults were part of the Ministry, the worldwide group responsible for the near apocalypse that brought the world to a halt some thirty years ago. Some of the groups were harmless folks who wanted nothing other than to live off the grid, away from the "sins of society." But others, which were part of the Ministry, were no better than the Nazis of old or the white supremacists whose goals were to rid the world of anyone who didn't fit their idea of a perfect civilization.

Josiah Talbert was one such person. He and his brother, Gideon, were the worst of the worst. Josiah had been the one to take Juliette, but it had been Gideon who kept her.

Had taken her child – Ryker's child – and given Mac to someone else to raise. Gideon was responsible for Elijah being taken away from Mac, all because one of Gideon's guards wanted Mac for himself. Ryker had to find Josiah and get Elijah back, if the boy was still alive. Until Lucy – War's daughter and family computer expert – located Josiah, Ryker had to focus on the other part of the family business, and that was their mercenary work.

Sutton's friend and former army buddy, Trenton Shepherd, started his own vigilante organization years ago, and now Ryker was headed to meet with the man. Feel him out to see if they were a good fit. When Sutton contacted Shepherd, the man invited Ryker to his office so Ryker could see for himself how things were run. That was Ryker's first clue the organization was completely different than Nexus. Ryker had no idea where Nexus's headquarters was located. He didn't know the person in charge. Secrecy had been their first rule. Handlers had code names. If he hadn't worked with Cassandra on a job, he'd never have known the former operative-turned-handler's identity.

It was almost three when Ryker arrived at the address given. He'd expected to meet Shepherd at a business location. Somewhere the building doubled as a front for something legitimate. Instead, the address was a large house sitting back off the road behind a tall, iron fence. Ryker rolled up to the gate and put his bike in neutral. There was no guard shack, but there were cameras watching his every move. Ryker removed his helmet, turning his face up so whoever was watching the security feed could see him clearly. A few seconds later, the gate swung open, and Ryker replaced his helmet before easing his bike down the long concrete drive. Before he could shut the bike off, the front door opened, and Shepherd stepped out onto the porch. The man was in his sixties, but he was as fit as anyone thirty years his junior. Gray hair was cropped close; steel-blue eyes smiled while still looking intense. He was dressed in dark jeans and an untucked, button-up shirt with the sleeves rolled back showing off corded forearms. The man hadn't let himself go, and Ryker appreciated that.

When Ryker removed his helmet and climbed off his bike, Shepherd grinned. "If I didn't know better, I'd think I was looking at your father."

"I'll take that as a compliment." Ryker ran his hand over his head, doing his best to get rid of the helmet hair.

"As you should." Shepherd was one of the humans who was aware of Gryphons. The fact that Sutton trusted the male with their secret said a lot about what kind of man he was.

Ryker held out his hand. "It's good to meet you, Shepherd."

"Likewise. Come on in. I hope you don't mind, but I asked Quinn to join us."

"Not at all." Ryker didn't mind. He wanted to meet the handler he'd be working with.

As Shepherd led Ryker into his home, he said, "Your father is one of the best males I know, and I expect the apples didn't fall far from the tree, if you'll pardon the saying."

Ryker smiled, appreciating the sentiment. "We like to think so. The five of us, while all different in personalities, do our best to emulate our father. He *is* the best man we know, and we live to make him proud." Ryker followed Shepherd, taking in the home. When they reached the office, a pretty woman looked up from where she was working at the desk. The female was early thirties, dressed in jeans and a fitted sweater. Her long, brown hair was pulled back in a low ponytail. She stood and held out her hand.

"Ryker Lazlo, I'd like you to meet my daughter, Quinn. She's in charge of our organization. I passed the mantle to her six years ago, much like Sutton turned over the MC to you." Shepherd stood aside while the two of them shook hands. Her grip was firm, like her countenance.

16

"It's a pleasure." Quinn gestured to the chairs across from her. "Please, have a seat."

Ryker took the one closest and set his ankle on the opposite knee.

"Shepherd shared a little about what happened with Nexus, but I'd appreciate it if you told me everything," Quinn said as she returned to the leather chair behind the desk. Ryker filled both father and daughter in on everything except the fact that he and Cassandra had been lovers.

"This isn't the first we've heard of Nexus being less than aboveboard. I'm glad you came to us. We can always use people with your particular skill sets. And the thing that sets us apart from them is I am the only handler. You won't be dealing with an unknown using an alias. I personally vet every request that comes through. Of course, you'll conduct your own due diligence once you accept the contract, and if you find something you believe I've missed, I not only welcome you discussing issues with me, I expect it. I'm not infallible or perfect. I would rather you share concerns if I miss something than for an innocent to be taken out. Having said that, it's rare I make that costly a mistake." Quinn pushed a piece of paper across the desk. "These are the terms of our contracts. I think you'll find the payout is generous." Ryker did a double take when he read the percentage. When he glanced at Shepherd, he was smirking.

"With Quinn being the only handler, we don't require as much on our end as an organization paying ten or more handlers. Our overhead is low, and we feel if we pay top dollar, we get top results in return."

"Do you have any questions?" Quinn leaned back in her chair, confidence clear on her face.

"Yes, when can we start?" Ryker was excited about working for the father-daughter team. The fact that Shepherd and Sutton were still friends after all these years was a bonus.

"Immediately." Quinn opened her desk and pulled out

17

a phone. She handed it over and said, "All contracts will be sent to you through this phone. The messages are encrypted, so you'll need to give me a sequence you wish to use to unlock them. Only you, Shepherd, and I will have the code, plus anyone you wish to share it with, say your second-in-command. All communication will come through this device. Should you wish to speak with me at any time, just send me a message. Normally, we don't invite operatives into our home, but our fathers go way back. You are the only associate who knows where we are. We'd like to keep it that way, so unless we invite you back, I'd prefer any future meetings be done elsewhere."

"That's understandable and not a problem. Until the last few assignments went astray, we never met anyone from Nexus. I don't foresee needing to meet back up."

"Excellent. If you'll choose your code, I'll make note of it in your file. Other than that, welcome aboard." Quinn stood and held out her hand. Ryker shook it, and the weight of the last months lifted from his shoulders.

With his new phone in his pocket, Ryker said goodbye and headed home. The ride back to New Troy was much more enjoyable until he ran into a storm. Ryker didn't mind a little rain, but the sky let loose with a downpour. The roads were slickest when they first got wet. He was used to it, but he didn't trust other drivers, so Ryker took the next exit. The town wasn't large, but it had more than just a truck stop. The strip of road boasted a few convenience stores, several hotels, and plenty of restaurants to choose from. Ryker was used to eating alone, and it had never bothered him. Until lately. Sure, he had his daughter to share meals with, and Mac was getting a little more comfortable going out the more she spent time with Lucy, Kerrigan, and Natalia. All three females were different, but they each gave Mac something Ryker couldn't. Something she'd never had, and that was friendship.

Having lived in a cult, McKenzie had endured a life

Ryker would never understand. He did his best to make up for the lost years, but it was hard with all the time he spent away from home. Rory did her best to make Mac feel like she was part of the family, but his daughter was still leery of leaving the house, even if she was going to visit her grandmother. Ryker hoped by getting Elijah back – because he would find the boy – that Elijah would bring Mac out of her shell. Now that he had gotten the club back in the mercenary game with the Shepherds, Ryker could return his attention to searching for Josiah, and in turn, Elijah.

Ryker pulled into a convenience store lot to get gas while letting the storm pass. He shut the bike off, crawled from the seat, and went about sliding his card and stuffing the nozzle into his tank. Ryker turned his gaze to the strip, searching the various signs for restaurants. Tires screeched and horns blared. Ryker waited for the crunch of metal, but it never came. What he did hear, however, was a man yelling.

"Anna! Get your ass back here." Ryker searched for an escaped pet, but what he found was a young woman running through the parking lot. Her eyes were wild, full of fear, and her hair and dress were plastered to her body. She ran past Ryker toward the back of the building. A few seconds later, a plain, white van barreled into the lot, and the driver jumped out once he was parked. He searched the area, and the way he fisted his hands told Ryker all he needed to know. If those hands caught up with the woman, they wouldn't be tender. Ryker replaced the nozzle while keeping an eye on the man.

"Is there a problem?" Ryker asked.

"Stupid wife. She's mental."

That was the wrong thing to say. If the woman did have mental issues, her husband shouldn't call her stupid. "She ran that way." Ryker pointed the opposite direction from where the woman had gone. He didn't understand why he did it, why he was getting involved.

He's going to hurt her.

His Gryphon liked to point out the obvious sometimes.

"Are you sure?" the man asked, looking past Ryker.

"Yep. I saw her double back and head for the Mexican restaurant."

"Fuck!" The man got back in his van and pealed out of the parking lot. Ryker waited until the vehicle was on the road before striding behind the convenience store. There was no sign of the woman, so he used his eagle's vision to search the area. He still didn't see anything, but he heard the slightest shuffle coming from inside the dumpster. Ryker lifted the plastic lid and peered inside expecting to see a rodent. Curled up among the garbage bags was Anna, looking like a drowned rat. An adorable, shaking, drowned rat.

"It's okay. He's gone." Ryker used a soothing voice, not wanting to cause any more trauma.

A set of red-rimmed eyes stared at him. "He'll be back," she whispered. If Ryker weren't a shifter, he probably wouldn't have heard her.

"Is there someone I can call to come get you? Do you need the cops?"

Anna shook her head. "They'll just take me back."

Ryker wanted to ask, "Back where?" but if she did have mental issues, he could guess the answer. "And you don't want to go back?"

"No. I'll never go back. They've kept me prisoner for too long. I'd rather die."

"Well, you can't stay in here." Ryker looked around to make sure they were alone. It wouldn't take a rocket scientist for the man to figure out Ryker was talking to his wife if he drove back around. "Your husband seemed worried."

"He isn't my husband," Anna seethed. She curled farther into herself if that were possible. "He's nothing more than a warden looking to recapture his escapee. If he finds me, he'll take me back. I can't." Her eyes were pleading, and Ryker cursed himself for caring, but that was his nature. It was why he and all the Gryphons had been created. To care for and protect humans.

"What's your plan? Do you have somewhere to go? You have money to get you there?"

Anna shook her head. "I-I didn't plan on running, but I saw an opportunity and took it. Please, you can't tell anyone where I am."

"Like I said, you can't stay here. How about I get you a hotel room for the night while you figure out your next steps?"

"Why would you do that? I don't have money, and I'm not having sex with you as payment."

Ryker cringed, but he couldn't fault the girl for jumping to that conclusion. Not in this day and age. "I'm doing it because it's the right thing. My family, we help people all the time. It's what we do. We get people out of bad situations and help get them back on their feet. My parents have a place you can stay for a while. They'll get you medical care if you need it. Medications or someone to talk to."

"I don't take medicine. Don't need it."

Thankfully, the rain had slacked off to nothing more than a drizzle. The back door opened, and a clerk came out carrying a garbage bag. She froze when she saw Ryker. "Uh…" The girl looked around, fear pouring from her body.

"You want me to help you with the bag. You're going to go back inside and forget you saw me," he instructed, using his Gryphon voice, the one that manipulated someone's mind.

"Can you help me?" the girl asked, handing over the bag. Ryker took it, and the clerk returned inside. When the door closed behind her, Ryker dropped the bag inside the dumpster, well away from Anna. He didn't want to use his voice on Anna, but time was of the essence. "You're coming with me. I'm getting you a hotel room and something to eat."

Anna climbed to her feet, but she couldn't get out of the container on her own. Ryker leaned over and lifted her easily. When he had her in his arms, his lion purred.

Not now.

But she smells delicious.

She smells like garbage.

Underneath that. She smells like home.

Ryker ignored his beast. This woman didn't need them sniffing her. She needed help. It wasn't going to be easy getting her to a hotel unseen on the back of his bike. He didn't have a spare helmet, and if the man from the van was in the area, Anna would be too exposed anyway, wearing a dress and torn pantyhose. "Stay here." He propped her up behind the dumpster, jogged to the front of the store, and moved his bike to a parking spot at the side of the building. As he walked back to where he left Anna, he pulled up the app for a car on his phone. While they waited, Ryker tried to ease Anna's fears.

"My name's Ryker. Ryker Lazlo. I'm taking you down the street to the Continental. I'll order room service and then I'll call my mom. She can bring you some clothes and anything else you need. Okay?"

"Yeah. Uh, thanks. I'm Rhiannon Spencer, but you can call me Rhi."

"Rhi? The man you were with called you Anna."

Rhi rolled her eyes. "That's what they call me. They thought Anna sounded more biblical. Less pagan."

"And are you? Pagan?"

"Does that matter?"

Ryker didn't get the chance to answer because their ride pulled up. He held the door open for her, then climbed in beside her. Since he already input the destination into the app, the driver pulled out of the lot, glancing in the rearview mirror. "Not many people call a car to go three

22

blocks."

"My bike wouldn't start, and I hate walking in the rain." Ryker gave the man his best scowl, which wasn't hard to do since it was his normal visage. The driver remained silent after that. Within minutes, they were out of the car and in the hotel lobby. Ryker checked them into a suite for three nights, since he didn't know how things would go with Rory or how long it would take his mom to get there. He signed his name and accepted the key cards, then placed his hand at the small of Rhi's back as he led her to the elevator.

They stood on opposite sides of the lift, which was good. Ryker didn't need her close. When he opened the door to the suite, Rhi didn't move. "I vow on all that's holy I won't hurt you," Ryker soothed, once again using his Gryphon voice. He needed her to trust him. She nodded once, then stepped into their room.

"Wow." Rhi walked around the living area, stuck her head in the bedroom, came back out, then stared at the sofa.

"Why don't you have a seat?"

"I'm all wet."

Ryker stepped into the bathroom, returning with several towels. He placed one on the sofa, then handed the others to her.

"Thank you." Rhi wrapped a towel around her dress and used another to dry her braided hair. She finally sat, twisting her hands in her lap. "Dang, that's a big TV."

Ryker thought it was small compared to the one in his own living room back home, but he didn't know Rhi's story or where she'd been held. She didn't seem dangerous, and she wasn't. Not to him, anyway. If she did have mental issues like the man suggested, she could be a threat to herself. Ryker would have to watch her closely.

CHAPTER THREE

Ryker

INSTEAD OF GRILLING her like he wanted, Ryker asked, "Are you hungry? Because I am." He found the room service menu and handed it over. "Pick anything you want."

"Oh, my god. I haven't had a cheeseburger in forever. And fries. I need all the fries."

While Rhi was gushing over the food choices, Ryker finally allowed himself to study the woman. She was young, early twenties. Long, dirty-blonde hair was braided. She wore no makeup, but she didn't need it. She had a natural beauty. Her eyebrows were a little bushy, like she'd never seen a pair of tweezers, but it didn't detract from her looks. Her dress was frumpy and ill-fitting. Her shoes were basic slip-ons, and something about them niggled at his brain. Big, blue eyes met his when she asked if she could get two orders of fries.

"You can have all the fries you want." In that moment, Ryker would give her anything she wanted, and he mentally chastised himself. Rhi wasn't his. She was a young woman in need of help, not anything else. She couldn't be anything else.

Yes, she can.

Shut it. We don't know enough about her.

I don't need to know more. She's ours.

Ryker ignored his Gryphon, even though he wanted to

24

agree. There was something about the woman that called to him for more than protecting her. "Did you settle on the cheeseburger?" Rhi nodded. "What do you want on it?"

"Everything. And a Coke. No, a milkshake. Chocolate. No, a Coke."

Ryker's heart broke for her. Had she been denied something as basic as food and drink choices? If she'd been held in an institution, she probably had to eat shitty food. He took the menu from her and decided on his own meal. The cheeseburger did sound good. He called room service and placed their order. When he asked for a six-pack of sodas and four orders of fries with extra ketchup, Rhi's eyes filled with tears.

"What's wrong?" He hung up the receiver and squatted in front of her. The need to touch her was great, but he kept his hands on his own thighs.

"It's been so long since I had junk food. I…" Rhi closed her eyes, tears rolling down her cheeks. "I don't know why you're doing all this, but thank you."

"You're welcome. I'm going to call my mom and let her know what's going on. Then I'm going to put you on the phone with her so you can tell her your sizes. I have to warn you, she'll probably outfit you like a biker chick. Jeans and boots are her usual dress code."

Rhi's smile was sad. "I miss wearing jeans, so I have no problem with that. Um, is it okay if I use the restroom?"

"Of course. You're not a prisoner, Rhi. You don't need my permission to move around. I would ask you don't leave the room alone, since we don't know if that man is still looking for you."

"James. His name is James, and I guarantee he's still looking. He won't dare go home without searching everywhere."

"Do you want to talk about it? You know what? Don't worry about that. For now, go use the bathroom. I'll call Rory, that's my mom, and then we'll eat. Everything else can wait."

"Thank you, Ryker Lazlo. I'm really glad you're the one who found me."

"Me too." Ryker stood and moved out of the way so Rhi could go to the bathroom. When she got to the door, she looked over her shoulder and smiled. It was full of appreciation, not anything else. It didn't matter, though. The reason for it still transformed her face, and Ryker merely inclined his head. His lion was purring, and the last thing he needed was his shifter getting the wrong idea. He was helping a human in need. Nothing more.

Liar.

Rhiannon

RHI SHUT THE bathroom door and leaned against it. Closing her eyes, she sent up a silent prayer to the goddess, thanking her for her freedom. For sending Ryker Lazlo to find her. It had to be divine intervention for someone like him to be the one to find her in the dumpster. If what he said was true, his family helped people in need, and there was no one needier than her. Pushing off the door, Rhi took a look at herself in the mirror. Somewhere along the way, she'd lost her head covering. Her hair had come loose from her braid, so she unplaited it. Instead of redoing it, she left it loose around her shoulders. It had been years since she'd been able to wear it down. Years since she'd been allowed to be who she truly was.

Since she told Ryker she needed to use the bathroom, Rhi took the time to pee and wash her hands. She was in serious need of a shower after hiding amongst the garbage, but that would have to wait until she had clean clothes. She didn't know where Ryker's mom was or how long it would take her to reach them. There were two plush robes hanging on the back of the door, but she didn't have deodorant, so she decided to wait a while. When she returned to the living area, Ryker was on the phone.

"Here she is." Ryker handed the phone to Rhi. "Talk to my mom."

"Hello?"

"Hello, Rhi. My name is Rory. How are you holding up?" Rory's voice was a soft, southern twang.

"Uh, pretty good. Except I need a shower. I stink."

Rory laughed, and the sound was bittersweet. Rhi hadn't heard her own mother's laugh in years. "Yeah, Ryker told me about you hiding in the dumpster. That was smart thinking on your part."

"I don't know about smart, but it worked."

"Tell me your sizes, and I'll stop and get you some clothes on the way." Rhi did as Rory asked, guessing at her size, but then she nervously looked over at Ryker. There were some things she didn't want to talk about in front of the handsome man.

Ryker must have read her mind. He stood from where he was sitting at the table and said, "I'm going to step out in the hallway a second."

When the door closed behind him, Rhi said, "If it's not too much trouble, I need some pads. I'm due to start my period in the next couple days."

"Not a problem. Ryker said your hair's long. Is there any special shampoo and conditioner you prefer?"

"I honestly don't know what's out there now. Where I've lived the last ten years, we made our own stuff. So, just get whatever's cheapest. Same with deodorant."

Rory made a humming sound. "I'll take care of everything. Sutton, that's Ryker's father, and I will hit the road here in the next little bit. If you're already asleep, we'll see you in the morning."

Rhi choked back a sob. How'd she get so lucky to be

found by these amazing people? "Please, don't rush on my account. You're already doing too much for someone you don't know."

"Nonsense. This is what our family does. If you think of anything else you need, just have Ryker call or text. I don't know your story, but I promise, everything's going to be okay now."

"Thank you. For everything."

"You're welcome. I'll talk to you soon." Rory disconnected, and Rhi stared at the phone. It had been ten years since she'd seen anything modern. Anything that wasn't approved by the elders. Cell phones weren't on the list.

Ryker strode in the room, holding the door for the man pushing their food cart. Ryker instructed him to put everything on the table. He tipped the guy, then motioned for her to join him. Rhi's stomach grumbled just thinking about what was waiting for her. When Ryker removed the domed lids, Rhi stared at all the food. It had been so long since she'd enjoyed a meal. She should be used to eating home cooking, even if it was prepared in massive quantities. It had been devastating, going from a happy teen with two parents to a miserable girl whose father lost his mind when his wife died. Rhiannon's mother had been a ray of sunshine, living her life as though each day could be her last. Daisy – Rhi's mom – had tried her hand at painting. She took drum lessons. She even went skydiving. But she was never happier than when she was in her garden. Rhi never minded helping her mom. Working with dirt, learning about the various herbs, that had been their thing. Something just the two of them did. Rhi's father never complained openly, but his mother did. Grandmother would call Daisy a witch. She would chastise David for allowing Daisy to influence Rhi in things that went against God's word. It wasn't until Daisy died that Rhi understood how much influence her grandmother had over Rhi's dad.

"Aren't you going to eat?" Ryker had one of the thick, juicy burgers halfway to his mouth.

"Yeah, sorry. Just lost in thought. Thank you again." Rhi sat down across from Ryker. It was tempting to sit next to him, but putting space between them was necessary for her sanity. Where she'd escaped from, unmarried men and women weren't allowed to eat together. They weren't allowed to spend time together. The preacher talked more about sins of the flesh than any other topic, but Rhi didn't think they pertained to her. Not once had she entertained an impure thought about a man. Until she was locked inside a hotel room with Ryker Lazlo.

Rhi took a tentative bite of her burger and groaned. It was better than she remembered. "Oh, man. This is so good." She dipped a couple fries in ketchup and shoved them in her mouth. She closed her eyes as she chewed, relishing the saltiness. All the food she'd eaten the last ten years had been bland and unremarkable. Next, she took a sip of the cold soda Ryker had poured over ice. It was so good she chugged half the glass before it burned her throat. When she let out a belch, Rhi slapped a hand over her mouth and looked at Ryker. His expression was a mixture of confusion and laughter. What she didn't see was condemnation. "I'm so sorry," she said anyway.

"Nothing to apologize for. My brother Hayden would give that a seven."

"A seven?"

"It had depth but not a lot of volume."

"Your brother rates belches?"

Ryker grinned. "He does. Hay is thirty-two going on twelve. He's still a kid at heart."

Rhi let that sink in. It was hard for her to remember how her life had been before her mom died. Burping at the table wouldn't result in a lecture or having food withheld as punishment. After eating half her food, Rhi was stuffed. She'd been taught not to waste her food, but the portions were never this large.

"You full already?"

"I'm sorry. I didn't realize the burger would be so big. I'll finish it. I promise."

"You don't need to eat it if you're full. It's not like it'll go to waste." Ryker took her half-eaten cheeseburger and put it on his plate. "I'm a growing boy," he joked and took a bite. At least she thought he was joking. There was nothing boyish about the man. He was ruggedly handsome with dark, messy hair and equally dark eyes. He wore jeans and black boots. Not the same kind some of the men did where she came from. These were scuffed leather, and they looked well-worn.

"After we eat, I need to go get my bike from the convenience store. Will you be okay here by yourself?"

"Sure. Can I watch television while you're gone?"

Ryker frowned. "Of course. You can do whatever you want. All I ask is you don't leave the room."

That wouldn't be a problem since she had nowhere to go. "Thank you. Is it okay if I turn it on now? I'm really excited to see what kind of shows are on these days."

"Rhi, how long has it been since you watched TV?"

"Ten years. When my dad and I went to live in our new home, we weren't allowed to have one." They didn't have anything that could be a distraction from the teachings of the Bible. Rhi had not been allowed to take any of her toys or books with her when they moved. Her life had ended the day she lost her mother in more ways than one.

"I'm sorry if I'm overstepping, but can I ask where your mom is?"

"She died when I was thirteen. My dad said it was a brain hemorrhage, but my grandmother said it was God's punishment. She never liked my mom because Mom was different. Grandmother called her nasty names because my mom refused to go to church."

"You mentioned earlier they called you Anna because it

30

sounded less pagan. Is that why your grandmother didn't like your mom? Because she wasn't a Christian?"

Rhi nodded. "Mom was a free spirit. At least that's what she told me. I never understood what she meant until later when someone called me that. I was always getting into trouble because I wanted to help in the garden, the way I helped my mom. I was laughed at when I talked to the plants. Mom said they were living things and thrived when you treated them as such. When I told my preacher that, he chastised me and wouldn't let me near the garden afterwards."

"Rhi, was your preacher in charge of where you lived?"

"Yes. Everyone thought he was a good man, but I thought he was a jerk. I used to get in trouble for talking to the boys. Before we moved, I had lots of boy friends. Not boyfriends, but friends who were boys. Our neighborhood was filled with them. I rode bikes with them. Played video games. We lived in a cul-de-sac back then. Everyone knew everyone, and it was normal for everyone to play together. We all went to the same school. Rode the same bus. I called their mothers 'mom' the same way they called mine that. Nobody cared that I talked to plants or that I liked to play in the dirt. They were my friends. But when my dad took me to live in our new home, I didn't have any friends. There were a few girls in my school, but they didn't like me very much because I was always getting in trouble. And if I got in trouble, everyone was punished."

Rhi didn't like thinking about those early days, so she picked up the milkshake and took a sip. When the chocolate hit her tongue, she smiled. "My mom used to make the best milkshakes. She always added extra syrup to the top. Said it was a little dose of love."

"She sounds like a wonderful person. Did she name you Rhiannon after the song?"

"She was the best, and yes. We would listen to music while we worked in the garden and sing all the old rock

31

songs. Stevie Nicks was her favorite singer." Rhi's heart still hurt thinking about her mom and the happy life they'd had. "I'm going to watch TV now, if that's okay." She didn't wait for Ryker to answer since he already said it was okay. She picked up the remote and hit the power button. Sinking down onto the sofa with her milkshake, Rhi got lost in clicking through the hundreds of channels. Ryker left to get his motorcycle, and only then did she let herself dream of a future away from her home and Brother Josiah. Away from the man who courted her so he could see if she would make a good wife. Away from the father who had taken another, Godlier, wife. A future where she could have a little house of her own where she could talk to the plants because they were living creatures. A place she could openly worship the goddess, the way her mom taught her.

When Ryker returned, he untied his boots and toed them off, setting them beside the sofa. He sat on the end opposite her. Rhi held out the remote, but he shook his head. "I'm fine watching whatever." He laced his fingers behind his head and stared at the TV. Rhi was more interested in watching him than the show about gardening she'd come across, but that would be rude. It would also give her body ideas she didn't think were wrong, no matter what Brother Josiah said. Her mom had talked to her openly about sex as soon as Rhi got her first period. Told her she was a woman even though her body would continue to blossom like the fragrant flowers in their garden. Daisy explained how Rhi would respond to boys differently as she got older and what would happen when she gave into those urges. Her mom never called sex ugly or sinful. She said with the right person it would be beautiful. Life-altering. But she also told Rhi she should be selective in who she gave her body to because it was a gift. One that should only be given to someone who would appreciate it. Nurture it. Respect it.

Rhi had never found someone worthy, but she

32

wondered if Ryker would be. He was older, but that meant he was experienced in the ways of the world. The world outside her former home. He was a man who rescued people like her. Him and his family. "Will you tell me about your family? You mentioned a brother. Is he the only one?"

"Not by half. I have six older sisters. Three sets of twins who live in Texas. That's where we're from originally. Then there's me. Maveryck and Warryck who are twins are next oldest. We all were born in Texas. Then we moved to New York, and Hayden and Kyllian were born here. My dad, Sutton, he formed a motorcycle club a long time ago. He handed the presidency over to me about twenty years ago. War has a daughter, Lucy, and his female's name is Kerrigan. Maveryck has a set of four-year-old twins – Major and Marshall. Those kids are so fucking cute. Mav's woman is Natalia. I have a daughter, McKenzie. She goes by Mac. She's only been in my life a few months, but that's a story for another day. Depending on what you decide to do once Rory gets here, you'll probably meet everyone at some point. The Hounds too. That's the name of our MC, The Hounds of Zeus. They're all great males, and every single one of them would protect you with their life. It's not just my blood family who helps those in need, but my biker family too."

"You mentioned your twin brothers have women. Do you have a woman? I mean if you have a daughter…"

"Mac's mom died a long time ago, but no. There's no one in my life now. I have too many responsibilities to worry about having a mate."

Rhi found it strange how Ryker spoke of the women as females and mates. She found it disheartening how he didn't have time for a woman. And just because he was the first man she came across outside her home, that didn't mean he was someone she should seek out as a companion. Why did that make her sad? He was gorgeous and kind. It wasn't just his looks; it was his heart she was attracted to.

Mostly.

Rhi didn't ask any more questions. She tried to focus on the television, but the events of her evening were catching up with her. She tried to stay awake until Rory got there, but her eyes wouldn't stay open. Rhi slid down, resting her head on the arm of the sofa, and exhaustion won the battle.

CHAPTER FOUR

Ryker

RYKER WAS CONVINCED Rhi had escaped a cult. She wore the same slip-on shoes he had seen when they went into Gideon's compound, and the way she described the preacher and all the rules... It all added up. Whether or not it was one associated with the Ministry, he didn't know. Ryker wanted to find out, but it was clear Rhi was tired. He didn't ask all the questions he was curious about. He was going to let Rory have that conversation. When Rhi asked if Ryker had a woman, he didn't miss the hope in her eyes, but he wasn't the male for her. He might want a mate, but Rhi had been sheltered the last ten years of her life. She was too young and naïve for someone like him. If Ryker did find a mate, she needed to be tough like Lucy or Natalia.

But she needs someone like us to care for her. Protect her. Love her.

No, she needs someone softer, like Kyllian.

Kyllian's a child.

So is she.

Look at her. Really look at her. She's all woman. Just because she's not wild like Juliette was doesn't mean she's not strong. Rhiannon has to be tough to have escaped from that bastard James.

Ryker should be pissed his Gryphon was comparing Rhi to Juliette, but he wasn't. He understood the need for a

35

mate. The need of connecting with another person. Yes, he wanted it. Enough time had passed since he lost his wife. He agreed with his beast that Rhi was strong, but Ryker didn't think he was right for her. She was most likely a virgin. That wasn't a bad thing. Ryker would be honored to be her first under normal circumstances, but Ryker wasn't a gentle lover. It's why Juliette had been perfect for him. She'd been wild and willing. It was that same untamed abandon that had drawn him to Cassandra. As with other lovers he'd taken over the years, Ryker sought out those who matched his penchant for down-and-dirty fucking, not gentle lovemaking.

Ryker was still sitting on the sofa watching Rhi sleep when his phone vibrated. It was a text from his mom letting him know she and Sutton had arrived. He responded with his room number and stood to gather himself. If anyone could read Ryker, it was his parents. Sutton more so than Rory. His father was adept at taking one look at someone and knowing where their head was.

He opened the door before they had a chance to knock. Rory hugged Ryker as she did every time she saw him or his brothers. His father was carrying several shopping bags, so Sutton lifted his chin. Rory walked over to where Rhi was sleeping and studied the young woman. Ryker couldn't talk freely with his parents in the living room with Rhi, so he motioned toward the bedroom. Sutton set the bags on the bed, and Rory began emptying them. While she placed the toiletries in the attached bathroom, Sutton leaned against the far wall.

"Tell us everything."

Ryker had already told them about Rhi running from James and hiding in the dumpster. He recounted their earlier conversations. "I have no doubt her father moved them to a compound. Whether or not it's part of the Ministry is yet to be determined."

Rory began putting the clothes in the dresser. "That

36

poor child. First, she loses her mother, then she's hauled off to live in a cult. I'd like to know what made her run now."

"I thought you could talk to her. She needs a woman's touch." Sutton stared at Ryker, eyes narrowed. Ryker knew what his father was doing – reading the situation. "Don't look at me like that, Pop. You know Mom is better equipped to handle this. It's what she does. What you both do. It's why I called you."

"Fair enough. We got a room down the hall. When she wakes up, give us a call, and we can all sit down over breakfast. Might I suggest you carry her to bed? She doesn't look comfortable on the sofa." Sutton smirked, and Ryker pinched the bridge of his nose. *Meddling Gryphon.*

Rory laughed softly. "She is pretty. And strong."

"And way too young. She's barely older than Mac, for fuck's sake."

"So? We know age is a number that means little in the scheme of things. But think of it this way; the younger she is, the more years you'll have with her." Sutton clapped Ryker on the shoulder. "See you in a few hours."

Ryker followed his parents to the door. Once it was closed, he turned and stared at Rhi. Her hair was fanned out over the arm of the sofa.

She looks like an angel.

His Gryphon wasn't wrong, and his dad was right; she looked like an uncomfortable angel, so against his better judgment, Ryker strode over and lifted her in his arms. She smelled like garbage, but underneath was her unique scent, something earthy and sweet, and Ryker had to admit it called to him. When she took a shower, it was going to be harder to ignore. Rhi stirred in his arms but didn't wake. She nuzzled his neck, her breaths tickling his skin. Ryker didn't linger. He took her to the bedroom and set her in the middle of the king-sized bed. He removed her shoes, then pulled the covers up. Rhi turned onto her side, her hair falling over her face. Ryker pushed the strands back, enjoying the softness. If she were someone different, he would imagine grabbing fistfuls of her long mane, tugging it while fucking her hard from behind. But she wasn't one of his lovers who knew the score. Who liked it rough. She was a young woman who'd been sheltered the last ten years and no doubt had been taught sex was something that should only happen between a married couple. Or at the least between a couple in love.

Rhi was a beautiful, naïve woman, and Ryker wasn't going to taint her innocence.

Rhiannon

RHI STARTLED AWAKE. It took her a few seconds to remember she wasn't at home. The previous day came barreling back, and she felt both elated and nervous. The clock on the bedside table showed it was after eight. That made her smile. Sleeping late wasn't allowed at home. Pushing the plush covers off, Rhi sat up and stretched. When she went into the bathroom to pee, there were full-sized toiletries lined up on the counter. *Rory.* Rhi was excited about meeting Ryker's parents, but first, she needed a shower. It was bad enough Ryker had been around her all evening, smelling the stench of trash. There was no way she was going to meet his parents in the same condition. She turned on the water, letting it heat. After peeing, she stripped out of her dress and pantyhose, gathered the things she needed, and climbed under the spray. Rhi took her time, enjoying the wonderful water pressure. While the conditioner sat on her hair, she shaved her legs and her armpits, singing *her* song. The one her mom took her name from. When she was finished, Rhi was loath to get out, but she was ready to meet Rory and Sutton. To find out how they were going to help her get away and start a new life.

Just as she turned the water off, there was a knock on the door. "Rory put your new clothes in the dresser," Ryker called out from the bedroom.

"Thank you. I'll be out in a few minutes."

"I'm going to order breakfast. Anything in particular you want?"

"Can I have pancakes?" Rhi had always loved her mom's pancakes. She had loved everything her mother cooked.

"Yes. Bacon or sausage?"

"Bacon, please."

"You got it."

Rhi waited until she heard the bedroom door close before she stepped out of the tub. Not that she thought Ryker would sneak back in to get a look at her naked, but she didn't want him to see her with no clothes on. Rhi's body was nothing special. If Ryker figured that out, he'd have no reason... *Stop.* She couldn't allow herself to get caught up in him. He was probably going to hand her off to his parents and be on his way. Rhi finished in the bathroom quicker than she wanted. She found the new clothes and underwear where Ryker said they'd be. The bras and panties were lace. They felt strange against her skin. Rhi chose a long-sleeved tee that was softer than anything she'd ever felt. She pulled on a pair of jeans that hugged her legs. It felt weird wearing them after so long of having to dress like every other woman. Even the married ones were required to wear the oversized pants and tops that did nothing for their figures.

Not wanting to keep Ryker waiting, Rhi towel-dried her hair, removed the tangles, and left it down to air dry. Ryker was standing by the window, looking out. He turned, smiling when he saw how she was dressed. "I hope the clothes are okay. I told you Rory would dress you like a biker chick."

Rhi looked down at herself. She was barefoot, so until she put on the soft leather boots, she thought she looked like a normal woman. The few women she came across when she and James made their weekly trips to the city were usually in jeans and sweatshirts or tees under jackets. She had only recently been allowed to leave home, so she hadn't been to the city during summer. For that, she was thankful. She'd definitely stand out if she'd had to wear her cotton pants.

"Rory and Sutton would like to join us for breakfast, if that's okay with you."

"It's fine. I'd like to thank her for all my new things. I'll have to find a job so I can pay her back."

"That's not necessary. Like I said before, it's what we do."

Before Rhi could argue, there was a knock at the door. Ryker went and paused only a second. Without looking through the peephole, he opened up to let a couple in. A couple who could in no way be Ryker's parents because they weren't old enough.

The woman was a pretty blonde dressed as Ryker had described Rory. The man was dark-haired like Ryker. The woman approached Rhi, assessing the clothes. "Hello, Rhi. I'm Rory, and this is Sutton."

"Uh, hi. You… thank you for the clothes. But…" Rhi didn't want to be rude about the couple's ages, but she had to ask. "How is it possible you're his parents. Is he adopted?"

Rory laughed. "Oh, I promise you I birthed him and all his siblings. Sutton and I have good genes, that's all. Now, why don't you come sit down and tell us about you and the man you ran from?"

A knock sounded on the door, and Ryker let in a young woman bringing room service. The woman kept eyeing Ryker, and although it brought out a jealous streak, Rhi couldn't blame her. Ryker ignored the woman's glances except to sign the paper she presented. When everything was spread out on the table, the four of them sat down. As Rhi poured syrup over her pancakes, she wondered where to begin.

"Coffee, dear?" Rory asked.

"Oh. I've never had coffee. Is it any good?"

Rory poured her a cup. "Personally, I can't live without it. There's only one way to find out if you like it or not. Some people like it black, some with cream or sugar or both. Take a sip, and if you don't find it to your liking, we can doctor it up until you do."

Rhi took a small sip. It was hot and bitter. She shook her head. "Nope." She added cream from a miniature pitcher and stirred it with her spoon the way Rory had. That was better, but she decided to try it with sugar. After adding a teaspoon, Rhi found it to be perfect. "Yes. I like it." Ryker was watching her. Something about his expression was off, but she figured it was because she didn't know how to act like a normal person. Rhi knew where she lived they didn't do things like most other people. She hadn't forgotten what it was like before her mom died and her dad carted her off to live with the church community.

"I'm not sure where to start," Rhi admitted after taking a bite of pancakes. She didn't want to talk right then. She wanted to enjoy her food while it was warm.

"At the beginning is always a good place," Sutton suggested. Ryker's dad was unlike any man Rhi had ever met. His voice was soft, like he didn't want to scare her. He had greeted Ryker with a firm hand to the shoulder, but the affection was there when he looked at his son. Something Rhi hadn't seen since her mother died. Where she'd been taken to live, affection had been discouraged. Only married couples were allowed to touch outside their cabins, and that was nothing more than holding hands. Even the kids didn't receive hugs or words of encouragement from their parents. Rhi hadn't had a hug in ten years, and as that thought hit her, she couldn't hold back the tears.

"What's wrong?" Ryker was kneeling by her chair before she could blink.

"Just thinking about my mom. Sorry." Rhi wiped her eyes and blew out a breath. Ryker returned to his seat, but not before he shared a look with his parents.

"Nothing to be sorry for." Rory patted her hand. "Talk can wait. Let's enjoy our breakfast first, okay?"

Rhi nodded, thankful for the reprieve. While she enjoyed the best breakfast she could remember having, Rory talked about her newest grandsons, Major and Marshall. Rory told Rhi how they'd been kept from Maveryck for the first four years of their lives and how the family was trying to make up for lost time. Rhi was fascinated. So much so she wanted to meet the little boys. She'd been around other kids when she was younger, but hearing how their family almost fought over spending time with the boys was both wonderful and bittersweet. It was clear these people were nothing like those she'd lived with the last ten years. They reminded her of her mother, and Rhi knew she was going to be okay.

When breakfast was finished, Rory added more coffee to Rhi's cup. Rhi mixed in more cream and sugar because black coffee was just nasty. The four of them moved to the living area. Rhi and Ryker took chairs, while Rory and Sutton sat next to each other on the sofa. Right next to each other. Rhi smiled at their closeness. That's how her parents had been before her mom died. Even with her grandmother harping on her dad about Daisy being "of the devil," David had loved her mom.

"My mom, Daisy, she was everything to me. She was what some liked to call a free spirit. My grandmother called her a witch. Grandmother didn't like it that my mom was pagan. It caused more than one fight in our house. Not between my parents, because my dad, David, he loved my mom. He saw nothing wrong with her tending our garden.

42

Or the candles she lit when she talked to the goddess and asked Her to bless our home. Our home *was* blessed until it wasn't. Mom died when I was thirteen from a brain hemorrhage. My grandmother said it was God punishing her for having the devil in her. My mom didn't believe in the devil, so I thought my grandmother was just being mean.

"Soon after we buried my mom, my grandmother convinced my dad he needed help with me, and she convinced him to take me to live with a group of super religious people. It was completely different from what I was used to. There were no televisions or radios. It was a little town all on its own where men and women had to keep separated unless they were married. Instead of living in a house with my dad, I was put in a cabin with two other girls. Both were older, and since they'd been there a lot longer, we didn't get along that well. They did as they were told, but I just wanted to go home. The only thing there was that remotely reminded me of home was the gardens. I would sneak off and talk to the plants. For that, I was punished. The preacher said it wasn't right, talking to the vegetables and herbs, but I knew better. Mom taught me they were living things, and living things thrive by being nurtured and cared for." Rhi took a sip of coffee to gather her thoughts.

"Ryker told us the man you were with, James, called you his wife."

"He wishes. Brother Josiah had approved our courtship. It was the only reason I was allowed to leave our community and accompany James to the city when he went on a supply run." The mood in the room instantly changed. Rhi could feel the charged energy, and she knew it wasn't good. "Please don't make me go back. I don't want to marry him. I don't want to marry anyone there," she whispered.

Rory stood and came over to kneel at Rhi's feet. The pretty blonde took Rhi's free hand in hers. "We would never

43

make you go back. Rhi, do you know a young man named Elijah?"

Rhi stared between the three of them. How did they know Eli? "Yes. He came to live with us several months ago. Brother Josiah told the congregation Elijah was a troubled soul and none of us were to speak to him. Said he had to do his counseling in silence. How do you know Eli?"

"He used to live in a compound similar to the one you ran from. Elijah and my granddaughter – Ryker's daughter – McKenzie, they fell in love. Mac had been promised to one of the guards, so they took Elijah away."

"What happened to Mac?" Rhi was afraid to hear the answer.

Ryker stood and strode to the window, looking out. Rory stared after her son a few seconds before answering. "Long story short, she tried to run away. She was caught, but not before being attacked by the dog tracking her. Also, she had gotten pregnant, and Gideon, Josiah's brother who was running their compound, took the baby and sold it to someone outside their group. Warryck was looking for a missing woman, and he found her when she was being chased the same way. He rescued her and then we went in and took down Gideon. Since you were also trying to escape, I'm going to assume you have no love for Josiah?"

"Not at all. I think he's a creep. My dad…" Rhi blinked back the tears. "He changed once we went to live there. I'd always been closer to my mom, but Dad, he uh, he listened to what Josiah said. Became distant and allowed me to be raised with all these new rules. I went from having friends I played with every day after school to not being allowed to speak to the boys. I didn't understand why things were so drastically different. I tried to talk to my dad about it, but I got in trouble for that too. I stayed in trouble for the first couple years, and I finally figured out how to keep my head down. I stopped talking. I did my studies. Learned all these stupid Bible passages I didn't believe in. I became the perfect, submissive woman I was expected to be, all while biding my time. I prayed to the goddess every day like my mom taught me to, but I did it in my head. While Josiah was shouting about the wrath of God, I was inwardly seeking the blessing of the goddess. I'm sorry if that's something you don't agree with."

"Oh, Honey. Your spirituality is as unique as you are. We don't believe in forced religion. Hell, we don't worship the Christian God, either. Let's just say, our family's beliefs are more aligned with yours, as we still believe in the old gods." Rory stood and went back to sit by her husband. "Do you have any family you want to reach out to?"

"No. My mom was an only child, and both her parents died when I was little. If my dad's mom finds out I'm no longer living where my dad is, she'd just take me back."

"Did your grandmother not live at the compound too?" Sutton asked.

"No, she came from a different community. I can't remember the name of the preacher where she lived. I always wondered why we didn't go live with her when we moved, but I was just a kid. She always told me I was to be quiet unless spoken to first."

"When we help people get back on their feet, it's when we've helped the compound as a whole. Since you're on the run and James will no doubt be looking for you, it might be best if we hide you out for a while. You can come stay with Sutton and me until we make sure James is no longer a threat."

"She can stay with me and Mac," Ryker said, still staring out the window.

"Ry—"

"I'm thinking she and Mac can help each other. Rhi knows about Elijah, and she can talk to Mac about him. Give her hope that they'll be reunited soon." Ryker had turned when he was speaking to his mom. They stared at each other, some unspoken conversation going on between them.

45

"Rhi, can you tell us where the compound is?" Sutton asked.

"No."

"No? Why are you protecting them?" Ryker asked, his face angry.

"I'm not protecting them. I can't tell you because I don't know. James made me wear a blindfold on the drive. I was only allowed to take it off right before we made it to town."

Ryker sighed. "I'm sorry. We've been looking for Josiah for a while now. Wait. We went to where the old compound was, but it had been abandoned. It was moved to a new location. You had to have been part of that."

"Yeah, that wasn't fun. We packed up everything a few months ago. But when they took us to our new home, we all were blindfolded. Josiah said it was for our safety. All I know is it takes about an hour to get from the compound, as you call it, to town."

"How do you know this if you're blindfolded?" Ryker crossed his arms over his chest. Rhi had to look away. The man, even when scowling, was too tempting.

"Because I counted the songs. Trying to get in my good graces, James allowed me to listen to the radio during the drive. I love music, or I did before we moved. Most songs are around three minutes long, and I began counting them so I would know when we were getting close to town."

"That was smart of you," Rory praised. Rhi wanted to go to Rory and hug the woman. She missed her own mom so much, and Ryker's mom looked like she would give good hugs. Rhi was torn. She wanted to go live with Rory and have a mother's touch, but she also wanted to stay with Ryker. She told herself it was so she could help Mac feel better about Elijah, but that would be a lie. She wanted to be wherever Ryker was. Rhi was infatuated with the broody man.

46

CHAPTER FIVE

Ryker

WHAT THE HELL was he thinking? Ryker didn't need Rhi living in his home. Now that she had showered, her natural scent, even though covered by bodywash and shampoo, was calling to him. It was stronger than even Juliette's had been, and that wouldn't do. Juliette had been his one love. He didn't get a second chance.

Mav and War found love twice. Why not us?

Ryker hated when his Gryphon made sense, but he wasn't going to argue with it. Yes, Rhi called to him, but he wasn't good for the young woman, no matter how good she smelled, how she sang like an angel in the shower, or how she looked at him like he was her hero. He had saved her from James. That's what she was feeling. Once she was around the others, Rhi would most likely forget all about him when she saw Kyllian and Hayden or any of the other younger Hounds. Ryker was a broody bastard. Why would she want someone like him when she could have a younger, more fun male?

He could put up with her long enough for Rhi and Mac to talk. To become friends and help each other start living again. Ryker had a job to do, and that didn't leave time for him to worry about being around Rhi that often. Thinking of his daughter, Ryker asked, "Who has eyes on Mac?" McKenzie never minded when Ryker wasn't home. She enjoyed being in the house by herself, doing whatever it was she wanted to in privacy. She preferred it, or so she said.

"Kyllian's taking her out on his bike today. I think our girl's getting the fever. Hayden said Mac wanted to learn to ride, and both of them are willing to teach her."

"Mac's going to learn to ride a motorcycle? That would be so cool," Rhi said.

"Have you ever ridden?" Rory asked.

"Not by myself. One of the boys I grew up with had a dirt bike. He doubled me sometimes, but I never drove it by myself. Not for lack of asking, though. Do you ride?"

"It's been many years, but I used to have my own bike. Well, I still do, although it's sitting at the clubhouse instead of at home in the garage."

Ryker could envision Rhi taking Rory's pink bike out, her long hair whipping in the wind behind her. He could also imagine her riding behind him, pressed against his back, holding on tight. *Fuck.* He needed to put some space between them before he did something stupid like put her on his bike for the ride home.

"I need to get back. My meeting with the Shepherds went well, and I'm ready to move forward." Ryker would take the first job Quinn offered the Hounds and get away from the temptation that was Rhiannon Spencer. "Rhiannon, do you want to go home with Rory and Sutton, or would you like to come stay with Mac and me?"

"Uh…" Rhi looked between the three of them, a blush staining her cheeks. Ryker shouldn't find it endearing, but he did. "Do you think Mac would mind? I don't want to be a painful reminder of her past."

Zeus, she is so sweet.

Ryker mentally pushed his beast. *Get a grip, big guy.*

I'd love to. Grip her around the waist. Put her on our lap and kiss her pink lips. Mmm.

"I think Mac could really use a friend right now. Considering you both went through something similar, I'm sure she won't mind." Ryker was counting on Mac and Rhi becoming friends, even if it would be hell for him.

"Okay, then. I'll stay with you."

Ryker ran a hand through his hair. He could do this. He could be around Rhi and keep it in his pants. "I'm going to hit the road. I need to stop by the clubhouse before I get home, so take your time."

"Let me walk you out." Sutton followed Ryker to the door and out into the hallway. "Before you get on the road, give Lucy a call. Hopefully with the information Rhiannon gave us, she'll be able to locate Josiah."

"Will do. I'm also going to text Kyllian and make sure he has Mac home before we all arrive. I want to give her a heads-up that we're going to have a houseguest."

"I know you think Rhi's too young, or you're too... something, but if your Gryphon is telling you to go after Rhi, listen to it. Life is too short, even with our extended years. And don't give me any bullshit about being too busy. I ran the MC and held down a job when I met your mother and helped raise eleven kids. Nor do I want to hear about her age. You've had the party girl. The strong one. Now, maybe it's time to let yourself be loved by the innocent one."

"Pop, you don't get it. I'm not interested in Rhi. Yes, she's pretty. Yes, she has stars in her eyes when she looks at me, but that's because I rescued her. If it had been you who pulled her from the dumpster, she'd be looking at you the same way. I'll introduce her to Kyllian." Zeus, why did that thought make him want to throw up? Kyllian was the gentlest out of all his brothers, even though he had a penchant for getting Maveryck in trouble.

"Okay, Son. I'll not bring it up again. Ride safe, and I'll see you at your house."

Ryker strolled out of the hotel. He checked his surroundings before straddling his bike. If Rhi was correct, James was still in the area. Then again, knowing what he did about the Ministry, Ryker didn't doubt James had returned to the compound and told Josiah about Rhiannon running. They moved a whole compound so they wouldn't be found. Now, they had someone who could possibly give the authorities information on the new location. He pulled out his phone and called Lucy.

"Morning, Uncle. What can I do for you?"

"Good morning, Little Dove. Can your favorite uncle not call just to say hello?"

Lucy laughed. "You could, but it's not your MO."

"True, and for that, I'm sorry. I'll try to do better in the future." Zeus, Ryker really was a bastard. "I have information that should help you find Josiah's compound." Ryker looked around, making sure there was no one in listening distance, then explained about Rhiannon.

"I'm on it. Hopefully by the time you all return, I'll have the location pinned down."

"Thank you. Also, if you would, check for any CCTV footage in the area and see if you can get video of Rhi and James. I'd like a photo of the man to circulate between the Hounds. If Rhiannon's right, they'll come back looking for her, if they haven't already. If we can catch them here in town, we'll be able to capture some of their men and question them about their operation."

"Will do. I'll talk to you soon."

Ryker thanked Lucy before hanging up. He hated everything his niece went through, but he was glad she was part of their family again. Glad she had a Gargoyle as honorable as Tamian St. Claire as a mate. His little Lucy, a queen. No, she wasn't his daughter, but he was the one who looked out for her while Warryck was off living his life away from the family. Now, both War and Lucy were back where they belonged. Thinking of daughters, Ryker sent a quick text to Kyllian telling him to bring Mac home before it got too late and why. Ryker wanted Mac to be there when Rhiannon arrived.

Ryker felt lighter than he had in months. The ordeal

with Cassandra and Nexus had thrown him into a tailspin, but now the Hounds would be working with Shepherd and Quinn. He was confident the father-and-daughter team would be a good fit with the work the Hounds did. Ryker couldn't wait to tell Mac the good news about Elijah. The boy was alive if Rhi was telling the truth, and she didn't have a reason to lie about the young man. They were one step closer to finding Josiah and shutting down that branch of the cult.

Ryker arrived at the clubhouse pleased to see many of the Hounds already there. Calling church was usually only done when they had something of utmost importance to discuss. This was more of an impromptu gathering to let them know about his meeting with the Shepherds. This affected them all, and Ryker wanted to assure them they wouldn't encounter the same shitstorm that was brought upon them while working with Nexus.

Sultan, his Sargent-at-Arms, got everyone's attention and sent them into the conference room. The Hounds gathered around the oak table with Mayhem sitting to his right and Sultan to his left. The only ones missing were Kyllian, who was still out with Mac, and Tank. Martina was ready to give birth, and family came first. No, that wasn't how most MCs worked, but the Hounds weren't like other clubs. In that moment, Ryker became Ryot, president of the Hounds.

"This won't take long. There are two things I wanted to share with you. First, I met with Trenton Shepherd and his daughter, Quinn. Shepherd is an old friend of Sutton's, and he and his daughter have been running an organization similar to Nexus for over twenty years. Going forward, we will be taking contracts from them instead of Nexus. They are not a large organization with various unnamed handlers. Quinn is the only one who'll be contacting me when they have jobs for us. Sutton trusts Shepherd, and I do as well. You've all had a short reprieve from our merc work,

51

and now that I've agreed to partner with them, we'll be getting back into it immediately. Any questions?"

"Is Quinn hot?" Havyk asked. The other Hounds chuckled, and Judge slapped Hayden on the shoulder.

Ryot grinned at his youngest brother. "She's not bad, but she's older than you and way too serious."

Hayden crossed his arms over his chest. "I'm not opposed to older."

Ryker shook his head, ignoring his brother. "Does anyone have a serious question?" Ryker waited, and every Hound remained silent. They trusted him to make the best decisions for the club. "Moving on to the next reason I called you in. On my way back from meeting with Shepherd, I stopped to get gas, and a female was running away from a man." Ryker recounted the story of Rhi hiding out in the dumpster and him getting her a hotel. "The female, Rhiannon, was running from Josiah Talbert's compound. Sutton and Rory are with Rhi now, and they're bringing her to my house. Rhi is close to Mac's age, and I'm hoping they will be able to help one another. In speaking with Rhi, she confirmed Elijah is alive and at that location. She was able to give us an estimate of how long it took to get from the compound to town, so Lucy is already searching for both the compound as well as any men in the area looking for Rhi. I'm meeting Sutton and Rory back at my house, and once Rhiannon is settled, I'm going to ask her more about the layout of the area as well as the men who act as guards. As soon as Lucy gets a location, I'll send two of you in to recon the area. Any questions?"

Hayden smirked, and Ryker pointed a finger at him, effectively shutting him up. The other Hounds laughed heartily, but Ryker didn't want his brother asking about Rhi. And wasn't that a punch to the balls? Ryker wouldn't claim the young woman, but he didn't want anyone else to either. "If nothing further…" Ryot banged the gavel announcing the end of the meeting. Most of the Hounds had families to get home to, but those who didn't hung around, chatting, drinking, and shooting pool.

Ryker left them to it as he strode out the door. Hayden was right behind him. "Wait up." Where Kyllian was the quietest and most reserved of all the brothers, Hayden was the goofball, but at the moment, he toed at a rock when Ryker gave him his attention. "I'd like the first job you get from Shepherd."

That surprised Ryker. Hayden was still learning about being a mercenary. He didn't hesitate to take jobs, but he never asked for one either, preferring to spend his time building bikes or working on his art. Something about his younger brother was off. "You okay?"

Hayden wouldn't meet Ryker's eyes. "Fine. Just ready to get back out there."

"You know you can talk to me, don't you?" Ryker often felt like the odd male out when it came to his family. Sutton had Rory. Mav and War had their twin bond, and now they had their mates. Kyllian and Hayden were close because they were the youngest. Ryker had their love, but being the asshole he was, most of his family didn't seek him out unless it had to do with MC business.

"Yeah, I know. I just…" Hayden blew out a breath and crossed his arms over his black leather kutte. When Ryker looked at his brother, really looked, he saw the sadness around his eyes. If they were alone… No, fuck that. This was his brother, and Ryker didn't give a shit who was watching. He stepped up to Hayden and pulled him into his chest, wrapping his arms around him. Hayden stiffened for a second, then he relaxed against Ryker. Hayden grabbed hold of Ryker's hips, his fingers squeezing into Ryker's sides.

"Talk to me," Ryker urged.

Hayden stepped back and cleared his throat. "I'm not sure how to explain it, but ever since Jenna brought the twins back to Mav, I've felt like something is missing in my

53

own life. I want that. The mate and kids. Going out and fucking for the sake of getting fucked has never been my thing. It's like every date I go on ends in the female getting mad because I'm not what they expected. Just because I'm a biker, they expect me to be and act a certain way. Hell, the last woman I asked out got pissed when I wanted to take her to dinner. I want someone who can see past the leather and the bike to the male who likes to have fun on occasion, but one who's a gentleman too."

"And she's out there, I promise. You'll find her when you least expect it." Rhiannon immediately flashed in Ryker's mind. As much as it pained Ryker, he said, "Come home with me. I need to get there and introduce Rhi and Mac. I'd like you or Kyllian to be the one to ask Rhiannon about her time at the compound."

"Why?"

"Kyllian's not nearly as abrasive as I am, and you have a way of making people smile. She's going to be telling some hard truths, and I'm going to get pissed off, grunt, and scare the girl."

Hayden grinned, even though the sadness was still in his eyes. "You're not wrong. Yeah, okay. I'll come with you." Hayden strode to his bike and climbed on. Ryker's Gryphon cursed him ten ways to Sunday, but Ryker knew he was doing the right thing. He wasn't the right male for Rhi. Hayden might not be either, but Ryker wouldn't stand in his brother's way if he and Rhi hit it off.

Rhiannon

THE CLOSER THEY got to Ryker's home, the more nervous Rhi got. Rory and Sutton had done their best to make her comfortable, and Rhi enjoyed talking with the couple. She still couldn't believe they were old enough to be Ryker's parents, good genes or not. If Ryker didn't look so much like his father, she would have chalked it up to him being adopted. She thought back to a book series she'd read when she was younger where a group of vampires had young-looking parents, and Rhi snorted at the thought of Ryker and his family being less than human. There were no fangs or sparkly skin. Ryker and his parents had enjoyed their meal. They walked freely in the sunlight.

Rory kept Rhi's thoughts busy with talk of all their grandchildren. Rhi didn't miss the wistfulness in the woman's voice when she spoke of her daughters who still lived in Texas. Rhi couldn't imagine Daisy moving hundreds of miles away leaving Rhi behind. She would have followed her mother to the ends of the earth to be near her. All six of Ryker's sisters had husbands and children. Maybe that would have been the one thing keeping Rhi from her mom — a family of her own. Ryker's stern face popped into her mind, but she knew he wasn't interested in her. How could he be? He was a badass biker. An older man with a daughter nearly Rhi's age. He probably saw her as a kid. Besides that, she had nothing to offer someone like him, or any man for that matter.

When there was a lull in the conversation, Rhi asked, "If Josiah finds me, can he make me go back?"

"No. You are of legal age and can make your own decisions. Lucy is already working on getting a copy of your birth certificate and Social Security card. If Josiah is looking for you, that helps us in finding him. Do you know of any others who aren't there of their own free will?" Rory asked.

"Other than Elijah? Not really. We were taught to keep our thoughts to ourselves. I kept to myself because nobody liked me."

"Because you're pagan?" Sutton asked.

"I never came out and said I worship the goddess. It's not that I'm ashamed of my spirituality, but when everyone around you believes something different, it's easier to keep it inside. I saw enough opposition from my grandmother when she spoke hatefully about and to my mom. Since she was the one who convinced my dad to go to Josiah, I knew better than to speak out. No, it was because I talked to the plants and trees when I first got there. The other kids thought I was weird, and the adults... Let's just say they called me worse names than the kids did."

"What about your father? Did he not try to protect you?" Sutton looked at her in the rearview mirror, his eyes narrowing.

"No. He told me to keep my head down and stay out of trouble. He went off with the other adults, leaving me to live with the kids. I rarely saw him after we entered the community."

"Rhi, I know you were young when your mom died, but do you know if your father was having financial troubles?"

"Not that I know of. He went to work every day. We lived in a nice-enough house in a good neighborhood. Mom didn't have a job outside the home, but I never heard him mention her getting one or that we didn't have enough money."

"What did your dad do for a living?" Rory asked.

"He worked with computers."

Rory and Sutton shared a silent look, and Rhi wondered what they were thinking. She didn't get the chance to ask about it because they pulled into a driveway and parked next to three motorcycles. Rhi looked out the window at the two-story house. "Is this Ryker's home?"

"Yes. He's already here, and so are Hayden, Mac, and Kyllian." Rory unbuckled and turned to face Rhi. "I want you to know you are safe now. You might get overwhelmed with our family, but I promise, every one of my sons, their women, and all the Hounds have your back. You are one of us now for however long you want to stay around."

56

Rhi's eyes watered, and she swallowed hard. It had been a long time since she felt like part of a family, but Rory's words rang true. Josiah's community was supposed to have been home, but it always felt like a prison. Sutton opened the back door to the SUV and held out his hand. Rhi grasped it, welcoming both the strength and warmth. He was a slightly older version of Ryker, and although quite handsome, Rhi didn't feel the same draw to him. Not that she would have sought a married man. She was merely making a comparison between the two men in her mind. During the three-hour drive, she had compared Ryker to all the men at the compound. Sure, some of the men had been nice-looking, but none compared to her biker. *He's not yours.*

Speaking of the man, Ryker was waiting on the front porch alongside a young woman Rhi assumed was McKenzie and two younger men. One was dark-haired like Ryker and Sutton, and the other was blond like Rory. From listening to Rory speak about her sons, Rhi knew the blond was Hayden and the other was Kyllian. Or Havyk and Kayos as they were also known as. Both were handsome, but neither held a candle to their older brother. When Rhi caught sight of McKenzie, she forgot all about the Lazlo brothers. Mac had a scar on her face. It was visible, but it didn't detract from her beauty. Her eyes were haunted, and Rhi vowed then and there to do everything in her power to see some happiness on the other woman's face. With Rory on one side and Sutton on the other, Rhi approached the steps.

CHAPTER SIX

Rhiannon

RHI SHUFFLED FROM side-to-side as Sutton introduced everyone. Both younger brothers had cute smirks on their faces. She'd already heard how playful Hayden was, but it seemed Kyllian had the same roguishness. Rhi ignored them both and gave Mac her attention. "Hi, Mac."

"Hi. Uh, my dad said you know Elijah?" Mac's voice was hopeful.

"As well as you can know anyone in a compound. But I saw him last week when I was leaving the dining hall. He didn't appear to be harmed, so that's a good thing, right?"

"Yes. It's a great thing. Come on in, and I'll show you around." Mac moved to the door and held it open. Rhi looked over at Rory, and the woman nodded her head, smiling. Rhi strode up the steps, ignoring the two younger brothers, but she couldn't stop herself from looking at Ryker. He returned her gaze briefly, then he turned to his parents. Yep, she was nothing to him other than someone he saved.

The inside of the house reminded Rhi of her old home. The living room had a comfortable-looking sofa, two recliners, a coffee table, and a large-screen television. She'd thought the TV at the hotel had been big. The floorplan was open, with the dining room and kitchen visible from where she stood. There was a sliding glass door leading out back, where Rhi could see lots of greenery. She couldn't stop her feet from carrying her that direction. She stared in awe at all the plants and trees. "Hello," she whispered.

"Who are you talking to?" Mac asked.

"The plants and trees. I've missed them terribly."

Mac opened the door and ushered Rhi outside. She looked at Mac. "Can I?"

"You're not at the compound, Rhi. You don't have to ask permission. The only thing you need to be mindful of is one or more of the Hounds can stop by at any time. I don't suggest walking around in your underwear." Mac grimaced.

"Got caught, did you?" Rhi grinned.

Mac rolled her eyes, but she smiled back at Rhi. "Yes. Not my best moment. I may or may not have thrown a glass of beer at Uncle Hayden. It's a good thing he has quick reflexes."

"You drink beer?" Rhi asked as they walked out into the yard together.

"Not often. I did it more because I could than because I like the taste of it."

Rhi knelt beside a large pot of pansies and stroked their leaves, whispering to them.

"Did you work in the gardens?" Mac asked.

"No. I was caught talking to the flowers when I first moved there, and after that, I wasn't allowed anywhere near the gardens. The only greenery I was allowed around were the vegetables in the kitchen."

"How old were you when you moved there?"

"Thirteen. My mother passed away, and my grandmother convinced my father I needed a godlier environment. My mom was pagan, and she taught me all about plants and gardening. I've missed digging in the dirt." Rhi looked around. "How long did it take you to get used to all this?"

"Who says I'm used to it?" Mac squatted next to Rhi. "I

59

was in love with Elijah, but Gideon promised me to one of the guards." Mac looked around, then leaned in and whispered, "Lewis, the guard, raped me. I didn't tell my family that. They think the baby was Elijah's, but he and I were never allowed to be alone together for more than a few minutes. It was then I really started causing trouble, and they took Elijah away. I ran the first chance I got, but some of Gideon's men and their dog chased me through the woods." Mac touched the scar on her cheek. "Then I was held in solitary, had my baby stolen from me and given up for adoption. I was all but branded a whore, and nobody was allowed to interact with me. Not even my family. Or, who I thought of as my family. Kerrigan was the first person to be nice to me and not judge me."

"Kerrigan, that's War's girlfriend?"

"Yes. She was kidnapped on the side of the road one night and brought to our compound because she looked like my mom. Gideon had a thing for redheads. Anyway, I'm still getting used to my freedom. Kerrigan and the others are trying to get me out of the house more, but I'm still self-conscious about my scar. Dad's offered to find a plastic surgeon, but I'm scared something will happen and I'll look worse than I already do."

"For what it's worth, I think you're gorgeous." Rhi stood and held out her hand to Mac. "How about we go back inside and you can show me where I'll be sleeping?" Mac allowed Rhi to help her stand, and the two of them left the peacefulness of the outdoors.

Ryker, his parents, and brothers were in the living room when they stepped through the door. "We're going upstairs," Mac said. Nobody stopped them, so Rhi followed. Mac pointed to a door on the right. "This is my room." Rhi peeked inside to see a tidy room with white furniture and a television mounted on the wall above the bureau. "That's the bathroom, and we'll need to share it," Mac said, pointing to the room on the left. It was as large as the bathroom at the hotel and decorated just as nicely. It was as neat as Mac's bedroom. Living at the compound, they didn't have much in the way of personal items. All toiletries, which they were required to share, were kept in a small closet. Rhi had no problem sharing with Mac. "And this is your room." Mac stood in the hallway so Rhi could go first.

"Are you going to laugh at me if I bounce on the bed?" Rhi asked.

"Nope. I did the same thing. These mattresses are heaven after the shitty cots we had to sleep on."

Rhi wasn't used to cursing, but it didn't bother her. It made her feel like Mac was settling into her new environment. She took Mac at her word and launched herself onto the bed, bouncing up and down like a kid. She flopped backwards and spread her arms and legs as though she were making snow angels. "Goddess, you're right. I might never get up again."

Mac leaned against the doorframe, smiling. "You want to know the best part about being here? It's the food. No more disgusting oatmeal."

"I embarrassed myself in front of Ryker at the hotel. I ordered way too much food, but it had been so long since I had a cheeseburger and fries. Then this morning I had pancakes and bacon. Oh, and I tried coffee too."

"I get it. Little things like ketchup on fries, flavored creamer for coffee, choosing pancakes over cereal. Hell, having cereal for lunch if I want it instead of a sandwich. I'm not much of a cook, but I'm learning. You mentioned the kitchen at the compound. Did you cook?"

Rhi sat up and slung her legs over the side of the bed. "No. Sometimes I had to do the prep work, but mostly I washed the dishes. I'm surprised they let me have a knife. I'm not an aggressive person, but more than once I thought about stabbing Marion. She's my dad's wife. They got married soon after we moved there."

"And I take it you didn't approve?"

"I couldn't understand how he got over losing my mom so quickly. It was like he forgot all about her. And me. I rarely saw him, and when I did, it wasn't like before when we were back at home. There were no hugs. No 'how was your day at school?' He became this stranger to me, same as all the other men." Rhi closed her eyes and let out a heavy breath.

"Are you ready to go downstairs? We can retreat up here when the family leaves."

"Yes. I'm sure they have plenty of questions about the compound." Rhi pushed off the bed, not ready to leave the softness. But she could enjoy sleeping on the lush mattress later.

Soft murmurs ceased when the two women reached the bottom of the stairs. Ryker was leaning against an unlit fireplace. Rory and Sutton were close to each other on the sofa, and the other two brothers were seated in the recliners. When Rhi and Mac fully entered the room, the brothers jumped to their feet.

"Rhiannon, please sit here," Hayden said, motioning to the chair. Rhi blushed at the gesture. It was odd having a man speak to her so freely. With Ryker, it had been from necessity after he saved her. Hayden's smile was sweet, but it didn't have the same effect as Ryker's broody gaze. Rhi took the offered seat and crossed her booted feet out in front of her. She glanced up at Ryker who was frowning at his brother.

"This is awkward," Kyllian muttered. "I'm getting drinks. What does everyone want?"

Rhi wondered why the brother found things awkward. Was it because she was an outsider? When the others told Kyllian what they wanted to drink, he looked to her. "Is there Coke?" she asked.

Mac took her uncle by the arm and pulled him toward the kitchen. "Yes, there is. Come on. I'll help."

"I'm sorry," Rhi blurted.

"You have nothing to be sorry for." Rory was sitting impossibly close to Sutton, almost in his lap. Her parents had loved each other, but even they hadn't sat so closely at night when watching TV together. She remembered them giving chaste kisses when it was time for her father to leave for work each morning, but she'd never noticed their need to constantly touch one another the way Sutton and Rory did. It was as if they gravitated to the other without thought. They had to have been together an awfully long time to have so many adult children. Rhi still couldn't get over how young they both looked.

"Rhi, do you feel up to answering questions about the compound?" Sutton asked.

"Yes. I'll do whatever I can to help you."

Kyllian returned with a glass of soda and handed it to her before he and Mac passed out everyone else's drinks. She clutched the cold glass in her hands after taking a sip.

"Gideon called his compound The Sanctuary. Did Josiah also name his compounds?" Sutton asked.

"Yes. He called his Haven, but he should have named it Hell." Rhi waved her hand in front of her when Hayden growled. "I'm sure most of the people who live there want to be there. They choose to live out in the middle of nowhere, following the rules of a tyrant. Tyrant? Is that the right word? School was so different than what I was used to. We learned math and grammar, but mostly we were taught the Bible. That was on top of the daily lessons with Josiah. In school, we mostly spent our days learning Bible verses. All of them were from the Old Testament. Whenever I would get into trouble, my punishment was to read in solitude. I chose to read from the New Testament, and it confused me as to why Josiah never spoke about Jesus. That is until I got older. Jesus was loving and cared about everyone, no matter who they were or what they did. That wasn't Josiah's message.

"We were taught the ways of the outside world are

63

sinful, and anyone who believes differently needs reforming. Luckily, I wasn't taken there when I was younger, or I might have agreed. I was thirteen, and I'd seen enough of what life was like on the outside. Maybe it was because I was young, but I had never encountered any of the bad he preached about."

Rhi took a sip of her soda and sneaked a look at Ryker over the top of the glass. When she caught his eye, he looked away. She really needed to let go of the crush she had on the man. His brothers were younger and also handsome, but there was something about the stoic man that called to her.

"How many people live at Haven?" Sutton asked. "And were there any guards walking the compound?"

"I'd say about two hundred including children. A lot more now than when my dad and I joined them. As for guards, yes. They patrol constantly. Then there are those who train the men in weapons and fighting with their fists. Men like my father who have jobs outside the community are excused from training, but those are few."

Ryker uncrossed his arms and took a step forward, pulling his phone from his pocket. "Your father is allowed to leave for work?"

"Yes. Josiah said my dad's work was important to the community, but I didn't see how. He works with computers, but electronics aren't allowed in Haven."

"Rhi, do you know where your father worked before he took you to Haven?" Hayden asked, sharing a look with Ryker.

"Somewhere with initials. FIA, or something like that."

"Your father worked for the GIA?" Ryker narrowed his eyes as though her words offended him.

Rhi was hesitant to answer. She didn't want the biker mad at her. "Yes?"

Ryker tapped a few buttons on his phone and held it out in front of him.

A woman's voice came through the speaker. "I was just about to call you."

Ryker set the phone on the coffee table. "Lucy, you're on speaker. I'm here with Sutton, Rory, Hayden, Kyllian, Mac, and Rhiannon. Rhi's dad, David Spencer, worked for the GIA."

"You're shitting me. And when you say worked, you mean works. At least he was still there when I left, and I doubt he quit in the last few months. He was another analyst working under Ramey."

"Why would someone who works for the GIA go live in a compound?" Kyllian asked.

"Rhiannon, how often did you see your father?" Sutton asked instead of answering Kyllian's question.

"Not often. Maybe once a month, and that was only in passing."

"Rhi, what do you know about the GIA?" Lucy asked.

"Nothing. Is this important? My father's job?"

"Oh, yes. The GIA, or Global Intelligence Agency, is the top government agency in the world. Your father has access to all sorts of information. As to why he went to live in the compound, I'm sure it was required of him. Now things are becoming clearer. As I told Ryker, I was just about to call. I pulled up CCTV footage of the area where Rhi escaped from James. The place is crawling with men in black fatigues. It's almost like they wanted to get caught on camera."

"What do you mean?" Rory asked.

"If I were covertly looking for a lost sheep, I wouldn't send in twenty men dressed in military gear. Not that they were armed in public, but they were impossible to miss. And if I was able to pick up their movement on the cameras, David would be able to access the same footage as well as go back to when Ryker helped Rhiannon."

"Are you saying they know we have Rhi?" Ryker pushed both hands through his dark hair.

"I would bet on it. Were you wearing your kutte?" Rhi

didn't know what a cut was, but Ryker's hands smoothed down the black leather vest showing the name of the MC across the back as well as his MC name and rank on the front.

"Yes. And if they saw me, they saw Rory and Sutton leaving with Rhi in their SUV." Ryker's eyes caught hers, and she wanted to shrink back from his anger.

"Calm down, Son." Sutton stood and closed the distance between him and Ryker, placing a hand on his shoulder. "Josiah already knows about us. The Ministry didn't get this far in the world without having eyes and ears everywhere. Taking down Gideon put us on his radar."

"Then that means Elijah is in danger." Mac paced the area between the living room and kitchen, her hands twisting together.

Hayden stepped into her path and grabbed her hands. "No negativity. Elijah's alive, and we will get him out of there." Mac's tears rolled down her cheeks, and Hayden pulled his niece into his arms, wrapping her up tight. Rhi wanted to know how they thought they were going to get past all the armed guards.

"We have our ways," Ryker said. Rhi jerked her head around to look at the man. Had she spoken aloud?

"I can see the question on your face. You mentioned the guards at Haven are armed, but we're not without our own resources."

Rhi shook her head. "It's not just the guards. Like I said, Haven isn't only a place people go to disappear or get away from the outside world. It's where the men go to train. The boys who are raised there are taught to shoot and fight at an early age."

"What about James? He didn't look like a guard."

"He's not a guard. He's a recruiter, whatever that means. I only know that because I overheard him talking to someone when we went out for supplies."

"He just walked up and spoke to a random person?"

Kyllian asked.

Rhi thought back to that day last month. "I don't think so. He had a piece of paper he kept looking at. We stopped at a house, and he went inside for a few minutes. I cracked the window so I could get some fresh air, and James told the man he was a recruiter looking for men to join the cause. I didn't catch every word he said, but that was the gist of it."

"What did the house look like?" Sutton asked.

"It was small and rundown."

Sutton scratched his chin. "It's possible David is using his computer skills to find men down on their luck and sending James out to recruit them. Rhi, did you ever see the man after that? The one James visited?"

"Yes. About two weeks ago, he came through the line in the dining hall."

"Lucy—"

"I'm on it. I'm going to need to reach out to Julian for a little help though. We all know what happened last time I was on the GIA's radar."

"If you aren't absolutely sure you can find out what David's doing without getting caught, we'll find another way. I won't see you going to prison, Little Dove," Ryker told his niece. Rhi was caught off-guard at the gentleness in the man's tone. She wondered what it would be like to have him speak to her with such affection. He glanced her way, and the hardness returned to his face. Rhi closed her eyes and told herself to forget about wanting to get close to the biker.

CHAPTER SEVEN

Ryker

RYKER WAS BOTH excited and pissed. Excited that they were one step closer to finding Josiah, but pissed that the man had someone like Rhi's father working for the cult. Knowing someone in the GIA was assisting the Ministry explained how they got away with so much. Was all of the agency crooked? Or was David Spencer like Ramey – a rogue figure who had infiltrated their ranks?

"The reason I was going to call was to tell you I'm having trouble getting a lock on the compound. The satellites I've tapped into are constantly being blocked. Now that I know David is working for Haven, this probably explains why I can't find the location. I don't know if he has a program in place or if he is sitting at his desk watching. Either way, I'm going to need help. It might be a long shot, but I suggest you send a couple Hounds undercover to follow the men who are in town looking for Rhi."

"I'll go, and I'll take Hawk and Spyder with me. Kyllian, you and Hayden stay here to watch over the women." Ryker had to get away from Rhi. Her furtive glances were messing with him, and his Gryphon was being a pain in the ass. It had been a long time since he and his beast were at such odds, and the sooner he got away from the woman, the better. Maybe with a little distance, Rhi would realize his younger brother was the better male for her.

You're an idiot.

Fuck you very much.

Ryker didn't look Rhi's way. He didn't want to give her any indication he was interested.

"If David's as good as I think he is, he probably has someone headed your direction," Lucy said.

"Then I'll double security on the house."

"Why don't you bring them here? My place is more secure, and Tamian can help watch over them," Lucy offered. It wasn't a bad idea. Ryker's house was in a busy neighborhood. Lucy's home was situated on twenty acres with a lake at the back. It would be much harder for Josiah's men to infiltrate her property.

Ryker turned to his daughter. "What do you say? Wanna go hang out at Lucy's for a few days?"

"I'm good with that."

Rory stood. "You go get packed, and your Pop and I will drive you and Rhiannon. Kyllian, you and Hayden can follow us." Rory turned to Rhi. "Your safety is important to us, and Lucy's home is the better choice as far as security is concerned."

"You don't have to sell me on the idea. I appreciate everything you've done, and I will find some way to repay your kindness." Rhi stood and began gathering empty glasses.

"You can leave those. I'll clean up later," Ryker told her.

"I'll help you, Rhi," Hayden offered, ignoring Ryker. His beast bristled, but Ryker tuned it out. He had brought Hayden along to be a buffer of sorts, and his plan was working. Too well. His younger brother seemed smitten with the woman, and Ryker couldn't blame him. He also couldn't watch the two of them together, so he turned his attention to the phone.

"Lucy, it looks like you're going to have company. Once

Mac gets her things together, we'll head your way."

"Sounds good. I'll see you all soon."

Ryker disconnected the call, then phoned both Hawk and Spyder, telling them to get ready to hit the road. Instead of riding their bikes, Sutton suggest driving one of the SUVs. The Hounds' vehicles were easier to blend in with other cars than their bikes were.

Ryker needed to say something to Rhi, but he didn't know what. He knew his parents and brothers would take care of her. Laughter brought his head up, and he looked over to where she and Hayden were coming out of the kitchen. Yes, Hayden was the better choice for the young woman, probably better than Kyllian now that Ryker knew his youngest brother was ready to settle down, but that thought stirred something ugly inside him.

He couldn't keep ignoring Rhi, so he turned to her. "I'm not sure how long this will take, but I'll come check on you when I return."

Rhi's smile was instantaneous and blinding. "You will?"

Ryker had the intense urge to grab her and kiss her. Make promises he had no right to make.

"Okay, I'm ready," Mac said, bounding down the stairs, breaking Ryker out of his wayward musings. Mac stepped up next to Ryker, and he pulled his daughter in for a hug. Touching Mac had been awkward at first, but over the last couple of months, things had become easier between them. For all Mac had been through, she was opening up to him more and more. The first time she told him she loved him had broken open something inside the frozen shell he called a heart. For so long, Ryker had been on the outside looking in. He loved his family, and they loved him, but losing Juliette all those years ago had hardened him to the world.

"Love you, Kiddo." Ryker pressed a kiss to the side of her head, and Mac's face morphed into her beautiful smile. The one that looked so much like her mother's. The reminder of his lost love no longer brought him to his knees. Having Mac in his life was the best thing that ever happened to him.

"Love you too," she whispered.

He glanced over the top of Mac's head when he felt eyes on him. Rhi was staring at the two of them with longing. His heart hurt for Rhi. She not only lost her mother's love when the woman died; she also lost the other person who should have been there for her, helping a teen grieve. But losing that other part of your heart when a spouse was gone... Ryker knew all about that. He liked to think if his situation had been similar, he'd never have abandoned Mac the way David Spencer did Rhi.

Hayden broke the spell by grabbing Mac's bag. "Come on then," he urged.

Ryker followed his family and Rhi outside. Hayden was there, opening the back door of the SUV for Rhi. Before she climbed in, she looked back at Ryker and smiled, giving him a small wave. Hayden looked between the two of them and frowned. He closed the door behind Rhi when she was safely inside the vehicle and inclined his head to Ryker in defeat.

Well, fuck.

Ryker spent the first half hour of the drive toward New Roseville telling Spyder and Hawk about everything that transpired as well as the conversation with Lucy. Now that they knew Rhi's father worked for the GIA, their quest for taking down the Ministry took on a new challenge, and it was one that didn't sit well with Ryker. In targeting the cult, they were also targeting Rhi's father. Someone such as Spencer didn't blindly follow a man like Josiah Talbert. It wouldn't surprise Ryker if David hadn't been helping the cult all along. They only had Rhi's version of the story, and that was one of a thirteen-year-old girl who'd just lost her mother. Not only had she been grieving, but she was young when her life had shifted on its axis. Rhi blamed her grandmother for the turmoil, but it could be she was projecting her trauma on someone who wasn't her father. The father who was supposed to love and support his daughter.

Ryker hated to think how this was going to affect Rhi. She had escaped the cult because she didn't want to marry James. She escaped to get away from the oppression. Her education was lacking. Other than working in the kitchen, the young woman had no life skills. She had been sheltered. McKenzie had been raised in the same fashion. For whatever reason, both young women seemed to have a good head on their shoulders despite what they were taught. Maybe it was because they both had lived outside the cult for a number of years before being dragged into their new lives. Rhi hadn't forsaken her pagan beliefs. She held tight to something that went against everything the Ministry stood for. She had run at the first opportunity. Both those things told Ryker Rhiannon was strong. No, she didn't have life skills, but she could learn, the same way Mac was learning. He could see the two women becoming fast friends, using their mutual experience in the cult as the catalyst that brought them together.

It was going on seven when Ryker turned off the exit to New Roseville. As he drove down the main thoroughfare, the three of them searched the area for any sign of Josiah's men. Ryker's skin prickled, and his Gryphon pushed against him. "We have company." The traffic was sparse enough for Ryker to notice when they picked up a tail. "Damnit!" He slapped his hand against the steering wheel.

"How are we going to play this?" Spyder asked.

Ryker turned into the parking lot of a steakhouse. "I'm not going to try to lose them and risk getting pulled over by the cops, so I say we meet them head-on. See what they have to say. If things get too bad, I'll use my shifter voice." Ryker tried not to use the Gryphon's gift of coercion too often, but sometimes it was necessary. The car that had been

72

following didn't pull into the parking lot, which surprised Ryker. He was sure they were being followed.

Spyder, who was sitting in the back seat, looked out the window. "Where did they go? Are you sure we were being followed?"

"Yes, I'm sure. They probably thought we didn't notice them and didn't want to give themselves away."

"Now what?" Hawk asked. "If they circle back around, and we leave, they'll know something's up."

"I say we go in, eat a steak, then regroup. They already know I was here when Rhi went missing. They more than likely have footage of her leaving town with Sutton and Rory. On the off chance they don't, I can play it off like we have business here."

The three of them strode into the restaurant, imposing even without their MC kuttes. Ryker and Hawk were both over six feet and muscled. Spyder was shorter at five-nine, but the male exuded power in the way he carried himself. The hostess's eyes widened, and like every time the Hounds were in public, surprise gave way to lust. The young woman tried to be subtle in her perusal of their bodies, but when she looked back up at Ryker's face, her cheeks blushed.

"Right this way." If Ryker had been alone, he'd have sat at the bar, but the three of them couldn't talk freely spread out. The table the hostess led them to was a round booth in the corner, giving them a view of the room as well as the front door. Ryker slid to the middle so the Hounds could protect him. Not that he needed their help in a fight, but over the years, they had studied other MCs, and the President was always guarded by lower-ranking members. They received many looks from the other patrons, but Ryker only noticed long enough to ensure there were no threats. Mostly, he was looking for members of the cult. Lucy said they were dressed in black, so they would be easy to spot. No one seated in the restaurant fit the description, so Ryker relaxed a little.

The waitress came and took their orders, stopping back by quickly with their drinks. Spyder was less talkative than usual, so Ryker asked, "You okay?"

The smaller Hound shrugged, tipping his longneck back, swallowing down half in one go. When he set the bottle down, he turned to Ryker. "I turned Heather loose."

That didn't surprise Ryker. Spyder wasn't one to keep a girlfriend long, but Heather had lasted longer than most. "Any particular reason?"

"She kept hinting at getting married. Said she's ready for kids. I'm not opposed to finding someone to settle down with, but it wasn't her." Spyder scrubbed a hand down his face. "I don't think I'm ever going to find the right one."

Rhi popped into Ryker's mind, but he shut that shit down right quick. No matter how much the pretty blonde called to him, she was too young. The server came back by with another round of beers, and Ryker spread his arm across the back of the bench. "You will. I believe there's someone out there for all of us."

Hawk barked out a laugh. "Who are you, and what have you done with Ryot?"

"Fuck you," Ryker responded with no heat. "Just because I'm alone now doesn't mean I want to be. Don't get me wrong. I loved Juliette with all my heart, but her memory doesn't keep my bed warm at night."

Hawk held up his bottle, and Ryker clinked it with his beer. "I hear you, man. I've been babysitting for Tank just so I can be around kids. How sad is that?"

"Not sad at all. It's all I can do not to kidnap Mayhem's twins. Those two are so much fucking fun."

Hawk laughed. "I about pissed myself when we went camping and Major tried to eat the fish he caught. I know they're too young to show any tendencies, but I'd bet my bike he's going to be a Hound."

Their food arrived, and as they ate, they all reminisced about the group camping trip and the antics of Maveryck's twins. For not being around the other Hounds' kids for the first four years of their lives, those two were making up for lost time. Natalia was the perfect mother for the boys, blood related or not. Ryker had missed out on seeing McKenzie grow up, and that was another reason he was hellbent on seeing Josiah Talbert brought down. The Hounds preferred to let the legal system handle the leaders of the Ministry, but Ryker would make the man pay.

"What's the plan?" Spyder asked when they finished eating.

"I say we check into a hotel, then slip out and do a little searching from the sky." Ryker loved being in eagle form. The freedom he felt when stretching his wings was like nothing else, except maybe riding his Harley. He flagged down the waitress, and once the check was paid, the three males slipped outside to their vehicle. Ryker drove to the same hotel where he'd spent the night watching over Rhi. It was the nicest one in town, and it also backed up to a tree line.

They made it the six blocks to The Continental without seeing any of Josiah's men nor the car that had been following. Ryker felt in his gut the men were still out there only hiding. Since they didn't know how long they'd be staying, Ryker got three rooms on the same floor. He had no problem sharing with the other Hounds, but it was easier if they had their own space. With the extra money they'd received from Natalia selling her family's estate, Ryker could afford to splurge.

Ryker's phone vibrated in his pocket. "Hey, Lucy. You got something?"

"As a matter of fact, I do. You need to be careful. I managed to get into David's system briefly, and I just watched you drive up to The Continental and go inside. If you were planning on doing any... scouting, I would suggest you rethink that plan. Ryker, he's using government satellites, and they're more powerful than anything I have access to. I've contacted Julian, but he isn't in a position to help me right now. Something is going down with the Gargoyles, and Tamian is thinking about heading to New Atlanta to help out."

"Fuck. Stay out of his system. I don't want you getting caught by the GIA again."

"Already out, but that means you're going to have to do things the human way."

Ryker wanted to ask about Rhi, but he didn't want Lucy to get the wrong idea. "I have to go, Little Dove. Thank you. For now, focus on the family." Ryker didn't specifically say Rhiannon, but he included her in the sentiment. "I'll handle this without getting you in trouble."

"Stay safe, Uncle."

"You know it. Love you, Lucy."

"Love you too." Ryker disconnected and put the phone in his back pocket.

"I take it we need to keep the eagles at bay?" Hawk asked.

"For now. David Spencer's using government satellites and knows where we are. We can't risk him seeing us shift."

"What's the plan then?" Spyder asked.

"We hunt." Ryker ran a hand through his dark hair, his thoughts bordering on feral. "We hunt until we find them and then I'm going to have a little chat with James and the lot of them. I'm going to 'suggest' they return to the compound, but not until they've told me all about Rhiannon's father. He's the one standing in our way at the moment. We're going to intercept him and keep him somewhere away from his computers. If he isn't watching us, Josiah won't see us coming."

"Do you think he'll try to move again?" Hawk asked.

"It's possible, but if he does, it'll take a while. I can't imagine moving an entire community can be done quickly. Rhi said the last move took a few months. She also said the guards are armed, and they train all the males to shoot and

76

fight. We need to get their guns. We can go hand-to-hand against them, but we're no match to rifles."

"Truth, but if James goes back and starts loading weapons, that won't go unnoticed." Spyder walked over to the window, pushed back the sheer curtain, and peered out into the darkening evening.

"You're right. I think we need to apprehend David, then, without him watching our movements, we can get to the compound. Let's find James or one of the others and find out as much as we can about the guards, their patrol schedules, and the number of weapons at their disposal."

"Looks like we don't need to go looking. Three males dressed in black are crossing the street."

Ryker and Hawk joined Spyder at the windows. "I have no doubt David hacked into the hotel's system to get our room numbers." Ryker strode to the wall and flipped the switch, bathing the room in darkness. There were no good hiding places for three large shifters. Spyder ducked behind the sofa, Hawk stepped into the bedroom, and Ryker flattened his back to the wall beside the door and waited.

CHAPTER EIGHT

Rhiannon

DURING THE DRIVE, Rory told Rhi about Lucy's life. Rhi was a little nervous. She hadn't been around any women who were smart and fierce since her mother died. And the fact that Lucy used to work with Rhi's father was intriguing as well as daunting. She wanted to know all about the man who had more or less abandoned her to help Josiah and his community. When they pulled through the iron gate and ended up in front of a large, stone house, Rhi let out a "Wow." She'd never seen something so extravagant. Rory had explained how Lucy's great-aunt and great-uncle adopted her, then upon their deaths, everything they owned went to Lucy.

Rhi looked around for Hayden, but instead of him helping her like he had before, he strode up to the house without looking back. It was Sutton who helped gather her things and escort her inside. Kyllian had grabbed Mac's bag, and the two of them bumped shoulders as they walked. Rhi wasn't jealous of their closeness, but she wouldn't lie to herself and say she didn't long for someone to joke around with. She had to remember she was an outsider. One who was only there long enough to figure out her future.

When they reached the top of the steps, a pretty brunette was waiting with an equally handsome man. "Rhiannon, I'm Lucy, and this is my mate, Tamian.

78

Welcome to our home."

Mate?

"Thank you. And please, call me Rhi. You have a beautiful home."

The inside of the house was even more spectacular than the outside. Rhi couldn't imagine living somewhere so grand. She looked all around, taking in the artwork, the sculptures, and the statues.

"Come on, and I'll show you where you'll be staying," Lucy offered. When they were at the top of the stairs, Lucy asked Mac, "Who peed in Hayden's Lucky Charms?"

"I don't know. Why? Did he say something?"

"No, and that's the problem. He came in the door, grunted, then strode right out the back."

"I think he's mad at me," Rhi said. "Although I don't know why. One minute he was smiling and joking with me, then the next he was frowning and ignoring me."

"Don't worry about it. I'm sure you didn't do anything wrong. He's probably focused on keeping you safe, and he takes his jobs seriously. Now, here you go." Lucy gestured to a door, and when Rhi stepped in, her eyes widened.

"Uh, are you sure? I mean, I don't need this much space." The bedroom was larger than four cabins put together.

Lucy grinned. "It's the smallest bedroom in the house. Lucius, my adoptive father, was of the mindset 'go big or go home.'"

"Well, a queen does need her palace," Kyllian said from the doorway. "Here you go, Rhi." The dark-haired Lazlo brother stepped into the room and placed her bags on the bed.

"Thank you."

Kyllian bowed with a flourish. "Anything for you." Mac shoved Kyllian, and when he stood upright, he winked at Rhi, smirking. "I'm going to find my brother and see what crawled up his ass. If you need me, just yell."

Rhi giggled at Kyllian's colorful words.

"My room is right across the hall. Why don't you unpack while I do the same, then I'll give you the grand tour," Mac suggested.

"Yeah, that sounds great."

"Rhi, you probably have a lot of questions about your dad, and I'll be happy to answer them all to the best of my ability once you get settled in. I'm going to get back to work, but if you need anything, come find me." Lucy squeezed Rhi's arm with a smile.

"Is everyone in your family this nice?" Rhi wasn't used to the friendly gestures and playful banter.

"Mostly. My dad and Kyllian are the least friendly out of everyone. Dad is coming around, and Kyllian... Well, I'm not sure what's going on with him. He's the quietest of the brothers, unless he gets together with Uncle Mav. Then he's a pain in Maveryck's ass. His words, not mine. But yes, our family is loving and generous. You'll meet War and Maveryck and their mates, Kerrigan and Natalia, eventually, and they're equally as friendly."

"I'm looking forward to it." Rhi unzipped her large bag and stored the few clothes Rory had bought her in the tall chest opposite the bed, all the while singing to herself. She then took the smaller case into the bathroom and unpacked her toiletries. It dawned on her then that everything she owned was reduced to two pieces of luggage, and all of it had been given to her by the Lazlos. They really were good people. Rhi placed the empty baggage in a closet bigger than her cabin had been.

Just as she turned to exit the closet, something shiny caught her eye. Thinking Lucy had dropped an earring or other piece of jewelry, Rhi bent down. It was a ring of sorts, and when she picked it up, the carpet beneath separated. Rhi dropped it, thinking she had ruined the carpet. She dropped to her hands and knees so she could investigate and found the ring was attached to a metal wire. Pulling the two sides of the carpet aside, Rhi stared at the metal square on the floor.

"Rhiannon? Oh, there you are," Mac said. "Did you drop something?"

Rhi looked over her shoulder and motioned for Mac to come closer. "I saw something shiny. When I went to pick it up, that happened." She pointed at the floor. Mac lowered herself to the floor and crawled up beside Rhi.

"Huh. I wonder what's inside."

"Should we open it?" Rhi asked. She felt like a little kid having discovered a secret compartment.

"Definitely not. Lucius was sort of a mad scientist. There's no telling what else he hid in the walls. We'll tell Lucy and let her investigate. Come on. I'm hungry, and Rory's in the kitchen."

"Is that a good thing?"

Mac stood, then held out her hand, helping Rhi to her feet. "It's the best thing. Rory's a great cook, and with you here, she'll be putting on the pig."

"Pig? You mean we're having ham?"

Mac laughed and linked elbows with Rhi as they found their way downstairs. "No. It means she'll be going all out to impress you. The Lazlos are originally from Texas; Rory has some funny sayings. That's one of them."

Rhi had already heard Rory's soft, southern twang, but Ryker didn't have it. He must have lost it in the past however long he'd been living in New York. Mac showed Rhi around the large house, ending in the kitchen where Rory was, indeed, putting together a large spread. Rhi's stomach growled from all the heavenly aromas.

Rory turned, smiling. "I heard that all the way over here. Mac, why don't you go call the boys in for supper?"

"What can I do to help?" Rhi asked.

"If you'd like to get the plates and silverware, that'd be wonderful. Plates are in that cabinet" — Rory pointed to the right — "and silverware is in that drawer by the fridge. Just place them by the stove. We're not getting fancy tonight."

"How did you put this together so quick?"

Rory pulled a pan of biscuits out of the oven. "I have a large group to feed, so I've learned some shortcuts over the years. I can teach you, if you'd like."

"Oh, I probably won't be around long enough for that, but I appreciate the offer."

"Where are you going?" Kyllian asked when he walked into the room.

"Uh, I'm not sure, but I can't live off your family's generosity forever. I guess I need to find a job, and..." Rhi had no clue what she was going to do. Lucy was getting her birth certificate, but Rhi had no experience except working in the kitchen.

"If you could do anything, what would it be?" Rory asked.

"Work with plants and flowers," Rhi responded without thinking.

"There are plenty of florists in the area. Maybe once the threat of Haven is over, you can look into working with one of them," Kyllian said as he reached for one of the biscuits. Rory smacked his hand. "Hey, what was that for?" He smirked at his mother before winking at Rhi. She didn't think he was flirting with her. At least, she hoped not. Not that Kyllian wasn't handsome, because he was. All the Lazlos were gorgeous in their own way.

Mac returned to the kitchen. "If the florist doesn't work out, you could always get a job singing."

Rhi frowned at her. "When have you heard me singing?"

"You sing all the time. Did you not realize it?"

Rhi shook her head, embarrassed.

"You have the most amazing voice."

"Oh, uh, thanks." Crap. She had forgotten how she used to burst into song at any given moment.

Rory handed Rhi a plate and told her to dig in before

the males got to the food. Rhi wasn't used to having so many options available, so she took small portions of everything, wanting to try it all. Rory directed her to the dining room where Rhi took a seat in the middle of the table. Lucy and Tamian joined them, and supper was both mouthwateringly delicious as well as entertaining.

"Hey, Lucy. Rhi found a hidden compartment in the closet upstairs," Mac announced during a lull in the conversation.

"I wasn't snooping, I promise." Rhi was mortified when everyone turned to stare at her. "I honestly thought it was a piece of jewelry. The ring was attached to some kind of wire, and when I picked it up, the carpet ripped."

Lucy smiled and waved her hand. "You didn't rip the carpet. It was designed that way. I found one in my own closet not too long ago. I meant to check all the rooms in the house for similar setups, but I got busy. What was in there?"

"Oh, we didn't open it. Mac thought it would be best to tell you about it."

"After supper, you're welcome to go see if anything is hidden there."

"Are you sure that's a good idea?" Tamian asked. Lucy's boyfriend had been quiet up until that point. There was something different about the man, but Rhi couldn't figure out what.

"I seriously doubt Lucius left any of his journals in the spare bedroom. Everything he had would have been in the lab." Lucy waved her fork. "I'm not worried." Lucy leaned over and pressed a soft kiss to the man's lips. The smile he gave Lucy made Rhi's heart flip-flop. What would it be like to so freely show love like that?

"Your computer is pinging," Tamian said, his fork halfway to his mouth.

"Thanks. Please excuse me," Lucy said as she stood from the table and left the dining room. Rhi hadn't heard anything, but she hadn't been paying attention to anything other than the food. Everyone went back to eating without Lucy, with Kyllian keeping the conversation going. Rhi really liked the man. He was charming and flirty, but he didn't make her feel self-conscious. He had been the same way with Mac, and she was his niece. Once they finished dinner, Rhi and Mac did the dishes while Hayden and Kyllian patrolled the property. Sutton and Rory left afterward but promised they'd return the next day. Rhiannon thanked them again for everything before they left.

"I love your family." Rhi scrubbed one of the pans. "I'd forgotten what it felt like having supper together."

"Just wait 'til they all get together. It's a madhouse, but I wouldn't trade it for anything. Even the Colins weren't like this before we went to live at the Sanctuary. And it's not because my family has money. It's because they care. Even the Hounds I've met are the same way. I expected a bunch of bikers to be rough and hardcore, but because of who they are, they're all about family."

"I'll admit I don't know anything about bikers. I don't know much about a lot of things. Everything I experienced before I was taken to Haven was limited, probably because I was young. I lived in a nice neighborhood where everyone knew everyone else. All the parents were still married with the exception of Mikey's parents, but his stepdad was nice. It's strange, coming back to the outside after ten years. Time moved on, whereas in Haven, nothing ever changed."

"I get it. Like I said earlier, I'm still getting used to all the changes. Getting to decide what kind of clothes I like, wearing makeup if I want, having toiletries that aren't homemade. Listening to music has been the best thing. There's this rock band I really like, and Tamian knows the lead singer. He's friends with the guy's father. I get to go backstage next time they're in town. You should come with me."

Rhi looked over at Mac. "Really? You wouldn't mind?"

"Why would I mind? I'd love to hang out with you."

"That's…" Rhi swallowed hard. It had been so long since she had friends. Maybe Mac felt the same way. "What job did you have at The Sanctuary?"

"Before everything went to hell, I worked with the animals. I always wanted to be a veterinarian, but since we weren't allowed to go to college, feeding the cows was the closest thing to it. Elijah worked in the barns, keeping them cleaned out and maintained. Everything was as perfect as it could be for us. We had plans to go to Gideon and ask to be allowed to get married, but Lewis decided he wanted me, and when I told Gideon no, that's when things went from bad to worse."

"Why don't you go to college now? You're plenty young enough. You can still become a vet."

Mac paused drying the dish in her hand. "I've considered it, but I don't think I could stand being around so many people. Even if I didn't have the scar."

Hayden sauntered into the kitchen and hopped up onto the counter next to Mac. "Haven't you heard? Scars are sexy." He wiggled his eyebrows at Mac, and she popped him on the leg with her cloth. His previous bad attitude was gone.

"Maybe on brutish males such as yourself." Mac finished drying the pan and asked Rhi, "What about you? Do you want to go to college?"

"No. I like Rory's idea of working at a florist. Eventually, I want a place of my own where I can have a garden, but that's just a dream."

"I don't think that's out of reach, especially if you work for the family. Rory and Sutton can always use people who've been on the inside to help those we rescue."

"You mean others like us?"

"Yes. Not everyone who lives within the Ministry wants to be there. Kerrigan—"

"Hide, now!" Kyllian yelled, storming into the kitchen.

"What the fuck?" Hayden jumped down from the counter.

"We have company. Four men just walked up the driveway, and from the way they're dressed, I have no doubt they're Josiah's men."

Lucy ran into the kitchen. "Mac, Rhi, come with me."

Rhi and McKenzie followed Lucy deeper into her home. She opened a door and took off down a set of stairs. When they reached the bottom, Lucy stopped at a bookcase, pressed something on the side, and the large shelf slid open. "Get in here. I'll be back as soon as I can."

Mac entered the tunnel without hesitation. Rhi didn't understand what was happening, but she didn't have a choice. Not if she didn't want to be sent back to Haven. When the bookcase closed, Rhi was glad the passageway was illuminated. "What is this?" she asked.

Mac grabbed Rhi's hand and led her away from the entrance. They walked for quite a ways before she stopped. "I don't want to risk being overheard. Lucy's father was a scientist. A geneticist. The room we came through, it was his lab. I'm not sure exactly what all he experimented with, but I do know not all of it was good. He built this tunnel so he could hide what he was doing from his wife, Lucy, and the outside world. If we keep walking a quarter mile, the tunnel ends at the edge of the lake on the other side."

"Is Lucy okay with what her father did?" Rhi asked.

"Not at all. When she worked for the GIA, her boss took her to an underground lab and had her continue her father's work after he died. Only Lucy wouldn't do it. She figured out what was going on, managed to escape, and then Tamian and the Hounds found her."

"I can't imagine finding out something like that about my dad. I mean, I don't know him anymore, but I hate to think of him doing something... wrong." Mac gave Rhi a funny look. "You don't have to say it. I just wish I could go back to being the naïve teenager. You know, before my mom died."

"Tell me more about her." Mac slid down the wall to sit against it.

Rhi was too nervous thinking about the men upstairs to sit, so she leaned a shoulder on the opposite wall in case she needed to make a run for it and told Mac about Daisy. "Somedays, it's hard to remember everything about her, and others, I feel like she's with me, here." Rhi pointed to her chest. "She was the kindest soul I've ever known, and it wasn't until Dad took me to Haven that I understood why my grandmother didn't like her. Mom was pagan, and my grandmother wouldn't abide her choices. I never once saw my mother cast a spell or anything like that. What little I know about witches comes from watching movies or TV shows when I was younger. I do know she worshipped the goddess instead of God, but I don't think that made her a bad person. Rory said your family worships the old gods, and from what I can tell, they're good people. They're out here in the world helping others, while my grandmother and dad are living out in the middle of nowhere, keeping to themselves."

Mac bent her knees and wrapped her arms around her legs. "My adoptive mom, Amy, she took me and Sparrow, their biological daughter, to church before we moved to the Sanctuary. I can tell you the sermons were different. I remember our preacher talking about Jesus and how he was kind and loving. It was none of the fire and brimstone stuff Gideon spewed day after day. The older I got, the more I realized that was his way of keeping his flock in line. If we didn't adhere to his teachings, we were punished. Then to find out both he and Josiah were the worst kind of men out there? Kidnapping women for their own pleasure? Josiah's the one who abducted my mom when she was pregnant with me. Gideon convinced his brother to give Juliette to him."

"But Josiah's married. Why would he want your

mom?" Rhi didn't understand much of the ways of the world, but even she knew that was wrong.

"Because he's a hypocritical, sadistic bastard? I don't know. These men – the leaders of these cults – think they're above the law. That's why they move out to the middle of nowhere and start their own communities. Ones where they make the rules. They go out and find people who are down on their luck and convince them the Ministry is a better way of life. They offer them somewhere to live without having to worry about paying bills and things like that. It's all bullshit. They take them there, give them a small cabin, and use them for free labor. Sure, they no longer have to worry about paying bills, but they also lose what freedom they had on the outside. But then, you know all about that."

"I do, and I hated every second of it. I got into so much trouble the first couple of years because I wouldn't give up on my mom's beliefs. Josiah refused to call me Rhiannon because he said it was too pagan, so he called me Anna. I got in trouble for talking to boys. I was disciplined for talking to the plants. I finally just stopped talking. It was a lonely existence, and when Josiah began letting James 'court' me, I knew I had to get out of there."

"I'm glad you did. I'm really glad my dad found you."

"Yeah, me too." Rhi didn't tell Mac how she felt about Ryker. She didn't want to ruin the tentative friendship they had started. Yes, the Lazlos were good people, McKenzie included, and Rhi didn't want to ruin everything by having a crush on the handsome man who rescued her.

Mac must have realized it, though. She smiled up at Rhi. "I think you would be good for him. I know he loved my mother, but he needs someone in his life to love now. He comes across as this stoic, angry man, but deep down, he's the best of all of them. He's strong. Honorable. A protector. He needs someone to remind him he doesn't have to sacrifice happiness to be the amazing leader he is. I think you should be that someone."

The sound of the bookcase being slid open echoed down the passageway. Mac jumped to her feet, placing herself in front of Rhi. The movement warmed Rhi's heart. Ryker wasn't the only protective Lazlo, and if Mac was giving her blessing, maybe Rhi could be the woman Ryker needed.

Chapter Nine

Ryker

Ten minutes passed and there was still no sign of the males. Ryker eased over to the window and pulled back the curtain just enough to look down to the street. The four males were running back across it. A nondescript SUV pulled up, and they hopped in, speeding away.

"Fuck! They took off in a vehicle like their asses were on fire. That can't be good." Ryker pulled his phone out. When Lucy didn't answer, he called Kyllian. He didn't answer either, so he dialed Hayden.

"We have company. I'll call you back." Hayden disconnected without explaining further.

Ryker wanted to throw his phone across the room but stopped at the last second.

"Havyk said they have company. That's all the fuck he said. How the fuck did they find Rhi?"

"What do you want to do?" Hawk asked.

"I'm calling Sutton. We're too far away. Fuck!" Ryker needed to calm down and trust his family to take care of Rhiannon. He didn't want to examine why he was so upset.

Because you know she's ours.

Not now.

Ryker dialed his father. When Sutton answered, Ryker stormed, "Where are you?"

"At home. Why? What's going on, Son?"

"Hayden said they have company and hung up. That's all I know. Pop…" Ryker swallowed hard.

"I'm on my way back. I'll call a couple Hounds to go with me." Ryker could hear his mom in the background asking what was wrong. Ryker ran a hand through his hair while he paced the room. Sutton told Rory to calm down, then he told Ryker, "I'll call you as soon as I know something. I'll keep them safe, Son. I promise."

"What if you're too late?"

"Your brothers and Lucy will protect the girls with their lives."

"That's what I'm afraid of. Fuck!"

"Ryker, stop. Let me call the others. Get on the road home and let Hawk or Spyder drive. That's an order."

It wasn't often Sutton pulled the alpha card, but when he did, Ryker knew to listen. "Yes, Sir. I'll be waiting." He disconnected and took a deep breath. "Sutton's headed over there now. He said for us to come home, and one of you are to drive."

Spyder held out his hand for the keys. "Let's go."

No one spoke until they were on the road. Ryker stared out the side window, his phone clutched in his hand. "We really need to find David. It's obvious he has better equipment at his disposal. If they get hold of Rhiannon…"

"Your family will protect her. You know that." Hawk cleared his throat. "Is there something more going on with Rhi than you wanting to protect her from Josiah?"

"What? No. I… Shit. Maybe. No. *No*. She's too young." And Ryker was a rambling mess. Yes, he wanted Rhi, but he wasn't the kind of male she needed. "She's a beautiful young woman, but there can never be anything between us. She needs someone softer around the edges, like Kyllian."

Spyder barked out a laugh. "Kayos? Soft? You really don't know your brother, do you?"

"What's that supposed to mean?" Ryker asked, harsher than intended.

"Kayos might be the softer spoken out of all your brothers, but that's where it ends. It's going to take a special female to tame that beast."

Ryker stared at the Hound, waiting, but the male didn't add anything. "Spyder—"

"Ryot, Kyllian's lifestyle isn't mine to share. If you want to know what your brother gets up to in the privacy of a hotel room or the back rooms of certain clubs he visits, you need to ask him yourself."

"Clubs? What kind of clubs is he visiting?"

Hawk leaned up from the back seat and set his hand on Ryker's shoulder. "Calm down, Ryot. It's nothing bad, okay? Let's just say your brother isn't exactly vanilla."

"How do both of you know this and I don't?"

"Do you share your sex life with him? Or any of the rest of us?" Spyder didn't give Ryker a chance to answer. "No, you don't. Not that we expect you to. We only know about Kayos because we go to the same clubs he does."

"Like fetish clubs? Are you telling me he – you all – are into BDSM?"

"Are you judging right now?" Hawk growled.

"No, of course not. Just... Fuck. How did I not know this?"

"Because it's really none of your business." Hawk leaned back, taking his hand with him. "What we do in our personal time is just that – personal. Some of us need more than a simple romp in the bedroom."

"So, what? You go to these clubs so you can beat your partner?"

Spyder sighed heavily. "It's not about beating someone. It's about giving or getting a different kind of release. Some like to wield a crop or whip, while others like to be on the receiving end. For some, it's about being tied up in ropes or bound to a bench or cross, giving complete control over to another person, trusting that person to take care of you while all you do is feel."

92

It took a lot to surprise Ryker, but Spyder's words had rendered him speechless. He stared out into the night, thinking about his younger brother dressed in leather and using a whip on someone helplessly tied up. Ryker wasn't completely clueless. He had heard of fetish clubs, but he'd never seen the appeal. Yes, he liked rougher sex, but the thought of actually hurting someone...

"I can hear your brain from here. If you have questions, just ask," Hawk offered.

"I have plenty of questions, but I'm not sure I want to know that much about Kyllian. What about Hayden? Does he go to the clubs too?"

"He went once, but it wasn't his scene. Hayden's the gentlest male I've ever come across in my life. And it's not because he's the youngest out of the five of you. He would make a good Daddy for someone with the way he likes to protect and nurture." Ryker snapped his head around at Spyder's words.

"Daddy?"

"It means—"

"I know what it means. Jesus fucking Christ." Ryker scratched at his beard. He felt like he'd fallen down the rabbit hole.

"I'm just saying, if you want someone gentle and loving for Rhiannon, Havyk is a better fit than Kayos."

Ryker didn't want to think about Hayden with Rhi. That made his skin itch. Or maybe it was thinking about Kyllian and some of the other Hounds living a lifestyle Ryker knew very little about. But their sexual proclivities had no effect on him or their club. As long as they did their jobs, which they all did, what they preferred in the bedroom or elsewhere wasn't any of his business. But knowing what they'd shared, he would never look at them the same way again. This information made him feel normal. No, that wasn't right. Their preferences weren't any less normal. When it came to sex and what someone liked, it wasn't abnormal, just different.

"I'm sorry if I came across as judgmental. Whatever you like is, like you said, personal. I think I'm just more shocked that I didn't know this about my brother."

"Well, you aren't exactly welcoming or forthcoming when it comes to personal stuff. And I say this as your friend, Ryot. You aren't the easiest male to get close to." Spyder reached across the console and squeezed Ryker's forearm. "Your family, both biological and the MC, we love you, Brother, and we understand why you are the way you are. Don't forget most of us have been in your life since before what happened with Juliette. Not only that, but you're our Pres. You carry the weight of us all on your shoulders, and we couldn't ask for a better leader. You stepped into some mighty big shoes when Sutton handed you the gavel, but you filled them well. More than filled them. Even if you hadn't been the oldest, I think Sutton would have chosen you to take his seat at the table, because you were the best male for the job."

"Spyder's right. You might be broody and keep things close to the vest, but you're one of the most honorable males I know, and I'd follow you to Hell and back again, no questions asked." Hawk clapped Ryker on the shoulder.

"Thanks. I—" Ryker's phone rang, cutting him off, and he was thankful for the reprieve. "Lucy? What's going on?"

"Everyone's safe, for now. Four of Josiah's men showed up, demanding we release Rhiannon. They said they knew she was here. I told them they were wrong and they could look around all they liked. I don't want to say any more because I don't know if our phones are secure."

"Are they still there?"

"No. Kyllian followed to make sure they left the area."

"Sutton was supposed to be on his way with backup."

"He's here. That's one of the reasons Josiah's men decided to leave. Four against six didn't seem like good odds, I guess."

"We're on our way back. We'll be there in little over an hour." Ryker wanted to know everything that happened, but if Lucy didn't think the line was secure, he wouldn't risk asking.

"Okay. We'll see you then." Lucy hung up, and Ryker let out a breath. "Pull over."

Spyder looked at Ryker to see if he was serious. "On the side of the highway or at the next exit?"

"Next exit. I want to check the car for trackers."

"Shit. Yeah, okay."

Ryker didn't trust Josiah Talbert as far as Marshall or Major could throw the human. Spyder took the next exit and parked behind a truck stop. The three of them got out of the SUV and searched the undercarriage for any sign of something that shouldn't be there. When they found nothing, Ryker motioned for them to get back on the road.

Hawk shut his door and sighed. "If Rhi's father is as good with computers as Lucy thinks, they wouldn't need a tracker to keep a lock on us. He can do that from behind his computer."

"Just another reason we need to get to the man. But we can't do that at GIA headquarters. Too much security."

"Then we ambush him between work and the compound. Lucy can tell us if there is an office other than in DC where GIA Headquarters is located. If not, that means it's at least a seven-hour drive. There's no way he commutes. He would have to have an apartment or house somewhere closer to the office," Hawk said.

"Depends on how much Josiah trusts him. If David is loyal, and it seems he is, then Josiah probably trusts him to spend time away from the compound." The other phone he carried pinged with an incoming message. Quinn. He raised his ass so he could peel the device from his back pocket. It was odd having an actual name and face to go with the sender of the email, but he appreciated it now more than ever. The job was straightforward. One Hayden could handle. His youngest brother was still in training, but Ryker trusted him to do the job, and Hayden had asked to be sent into the field. Ryker accepted the contract, but he didn't forward the email to Hayden's phone. If they were compromised, he didn't need the knowledge of their mercenary work falling into the wrong hands.

"We just got our first contract from Shepherd."

"You want one of us to take it?" Spyder asked.

"No. I'm giving it to Havyk. He asked for it."

"Is he okay? He's seemed a little down lately."

"We had a talk earlier. It seems seeing War and Mav finding mates has Hayden wishing for love of his own."

"That's understandable," Hawk said, sighing. Ryker didn't understand the BDSM lifestyle. He wondered how you could find a mate somewhere like a fetish club, but maybe that wasn't why they went there. Maybe they chose to let loose a little until they found their mate. The rest of the ride was made in silence, and when they pulled into Lucy's driveway, Ryker tensed. He knew the reason but refused to address it. Hayden and Kyllian met them at the SUV.

"Lucy said the phones might be compromised. If that's the case, do we know the males didn't hide bugs inside the house while they were looking for Rhiannon?"

Kyllian crossed his arms over his chest. "They did, actually. We found three of them, but until we get a sweeper in here, we aren't taking any chances. We need to move Rhiannon somewhere else. Somewhere she can speak without giving herself away. Hiding out in the tunnel isn't an option."

"Where is she now?"

"In the game room with Mac. They're trying to shoot pool without giggling. I turned the music up pretty loud so any noise they make will be drowned out," Hayden said.

"Is Sutton still here?"

"Yes. He, Legend, and Brick are keeping an eye on the perimeter. I'll go get him." Kyllian jogged off toward the

96

back of the house.

Ryker turned to Hayden. "I have a job for you. Since the phones might not be secure, I didn't send the information to yours. I'll use Lucy's printer and give you a paper copy. First thing tomorrow, I'm going to get a cache of burner phones we'll use for our merc jobs."

"That can wait until you talk to Pop. We need to figure out where to take Rhiannon first."

Kyllian returned with their father, and Lucy joined them outside. "I have an idea," she said. "We need somewhere safe for the girls, and I have the perfect place. Tamian's parents' house is a fortress, and Josiah would never know to look for Rhiannon there."

"Where is Tamian?" Ryker hadn't seen the Gargoyle since they returned.

"He's on his way to New Atlanta." Lucy slid her hands into her pockets. "He was torn about staying, but I convinced him we could handle things here."

"Say we do take the girls to Xavier's. Won't Rhi's father be able to track our movements?" Ryker asked. He didn't want to trust the woman's safety to anyone else, but that was jealousy speaking. Tamian's father was a full-blooded Gargoyle, and he loved Lucy. She had spent quite a bit of time with Xavier and Elizabeth, and Ryker knew Rhiannon would be in good hands with the male. Ryker had a job to do, and that meant he had to put aside his personal feelings. Feelings he was all too aware were getting deeper by the second. He didn't want to claim the female, but he also didn't not want to. Ryker had never been so conflicted in his life. "How are you going to explain the fact that Xavier and Elizabeth look the same age as Tamian? At least with Pop and Rory, they appear a little older than us."

"Well, we could tell her the truth. Or you could use your Gryphon voice on her. Either way, it's a chance we're going to have to take. You know I don't mind her being here, but what happens if we don't find all the bugs and

97

they hear her talking? They'll come back, and the next time, I doubt they come unarmed. If we use the tunnel, we can get her to the other side of the lake where there's enough tree coverage to obscure our movements."

"I don't like the idea of sending her to live with strangers." Ryker scrubbed his hands through his beard.

"They're no more strangers than the rest of us. She trusted you to keep her safe, and if you tell her this is what's best, she'll believe you. Unless you have a better idea?" Lucy narrowed her eyes at Ryker. His niece was feisty, but she was also smart. And she was right; Xavier's home was secure. But it was also over an hour away.

We will go with her.

We have a job to do.

Nothing is more important than protecting our mate.

She's not our *mate.*

I say she is.

"Ryker?" Lucy called his name, probably not for the first time.

"Sorry, just arguing with the beast."

"If it makes you both feel better, you can go with her," Lucy added.

"I have a job to do, and I can't do that babysitting Rhiannon."

Someone gasped, and Ryker didn't have to look to know who it was. By the time he did look toward the house, Rhiannon was already through the door. Mac scowled at him.

Rhiannon

RHI'S NERVES WERE shot. When the door to the passageway

opened, she wanted to run. Far. But it had been Lucy telling them the coast was clear. Even though Josiah's men were gone, the house wasn't safe for Rhi to talk freely, so she went back to being silent. It was like being back at Haven all over again. Josiah Talbert was still controlling her life, and she hated him for it. Her mother had taught her hate was a harmful emotion. It was negative energy which poisoned the mind. Without her mother guiding her, Rhi had allowed hatred into her heart and soul. If Daisy were still alive, she would find a way to cleanse the negativity. Since she was gone, it was up to Rhi to wash away the bad energy.

Mac was doing her best to keep Rhi occupied until they figure out where Rhi could go that was safe. Hayden had asked Mac to shoot pool with him, only instead of grabbing a stick for himself, he handed it to Rhi and pointed at the table. He then turned the music up loud so she and Mac could whisper to one another. Rhi hadn't shot pool since she was a teenager, and then she hadn't been any good at it. Mac wasn't much better, but at least she could break the balls and scatter a few. Rhiannon's cue ball ended up missing the others more often than not until Hayden showed her how to do it properly. He had aligned his large body behind hers, wrapping his arms around her. If that had been Ryker, Rhi would have probably fainted. Since it wasn't, she paid attention and finally got the hang of breaking.

Lucy had brought in snacks and sodas earlier before disappearing back into her office. Hayden and Kyllian, along with Sutton and two other large bikers, patrolled the grounds in case Josiah's men returned. It was late, and Rhi was tired. It had been a long, trying day, and she was ready for it to end. She was afraid if she went to sleep, her first taste at freedom in ten years would disappear and she'd find herself back at Haven, but she could barely hold her eyes open. She placed her pool cue in the rack and motioned upstairs to Mac. Mac nodded and grabbed Rhi's hand, pulling her through the house toward Lucy's office. Mac grabbed a pen and notepad.

"Let's go find Lucy and tell her we're going to bed."

Rhi nodded, then followed Mac through the house. When they didn't find Lucy anywhere, they looked out the front window to find she was talking to Ryker and all the other bikers. Rhi's heart sped up at the sight of the man. She wanted to run to him. To feel safe in his arms. She and Mac stepped out onto the porch.

"I have a job to do, and I can't do that babysitting Rhiannon." Ryker's words were like a slap to the face.

Rhi clapped a hand over her mouth before running back inside. She didn't stop until she was in the bedroom where her clothes were. She knew Ryker was out of her league, but to hear him say he considered watching over her as babysitting hurt. Deeply. She hurried into the bathroom and closed the door, sliding against it until she was sitting on the floor. Why couldn't she remember she was nothing to him other than some poor little girl he rescued? Why did her heart so desperately cling to thoughts of being with an older man who had a daughter almost her age? Why couldn't she have a crush on one of his younger brothers? But this felt like more than a simple crush. Rhi was drawn to him and had been since he found her in the dumpster. When he pulled her out of the container, something inside told her he was the kind of man she'd been dreaming of ever since she realized boys could be more than someone to play video games with.

Maybe it wasn't her age. Maybe it was because she had nothing to offer Ryker or any of the Lazlo brothers. They had rescued her. The whole family was doing everything they could to protect her. Wasn't that enough? The only good that came from them helping her was the fact that Mac now knew Elijah was alive. Rhi couldn't even tell them where Haven was.

Rhi needed to get her head out of her ass. She needed to

get away and start a life somewhere else. Somewhere far away from Haven, Josiah, her father, and Ryker Lazlo. She had brought nothing but trouble to their door. Climbing to her feet, she returned to the closet and retrieved her bags, filling them with the clothes and toiletries Rory had bought her. One day, she would find a way to repay their kindness. Until then, she would take her trouble elsewhere. Rhi grabbed her things and slipped silently down the stairs, continuing until she reached the lab and its secret passageway. Rhi wasn't in shape, so by the time she jogged the quarter mile to the other end of the tunnel, she was winded.

There was a keypad on the wall, and she had no idea what the code was. The lights were green, and that meant go, didn't it? She approached the large metal door. If she couldn't get out, she would have to return to the house and face the man who didn't want her around. Rhi grabbed the handle and twisted, then put her shoulder to the cold surface and pushed with a grunt. When it opened, she sucked in a lungful of crisp, night air. Rhi hitched her bags higher on her shoulder and stepped out into the night. The heavy, steel door closed with a bang, making her jump.

What little moonlight shone through the trees was enough for her to see the dirt path skirting the lake. She knew she didn't have much time before Mac came to check on her, finding her things gone. Rhi hurried down the path as quickly as she could and not trip. The farther away she got from the house, the harder her heart pounded. She should turn back. She should trust Mac and Lucy and Sutton to keep her safe. She didn't need Ryker. She didn't need him to babysit her. She could tell him she didn't want him around, and she knew he'd leave her alone. Let the others in his family watch over her. That's what they did. They helped others like her in similar situations. She had no money. She had no way of getting anywhere other than on foot and then she had no paperwork or identification allowing her to get a job.

Great. Way to think things through. No wonder Ryker thinks you're a baby.

Realizing her error, Rhi turned back toward the door. She got two steps in when someone stepped into her path. "Hello, Anna."

He expected her to be silent, but Rhiannon did the one thing she couldn't ever remember doing – she screamed.

CHAPTER TEN

Ryker

"FUCK!" RYKER TURNED his face toward the moon and let out a deep sigh. He knew he needed to go after Rhi, but he didn't know what to say to the female.

"You can be a real dick, Dad."

Ryker faced his pissed-off daughter. "Tell me something I don't know, Mac."

"Rhiannon has been through hell. Not just today, but every day for the past ten years. She hasn't had anyone she could count on since her mother died, and now she probably feels like a burden. I saw the way she looked at you, and yeah, she might be young and naïve, but you could do a lot worse. That woman would have been good for you. Good *to* you. But you have this need to keep everyone at arm's length. Your job is important, but one day, you're going to realize it isn't the most important thing in the world. Family is. Love is. Even someone like me knows that. So you go do your job, and I'm going to go see if I can repair the damage you've done." Mac stormed off toward the house.

"She's not wro—"

"Not now, Hayden. Yes, I'm a dick. We all know that. I'm sorry I hurt her feelings, but she doesn't want me. What she's feeling is nothing more than hero worship. It'll pass. She'll get over this crush and find someone who's right for her. Someone her own age. Now, let's figure out how to get her to Xavier's without her father and Josiah figuring out where we've stashed her. Lucy, you seem to have this all figured out, so why don't you tell us your plan?"

Lucy was glaring at him. Great. Now his Little Dove was pissed at him too.

"I'm going to call Xavier. You" — Lucy stabbed a finger at his chest — "go fix your shit."

The Hounds, his father, and brothers were silent, and Ryker was embarrassed. That pissed *him* off. He had no reason to be embarrassed. He was a fucking Gryphon. President of the Hounds. Yes, he hurt the woman's feelings, but he did have a job to do. It was his responsibility to keep both his family and his MC on the right track. Keep them focused on the things that mattered, like hunting down the fucking Ministry. Getting them mercenary jobs to keep the money coming in. Keeping his family safe. If he had to be a dick to do it, so be it.

Ignoring the looks the other males were giving him, Ryker said, "We're going to need — "

"Stop." Sutton motioned to the other Hounds. "Go patrol the area." Sutton was no longer president of the MC, but his authority wouldn't be denied. When they were alone, his dad asked, "What's this really about?"

Ryker knew better than to lie. "I can't have her, Pop. I had my one shot with Juliette."

"Are you telling me what War has with Kerrigan isn't real? Or Mav doesn't love Natalia?"

"No, of course not. But War isn't president of the MC. Mav's my second, but neither are responsible for getting the merc jobs. Making sure the family is taken care of."

"Are you saying I didn't do my job because I had your mother in my life?" Sutton didn't wait for Ryker to answer. "If Juliette were still here, would that affect your job? The way you handle your responsibilities?"

Ryker huffed. "No." He hated when his father made

him see reason. "I get it. But what if I'm right and she's only seeing me as the hero who saved her? What if I give in to my feelings, then she decides I'm too stern? Too rough? Too much to handle?"

"You show her the softer side of you. The male deep inside you were before you lost Juliette. The male who used to laugh and joke with your brothers. The one who used protecting your mother as an excuse so you could spend time in the kitchen with her where it was just the two of you. Show her the real Ryker Lazlo. Don't let her youth and naivety get in the way of something you know in your heart you deserve. Let it guide you back to the man you were before. Let her show you the good she has inside from being her mother's daughter and worshipping her goddess. Let her surprise you with her strength because it's in there. She wouldn't have gotten away from the cult if she weren't strong."

"What if I don't remember who that Ryker is?"

"Then let her remind you. Rhi is—"

"She's gone!" Mac ran out the door. "I can't find her anywhere."

"Hounds!" Ryker shouted, and the other males were back by his side within seconds. "Rhi is missing. Spread out. She couldn't have gotten far." The males took off running in different directions, but Ryker went to his daughter. Mac was shaking. "Mac—"

"No! You go find her. You did this, and only you can make it right." Mac ran back into the house, and he followed.

The first place he went was to the bedroom where Rhi was supposed to sleep. The door to the closet was open, but it was empty. The bathroom was void of toiletries, and the dresser drawers were open, also empty. All her things were gone. His Gryphon roared inside his head, and it was all Ryker could do to keep it from taking over and shifting. That wouldn't help the situation. At all. Ryker ran back downstairs to the office where Lucy's security monitors were.

"I don't see her anywhere," Lucy muttered. The screens showed the outside of the property. She tapped the keyboard a few times, and the screens switched over to the inside of the house. The feed blurred as Lucy rewound it. There on the monitor was Rhi with both bags. She hurried down the steps and turned down the hallway which led to... "The basement. Shit! She took the tunnel!" Lucy jumped from her chair and took off with Ryker on her heels. The bookcase was angled away from the wall, so in no time, he and Lucy were racing down the passageway. Before they reached the door at the other end, a scream rent the night, somewhere on the other side of the door.

Ryker's lion roared, halfway shifting. His sharp canines elongated, and his mane shook around his head. Ryker wrenched the door open, afraid of what he'd find on the other side.

"Let go of me!" Rhiannon yelled, and Ryker lost control. His lion was fully formed as he bound down the path where a man was dragging Rhi through the woods. The man – James – turned, Rhiannon in front of him as a shield, his arm outstretched.

"Ryker, no!" Lucy yelled.

Too late, Ryker saw the gun. The bullet slammed into his side, knocking him off course. He landed hard, but his Gryphon wasn't about to give up. It tried to shift, unable to fully do so. Rhiannon screamed, and James pointed at him again.

"What the fuck?" James asked as Ryker shifted back into his human form.

"No!" Rhiannon shoved against his arm, and the next shot went wide. A large eagle flew down from the trees, talons grabbing onto the man's hand holding the weapon. Rhiannon dropped to the ground and crawled over to where Ryker breathed through the pain. Having shifted

106

without thought, he was naked.

"Oh, goddess. Please, please, please," Rhi chanted, pressing both hands against the wound. Ryker hissed, and Rhiannon jerked her hands away. "I'm sorry."

"No! Keep your hands on him!" Lucy yelled. Ryker turned his head toward his niece's voice. She had the man on the ground, a knee in his back, and a talon clutching his neck. Rhiannon put her hands back on Ryker's side, and he did his best not to pass out.

"What are you?" she whispered. "Y-you're not human."

"We're Gryphons," Ryker managed to choke out. Several eagles flew overhead, and one lion bounded through the woods. "Pop," Ryker groaned upon seeing the white fur of his father. The lion padded over to Ryker and nudged his face. "I'm fine. Go help Lucy." Sutton disappeared into the trees, and a minute later returned in human form, wearing nothing but jeans.

"Anna! Get away from him! He's a monster!" James yelled.

"No! You're the monster," Rhiannon returned. The heat from her hands was like a soothing balm. The pain had lessened as soon as she touched him. *Right.* The blood loss had him imagining craziness.

"I'm your husband, and I command you to get over here and help me."

"You are not my husband, and you never will be. These people have shown me more care in the last twenty-four hours than you have in the last few years. I'll take my chances with them." Rhiannon looked down at Ryker. When she smiled at him, something inside shifted. Before he could figure out what it was, Hayden and Kyllian were at his side. Kyllian dropped a shirt over his groin, covering him from Rhi's gaze.

"You can move your hands now," Kyllian told Rhi. When she did, Kyllian pressed a cloth of sorts against the wound, and the pain returned in full force. "We need to get

107

you to the hospital."

"No. Call... Rev." Ryker didn't want the police involved, and that's exactly what would happen if he went to the emergency room. Zareck "The Reverend" West was a doctor and one of the Hounds.

"I did, but you're losing a lot of blood, Brother."

"Not... hospital," Ryker choked out. His eyes were getting heavy. Too heavy. He focused on Rhiannon who had tears rolling down her pretty cheeks. "S'okay, Angel," he muttered right before he passed out.

Rhiannon

RHI WAS PRETTY sure she'd fallen and hit her head. That, or James had drugged her. There was no way men could turn into lions and eagles and whatever it was Ryker had been. He said he was a Gryphon, but she didn't know what that was. It was like his body couldn't figure out if it wanted to be a lion or an eagle, and it was trying to be both at the same time. But that wasn't possible. Except it was, because she was awake, Ryker was bleeding, and Lucy had an eagle's talons clutching James's throat. Hayden, Kyllian, Sutton, and four other men Rhi had never seen were all wearing nothing but jeans. Ryker had called the white lion "Pop," so that meant Sutton was a Gryphon too.

"Ryot, stay with me." Kyllian slapped Ryker on the cheek, trying to get him to wake up.

Rhiannon crawled around to the other side, ignoring James and whatever Sutton was doing to him. She focused her energy on Ryker, placing her hands on his arm. Rhi closed her eyes and asked the goddess for help. She ignored the yelling behind her and focused her energy on Ryker. Ignored the blood. Goddess, there was so much blood. She

108

squeezed her eyes closed and imagined every good thing in the world, sending the positive vibes into Ryker's skin. A new voice met Kyllian's as they inspected the wound, but she still concentrated. It was something her mother had taught her to do with a dying plant. Daisy had brought many plants and flowers back from the brink with just a thought. It had been ten years since Rhi had tried it. No, that wasn't true. She had done it at Haven, and that's when the name-calling started.

"Rhi." Kyllian was trying to get her attention, but she had to focus. "Rhiannon, you can let go now."

"No. Need to concentrate."

"No, you don't. Look."

Rhi opened her eyes to find Ryker staring at her. "Hey," he whispered.

"Hi. I, uh…" She looked down where the bullet punctured his side. The blood had stopped flowing, and a man she'd never seen before was staring at her as well.

"How did you do that?" the man asked.

"Do what?"

"Stop the bleeding. I mean, it was a through-and-through, so the bullet wasn't lodged inside, but it should still be bleeding. You stopped it, didn't you?" He wasn't accusing her, exactly.

"I just wanted to help. I was trying to take his pain away."

"You did," Ryker said. "When Kyllian replaced your hands with the T-shirt, the pain came back. It was like magic. Your magic."

"Oh, I wouldn't call it magic. More like transference of positive energy. My mom taught me how to do it with plants, and I hoped it would work with you. I've never tried it on a human before. Or Gryphon."

"She knows?" the stranger asked.

"She knows," Ryker replied, still staring at her. Then he smiled. It was the first time she'd seen it, and it was

109

glorious.

"I still need to get you stitched up. Let's get you back to the house. It's going to hurt because we're going to have to carry you."

"I can walk, Rev," Ryker argued.

"You probably can, but you shouldn't."

Rhiannon stood and looked around. James was nowhere to be seen. "What happened to James?"

"They took him back to Lucy's to interrogate him," Kyllian answered. "I hate that he shot Ryker and almost kidnapped you, but now we'll use him for information."

Rhiannon didn't want to know how they planned to get said information from him, but she honestly didn't care. He had tried to take her, and he shot Ryker. For that alone, she hoped the others roughed him up a bit.

With a lot of fussing on Ryker's part and a little coaxing on Rhi's, Rev and Kyllian helped Ryker back through the tunnel after giving him a pair of jeans to put on. When they reached the door leading inside, James was yelling. As soon as Rhi stepped into the room, he stopped cursing and began begging.

"Anna, please. You have to help me. Your father—"

"My name is Rhiannon. And David stopped being my father the moment he took me to Haven. Do yourself a favor and cooperate. Or don't. I don't care." She ignored his further pleadings and followed Ryker and the others up the stairs to the bedroom she'd been given. That seemed like a lifetime ago. Mac and Lucy were standing on the far side of the room, and when she entered, Mac raced to her, pulling her into a hug.

"God, I'm so glad you're okay," Mac mumbled against her hair.

"Me too." When Mac released her, Rhi looked down at the blood on her hands. "I need to wash up, but my things..."

Mac pointed to her bags on the floor by the closet. "Go.

I'll keep my dad company while you shower, then you and I are going to have a long talk."

"Okay." Rhi didn't care if Mac yelled at her. She had been stupid for running. She deserved a good scolding. By the time she was out of the shower and changed into clean clothes, only Ryker and Mac remained in the bedroom. Ryker was propped up against the headboard, still shirtless, and Mac was sitting beside him, holding his hand.

"Mac, will you give us a minute?" Ryker asked.

"Sure." Mac leaned over, kissing her father on the cheek before standing. "Rhi, I'll be in my bedroom. Come find me… Or don't." She smiled at Rhi before closing the door behind her.

"Rhi," Ryker started, but paused. She had never seen him unsure. Mad, yes. Stoic, yes. Hesitant? She didn't think so.

"I'm sorry. I never should have run. Wait, is it safe to talk in here? I thought I was supposed to be quiet."

Ryker held out his large hand, and Rhi stared at it for only a couple seconds before she slid her smaller hand against his palm. Ryker tugged her closer, so Rhi sat down on the edge of the bed, mindful of his injury. What she saw didn't make sense. "Your side is… Where's the hole?" Rhi reached out to touch his skin but yanked her hand back at the last second.

"That's one of the perks of being a shifter. We heal quickly. But not this quickly, normally. I think whatever it was you did to me helped speed the process along."

"I didn't do anything," she lied. Her mother had warned her to keep her gift a secret.

"I think you did. I could feel the warmth from your hands. And like I said before, the pain receded when you touched me. It was amazing."

"You're not mad?" Rhi kept her eyes lowered.

"Why would I be mad? You have something special inside you, and you used it to help me. I'm grateful is what I

111

am."

"Oh. Okay, then." Having to tamp down her gift for so long had become second nature. Josiah hadn't appreciated it. Had called it sinful even. Rhi wasn't used to being praised for it.

"As for talking freely, one of the Hounds came in while we were dealing with James and checked the house. All the bugs have been moved down to the dining room for now."

"Then can I ask about Gryphons? That's what you called it, right?"

"Yes. I have to say you're taking the shifter thing awfully well."

Rhi shrugged. "I saw the evidence with my own eyes. When you were hurt, your body was changing, like it couldn't decide whether to be a lion or an eagle."

"Gryphons are both. Fully formed, our upper body is that of an eagle and the lower half is a lion. We can shift into either depending on the situation."

"Your wings were blue. Are they all that color? They were really pretty." Rhi had only seen them briefly, but she thought they were spectacular in a scary, something-out-of-a-science-fiction-movie way.

"Not all. Gryphons have the ability to call on one of the elements, and mine is water, thus the blue wings."

Rhi still hadn't looked at Ryker, afraid of what she'd see. She hadn't forgotten why she took off in the first place.

"Rhi, look at me." When she did as he asked, she was surprised by the softness in Ryker's eyes. "I'm sorry for what I said about babysitting you. I promise I don't feel that way. What I feel is complicated." Ryker blew out a breath and looked up at the ceiling for a few seconds before returning his gaze to hers. "I'm under a lot of pressure. My family tells me I'm too stern. Too focused, but it's the only way I know to be. I feel responsible for every single member of both my family as well as the club, and I take that responsibility seriously. My feelings for you are conflicted. I felt drawn to you the moment I saw you in that dumpster, and I didn't like it."

"I'm sorry. I understand I'm just some girl you rescued." When Rhi tried to pull her hand out of Ryker's grip, he tightened the hold, and Rhi stopped talking. She turned her head so he wouldn't see the tears forming.

"No, you are the *woman* I rescued, but it's more than that. I had a wife, Mac's mom. She was taken away from me by Josiah. Given to his brother where she was forced to live much the same way you and Mac were. Mac was taken from her mom and eventually given to her adoptive parents so that Gideon could keep up the charade of being a good man. Juliette also ran away, but unlike you, she lost her life. That was twenty years ago. I was informed she died in a fire. For the longest time, I mourned the loss of my wife and unborn child. I was angry. Angry at myself for not being here when she needed me. Angry at Zeus for taking them away from me. Just angry period. I started seeing someone not too long ago. It wasn't serious. We hooked up once a month for sex. Nothing more. Then I found out she was using me to get back at someone else." Ryker stroked his thumb across the back of Rhi's hand, and that little bit of affection helped stem the tears.

"Before I knew she was using me, it was a perfect relationship, if you can call it that. It was sex with no strings. No attachment. I didn't want the feelings that go along with a relationship. I wasn't ready for that. Even after twenty years, I thought Juliette was the only mate I'd ever have."

"Mate. I've heard that more than once. Is that what shifters call their partners?"

"Yes. Some are true mates where we complete a bond, and others are wives, husbands, girlfriends, or boyfriends, the same as human partners. The bond isn't as deep. Juliette was my mate. My bonded mate, and I thought that was it for me. But my brother Warryck, he found his bonded mate twice. Once with Lucy's mom, and now with Kerrigan.

When I saw you, I felt something I haven't in a long time, and it scared and confused me. When I lost Juliette, I resigned myself to being alone the rest of my long life, then I saw the most beautiful woman hiding in a dumpster. My Gryphon claimed you then and there, but I fought with it."

"So it's part of you but it isn't?" Rhi didn't understand how all the shifting stuff worked.

"Sort of. The Gryphon can act and think for itself and usually only does that when it's not in agreement with its human counterpart. When I saw James trying to take you away, my Gryphon took over. All it cared about in that moment was getting to you. To keep you safe."

"I take it Gryphons are a secret from the rest of the world?"

"Mostly. There are a few humans aware of our existence who aren't mates."

"Aren't you worried about them exposing you?" Rhi shifted so her thigh was touching Ryker's. He was still holding her hand, and she took that as a good sign.

"Gryphons have the ability to alter human thoughts. If we fear someone will 'out' us, we wipe what they know from their mind."

"Does that mean you can make someone have feelings for you that wouldn't normally be there? Or take away feelings you didn't want someone to have?"

"Absolutely not. We only remove the knowledge of us being shifters. We use our ability for our safety or the safety of the human. I will admit I used my voice on you when you were in the dumpster. I convinced you to let me get a hotel room. I only did it because I needed to get you somewhere James wouldn't find you, and you didn't know me enough to trust me. I would never use my voice to take away your free will."

"That's comforting. You mentioned a long life. How long is long?"

"Most Gryphons live a few hundred years if they aren't

114

taken out by, say, a bullet." Ryker smiled, and Rhi couldn't help but return it, even if he was playing off him being shot by James.

"How old are you, if you don't mind me asking?"

"I'm forty-eight."

"You sure don't look it. And your parents?"

"My dad is one hundred five, and Rory is one hundred three. The sisters I told you about are all in their eighties. They don't look any older than I do."

"That's—" Rhi couldn't hold back the yawn that escaped. She covered her mouth, then shook her head. "Sorry, that's amazing."

"You've had a long day. I'm going to let you get some sleep. Tomorrow, I'll probably be taking you to Tamian's parents' place. It's more secure, and Josiah knows nothing about it. You'll be safe there until we can take down Haven." Ryker pulled Rhi's hand to his mouth and kissed her knuckles. "We'll talk more later, okay?"

"Okay." Rhi wanted to ask him to stay, but she needed time to think about everything she'd learned about him and Gryphons. She had so many questions, but they could wait.

Ryker slid off the bed and turned down the covers. Once Rhi was snuggled underneath the soft sheet, Ryker leaned over and pressed his lips to her forehead.

"Goodnight, Rhiannon."

"Night." She watched him walk to the door with no indication he'd been shot. She was admiring the way his butt filled out his jeans until he turned out the light and closed the door behind him without looking back.

Rhi sighed into the dark room, a smile spreading across her face as she pressed the knuckles he'd kissed to her own lips.

CHAPTER ELEVEN

Ryker

RYKER WANTED TO stay with Rhi. Now that he had accepted the possibility of having her in his life, he wanted her by his side. Wanted to spend time getting to know the young woman. Sutton's words had shaken him. Made him see he was being obtuse. When Rhi placed her hands on him, pushing her energy into his body, it was as though she was sharing her soul with him. Ryker had never felt anything as magical. It was the only way he knew to describe the sensation. He likened it to when Juliette informed him she was pregnant, and even that didn't compare.

Juliette.

He had loved Mac's mother with his whole being, and she would always be his first love. She would forever hold a special place in his heart. That didn't mean he couldn't love again. Love someone completely different than the wildcat Juliette had been. There was so much more to Rhi than met the eye, and he wanted to find out everything about her. Mac had chastised him while Rhi was in the shower. Had practically given him her blessing to pursue Rhi. Ryker had already made up his mind to allow himself to do just that, but hearing his daughter tell him she was more than okay with it made him feel better about his decision. But first, he had to ensure Rhi's safety, and that meant dealing with James and the Ministry. He also had to find out what Rhi wanted.

When Ryker reached the basement, things were quiet. James was still tied to the chair, but he was staring off at nothing. "What's going on?" Ryker asked Sutton.

"Just waiting on you. I didn't want to start the interrogation until you were here to listen, but I got tired of his threats, so I voiced him to be quiet. Everything okay upstairs?"

"Yes. At least it will be once this shit is all over. Let's get on with it." Ryker gestured for his dad to proceed.

Sutton moved to stand in front of James. "You will only speak when spoken to, and you will tell the truth calmly. How long have you been part of Haven?"

"Eight years."

"And what is your role within the community?"

"I'm a recruiter."

"Meaning?"

"Brother Josiah gives me names and addresses, and I go speak to the person or family and convince them to join us."

"Where does Josiah get this information?"

"From David."

"What else does David do for Haven?"

"He uses his computer to hide our existence. Gives people new identities. Moves money around."

"Where does Haven get its money?"

"Mostly from the men who have jobs on the outside. David takes their paychecks and invests them."

"How many men have jobs on the outside, and what is it they do?"

"I'd say ten? Not sure exactly. Other than David, I know one's a banker, one's a retired doctor, and one is a former cop."

"Where do you get your weapons?"

"David brings them in, but I'm not sure where he gets them."

"What is the purpose of Haven?"

"To raise a community of likeminded men who want to see the world changed for the better. To ensure future generations are the leaders the world needs. Ones who are Godly and lead the communities in weeding out the criminals and less-than-desired."

"What makes someone less-than-desired?"

"Someone who doesn't walk the path to Heaven. Someone who doesn't believe in God. People who live immoral lives, thinking it's okay to lead others astray."

"You mean someone like Josiah who kidnaps women and gives them to his brother to use? Someone who holds young men and women against their will? Someone who sells babies to another family so his flock doesn't know the mother was already married?"

"Brother Josiah says sometimes you have to get your hands dirty doing the Lord's work."

"Rhiannon didn't want to marry you, yet you continued to pursue her against her will. Is that Godly?"

"Anna had the devil in her. It was my task to show her how a righteous man behaved. To show her the error of her ways. To get her to believe in the one true God."

Ryker took a step towards James, but Sutton held up his hand. "You're saying a righteous man takes a woman against her will? Did you touch Anna?"

"No. I was courting her. I wasn't allowed to touch her because we weren't married."

"Why would you want a woman who doesn't want you?"

"She didn't know what she wanted. She was raised by a sinful mother who told her lies about how real men behave."

"But David is her father. Are you saying he wasn't a real man?"

"David was weak. It took a righteous woman to show him his path."

"Tell me about Haven. Where is it located? How many

live there? How many guards do you have?"

"It's twenty miles east of New Roseville. There are about three hundred members right now. Most of the men are guards. The boys are in training."

"Other than the guards, are there security measures in place to keep people out?"

"David keeps watch over the area with drones. He has them programmed to alert Josiah if someone gets too close to the perimeter."

"Where is David's office?"

"In New Brunswick. Sometimes he has to fly to New Washington for meetings, but mostly he works out of New Brunswick."

Sutton turned to Ryker. "Anything else you want to know?"

"Ask him about Eli."

"Do you know a young man by the name of Elijah?"

"There are two Elijahs. One is a boy of about six, and the other came to Haven a few months back. Brother Josiah told us he was a troubled young man and we were to stay away from him."

"What is the older Elijah's role within the community?"

"Nothing really. He's held in solitary most of the time for causing trouble. When he's let out, he works cleanup, but that only lasts for a few days until he's put back in confinement."

"Where is he held when he's in trouble?"

"There's a holding cell under the smallest barn."

Ryker growled low in his throat. When he found Josiah, he was going to make the bastard pay.

"Is he treated badly when he's in this cell? Is he fed?"

"He's fed once a day but otherwise left alone."

"Is he the only one who is confined to a cell?"

"Now he is. There was another boy, but I haven't seen him around in about a year."

"What do you think happened to this other boy?"

"Brother Josiah took him away. Probably to his father-in-law's community. That's where the more troubled souls end up."

"Who is Josiah's father-in-law?"

"Abraham Goodman. He's the leader of the elders."

Sutton turned away from James, his expression between elation and a quiet storm. This name meant something to his dad. When he composed himself, Sutton turned back to James. "Why did you come back here after the others left tonight?"

"Because I knew Anna was here."

"How did you know?"

"By the tracker."

"What tracker?" Ryker strode to stand in front of James and tipped the chair back, leaning forward until their noses were almost touching.

"The one her father had put in before they came to Haven. Brother Josiah convinced David to let me have the device it's linked to since we're going to be married."

Ryker's beast pushed against him, wanting to tear James apart. He was close to turning it loose.

"Where is this device now?"

"In my pocket."

"Get it. Now," Ryker shouted. With James's arms tied to the chair, it took him a second to dig it out of his back pocket. Ryker watched James carefully to make sure it wasn't a trick. When the man pulled out a small, black box, Ryker grabbed it, dropped it to the floor, and smashed it under the heel of his boot. "Are there any more of these devices that can track Rhi?"

"Who's Rhi?"

"Anna. Are there any more?"

"Not that I know of."

Ryker paced the room that used to be Lucius's lab. He had to get his beast under control before it tore James apart one limb at a time. He was aware of the Hounds tracking his movements, but he also felt their ire. None of them liked the fact that innocent women were treated the way they were in these cults, but when that woman was family? They liked it even less. And Rhiannon became family the moment Ryker pulled her from the dumpster.

"One last question." Ryker stopped pacing in front of James but kept a few feet between them. "Do you know who David's mother is?"

"Sure. She's Abraham's wife."

"That can't be right. Abraham's last name is Goodman. David's is Spencer," Sutton said.

"Abraham isn't David's father. He married Ruth after his first wife died."

Sutton motioned for Ryker to follow him up the stairs. "I think we have everything we need to form a plan. Do you want to send him back, or…?" Sutton was silently asking if Ryker wanted to take the man out, but this wasn't a mercenary contract. Did kidnapping warrant a death sentence? As much as Ryker wished it did, he couldn't in good conscience kill the man. "He did shoot you," Sutton reminded him.

Ryker ran a hand down his face. When he was on a job as a mercenary, he had no trouble taking out the mark. So why was he hesitating now? Rhi's pretty face came to mind. Would she want him to kill the man? Would she think less of him if he did? Since she was standing outside the door listening in, he held up his hand, silencing his father. Sutton smirked, and they both turned to see if she would remain hidden or join in the conversation. They didn't have to wait long.

"If you can't shoot him, I will," Rhi said from the doorway leading to the kitchen. "Sorry. I didn't mean to eavesdrop, but I couldn't sleep."

"You could shoot James?" Sutton asked.

"Yes. He tried to kidnap me, and he shot Ryker. He intended to kill him. That's not okay."

Sutton grinned at Ryker with one eyebrow raised as if to say, "See? She's strong."

"What would your goddess think?" Ryker asked.

Rhi sighed. "You're right. If I killed him, that would return to me threefold, if not more. I've had enough bad to last a lifetime." She cocked her head to the side. "But you don't answer to the goddess, so do what you need to do." She gave Ryker a tight smile and walked off toward the stairs. When she was out of sight, Ryker turned to his dad.

"Let him go, *but* give him instructions to leave town and not return to Haven. Make sure he never speaks to anyone about what happened tonight, about Rhi, about anything related to her or the Ministry."

"I can handle that. Why don't you go see if you can't help your female get some sleep?" Sutton winked.

"Sleep is going to have to wait. We need to get the tracker out of Rhi. Just because I smashed the device doesn't mean there isn't another one out there. I'm going to find Rev."

Rhiannon

RHI HADN'T BEEN able to sleep, so she unpacked her bags, again, then decided to get something to drink. When she overheard Ryker's conversation with Sutton, she paused to listen before making her presence known. No, her goddess wouldn't want Rhi to kill anyone, but the man had tried to kill Ryker. Shouldn't he be punished for it? If she hadn't known Ryker was good before that, she did now. He was willing to let James go, but not before wiping his memory of what he'd seen. Ryker said he used his Gryphon voice on her when she was hiding out, but had that really been the only time? She hoped so. She couldn't think of anything she'd said or done that was out of character.

Flopping down on the soft bed, Rhi closed her eyes. She'd never had trouble sleeping before, but she'd also never had as crazy a day like this one either. The most exciting part was Ryker admitting to wanting to be with her. Rhi didn't know what to do next. She had no experience with men. Not the kind that mattered in this situation. Other than the chaste kisses Bobby Carmichael had given her when she was thirteen, Rhi had no idea what went on between two people in a relationship. Couples at Haven weren't allowed to show affection other than holding hands. Her mother had talked to her about sex, but it had only been to tell her to give her body to someone who cared for her deeply. She didn't know if Ryker was that man. He said he was done fighting his feelings, but did that mean he wanted a relationship or something more casual?

Rhi hated her father more in that moment than she ever had. If he hadn't taken her to Haven, she would have had a normal life where she and her friends would have fallen in love with cute boys at school. Gotten their hearts broken but learned from the experience and tried again. She would have gone on dates. Real ones where the guy picked her up and took her to a movie. Took her to prom. Made out with her in the garden while her dad was inside watching television. Or maybe her father would have been overprotective and refused to let her be alone with boys. She didn't blame her mom for dying. It wasn't Daisy's fault she got sick. If her mom hadn't died, Rhi's life might not have been perfect, but it would have been a lot better.

Then again, if she hadn't been taken to Haven, she never would have had to escape and be rescued by Ryker. Daisy always said everything happened for a reason, so maybe Ryker was the reason Rhi had to endure ten years at Haven. She had to see the bad to appreciate the good that was the Lazlo family. And they were good, even if they were Gryphons.

Gryphons!

Holy crap! Ryker could turn into a gorgeous lion. That should scare the crap out of her, but it didn't. It was exciting. And *sexy*. The way he'd gone all growly when he lunged for James. The Gryphon part wasn't nearly as sexy, but that was probably because Ryker had been hurt and couldn't fully shift. She had to admit she wanted to see him at least once in his Gryphon to know what it looked like. Rhi giggled. She couldn't help it. Her life had gone from miserable and mundane to exciting in less than a day. She might not like James, but she was glad it had been him to set his sights on her or else she might never have had a chance at escaping, since he was one of the few men she was aware of who left Haven with any regularity.

When her stomach twinged, Rhi knew what that meant. Her periods were like clockwork. She climbed off the bed and went to the bathroom to find the pads Rory had bought. Unlike the cloth ones she'd been forced to use at Haven, she found the pack of disposable ones like her mother had bought her. She'd tried tampons, but they made her cramps worse. After putting one on, she returned to bed and thought back over what happened with Ryker. He said Rhi's hands helped with his pain. Rhi had tried using her gift on herself, but it never worked. Maybe it was because both the energy and pain were on the inside, and to use her power, she had to push the energy outward the same way she'd done when she focused on Ryker. Or maybe it was a gift from the goddess she was supposed to share with others and not use for herself.

She had just about nodded off when the door opened and Ryker stalked in. "Sorry to barge in, but this can't wait. Do you know where your chip is?"

Rhi sat up and pulled the covers up under her arms. "Chip?" She looked at Ryker, frowning. "What're you talking about?"

Ryker swiped his hand through his hair. "Your father

124

had a tracking chip implanted somewhere under your skin, and we need to get it out of you. Come on, let's go downstairs." Ryker turned his back, and Rhi climbed out of bed, grabbing her clothes. She went into the bathroom and changed.

When they got downstairs, the dining room was full of people. Ryker pulled the chair out for her. "Do you remember going to the doctor for anything before you went to Haven?"

"Yes. David said I needed some immunizations. He took me to some doctor I didn't know. He had a chip put in instead?"

"Yes. That's how James knew you were here. He gave me the tracking device, and I destroyed it. We aren't sure it was the only one, so we need to find the chip and remove it. What do you remember about where the doctor stuck you?"

Rhi touched the back of her neck. "He gave me a shot in the arm, but then he said he needed to remove a mole from my neck – here," she said, pulling her hair over one shoulder so she could show Ryker the spot below her hairline. Ryker's breath was warm on her neck when he leaned closer to look, running the pads of his fingers over her skin.

"I'm sure it's miniscule. I can't feel anything." He sat back up in his chair. "Rev is going to remove it before we hit the road. I won't have anyone able to track you to Xavier's."

"You're going to have it cut out?" Rhi wanted it out, but there had to be a better way.

"Depending on the size, he might be able to extract it with a needle," Lucy said.

"That's not much better. But…" Rhi blew out a breath. She could do this. She had to do it. "Yeah, okay."

"Good girl," Ryker said, kissing her temple. Everyone was staring at them. Mac was smiling, Kyllian was smirking, but Hayden was frowning. "Rev is waiting on his wife to get here to help, so we have a few minutes."

"Would you like some water?" Lucy asked.

Rhi didn't know if she could keep anything down, so she shook her head. "No, thank you." Knowing her father did that to her without her knowledge made her nauseated. How could the same man who had been there for the first thirteen years of her life become this stranger? Ryker placed his hand on Rhiannon's neck and rubbed. She wanted to smile, but she just couldn't. Rhi pushed back from the table and stood. "I need some air." She took off out the back door, not stopping until her feet touched the ground. Rhi squatted and spread her hand over the grass, letting the earth's energy flow through her. She hadn't been outside long when the back door opened, and Ryker and Rev stepped outside.

"Hey, Rhi," the Hound said, looking nothing like a doctor and everything like a biker. There was a pretty woman with him, and she was smiling at Rhi like they'd been friends forever.

Ryker walked over and held his hand out. Rhi took it so he could help her to her feet. "Come on. I'll introduce you." Ryker laced their fingers and tugged her toward the other couple. "Rhiannon, this is Bethany, Rev's wife. Bethany, Rhi."

Instead of shaking hands, Bethany pulled Rhi in for a hug. The woman was older than Rhi with her long, dark hair braided down her back. She was dressed in jeans, leather boots, and jacket. That made sense if she rode with her husband. Rhi wanted a leather jacket.

"It's so nice to meet you," Bethany said when she pulled back. Her hands were on Rhi's biceps as she looked Rhi over. "Zareck was right; you are special." Bethany winked before going back to her husband.

"Zareck?"

"That'd be me. My given name," Rev explained. "Now, are you ready to have your tracker removed?"

No. "Yes. I don't want my father to have any way of

finding me. I still can't believe he did that. I mean, what kind of man puts a chip in his own kid?"

"The kind with something special to lose," Bethany said. "Not that I agree with it. I think it's the worst kind of manipulation. Rhi, does your father know about your gift?"

"Not really. At least I don't think so, unless my mom told him. But I never used it around him."

"Did you ever do anything extraordinary before your mom died?" Rev asked. "Like bring a dead plant back to life?"

"Oh, yeah. Plenty, but that was something just between Mom and me."

Rev and Ryker shared a look, and Ryker placed his hand on Rhi's shoulder. "I have a feeling he found out somehow."

"What does that have to do with putting a tracker in me?"

"Either he wanted to keep you around in case he needed your gift at some point, or he didn't want your gift getting in the wrong hands. If others knew what you're capable of, they could exploit you."

"But I can't really do anything other than heal plants."

Ryker narrowed his eyes. "That's not true. Maybe you haven't tapped into all your gift is capable of, but I know personally there's more to it than what you realize. You used it on me. Your energy was like an instant dose of morphine."

"What's that?" Rhi hated being stupid. No, not stupid – uneducated.

"It's a potent pain killer. Usually only given in the hospital because it's so powerful. I have to ask, have you ever turned your energy on an injured animal?"

How could he possibly know that? "What makes you ask that?"

"Your gift is special, just as you are. I just wondered if you ever attempted to help a stranded bird or some other

127

small animal, just to see if you could."

Rhi hesitated to answer, thinking back about the baby bunny that was injured. She hadn't known about her gift at that point. All she knew was she really didn't want it to die. She also remembered the promise she made her mom, but Daisy was gone, and her father had lost his mind. In that moment, she decided to trust Ryker and his friends. "There was one time, I was probably five or six. I found a bunny that was bleeding. I don't know what had happened to it, but I knew it wasn't good. I sat on the ground with it, protecting it from other animals. My mom was frantic when she found me. She asked what I was doing, and when I told her I was taking care of the bunny, she looked at me like I was the best kid ever. She told me my gift was special, just for me, and I couldn't ever tell anyone about it."

"What happened to the rabbit?" Bethany asked.

"It got up and hopped away. Every day, I went back to that part of the woods looking for it. One day, about a week later, I saw the baby with a larger rabbit I figured was its mother. I knew it was my bunny because one of its ears was white. When it saw me, it hopped over to where I had knelt down, watching it. It sniffed my hand before returning to its mom."

"I'm surprised your father didn't try to exploit your gift," Ryker said.

"I'm not. His mother, my grandmother, convinced him what I had in me was of the devil. That I was a freak and a sinner, and instead of saying I had a gift, she told my dad he had to get me somewhere I could be healed."

"I hope you didn't believe your grandmother," Bethany hissed. "You are everything good in this world. I know this, and I've only just met you."

"Thank you." Rhi wiped at a stray tear. It had been too long since she had someone on her side. "I didn't believe it. My mom was everything to me, and if she said I was good, nobody could convince me otherwise. It's her words, her love, that I've held onto all these years."

"Your mom sounds like she was as special as you are. I'm sorry you lost her." Bethany stepped up and hugged Rhi tight in her arms. Rhi clung to the other woman. She wasn't old enough to be Rhi's mom's age, but in that moment, she felt as though her mother were with her.

Rhi reluctantly pulled away and wiped her face. "Let's get this over with."

Ryker wrapped his arm around her shoulder, kissed the side of her head, then led her inside. They stopped in the dining room where Rev directed Rhi to sit. Several items were already spread out on the table, but Rhi opted not to look too closely at the instruments. "How are you going to know where the tracker is?"

"I'm going to do an ultrasound on the area. Once I pinpoint the location, I'll use a magnetic scope. I'll deaden the area first, but you might feel a little pulling."

It was Bethany who moved Rhi's hair out of the way, using a giant clip to pin it on top of her head. She then moved a chair directly in front of Rhi and sat down, grabbing Rhi's hands. Rhi smiled. "Tell me about yourself."

"Let's see. I'm originally from California. I'm an only child, like you, and I also lost my mom when I was young. She was a nurse, and I wanted to be just like her, so I followed in her footsteps. That's how I met Zareck. One look at the handsome doctor doing his residency and I was smitten. Three months later, we were married. Two years after that we had our son, Zane, then four years after Zane we had Zoe. Yes, I know, the zees are a bit much, but what can I say?" Bethany looked over Rhi's shoulder and winked at her husband. "The kids are eighteen and fourteen now."

"Are you still a nurse?" Rhi was focused on Bethany and not what Rev was doing.

"Yes, but only part time. I like being home when the kids get out of school."

"Are the kids Gryphons? Are you?" Rhi wasn't sure

how that worked.

"I'm not. And since I'm human, the kids had a fifty-fifty shot at it. Turns out both of them are shifters. That was another reason I didn't want to work full time. I wanted to be there for them while they got used to their new bodies. I don't understand what it's like to shift, but I have been around enough of the other kids to watch them struggle getting their Gryphons under control during the first year or so. Zane's a pro at it, but Zoe's still struggling. Going through puberty and shifting is hard on her, but she's strong."

"Just like her momma," Rev said warmly. Bethany beamed at her husband's words, and it was a beautiful sight.

"Okay, Rhi. I've found the tracker. Now comes the uncomfortable part."

"I'm ready." And Rhi was. She had a strong woman holding her hands and Ryker standing by her side. She would tolerate any discomfort if it meant keeping her new family safe.

CHAPTER TWELVE

Ryker

RHIANNON WAS A trouper. She never flinched while Rev was removing the chip from her neck. Bethany had been a big help, keeping Rhi's mind on other things. Ryker admired Rev's wife. She had shown Rhi nothing but love since she met the younger woman. Rhi needed positive women in her life. Women like Bethany who saw the good in Rhi and Mac. Someone who didn't judge others based on a belief system not everyone held.

Mac, who was standing in the doorway watching, had been on the receiving end of acceptance for the last few months, and she was slowly becoming her own woman. Ryker was proud of his daughter. He knew Juliette would be too. As a parent, he wanted Mac to find her own happiness, and he vowed to make that happen by finding Elijah. Ryker didn't know what type of man Elijah was, but if he brought Mac joy, he had to have some redeeming qualities no matter if he lived at the compound or not. According to Mac, Elijah had been one of those who spent most of his life at the Sanctuary. Other than falling in love with McKenzie, the young man had never been in trouble. He was being punished for loving someone another man coveted. As with Rhi, Elijah's parents had handed their child over to be raised by the leader of the cult instead of protecting him and loving him as was their duty as parents.

Ryker thanked Zeus every day Mac had been returned to him. She was still finding her feet on the outside. Figuring out what she wanted to do. He offered to pay for college so she could become a veterinarian. She didn't feel comfortable around a lot of people, so he was trying to encourage her to take online classes. If she didn't want the full load of becoming a veterinarian, she could be a vet tech and still work with animals. Ryker knew she was only focused on Elijah, and he understood that more than most. When Juliette had been taken from him, she was all he could think about until he got word she had died. Then the grief set in. Focusing on life was nearly impossible when that person who meant most to you was no longer there to share in your life.

Now, he had Rhiannon to share in his future. For the first time in twenty years, Ryker felt lighter. Freer. Even with the threat of someone finding Rhi and trying to take her away from him. He'd die before he let anything happen to her, and he wasn't ready to cross over just yet. He had a lot of living to do, and he wanted to do that with Rhi by his side. Like Mac, she had a lot to learn about living in the real world, but he was determined to be the one to show her everything the world had to offer.

Once Ryker knew Rhi was okay and the chip had been removed, he stepped away to call in the Hounds to meet at Lucy's. He gave War and Mav the option of staying home, but both were ready to hit the road with them. Both were equally pissed they hadn't been called before then about what was going on with Rhi and Haven. Ryker apologized, then explained how everything happened quickly. Kerrigan was going to visit with Natalia and the twins while War and Mav were away. Major and Marshall had demanded to talk to Ryker while Mav was on the phone with him. Ryker was surprised they were still awake. Speaking to the boys, listening as they rambled on about everything had Ryker wishing for his own little Hounds. Rhi was young enough to have children with Ryker, but he didn't know if that was something she wanted. There was still so much he didn't know about his female. He wished things were different. That he wasn't getting ready to drop her off with Xavier and Elizabeth for a few days. Ryker already missed her.

When he finished his calls, Rev was waiting for him. Rev palmed the small transmitter. "Want me to destroy it?"

"No. There was a reason David put it in Rhi's neck when she was so young. I doubt he handed the only locator over, so while I'm driving her and Mac to Xavier's, I'm going to have a couple Hounds take the transmitter and head toward New Roseville. I have a feeling someone from Haven will follow the beacon. If not them, then David himself. We'll set a trap for whoever comes looking and destroy their device."

"You want me to do it?"

"No, you've already helped enough. Take Bethany home for now. Thank you, Rev."

"No thanks needed. I'm really happy for you. There's nothing like the love of a good woman to get you through the days, and Rhi's a good one. I can tell."

"Yeah? How's that?"

"Bethany likes her." Rev grinned. "My female is the best judge of character."

"Is there anyone she doesn't like?"

"Yes. She couldn't stand Digger."

Ryker didn't want to think about the Hound who had betrayed them. "Is there anyone else she needs to warn me about?" Ryker asked with sincerity. He knew Gryphons and humans alike had special gifts. Maybe not as special as Rhiannon's, but he would never discount Bethany's ability to read people.

"Not that I know of. At least none of our family. She meets plenty of people out and about she steers clear of though."

"Am I interrupting?" Bethany asked from the doorway.

133

She had taken over for Rev and put a couple stitches in Rhi's neck after the chip was removed.

"Not at all. You finished up?" Rev held out his hand, and Bethany joined her Hound.

Ryker looked toward the door, searching for Rhi.

"Yes. Your girl stepped outside for a second," Bethany told Ryker. "She said she needed a moment. Something about seeing the trees?"

"Nature grounds her. Thank you both for everything."

"I like Rhi a lot. When this mess with Haven is all over, I'd love to spend more time with her."

"Thanks, Bethany. I'm sure she'd love it too. She hasn't had a lot of positive females in her life since her mom died."

"Not that I want to replace her mom, but I have plenty of love to offer."

"Thanks again. I'm going to find her so she can get some sleep."

Rev kissed the top of his wife's head. Ryker had often been a little jealous of the Hounds who had good women in their lives, but now, he didn't need to be. After they said their goodbyes, Ryker went outside. He searched for Rhi everywhere, but when he didn't see her outside, he headed upstairs to her bedroom. That's where he found her, curled up and sleeping peacefully. He warred with his heart and his head about climbing into bed with her, but his heart won out. Slipping out of his shirt, Ryker slid in next to Rhi and pulled her back to his chest, snaking an arm around her waist. He went to sleep with his nose buried in her hair.

Rhiannon

EXHAUSTION FINALLY TOOK over, and after stepping outside

for a few minutes, Rhi went back to her bedroom and slipped off to sleep, relishing the comfortable mattress and the soft bedding. Her neck ached, but it wasn't enough to keep her from drifting off. Lions and eagles plagued her dreams, along with the feeling of being wrapped in a safe cocoon. She never wanted to wake up. Rhi wanted to stay in Lucy's house where she was protected by creatures. Lovely, handsome, fierce beings. One being in particular. Rhi wanted to know what it was like to be kissed softly the way Tamian kissed Lucy. To be looked at the way Sutton gazed upon Rory as if she were the most precious gift ever bestowed. To have Ryker teach her about intimacy between adults. To have him claim her as his own, wanting to keep her for as long as she lived.

The weight against her stomach was odd. At first, she thought it was cramps, but the pressure was coming from the outside. Keeping her eyes closed, Rhi roused slowly, taking in not only the pressure against her stomach, but the heat at her back. That heat was coming from a large body pressed against her. She didn't have to look to know Ryker was spooning her, and she wanted to wake every morning just like that.

Rhi wished she knew what to do. Did she turn over and kiss him? Reach back so she could touch him, letting him know she was awake? Did she lie still so he could continue to sleep and she could enjoy being held for the first time?

Ryker tightened his arm around her before nuzzling her neck with his lips. "Good morning," he husked. The breath against her skin sent tingles throughout her body. It was a sensation she'd never experienced, but she'd never had Ryker Lazlo showing her affection.

"Good morning." Rhi pulled her arm from under the covers and placed her hand on his. Ryker threaded their fingers and held them against her chest. He was precariously close to her breast. If she moved just the slightest, he would rub her nipple. Did she want that? Yes, she did. But she didn't want to seem too forward and give him the impression she was ready for sex. Oh, she wanted him. Rhi knew those tingles were her body telling her brain she wanted Ryker to strip her down and make love to her, but her brain was strong enough to not give in. Yet.

"Did you sleep well?" he asked.

"Yes. This bed is wonderful."

"I suppose it is after sleeping on nothing more than a cot for the last ten years."

"How do you know that?"

"I saw Gideon's compound, and I can't imagine Josiah's was any different. The buildings were similar, so I figured the insides were outfitted the same way."

"What's the plan? Am I still being taken to Tamian's parents'?"

"Yes. Lucy called them, and they're looking forward to meeting you and Mac. It won't be for long. Now that we know where Josiah's compound is located, we'll be able to get in and take him down."

"What about my father?"

"That depends on you."

Rhi unclasped their hands and rolled over so she could look at Ryker. That was a big mistake. Ryker in the morning with his bed-rumpled hair and sleepy eyes was even better than a put-together Ryker. His chest was bare. Rhi hadn't seen a lot of men's chests, other than her friends' back when they swam together, and they had been boys. Her father's didn't count. But Rhi knew Ryker's was something special. His full lips were right there, begging to be kissed, but she didn't want to prove how lacking she was, so she focused on his eyes.

"If my father willingly went to live with and work for Josiah, I don't suppose he's a good man."

"No, he's not. For that, I'm sorry." Ryker brushed a strand of hair away from Rhi's face, and she leaned into his touch.

"That's nothing for you to apologize for."

"No, but I'm sorry that's the type of father you have. You deserve so much better." Ryker's eyes were soft, but she didn't see pity in them. Only warmth and honesty.

"I'm sure other kids had it worse. Honestly, I don't care what happens to him. I stopped loving him a long time ago. Stopped thinking of him as my father the first time he ignored me when we passed on the street. Hated him when he allowed Josiah to take me away from what I loved most – being outside. Not being allowed to go anywhere near the gardens or the woods, that was the worst punishment imaginable for someone like me. It was like taking a bird from the sky and clipping its wings so it couldn't fly."

"I have the perfect spot in my backyard for you to grow a garden. You're welcome to dig up the whole yard if you wish."

"Really?"

"Really. I know we got off to a rocky start, but I want nothing more than to make you happy. I want to give you back your wings and watch you fly."

Without thinking about it, Rhi leaned forward and pressed her lips to Ryker's. It was clumsy and awkward, until Ryker took control. He rolled Rhi to her back, his body sliding over hers seamlessly. Propped on his forearms, Ryker studied her face, his eyes darkening. He covered her mouth with his, angling his head to the side. He didn't try for more than soft pressure, nor did he use his tongue. It was sweet. Almost too sweet, but she appreciated him going slow.

When he pulled away, Ryker rubbed his nose against hers. "I'm going to do my best to take things slow. I don't want you to think this is all about sex. Yes, I want you. You're a beautiful woman, but I want to do this the right way. Get to know you and let you figure out who I am. I want you to be absolutely sure I'm the male you want for the rest of your life, because if I claim you, it will be

137

forever."

Rhiannon ran her fingers through Ryker's short beard. He was willing to take things slow for her sake, and that proved to her the type of male he was – honorable. It was a word she'd heard more than once since meeting the Lazlos, and she was coming to learn it applied to all of them. James had called them monsters, but they were anything but. Monsters were the things of nightmares. Ryker and his family were the good guys. They might be able to shift into something other than human, but inside, they were good. They didn't kill just because they could.

Someone knocked on the door. "Breakfast is ready," Mac called out.

"As much as I would love to stay in bed with you all day, we need to get moving. After we eat, I'll help you pack your bags." Ryker kissed her quickly, then rolled off the bed. He pushed the covers down and held out his hand. His eyes darkened as he raked them down her body. She was wearing shorts and a tank top, so lots of skin was on display. He reached out a fingertip and trailed it down her bare leg. Goosebumps rose on her skin, and Rhi bit her bottom lip. Ryker adjusted his penis. Rhi could see the outline of it behind his jeans, and she wanted to know what it looked like. She wanted to touch it. To see Ryker's reaction when she did.

"Stop looking at me like that," he demanded. Rhi blinked, moving her eyes from his crotch to his face, afraid she'd done something wrong. "I'm trying to do the right thing here, but you're too tempting for your own good." He grabbed his T-shirt off the end of the bed and tugged it over his head, covering all his glorious skin. "Get dressed. I'll see you downstairs." Ryker kissed her again and then he was gone.

Rhi's heart was racing. *He thinks I'm tempting.* She giggled as she stood to get dressed, wondering if most grown women giggled or if they were supposed to laugh huskily. Ryker had taken issue with her age, and Rhi didn't want to remind him of it every time he turned around. She tried to remember her mother's laugh. Around Rhi, it had been soft yet genuine. Around her father… Rhi couldn't remember her parents sharing any moments that joyous between the two, and that hurt her heart. Daisy had been the best mother in the world, and she deserved to have laughed with her husband. Just another reason for Rhi to hate her father.

After brushing her teeth and taking care of personal business, Rhi pulled on jeans and a long-sleeved tee. Since it was warm inside the house, she padded barefoot downstairs. Several voices talking at once sounded from the dining room, and when she passed through the door, everyone got quiet. She looked down at herself, then behind her. "What?"

Lucy smiled and took Rhi's hand. "Ignore them. They act like they've never seen a beautiful woman before."

Rhi's face warmed, but she ignored it as Ryker placed his hand on her back and led her to a seat at the table. He headed to the kitchen, and when he returned, he had two cups of coffee. The one he placed in front of her was creamy, and she knew before she took a sip it would be sweetened. Lucy, Mac, and Kyllian brought in platters and bowls. When they were seated, everyone passed the food around.

After breakfast was over, Rhi offered to help Mac with the dishes. Ryker had said they needed to get on the road, but Rhi wasn't ready to go. She still needed to pack her bags. At the rate she was going, she might as well leave them packed. Ryker came back to the kitchen just as Rhi and Mac finished the dishes.

"Come on. Let's get you packed." Ryker laced their fingers together as they headed upstairs. Rhi couldn't remember the last time she'd held hands with someone, but she liked it. She enjoyed the connection with this male. Now that she was aware of Gryphons, she understood why the others used that term – male. Because they weren't men exactly. They looked human, but they had an animal hiding inside.

When Rhi stepped into the closet, she stopped where the hidden compartment was. "Everything okay?" Ryker was closer than she expected.

"Yes, just trying to decide whether or not to open that," she responded, pointing to the floor.

Ryker squatted beside her legs and pulled at the handle. The floor opened, and inside were a couple of leather-covered books. Ryker fished them out, flipped open the covers, and let out a "hmm." When he stood, he tucked the books under his arm. "I'll get these to Lucy. They're definitely more of Lucius's work."

"She said genetics or something. What does that mean?" Rhi's education had been lacking. Just the basics required followed by mostly Bible study. She doubted the lot of them would pass the normal high school levels.

"Basically, the internal makeup of people or animals. What makes them alike or different. Why you have blonde hair and mine's dark. Why some people can naturally run faster or are stronger. But in his case, I think Lucius was trying to figure out how to take Gryphon genes and add them to humans to make them stronger. He worked for Lucy's boss at the GIA, and when Lucius died, her boss wanted Lucy to continue Lucius's work. He forced her into a secret lab, threatening her with jail time if she didn't do as he wanted."

"Jail time?"

"Lucy was good with computers. She got caught hacking somewhere she wasn't supposed to be. The GIA gave her the option of working for them using her skills or going to jail. She chose option A, but then Ramey got hold of her when the other scientists he hired couldn't crack Lucius's codes. He thought since she had trained with Lucius, she would be able to carry on where Lucius left off."

"And did she?"

"No. She managed to escape, then the Hounds, with Tamian's help, shut down the lab."

"What happened to her boss?"

Ryker sighed. "Monk happened. He's one of us, and he was in love with Lucy. When she didn't return his affections, he took off. With my blessing," Ryker added.

It didn't take long for the two of them to put the few clothes and toiletries she had in her two bags. Ryker carried them downstairs along with the journals, which he gave to Lucy. When Lucy opened one of them, she frowned, biting her lip. What little of the writing Rhi had seen didn't make sense, but it shouldn't, seeing as how she was barely educated. Was that how Ryker saw Rhi? A stupid girl with no real-world experience? It had to be because it was the truth. She walked over to the back door and looked out. Some of the trees had lost most of their leaves, but the evergreens were still rife with color. Not knowing when she'd get another chance, Rhi went outside.

A soft breeze carried the different scents from all the flora to her nose, and Rhi inhaled deeply. "Hello. I have missed you all so much," she whispered. Soft responses came from all directions. Rhi knelt, running her fingertips across the neatly manicured lawn. The soft sigh she received in response filled her soul. She wanted to strip her clothes off and lie against fading grass, but that would have looked weird to Ryker and his family, so Rhi refrained. She stood and walked around to different trees and plants, touching each one with reverence, losing herself in the peacefulness of being one with nature. She prayed Ryker had been truthful when he told her she could plant a garden at his house. Her fingers itched to dig in the soil. To sow seeds and nurture them, then watch the seeds grow into useful herbs, fruits, and vegetables.

Rhi felt the air shift, alerting her she wasn't alone. It wasn't a bad change, just different. Somehow, she knew it was Ryker. She looked over her shoulder to find him standing at the edge of the patio, watching her. Touching as much of the foliage as possible, she whispered a thank you to the goddess for allowing her the gift she'd been given before heading toward the house.

CHAPTER THIRTEEN

Josiah

"HAVE YOU FOUND her?" Josiah paced, only stopping to glare at David before resuming the path he was making through his living room.

"James is the one with the tracker. Find him, and you'll find Anna."

"I'm not the one with the government's super computers at my disposal." Josiah stopped when Nadine shuffled into the room. "What are you doing in here? You know to remain in the bedroom unless I call you." His wife didn't approve of having Anna at the compound, but that wasn't her decision. Nothing about what went on at Haven required her approval. Women were meant to be seen, not heard. Same as the children.

"I was going to start breakfast. I didn't realize you had company." Nadine looked at her feet and turned back toward the bedroom. The one she slept in. It had been many years since they shared a bed, for sleeping or otherwise. Josiah couldn't stand the look of his wife. Couldn't stand to touch her. She'd long ago lost her youth and her appeal. But sometimes a man had needs, and putting her on all fours turned away from him was the only way he could stomach having sex with her. If she wasn't Abraham's daughter, Josiah would consider getting rid of her and finding a younger wife.

Once she was out of earshot, Josiah turned to David. "Like I was saying, you have the best computers at your disposal. If you can't find one girl, what good are you?"

David stood up to his full height, but Josiah wasn't scared of the man. He wasn't scared of anyone. He was the leader of the biggest and deadliest community within the Ministry. Bigger men than a computer user had tried and failed to take Josiah down.

"Since you can't locate your daughter, get to work on finding out where James disappeared to. The other men returned without him, so he either went back to the house alone or something else happened. I want to know what. Now, get out of my sight and don't come back until you've located them both."

David inclined his head and took his leave without a word. Men like David Spencer thought they were indispensable. They weren't. The only reason Josiah allowed David to reside at Haven was because of his daughter.

Anna. Now there was a woman Josiah would like the chance to break. To show her the true path. He had thought James was worthy of the task, but now he wasn't sure. He didn't like the fact that James hadn't returned, even without Anna. The tracker assured them where Anna was hiding out, but the men who returned said they searched the home and couldn't find the girl anywhere. Josiah was tempted to pay Karsyn Daily a visit himself. The men had assured Josiah the woman was honest with them and allowed them to search every inch of her home and property. Either they were lying, or Anna really wasn't there. He trusted the team he'd sent. If he didn't, he needed to find new men to lead his army. They were the best he had. No, the tracker must have been faulty.

Or James led them to the wrong house on purpose.

If that was the case, James Kirby was a dead man.

144

Ryker

WHEN RYKER HEADED outside to look for Rhi, he found Lucy pacing.

"Little Dove? Are you okay?"

"No. Yes. Maybe? Shit. These two journals? I think Lucius was onto something. Something huge. Like prolonging life huge."

"What do you mean?"

"I thought all of his research was geared toward making humans into super-soldiers, but these two journals have notes relating to longevity. I need to study these more in depth. Ryker, if what I've read so far isn't just mad scribblings, it might be possible for the human mates to match our lifespans."

"That's…" Ryker wouldn't get his hopes up, but if Lucy was right, the possibility of Rhiannon living as long as he did meant he wouldn't have to watch her die while he lived a couple centuries longer without her.

"I know. But don't get your hopes up yet. I need to do more research. With you taking Rhi and Mac to Xavier's, and with Tamian gone to help his Clan, I've got nothing but time. Don't worry, though. I'll still be available to help with anything you need regarding Haven."

"James gave us the information we need to find the compound. You do whatever it is you need regarding Lucius's work. It's too important not to give it all your focus. I'm going to have Shadow and Ace watch over your house, just in case some of Josiah's men decide to return. I won't leave you unprotected." Lucy was used to having Hounds watch over her. Usually Ryker left that up to

Kyllian and Hayden, but the two of them tended to want to hang out with Lucy. All the Lazlos loved War's daughter, but she needed to focus without being bothered.

"Thank you. And if I need help, I know just the male for the job. But that would require me to travel back to New Atlanta, unless I can convince Tamian's uncle to come here."

"You're talking about Jonas Montague?"

"Yes. Who better than the male who created my mate? If he can create a clone, he can help figure out Lucius's notes."

"Why don't you call Tamian? Have him talk to Jonas."

"I will once I make sure this isn't all nonsense." Lucy was vibrating with energy. Ryker was so very proud of his niece. She was the smartest out of all their family. Lucy hugged the journals to her chest as she left him to go find his female.

Ryker stood on the patio, letting Rhi have a little extra time with her trees. At first, he thought she was talking, but the closer he got, he heard the most beautiful voice, singing an old rock song. As if she knew he was watching, Rhi turned around and smiled. It didn't quite reach her eyes, and he wondered what was bothering her. She said something he couldn't hear before walking toward him.

"Hi." Rhi stopped with a foot between them, but Ryker reached out and tugged her closer. He settled his hands tightly at the small of her back so she was flush against his chest. Ryker inhaled her hair still piled on top of her head, and Rhi tightened her hold around his waist.

"You can feel them, can't you?" Ryker asked. "And I don't mean just with your hands. You feel them in here." He touched her chest.

"Yes. They are as much a part of me as your Gryphon is you. They were the only things that gave me hope after my mother died, and David and Josiah took them away from me."

"Never again. From now on, you will have access to all

146

the plants you want. If there aren't enough at my house, I'll buy a piece of property surrounded by trees, and we'll build a new house."

"You'd do that for me?" Rhi's voice quivered.

"I would. Now that I have my head out of my ass, I've found I will give you the world if you ask for it."

"Why? What changed?"

"I saw you. When I was shot and you placed your hands on my wound, something happened. My body was cold from the shock of the bullet, but your warmth infused me, wrapped around every part of me, and it opened my eyes to who you really are. On the surface, you are Rhiannon Spencer, a young woman who has no experience in the outside world. But deep down, you are my Rhi, a strong woman who survived in a world with no warmth, no plants or trees to nurture. You endured something that goes against your nature, and you're still beautiful on the inside. That warmth thawed my cold heart, making it beat stronger and faster. You make me want to be a better male. A better Gryphon."

Rhi blinked back tears, and Ryker hugged her close. "How's your neck?"

"It's a little sore, but Rev and Bethany were gentle. I really like her."

Ryker smiled against her cheek. "She likes you too. Bethany's a good female to know, so any time you want to visit with her, all you have to do is ask."

"That would be nice. Between her and Rory, it's like having two mothers. Not that I think of them as old. It's just they're both so much like Daisy. Makes me miss her a little less."

Ryker couldn't understand why the women at Haven hadn't taken Rhi in and nurtured her the way a young girl should have been, but there was a lot about the cult he didn't get.

"I didn't know you could sing like an angel. Your voice

is beautiful."

"When did...?" Rhi shook her head. "I get lost in my thoughts and start singing. It's something I used to do when I was younger."

"You should do it more often." Rhi blushed, so Ryker changed the subject. "Are you ready to ride? I hate to be separated from you, but the sooner I get you and Mac to Xavier's, the sooner I can find the compound and make sure you aren't looking over your shoulder any longer."

"I'm ready." Rhi looked up at him, and Ryker took advantage of their closeness. He pressed his lips against hers, relishing in the softness. His Gryphon purred in his chest, content in the knowledge she was theirs.

Ryker led Rhi to where the Hounds were gathered. He introduced her to those she hadn't met. War and Maveryck welcomed her to the family, the same way they'd made Mac feel welcomed. Ryker was blessed when it came to his siblings. He hadn't seen his sisters in several years, but he knew the six of them would be just as warm to his mate. *His mate.* Yes, that felt right.

Our *mate, dickhead.*

Yeah, yeah. Ryker mentally gave his beast an eye roll.

Ryker's phone vibrated. Not his personal phone, but the one Quinn had given him. Several Hounds, along with most of his brothers, were gathered, waiting for their instructions.

"Give me a minute," Ryker said as he read the incoming contract. Hayden had already accepted a job, and the one Quinn sent was perfect for Kyllian.

"Kayos, can I talk to you a second?"

Kyllian stepped away from the group, and Ryker handed him the phone. Kyllian read over the contract. "This one mine?"

"If you want it. If you'd rather follow us to Xavier's, I'll give it to someone else."

"No. I want it."

"Then it's yours. I'll send the email to Lucy's printer."

148

"Thanks. I won't let you down."

Ryker pulled his brother in for a quick hug. Kyllian hesitated briefly before hugging him back. Ryker wasn't the most demonstrative one of their family. Okay, he was never one for showing affection, but something in him had loosened up over the last twenty-four hours.

Ryker didn't say anything else. Kyllian knew what to do. He released his brother and turned to the rest of his family. "Kayos is taking another job with Shepherd. Legend and Brick, I want you to remain here and watch over the house. Lucy has some important work to do, so she's going to be preoccupied. Spyder, Hawk, I want the two of you to take the chip Rev removed from Rhi's neck and head back toward New Roseville."

"You're thinking there's still a receiver out there?" Maveryck asked.

"Yes. I think there's more to the reason David had it put in than what James was aware of. If I'm right, David will be the one tracking it this time."

"What do you want us to do with him?" Spyder asked.

"Hold him or anyone else who comes looking for Rhi. Once I drop her and Mac off, I'll head that way. Regardless, I'll meet you there so we can locate the compound. We need to do some recon and make a plan for taking Josiah down."

Ryker handed Spyder the chip, and he and Hawk left to hit the road. Legend and Brick headed outside to guard Lucy's house. "Ace, you're with me and the women. Mayhem, if you would, ride my bike. I'll be taking it from Xavier's on to New Roseville, then you can ride back with Ace. Sultan, you, War, and Ripper ride with Mayhem. The rest of you take the other vehicle. I don't expect to need a decoy, but I'm not taking any chances. Any questions?" When no one spoke up, Ryker said, "Let's ride."

Ryker handed Ace the keys, then he helped Rhi into the back seat. He slid in next to her while Mac got in the passenger seat.

Mac turned the radio down. "I've never met a king before. I've never met a lot of people, but this is exciting."

"A king?" Rhi grabbed Ryker's forearm. "Tamian's father is a king?"

"Yes. Gryphons aren't the only shifters in the world. Tamian and his father are Gargoyles. Where Gryphons shift into animals, the Gargoyles retain their human visage, but they have wings, fangs, and claws. Their skin is virtually impenetrable. They also have Clans with a king. Xavier is King of the Italian Gargoyles. Tamian will one day take over, and Lucy will be their Queen. Here in the States, Rafael Stone is King. Tamian's sister, Tessa, is mated to one of Rafael's brothers. I had the pleasure of meeting Rafael and his Queen, Kaya, when we were searching for Lucy. They were both gracious and down-to-earth. I'm sure Xavier will be as well."

"If you say so," Rhi muttered. "Do the Gryphons have kings and queens?"

"No. We have strong alphas the others turn to if they have problems. Sutton is the alpha in the Northeast. One phone call from him can usually solve any problems that arise. Most Gryphons are peaceable and do what they were created to — protect humans. Just like with humans, though, there are bad Gryphons and Gargoyles. Several months ago, Rafael's Clan had to battle with the Greek King. Alistair happened to be Rafael's uncle, and the male was making life difficult for Rafael and his family. They took down the Greek, and some of his Clan have relocated to the States to carry on trying to take Rafael's throne. That's why Tamian returned to New Atlanta. He wanted to check on his sister and his great-uncle, Jonas Montague."

Rhi sucked in a breath. "I know that name. He's the man who created the first clone. Josiah talked about him during some of his sermons. Said Jonas had caused the apocalypse by playing God. Tamian's great-uncle is the same Jonas?"

150

"He is, but he didn't cause the apocalypse. That was all the Ministry's doing. Men like Josiah were the ones playing God. To cause as much destruction at one time, they had to have been planning to take the world down for years. Worldwide chaos doesn't happen on a whim. Yes, the apocalypse happened soon after Jonas created Tamian, but it wasn't Jonas's fault."

"Wait! Tamian was the clone?" Mac asked.

"I thought you knew that." Ryker felt sure Lucy would have shared that with Mac during their many talks.

"Uh, no." Mac sounded hurt.

"I'm sure Lucy would have told you eventually. It's not a secret within our family, but it isn't common knowledge any more than Gryphons and Gargoyles are real. Until Lucy and Tamian met, the Gargoyles weren't aware of Gryphons."

"Are there any other types of shifters?" Rhi asked.

"Not that we're aware of, but that doesn't mean they don't exist. The only reason Gryphons knew of Gargoyles was because many years ago, a Gryphon saw a Gargoyle flying. The Gryphon didn't share the secret of our kind, but he did promise to keep the truth of Gargoyles from humans. He passed the knowledge to his son, who in turn passed it to his son and so on. The truth spread, but as far as I know, no one outed them to humans. It's easier for Gryphons because we turn into lions or eagles. Rarely do we shift into our full Gryphon."

"You did. Or at least you tried," Rhi reminded him.

"That's because you were in danger. My Gryphon took over trying to protect you."

Rhi smiled inwardly but decided not to ask Ryker the reason. Instead, she chose a different topic. "Bethany said the kids have a fifty-fifty shot at becoming a Gryphon. Mac, I take it you aren't one?"

"No, thank god. Not that I wouldn't want to be one, but can you imagine shifting for the first time living at one of the compounds? Not only would I have freaked out, not knowing what was going on, but I'd have been shot on sight for heresy." Mac rolled her eyes, but she shivered too. "So, who's stronger? A Gargoyle or Gryphon?"

"We don't know. Tamian got into a fight with one of our Hounds who thought he was protecting Lucy, but she shifted and was protecting Tamian since they are fated mates. Remember I told you about Gryphon voice?" Rhi nodded. "Tamian has the same type of ability, and he commanded Monk to stand down before any of them got hurt."

"What's a fated mate?" Rhi asked.

"With the Gargoyles, the fates choose one perfect being for each Gargoyle. They can fall in love with someone else, but it isn't as true a love as that of their fated mate. Once they find that one, there is no other for them. Ever. It's only been in the last couple hundred years the Gargoyles have mated with humans. That was another reason the Greek King had such disdain for Rafael and his family. Once the bond is complete, the human stops aging, much like their Gargoyle. When you meet Tamian's mother, you'll see what I'm talking about. Elizabeth stopped aging as soon as she and Xavier completed their bond."

Rhi bit her lip, looking past Ryker out the window. "Does the same thing happen with Gryphon mates?"

"Sadly, no. Gryphons stop aging around the forty-year mark, but our mates, if human, continue aging." Ryker thought about Lucius's journals. "However, Lucy's father – adopted father – was researching this very subject. That's what was in those journals we found. According to Lucy, he might have figured out a way to prolong human lives. Lucy mentioned reaching out to Jonas to see if he can help her decipher Lucius's notes."

"Isn't that also playing God?" Rhi asked.

"I guess that's one way of looking at it. Would you not want to live a longer life if given the opportunity?"

Rhi stretched out her hand and ran her fingers through Ryker's beard. "If it meant I got to live as long as you? Definitely."

CHAPTER FOURTEEN

Rhiannon

RHIANNON WAS IN a dreamworld filled with shifters, clones, and mad scientists. Shifters who lived hundreds and thousands of years. Scientists who could clone a human. Meeting that clone. Being taken to his parents' home. The home of a king. Lucy becoming queen when Tamian was named king. How was this her life now? Not only that, but she'd gone from being forced to marry someone she couldn't stand to having a man who was so much more than she could have ever dreamed of.

They spent the rest of the drive asking each other questions, with Ace and Mac joining in the conversation. Mostly, she and Mac compared notes on their time at the compounds. More than once, she squeezed Ryker's hand. Whenever they would mention something he didn't like, Ryker would tense up, grind his teeth, or growl low in his chest. After hearing all of Mac's story – about Elijah, the baby, being chased through the woods and attacked by a dog – Rhi thanked the goddess her ten years had been nothing nearly as traumatic. The worst thing that happened to Rhi was being kept inside. Even enduring time spent with James didn't come close to what Josiah's brother had done to McKenzie. That just went to prove that there was always someone worse off than you.

When they reached their destination, Rhi couldn't

believe her eyes. If she thought Lucy's house was grand, it had nothing on the Montagnon estate. Tall, stone walls surrounded the property. A secure, iron gate guarded the entrance. The house itself wasn't as tall as Lucy's, but it spread out in every direction. She wondered if they gave out maps. A couple so gorgeous they could have been models met them out front. The man was tall with dark hair and eyes, much like Ryker. He had on a pair of black dress pants with a white, button-up shirt. The woman was shorter with long, red hair. She had on a pair of well-worn jeans and a chunky sweater. Where he was serious with a hand on the woman's shoulder, she was smiling and clasping her hands together. After the whole lot of them exited the vehicles and climbed off their bikes, the couple stepped forward.

"Welcome to our home. I'm Xavier, and this is my mate, Elizabeth."

"Should we bow?" Rhi whispered to Ryker, and Xavier laughed, transforming his face into something exotic.

"No need for formalities, Rhiannon. Here in the States, I'm just Elizabeth's mate and Tessa and Tamian's father."

"Xavier, it's a pleasure. I'm Ryker Lazlo." Ryker went around, making all the introductions on behalf of the Hounds. "I can't tell you how much I appreciate you allowing Rhi and Mac to stay here. We'll do our best to handle business with the cult as soon as possible."

"I know from experience the necessity to hide a mate." Xavier gestured to the property. "It's why I built this fortress. To keep Elizabeth safe from her husband. I know you want to get business handled as quickly as possible, but don't rush on our account. Elizabeth misses having our children around, so Rhiannon and McKenzie will be in the best possible hands."

"If you'll allow me," an older gentleman said, stepping out of the house. "My name is Manny, and I will be happy to retrieve whatever luggage the young ladies have brought with them."

"I'll help you," Ace offered while Xavier and Elizabeth showed everyone else into their home.

"Holy shit," Mac whispered. "I mean… I'm sorry. That was rude." She blushed and hid behind Maveryck.

"It is quite a bit at first, but you'll get used to it," Elizabeth said. She led them into a large room with a sunken seating area. "As much as I love my home, this is my favorite room. Please, help yourself to the buffet. I told Myra you probably wouldn't be hungry, but she insisted on creating a smorgasbord."

She wasn't wrong. Along the far wall, a long table was filled with more food than Rhi had ever seen in her life.

Maveryck was the first one to take her up on her offer. "Thank you. And Xavier, please don't take offense, but your mate is just as beautiful as your daughter. I met Tessa when she and Tamian were helping us look for Lucy."

"No offense taken. I'm well aware of my mate's beauty. I'm also happy that is where the similarity between her and Tessa, as you call our daughter, ends. Andrea's penchant for trouble would cause a lesser male to have folded many years ago."

"She's not *that* bad," Elizabeth countered.

Mav snorted, and Xavier nodded. "See? Even Maveryck knows how she is. The fates knew what they were doing when they deemed the warden of a penitentiary her mate. But enough about our daughter. Elizabeth, why don't you show the ladies to their rooms so I can chat with Ryker?"

"Girls, grab yourselves a plate and bring it with you. We've been kicked out of the badass club," Elizabeth said with a wink.

Rhi looked up at Ryker, and he leaned over and kissed her temple. "I'll find you before we leave," he whispered. She and Mac did as Elizabeth suggested and filled heavy plates with all sorts of food. Rhi had no idea if she liked any of it, but she wasn't going to pass up the opportunity to taste as much of it as she could.

While they walked down a long hallway, Elizabeth chatted openly. "I'm so happy you both are here. Lucy told me a little bit about each of you, but I'm hoping you'll do me the honor of telling me your story in your own words. I'll also share with you how Xavier and I came to be mates. While you're here, please think of this as your home. I miss Andrea something fierce, so it's good to have you here with me. I know I'm no replacement for either of your mothers, but I'd like to at least be a friend. So, please, while you're here, call me Beth."

"If her name's Andrea, why does she call herself Tessa?" Rhi asked.

"Her job within the family required her to use aliases. Tessa is one of many, but for some reason, it stuck. Tamian always called her Andi. Still does. Here we are. Thank you, Manny."

"You're welcome, ma'am. And if either of you want the real scoop on Tessa, come find me."

"Manny!"

"What? Miss Elizabeth, you know Tessa spends a lot of time with Lawrence and me."

Elizabeth sighed, but she was grinning. "I know my own daughter very well, thank you. Now, you ladies are welcome to check out your rooms and relax, or I can give you the nickel tour. Although, as big as our home is, it might be a quarter with inflation."

Rhi turned to Mac and raised her eyebrows. Mac might be younger, but she had been on the outside longer, thus she knew better how to interact with others. Mac inclined her head toward the door, and Rhi nodded. "We'll take the tour. We can check out our rooms later."

"Excellent." Elizabeth took them first to a patio just outside their rooms, giving them a chance to eat the food they had carried from the sunken room.

Rhi moaned with each bite she took. "This is amazing. I haven't had food this good in forever. Don't get me wrong.

157

Lucy's a great cook, but this is stuff dreams are made of."

"Myra's a wonderful cook, and she loves to teach, so if either of you are interested, feel free to spend as much time in the kitchen as you like. I've tried, but I just can't get the hang of it."

"I might take you up on that, but I think Rhi here is going to want to spend all her time outside."

"You enjoy the outdoors?" Elizabeth asked Rhi.

"It's where I'm most comfortable. Nature grounds me."

"Then you'll be quite grounded because we have lots of plants in both the solarium and the greenhouse out back. They thrive thanks to Manny's husband, Lawrence. Maybe you and he can have a chat?"

"I'd like that very much."

Once Rhi and Mac finished eating, Elizabeth showed them around the large structure, and Rhi was surprised to see all the photos of Tamian and a girl who must have been Tessa. The redhead started out as a beautiful baby and became more stunning the older she got. Elizabeth regaled them with stories of her first husband and how he thought Tessa was his child. How the man, Gordon Flanagan, lost his mind when Xavier took Elizabeth and both babies, hiding them out. The horror of what the man had done, creating the Unholy – men who were turned from human to monsters in trying to create super soldiers – shocked Rhi. She admired a woman she'd never met and hoped one day to get the opportunity.

"Uncle Maveryck was so smitten with Tessa when he first met her. If it wasn't for the fact that she already had a mate, I think he would have followed her anywhere," Mac said.

"She has that effect on people. My Andrea is so full of life. I know she's a grown woman, but I miss having her around. As soon as Tamian takes over the throne, I'm hoping to convince Xavier to buy us a place in New Atlanta so I can be closer to her, at least part of the time."

"I know if I had a mother like you, I'd want that," Mac said.

Elizabeth placed a hand on Mac's scarred cheek. "Thank you. Now, let's go see if the males are finished planning."

Rhi wasn't ready to say goodbye to Ryker, but she knew he had a job to do. She wouldn't be safe until he found Josiah and took the man down. Why Josiah was so focused on her didn't make sense, though. She was no one special. It wasn't like she could tell anyone where Haven was located, and as far as she knew, he wasn't aware of her gift. Her father didn't know what she was capable of either. When they got to the living room, it was empty except for Ryker and War. Ryker held out his hand, and she took it.

"You okay?" Ryker brushed her hair back from her face.

"Yes. Elizabeth is really nice, and this house is crazy huge. I'm sure by the time you get back, I still won't have seen all of it. We'll be fine here, won't we, Mac?"

"Yep. I'm going to spend time with Myra. Maybe I'll learn how to make some of this delicious food."

"We're going to hit the road. You're in the best hands here, but if you need me, just call. I'll get back as quickly as possible." Ryker cupped Rhi's face and pressed his lips to hers. She snaked her arms around his waist, and she set her cheek to his hard chest, Ryker hugged her back. Rhi never wanted to let go, but she knew she had to. Releasing him, she stepped back.

"Thank you. I'm not sure why Josiah's targeting me, but I know you'll figure all this out. I'm ready to get started on my new life."

"You don't have to thank me. Take care of yourself. Mac, come give your old man a hug." Ryker held his arms out for his daughter, and she replaced Rhi in Ryker's arms. Rhi waited for the jealousy to kick in, but it didn't. She would gladly share Ryker with his daughter. She knew what it was like to need a parent's affection, and she would never want to take that away from McKenzie.

They walked the males to the door and stood on the steps as they watched them all drive away. Ryker on his bike was the sexiest thing Rhi had ever seen in her life. She hoped to one day ride on the back with him. "What's it like?" she asked Mac. "Riding on the back of a Harley."

"It's awesome. All that power beneath you as the wind whips your face. They call it riding the wind, and that's the best way to describe it. Uncle Hayden is building me my own bike."

"I think I'd like to learn to ride too. I guess I need to learn to drive a car first, though."

"I can help you with that," Manny said as he joined them.

"Riding a motorcycle?" Rhi asked.

"Heavens no. Driving a car. I taught Tessa to drive. If I can survive that, I can surely teach you as well."

"Was she a bad driver?"

"Oh no. She took to it quickly. Too quickly. By the time she was fourteen, she was speeding through town with me holding on for dear life. I don't think the word slow is in that child's vocabulary. She's always been wide open."

"You'd really do that?" Rhi asked.

"I'd be honored. Miss Elizabeth isn't the only one who's missed having Tessa around. She's like a daughter to Lawrence and me. If I'm being honest, I'm not sorry you've been brought here for safekeeping, only the circumstances under which you both are here. Lawrence has his greenhouse to keep him busy, but now that the threat to Miss Elizabeth is gone, Master Xavier does all his own driving. The only time I feel useful is if he's out of the country and Miss Elizabeth wants to go to town, which isn't often. Listen to me. I must sound like the most pitiful manservant on the planet."

"No, you don't. You sound human," Mac said.

"I would love for you to teach me to drive, Manny," Rhi

added.

"Then let's get started!" Manny clapped his hands together, his smile wide on his handsome, older face. Rhi's heart hurt for the man. It sounded like his life was missing something. A Tessa-sized something. If she could fill the void, she gladly would.

Manny led them back inside to where Elizabeth was curled up in the living room with a book. "Miss Elizabeth, I'm going to teach our young Rhiannon how to drive."

"Oh, that sounds like a wonderful idea. Mac, do you want to go with them, or would you rather spend time with Myra in the kitchen?"

"The kitchen. I want her to show me how to make those puffy, meaty things."

Elizabeth laughed. "The Beef Wellington bites are some of my favorites too. Come along. I'll sit with you so I can be the taste-tester. Manny, please stay on the property for now."

"Yes ma'am. Come along, Miss Rhiannon."

David

"KARSYN DAILY, MY ass. What are you up to, Lucy? And how did Rhiannon end up with you?" David had been surprised to locate Rhi with Lucy Ball, a former fellow agent. He was well aware of Lucy's aliases, as well as her family of bikers. They were the ones responsible for taking down Gideon's compound, but that didn't explain how his daughter had ended up with them. It was possible it had been a coincidence, but David didn't believe in those. He believed in facts. What could be seen and manipulated with code. He had to give it to Lucy; she was much better with a computer now than she had been when she worked for the GIA. Not as good as him, though.

161

David bypassed the cabin where his wife waited for him. He almost felt sorry for Marion. The woman had been raised in Haven and was the least likely to speak out about him staying gone so much. She bought into everything Josiah taught. Why wouldn't she? It was all she knew. She was the perfect, dutiful wife. Waiting at home – if you could call a small cabin with no amenities home – keeping the modest place pristine. Reading her Bible when she wasn't working in the garden. A job Rhiannon should have had.

David had to find his daughter. Get her away from Lucy and the Hounds of Zeus before they ruined everything. When he finally reached his apartment, David was ready to climb out of his skin. He went straight to his computer. He hadn't been truthful with Josiah regarding the trackers. James had the one handheld device which could locate the chip in Rhi's neck, but the program on David's computer could do the same thing.

He pulled up the program. "What the...? That's not possible. Unless..." One of the chips was moving toward New Roseville while another was about an hour north of New Troy where Lucy's house was. They must have found the one in her neck. If that was the case, why hadn't they removed the other one?

Using the government's satellites, David focused on the one closest to Lucy's home. What he saw made no sense. One of Rhi's chips was currently located on a large estate. David quickly searched for the owner. Of course it would be owned by a corporation. Only those people with nothing to hide held deeds in their own names. Using satellite imagery, he zoomed in on the house. There was movement outside. Two individuals walking toward an outbuilding – the garage. David zoomed in closer, and yes! There she was. It really was helpful having the most sophisticated equipment at his disposal. He was three hours away. If he activated the chip in her leg now, it would take about half an hour to take effect, and probably another hour before panic set in. That still left an hour and a half, but he had no choice. He gathered the necessary paperwork before hitting the button that would bring his daughter back to him.

When David was in the car and on the road, he called Josiah. "There are four Hounds currently sitting in The Continental. Do with that what you will." He hung up before the bastard could bark any orders at him. Even if the leader of Haven called back, David didn't plan to answer. He had his own problems to deal with.

Rhiannon

RHI FOLLOWED MANNY out to the garage. She might not have been in the outside world for ten years, but she knew a powerful car when she saw one. Or ten. The garage held several sleek vehicles, all shiny and expensive looking. "Uh, Manny. I can't drive these. Don't you have an old beater or something?" At least that's what she thought a banged-up car was called.

"Nope. No beaters here. We'll take the Rolls. It's not as fast as the others, plus it's more durable. Just in case."

"Just in case? Manny —"

"Nope. No, ma'am. Get your pretty self over here." He held open the driver's door, and Rhi slid into the soft, leather seat.

Manny joined her and handed her a key. "Here's what you do first..." The man was patient as Rhi got the hang of driving around the property. "You're doing great," he told Rhi. She wasn't going fast, but she was driving. It wasn't that hard, really. But going up and down the long driveway was different than being on the road with other cars.

"Thank— ow!" Rhi gasped when a pain shot up her left leg.

163

"What's wrong?"

"My leg…" Rhi felt like she was going to be sick.

"Pull over and put the car in park." Manny waited until Rhi did as instructed, then he was out of the vehicle and around to her side, pulling the door open. "Which leg is it?"

"My left one. There," she pointed to a spot just above her ankle. "It feels like thousands of ants are moving around."

"Let's get you back to the house. Can you scoot over?" Rhi nodded as she breathed through her mouth, trying desperately not to throw up. While he drove, Manny pulled out his phone. "Master X, something is wrong with Miss Rhiannon. She has a sharp pain in her left leg. I'm bringing her to the garage. We'll be there in approximately twenty seconds."

When Manny stopped the car, Xavier was there to open the passenger door. "May I pick you up?"

"Y-yes," she stuttered, her teeth chattering. Her body was freezing.

Xavier lifted her easily and gently carried her inside. He didn't stop until he was in her bedroom. Elizabeth and Mac were already there waiting. Xavier placed her on the bed and then he sniffed the air. Rhi thought that was peculiar until he said, "It smells like poison. Rhi, may I look at your ankle?"

She nodded and wished she hadn't. "Gonna… be… sick…" Rhi leaned over the side of the bed and vomited into the garbage can Manny was holding. Someone was holding her hair out of the way and rubbing circles between her shoulder blades. When she had nothing left on her stomach, Rhi sat up, her head still spinning. Elizabeth rushed from the room while Manny adjusted the pillows behind her back.

Elizabeth returned with a glass of water and a cold, damp washcloth. "Here," she said, holding out the glass. "Take a few sips." Rhi reached for the glass, but she was too

164

weak to grasp it. Elizabeth held it to her lips, and Rhi drank tentatively. It had been a long time since she'd thrown up, and she didn't want to do it again any time soon.

Mac sat next to Rhi. "Can't you… you know?" She waved her arm over Rhi's leg where her jeans had been sliced open at some point.

"No." Rhi's voice was barely a whisper.

"Can't she what?" Elizabeth asked.

Mac looked at Rhi, and Rhi nodded once, so Mac explained. "Rhi has the gift of healing. My dad was shot, and when Rhi placed her hands on him, it took the pain away."

Elizabeth took Rhi's hand. "Is that something you can do now?"

"No. I have to push the energy out of my body into whatever I'm trying to help. The energy is already doing what little it can to ease the pain."

"I'm calling Dr. Marks," Xavier announced and left the room.

Rhi closed her eyes and concentrated on breathing through the pain. Her body was getting cold.

"Manny, what happened?" Elizabeth asked.

"She was driving when the pain came over her. She didn't hit her leg on anything, so I have no idea. Master X said it smelled like poison, so whatever it is —"

"Shit. It's probably from the bug," Mac said. "Sorry about the language, but her father had a tracker implanted in her neck. One of the Hounds removed it last night. Maybe he didn't get it all? Or maybe something from it leaked out when he removed it."

"Where was this tracker?" Xavier asked, striding back into the room.

"In her neck."

Xavier sat on the bed. "Rhi, I'm going to look at your neck, if that's all right?"

Rhi leaned forward, but she had to grab onto Mac to

keep from face planting on the floor. Xavier pushed her hair out of the way and inhaled deeply.

"No. There is no indication of anything residual besides whatever they used to numb the area. Whatever is causing this is definitely coming from the area above her ankle. My guess is there was another tracker or something worse implanted there. Dr. Marks is out of town, so we're going to take you to the hospital."

Rhi tried to respond, but she couldn't force the words through her chattering teeth. She was so cold. She wanted warmth. Wanted... Ryker.

CHAPTER FIFTEEN

Ryker

RYKER KEPT WAITING for Spyder or Hawk to send him a text. It was possible David was in New DC working. It was also possible there wasn't another device capable of tracking the chip. The closer to New Roseville he got without hearing from either of them, the more his beast pushed against him. Ryker didn't like leaving Rhi any more than the Gryphon did, but he had a job to do, and if a Gargoyle King couldn't keep her safe, no one could.

Signaling to Sultan, they took the next exit. His sergeant-at-arms had insisted on riding with Ryker, and he was happy to have the company. Spyder and Hawk were waiting at a small park on the edge of town. Both were leaning against their bikes. "Nothing?" Ryker asked as soon as he shut his motor off.

"Nada. Maybe there was only one device," Hawk replied.

"Maybe, but I doubt it. I'd bet David kept it, but he's busy at the GIA. We'll keep the chip on us and hope he comes for it sooner or later. For now, we'll go ahead and recon the compound."

Spyder stood and stretched his arms overhead. "I already did a flyover. Either they aren't expecting us to come after them, or they're confident in their abilities to stop us. It was business as usual. People were going about their lives like nothing was amiss."

Ryker placed his helmet on the mirror. "Josiah's faith in David must be high. Tell me about the guards."

Spyder crossed his arms over his chest. "There were twenty guarding the perimeter and probably double that roaming the streets. All were armed."

"Shit. This is going to be more difficult than taking down Gideon was. I still think getting to David is the key. He's the one keeping them hidden. He's also the one supplying them with guns. We need to get in there and take their weapons."

Sultan ran a hand over his shaved scalp. "How do you suppose we do that? None of us are armed."

"Did you get a look at the building where the guns are located?"

"Yes. It's just as James said. A barn, smaller than the others, with a door on each end. There is no hayloft, so we can't use the second story as an escape. The higher windows aren't large enough for us to get in or out of."

Ryker sighed. "As bad as I hate to say this, we might need to turn this over to the FBI."

"And tell them what?" Hawk asked. "We don't have proof of what they're doing."

"We have Rhi. She can attest to what she knows. Plus, I think the feds would be interested in finding out an agent for the GIA is aiding them. They want the Ministry as badly as we do, and if a government agent is aiding and abetting, that's grounds for treason."

"True, but David is smart. He's been playing both sides for at least ten years. That's a long time to go without getting caught. Do you think that's why they want Rhi back? Because of what she could know?"

Ryker narrowed his eyes at Sultan, thinking about what Rhi had told them. "I don't think that's it. At least not all of it. Why would a father put a chip in his teenage daughter before they went to Haven? She was just a kid back then. She had no idea what was going on. For the most part, Rhi has been kept indoors, away from the guards and the training."

"What about Elijah? If we turn this over to the feds, he's going to get caught in the middle."

Ryker hadn't forgotten about Mac's boyfriend, but his focus had been on the bigger picture. "We need to figure out which building his cell is in since he spends most of his time in solitary. James said it was the smallest barn. We'll go in under the cover of night and observe. We don't know the kid is in solitary at the moment. They have to feed him at some point, and I doubt there's a kitchen in the barn, but I could be wrong. This is going to take more than just one night. We need to observe without being seen."

Spyder returned to leaning against his bike. "The smallest barn is set off by itself, so that's a plus. There are plenty of trees close by where we can watch. I didn't see anyone going in or out, but I wasn't there to scope out the buildings, only the guards."

"Let's head back to the hotel. I never checked us out, so the rooms are still ours. We'll order in lunch, then wait for dark."

With Ryker in the lead position, Sultan took Mav's usual spot, and Spyder and Hawk fell in line behind them. It didn't take long to get to The Continental seeing how New Roseville wasn't a large town. When they passed the convenience store where he met Rhi, Ryker found himself smiling. What a difference a couple of days made. Before, he'd been wary and a little jealous of the Hounds who had wives and kids. Ryker had Mac in his life, but he'd missed out on her formative years. He was doing his best to make up for it, but like War, having a grown daughter was different than watching your child grow into their own person. At least the twins had been returned to Mav at a young age.

169

Now, Ryker had a beautiful, sweet woman to call his own. Her inexperience still worried him, but if she was meant to be his, he would find a way to make it work. He didn't know whether or not Rhi wanted children. He prayed she did, and he would gladly give them to her. He wanted the chance to watch a son or daughter grow. Witnessing all their firsts. Rhi had a good heart, and he knew she would make a wonderful mother. Ryker didn't care if their children followed his family in believing in the old gods or worshipped the goddess as Rhi did. Ryker thought children should be allowed to choose their own path as long as they were honest and caring. Where Rhi never faltered in her trust in the goddess, McKenzie had given up on any type of deity after what she went through.

Ryker told Sultan what he wanted off the room service menu, then went to stare out the window. Just because Josiah's men hadn't followed the chip didn't mean they weren't watching the town. Josiah's compound was different than Gideon's had been. Ryker knew from his own life how brothers weren't the same, even if their goals were. Both men were liars, using the guise of being preachers to command how everyone lived. Ryker had seen other Ministry compounds, and most were somewhere in between the two led by the Talberts. Gideon had no weapons to speak of, and Josiah had a small army. Maybe it was because Josiah had a government agent working for him.

Wanting to know more about the male, Ryker called Lucy. "Hey, Little Dove. What can you tell me about Rhi's father?"

"Honestly, not much. When I was at the GIA, I wasn't privy to what the other hackers were working on. I had been told we were all doing the same job, and if that were the case, he was probably working with Josiah, giving him all the information the rest of us dug up on the Ministry. I did my best to keep my head down and stay off anyone's radar."

170

"Do you think it's possible he's undercover?"

"Not if he's supplying Haven with guns."

"I've heard Sutton talk about agents who had to get deep in their undercover persona." Ryker knew he was reaching, but he wanted to understand Rhi's father and his motives. "If that's the case here, ten years is a long time to be undercov— Luce, I need to go. I see movement outside."

"Be safe."

"I will." Ryker disconnected but kept his eyes on the two men walking toward the hotel. "We have company," he told the Hounds.

"While we were waiting, I found the stairs to the roof. We can strip in the stairwell and shift as soon as we get through the door," Spyder said.

"Or, we could go down to the bar. They're not going to attack in broad daylight," Sultan countered.

"Both ideas have merit, but I think I'd like to meet them head-on. See if they approach us. Let's take the back stairway. If they're looking for us, they'll either use the front stairs or the elevator. We can bypass them and head to the bar." In less than a minute, the four Hounds were on the lower level of the hotel sitting at a high-top table. The bar wasn't busy, so they were served quickly. Their waitress – Emberlynn – did her best to flirt with them, and Spyder, being single, soaked it up. He winked at the pretty woman, flashing straight, white teeth.

When Josiah's two men stuck their heads in the door, their eyes widened when they found the Hounds. Ryker stood and walked in their direction. The two men looked at each other, obviously surprised to see the man they were looking for coming toward them. "Won't you join us?" Ryker asked, using his Gryphon voice. If he had to, Ryker would eliminate Josiah's guards two at a time. Spyder and Sultan stood, and Ryker motioned the men onto the vacated stools.

"What can I get you to drink?" the waitress asked,

standing closer to Spyder than was socially acceptable for someone who was working. If the glint in his dark eyes was any indication, the Hound was enjoying himself.

"We don't drink," the human closer to Ryker sneered.

Spyder took the server by the elbow and pulled her gently away from the table. "This is a business meeting, Emberlynn. If you wouldn't mind giving us a little privacy? I promise to make it up to you."

"Oh, of course…?"

"Spyder," he said, tapping the name patch on his kutte.

"Spyder," she repeated. "Got it. But if you need anything, just whistle." Emberlynn sashayed off with Spyder's eyes on her ass. Ryker rolled his eyes, then turned his attention back to Josiah's men.

"What are your names?" Ryker asked the one closest to him.

"I'm John. This is Paul."

"Where are George and Ringo?" Spyder asked. Hawk rolled his lips inward to keep from laughing. Sultan crossed his arms over his chest, but he was looking at his feet. Ryker loved Spyder's smartass nature, so he let the joke go.

"George is at Haven, but we don't know a Ringo," Paul said.

"Why are you here?" Ryker asked, toying with the label on his bottle.

"Josiah told us to find the Hounds," John answered.

"Well, here we are. What are you going to do with us?" Ryker sat back on his stool, crossing his arms over his chest.

"We're supposed to take you out."

"On a date?" Spyder quipped. Even Ryker couldn't hold back his smile at that one.

"What? No. We're not queer. That's wrong." Paul scrunched his nose like he smelled shit.

"Says who? I happen to think I'm a great catch. Any woman *or man* would be lucky to land my ass," Spyder taunted.

"You should come with us. Let Brother Josiah teach you the true path to righteousness."

"I think I'll pass. My god is perfectly fine with how I conduct myself. Why does Josiah want Anna so bad?"

"Because she belongs to James."

"Actually" — Ryker leaned forward — "she belongs to me."

"You? But you're a heathen. Anna is pure, and she should be with someone who leads a clean life."

"How do you know I don't? You know nothing about me other than what Josiah has told you, and he doesn't know me either. As a matter of fact, I bet you don't know who *he* is. Who his brother is. But I'll tell you. He's the man who kidnapped my wife. My pregnant wife. *Then* he gave her to his brother, Gideon. Gideon took my baby and gave it to his family to raise so his flock wouldn't know he had a married woman living with him. Josiah is the one who took my daughter's boyfriend away from Gideon's compound just because one of the guards wanted my daughter for himself. My daughter who was in love with another man and pregnant with his baby. Gideon then took her child, my grandchild, and put it up for adoption. Do those two sound like holy men to you? Because let me tell you something, if they do, you will burn in Hell right along with them."

"That can't be true," Paul muttered.

"Oh, but it is. I have no love lost for your so-called preacher. He uses the Bible to hide behind his true agenda. Why would a peaceful compound need to be so heavily guarded? Why train boys into killers if there wasn't a hidden agenda? Why send you to *kill* four unarmed men? That doesn't sound very Christian-like to me. But from what I understand, Josiah doesn't preach Christ's message of love, tolerance, and forgiveness. He focuses on the old text because it suits his needs."

"How do you know about what's in the Bible?" John asked.

173

"I'm not as much a heathen as you believe. Now, here is how this is going to go. You are going back to Haven. You are going to get Elijah out of solitary, and you are going to bring him back here."

"How are we supposed to do that?" John asked.

"You look like smart men. You'll figure it out. While you're doing that, you're also going to grab a case of guns and ammo. When you get back to the compound, you will not tell anyone what we've spoken about other than to say we want to make a trade, and that is only if you get caught. Otherwise, say nothing to anyone. Get Elijah. Get the guns and ammo. Bring them to me. If you aren't back here with what we've requested, we'll tell Josiah you let Anna get away. Do you understand?"

"Yes," both men responded in unison.

"Good. Now get out of here." Ryker reached for his drink and downed it after the two humans left the restaurant.

Spyder let out a whistle, and Emberlynn turned his way, grinning. "Another round, Doll," he called out.

"Do you really think that plan will work?" Hawk asked.

"Probably not, but it's worth a shot. If we can get Elijah without having to go to Haven, I'd prefer it. As much as I would like to take the bastard down myself for what he did to Juliette, Sutton convinced me we're up against a group of hostile men with guns. My revenge isn't worth risking all our lives. If John and Paul bring the guns, we'll record the transaction on video, get them to confess, and turn it all over to the feds. They have both the manpower and firepower to go up against Josiah where we do not."

"I agree. We've never come across a compound this heavily guarded." Sultan moved out of the way for Emberlynn to set their new drinks on the table.

"You fellas hungry?"

"Oh, shit. We ordered room service. Can you call to the kitchen and have them bring it in here instead?" Spyder asked.

"Sure. What's your room number?" she asked with a sparkle in her eyes.

"Three fourteen." Spyder looked down at Emberlynn's chest and licked his lips. Then he leaned in and whispered, "How do you feel about spankings?"

The waitress's cheeks turned red, but fire flashed in her eyes. If Ryker hadn't seen it for himself, he never would have believed it. Sultan was looking back and forth between the two of them, probably trying to figure out what the fuck was going on. He must not have been privy to Spyder's and Hawk's lifestyle outside the club.

"Close your mouth, Sarge," Hawk said to Sultan.

"What is going on right now?" Sultan looked over his shoulder where Spyder was following the waitress to the kitchen door. He leaned in and whispered something in her ear, and Emberlynn threw her head back, laughing. She slapped Spyder on the arm and pushed through the swinging door.

Spyder returned to the table with a little more swagger in his step than usual. For one of the smaller Hounds, his attitude made up for his size.

"I think I'm in love." Spyder had a dopey grin on his face.

Sultan narrowed his eyes but didn't say anything because Emberlynn returned with their food. After setting their plates in front of them, she asked if they needed anything else while looking at Spyder. He surprised Ryker when he traded his flirting for politeness and told her they were all set. Ryker just shook his head. Jude "Spyder" Sterling was an enigma, and with every new piece of information Ryker found out about the Hound, the more he realized he really didn't know the male at all. They had been friends and fellow Hounds for many years, but Ryker had kept to himself for most of those. When he thought about it, he didn't know any of the Hounds, other than his brothers, as well as he should.

"Is settling down something you want?" Ryker asked.

"Of course, but I'm not going to until I'm sure the female is perfect in every way."

Sultan wiped his mouth on his napkin before asking, "What type of female is perfect in your eyes?"

"She would have to have a sense of adventure, because my female will want to ride on my bike everywhere we go, unless it's to a fancy restaurant. She will need to love kids and dogs because I want lots of both. She has to have a bit of a wild streak when it comes to sex, because I... No, you don't need to know that part. And she has to get along with my mom." Ryker had to agree with Spyder's assessment, especially when it came to his mom. Rory's opinion mattered. War had learned that the hard way.

"So, when you asked the waitress about spankings, you weren't kidding?" Sultan asked.

"Nope. It's better to get certain topics out there immediately. If she had bristled at the thought, I would know right away there's no need to continue flirting with her."

"That does make sense." Sultan stared across the room, his eyes unfocused. Ryker understood his friend's silence. Spyder might seem like a wild child, but his wisdom was sound. With the exception of Emberlynn bringing more drinks, the rest of the meal was eaten in contemplative silence until his phone rang.

"Xavier? What's wrong?"

CHAPTER SIXTEEN

Rhiannon

RHI WOKE TO loud, angry voices. One was a voice she never wanted to hear again. She tried to sit up, but gentle hands pushed her back against the bed.

"Easy, Rhi." Elizabeth brushed Rhiannon's hair back from her sweaty face. At least she wasn't freezing any longer.

"What's going on?" she asked.

"Your father is trying to get past Xavier."

"I don't want him here. Please, don't let him anywhere near me," Rhi begged.

"You're an adult, Sweetheart. He can't make you go," Elizabeth assured her.

"I have the paperwork saying I'm her power of attorney as well as her medical proxy. My daughter is in no state of mind to make decisions!"

"And how do you know what is wrong with your daughter? No one called you," Xavier countered.

"The hospital called since my name is listed as her medical emergency contact," David said.

"Mr. Spencer, no one from this hospital called you," a third voice stated. "Rhiannon isn't in a coma. She isn't in distress. We have the situation under control, and if you don't leave peacefully, I'll be forced to call security."

"This is bullshit. I want to see my daughter."

177

"But she doesn't want to see you," Xavier growled. Rhiannon had heard that tone when Ryker was pissed. It was nice to have someone stand up to her father on her behalf.

"Get your hands off me! Rhiannon! You cannot keep me away from my daughter."

"I can, and I will. She is an adult capable of making her own choices, and it's her choice not to see you."

David's voice was loud even though it sounded farther away than it had initially. "I'm calling the police."

"You do that, but do it somewhere else. You're disturbing the patients," the third voice said.

"You have no right to keep me from seeing her."

"As Chief of Staff, I have every right. My hospital, my rules. Now, unless you want *me* to call the police, you need to leave. Quietly."

"This isn't over," David snarled.

The voices quieted, then Xavier came into the room looking calm. He was joined by an older man who was anything but calm.

"Ah, Rhiannon. You're awake. I'm Dr. Chastain. How are you feeling?"

Rhi looked down at her hand where a tube was sticking out. Her left leg was numb, but the pain was gone. "Better. Uh, what happened?"

"We removed a chip from your left ankle, and we are giving you both pain medication and an antiserum for the drug."

"My father drugged me?" Rhi couldn't breathe. She knew he had turned dark, but...

"Rhi, look at me. Breathe with me," Xavier commanded. She looked up at his handsome face, which was blurry from her tears. "That's it, breathe in and hold it. Good, now let it out." Xavier urged her to inhale several more times, and finally she didn't feel like she was going to pass out. "We don't know that for certain. What we do know is the chip

178

either malfunctioned or was triggered."

"Rhiannon, the drug in your system wasn't enough to kill you. That might not make you feel better, but we do have it under control. You'll feel the effects for a while. Numbness in your leg and possibly your hip. Once the antiserum runs its course, you'll be able to walk."

"What kind of drug was it?" Not that she knew anything about different drugs, but she wanted the truth of what her father had done. More importantly, why?

Dr. Chastain looked at Xavier, his face unreadable. "Please, just tell me," she begged.

Xavier took Rhi's hand. "It's a rare paralyzing agent. One that most humans don't have access to. If enough of the drug was introduced into your system, it could have rendered you immobile. In other words, you would have been completely paralyzed. Given the small amount present, we believe it was only meant to cause panic and bring you to the hospital. Since your father arrived soon after we did, he had to have known the drug had been triggered, because like Dr. Chastain said, no one called him. Since you've never been a patient at this hospital, they had none of your records. No authorization or medical contact. I explained a little of your history to Dr. Chastain, and we were able to keep your father away from you."

"He's not going to stop," Rhi whispered.

"You don't need to worry about that. I've called in some friends of mine, and they will guard the house and property until it is deemed safe for you to leave." Xavier didn't have to say what kind of friends. He meant Gargoyles. Gargoyles whose skin was impenetrable to bullets.

"When can we go back to your place?" Rhi wanted to be surrounded by Gargoyles. Protected from her father and Josiah and anyone else related to Haven.

"We will need to monitor you closely. The drug should be completely out of your system by this time tomorrow, so until then, you'll need to remain here," Dr. Chastain explained.

"Have you called Ryker?" Rhi asked Xavier.

"Yes."

Rhi sank back into the pillow and closed her eyes. The doctor spoke with Xavier in low tones, but Rhi didn't bother trying to listen. Her leg wasn't the only thing that was numb. Her heart was trying to freeze inside her chest. How could her father do this to her? He had all but ignored her for ten years, so why was he so interested in her now? It had to be her gift. That was the only thing that made sense, and even that was far-fetched.

"She needs to rest," Dr. Chastain said. "I'll allow you all to remain in here with her because of the circumstances, but please don't upset her. That will slow the healing process."

"We'll make sure she sleeps," Elizabeth assured the doctor.

Once Dr. Chastain was out of the room, Xavier stepped up to the bed. "I told Ryker what was happening, because if I were in his place and no one informed me my mate was in trouble, I would tear the world apart. I did convince him you are safe and he should remain where he is. The sooner he takes care of Josiah, the sooner the two of you can be together. He left you in my care because Lucy trusts us to take care of you. There is nothing Ryker can do for you that isn't already being done. It took a bit of arguing and assuring him you're going to be okay, but he agreed. I promised him I would keep him updated on your condition. Now, like the doctor said, you need to get some rest." Xavier dimmed all the lights in the room and closed the blinds. Mac was sitting in the corner biting the side of her thumb, but when she looked at Rhi, she smiled. Xavier sat on the small sofa and pulled Elizabeth down next to him.

Rhi's eyes, even though they were already closed, got heavier. She didn't try to fight sleep. If that would help her heal faster, then she welcomed it.

"David, that's crazy."

"I know what I saw, Daisy."

"No, you don't. What you saw was my daughter caring for a wounded animal. Nothing more."

"Oh, now she's your daughter?"

"You know what I mean. The only thing special about Rhiannon is the size of her heart."

"Look, I'm not the only one who knows. My mother… We have to protect Rhi."

"Protect her from who? And, wait. Your mother knows? What did you tell her?"

Daddy sighed, rolling his head around his shoulders. "Daisy, please."

"Rhiannon is a normal child. She cares about everything around her. Nothing more."

"I thought pagans weren't supposed to lie? You think you're so much better than the rest of us."

"I never said that. Don't use your mother's words against me. It won't end well for you."

"Are you threatening me?" Daddy got in Momma's face, and Rhi shrank back where she was hiding. She'd never seen her parents fight before.

"What's going on in here?" Grandmother appeared out of nowhere. And she called momma a devil.

"Nothing for you to be concerned about. How did you get in here anyway?" Momma asked.

"Everything to do with my son is my concern. As for your door, I have a key. Now answer me."

"I don't have to answer you. You aren't my mother or my boss." Momma turned to walk away, but Grandmother grabbed her arm. "Let go of me."

"You need to watch yourself, Daisy."

"And you need to let go. Now." Momma jerked her arm away from Grandmother and ran from the room.

"She threatened to leave you, David. You have to do something."

"I can handle my wife, Mother. Now, why are you here?"

181

"Abraham is ready to put her power to the test. He is getting impatient."

"Your husband is your problem."

Grandmother slapped Daddy across the face. "Don't you ever speak to me that way again. You forget who I am."

"No, I know exactly who you are."

"As the husband, it is your place to lead this household. Daisy will go where you tell her to, if not... Handle your wife, or I will."

Grandmother left, and Daddy followed. Rhi waited until she was sure they were both gone before she went after her momma. When she found her, Rhi walked up to her and wrapped her little hands around her momma's wrist where Grandmother had grabbed her, sending her love out of her body into her momma's.

"Thank you, my little flower. I love you more than all the plants and trees. I love you more than the sunshine."

"I love you more than the moon and the stars," Rhi said back.

"It's going to be okay. I promise I'll always take care of you." Momma pulled Rhi into her chest and held her close, stroking her hair.

No. Momma was dead, so who...? Rhi opened her eyes to find Elizabeth sitting beside her bed. It was her pushing Rhi's hair away from her face over and over.

"Hi," Rhi said, her voice rough from sleep.

"How are you feeling?"

Rhi searched her body for the pain but found it was gone. "I'm okay. Just ready to get out of here."

"Dr. Chastain said you can go if this round of bloodwork comes back negative. Here," Elizabeth said, holding out a cup with a straw. "You need to drink plenty of fluids."

Rhi sipped the water, the cool liquid soothing to her parched throat. Elizabeth smiled, and it reminded Rhi so much of her mother's warmth. "I was dreaming about my mom. You remind me of her. Not in your looks, but the way you take care of me. I... I don't think David is my father."

"What makes you think that?"

"The dream, it was more like a memory. And something my mom said about me being *her* daughter and David arguing with her about it. She was trying to keep my gift a secret from him, but somehow, he knew, and they fought. Then my grandmother came in, saying how Abraham was getting impatient. It wasn't long after that when my mom died."

"How did she die?"

"A brain hemorrhage. At least, that's what David told me."

Elizabeth got a funny look on her face, but she masked it quickly, her sweet smile returning. The doctor and Xavier entered the room, and Elizabeth stood, pulling Xavier off to the side, whispering. Rhi's attention turned to the doctor when he blocked the couple from her view.

"I have wonderful news. Your blood is all clear, so you can go home."

Rhi didn't bother to tell him she didn't have a home. Ryker had told her he wanted them to be together, but what if he changed his mind? He had more important things to do than babysit her. Yes, he apologized for saying that, but it was the truth. Someone had to look out for her because she wasn't capable of caring for herself. She had no home, no money. Even now, she was relying on Tamian's parents to watch over her.

"I thought that would make you happy," the doctor said when she didn't respond.

"What's wrong?" Elizabeth returned to her side, grasping Rhi's hand.

"Nothing. I'm just happy to hear the good news," she lied.

Xavier stepped up next to his wife. "Rhiannon, I've arranged it so you're going to leave here in an ambulance. I have two of my males outside the door. One will drive while the other rides in the back with you. We're hoping if David is watching, he'll be waiting for you to leave by the

183

front door. Elizabeth, McKenzie, and I are going to leave together and hopefully make him think you are still here. It will buy us some time to get you somewhere safe."

"You shouldn't have to go to all this trouble. Not for me."

"Dr. Chastain, if you would get Rhiannon's discharge papers together, I'd like to get her moved as quickly as possible."

"Of course. I'll have the nurse come in and remove the IV. By the time that's taken care of, the paperwork should be ready. Rhiannon, it was a pleasure to meet you." He patted her arm before leaving the room.

Xavier sat down in the chair next to the bed. "Rhiannon, this really isn't a lot of trouble. We have the means to hide you until Ryker can take care of business and return. Please, don't worry about anything."

"Do you trust the doctor?" Elizabeth asked Xavier.

"Yes. I explained to him David is a member of a cult, and we are keeping Rhiannon safe from having to return. I also offered him an exorbitant amount of money to keep silent."

The next hour was a flurry of getting Rhi out of the hospital. The male riding with her in the ambulance was large like Xavier and just as handsome. Stefan introduced himself once they were on the road, then he was quiet but attentive. He was dressed in an EMT uniform so if anyone saw him getting into the back of the ambulance, it wouldn't cause suspicion. She was taken to a nursing facility where once inside, she changed into the clothes Mac had been wearing. Somewhere, they had found her a short, auburn wig. From a distance, no one would be able to tell the woman exiting the building was Rhi. According to Lucy, David had access to some powerful tools, but hopefully by her leaving in the ambulance, he would be thrown off long enough for them to return to Xavier's.

The SUV wasn't one Rhi had noticed in the garage

when Manny was showing her the cars. When Stefan opened the back door for her, Rhi smiled. It wasn't Elizabeth and Xavier inside, but Manny and another man she assumed was his husband.

"Hop in, Miss Rhi." When she was seated, Stefan climbed in next to her and pointed to her seatbelt. He really was a male of few words. "This is my husband, Lawrence. Lawrence, Rhiannon."

"It's a pleasure to meet you, Rhi."

"Same to you. I don't think you said, but are you two Gargoyles?"

"Nope. We're as human as you are, but my family has been with Xavier's for hundreds of years. Myra is a cousin on my dad's side." Manny pulled the SUV out of the parking lot, while Lawrence and Stefan both looked all around. Half an hour later, they pulled up to a gate that wasn't Xavier's.

"Uh, Manny? Where are we?"

"This is my place," Stefan said. "There were drones flying over X's house, so he asked me to bring you here. He, Elizabeth, and McKenzie are waiting for you inside."

Rhi's eyes filled with tears. "This is too much," she whispered.

"Oh, Sweetheart, keeping you safe is never too much. You're family," Manny said.

"But I'm not."

Manny pulled the car inside a large garage. When he shut off the motor, he unbuckled and turned around to look at her. "Yes, you are. Family isn't always blood related. It's the people who care about you. Those who would do anything in the world for you. That's who we are. We might have just met you, but you're important to the Lazlos. Lucy is one of them, and she's Tamian's mate. Tamian is one of ours, so that makes Lucy just as much our family and in turn, you too. Not only that, but both Gargoyles and Gryphons were put on this earth to protect humans. It's what they do. Now, you have both watching over you. You might as well get used to it, because like I said, we are now your family."

A side door in the garage opened, and Xavier filled the frame. "Everything okay?" His voice was muffled through the closed car window, but Rhi still understood him.

Manny opened his door and got out, then opened Rhi's door for her and helped her out. "Yes. Just explaining to Miss Rhi how family works."

Rhi was still a little weak, so she held onto Manny's arm as they walked inside Stefan's home. Rhi had expected the same opulence as Xavier's house, but even though it was large, it was homey. Lived in. There were no statues and crystal chandeliers. Rhi wasn't afraid to sit on the sofa for fear of getting it dirty. Mac and Elizabeth were seated at a long bar that separated the kitchen from the dining area.

Mac laughed. "Nice wig."

Rhi reached up and pulled it off. Manny was there to take it from her. "I'll just put this away for now."

A pretty brunette was at the counter making sandwiches. She smiled and said, "Welcome to our home, Rhiannon. I'm Claudia, Stefan's mate. Are you hungry? Or would you like to lie down and rest?"

"A sandwich would be wonderful. Thank you for opening your home to me."

"It's what family does. What do you like on your sandwich?" Claudia asked.

"Whatever you're making is fine." Rhi didn't want to put these people out any more than she already was. She'd eat peanut butter and be fine with it.

The four women, along with Manny and Lawrence, sat at the dining room table. It was obvious by the way Manny got drinks for them all this wasn't the first time he had been in Stefan and Claudia's home. The conversations added to that proof. Manny asked about Claudia's grandchildren, and after they finished eating, Claudia produced photos to show everyone. It surprised Rhi when she saw the kids in the pictures were teenagers. Claudia, like Elizabeth, didn't look old enough to be a grandmother. She was a little envious of the fact that they would live hundreds of years. She remembered the question Ryker had posed about living a long life, and in that moment, Rhi knew she would jump at the chance if Lucy were able to come up with a way to make that happen.

Weather in Upstate New York was chilly in the fall, but the sunroom at the back of the house was toasty when they retreated out there after lunch. Several males, including Stefan, were outside. Xavier, however, was sitting inside next to Elizabeth. She wondered if it was because he was a king. Did he have an army of Gargoyles protecting him? It was still such a foreign concept for Rhi, knowing these males were other than human. She had seen Ryker shift into his lion and attempt to shift to his Gryphon. She couldn't wait to see him in all his Gryphon glory.

The longer Rhi sat in the warm room, the heavier her eyes became. She tried to stay awake, not wanting to be rude. "Why don't I show you to one of the guest rooms where you can rest?" Claudia suggested.

"I'm sorry. I guess I'm not one hundred percent," Rhi admitted.

"No need to apologize. You've been through a traumatic experience. It's understandable." Claudia held out her hand, and Rhi took it. Claudia directed Rhi back inside and up the wide staircase to where the bedrooms were located. "Here you go." The room was large, like the one at Lucy's house, but it was well used. "This is my granddaughter's room when she stays over. I hope it's okay."

"It's perfect. Thank you, Claudia. For everything."

Claudia palmed Rhi's cheek. "Like I said, it's what family does. If you need anything, all you have to do is call out. I'll hear you."

"Really?"

"Yes. Gargoyle hearing," she said with a wink.

"Wait, you're…?"

Claudia lengthened her fangs, grinning. "Sure am." Her fangs disappeared just as quickly. "Rest up. We'll be downstairs if you need anything."

Rhi slipped off her boots, turned down the covers, and climbed underneath. Exhaustion claimed her quickly.

Chapter Seventeen

Ryker

RYKER COULDN'T CONCENTRATE. While he and the Hounds waited for John and Paul to return with Elijah, he paced the room, thinking of Rhi and what she was going through. One thing was certain – Ryker was going to tear David Spencer apart when he got his hands on him. What kind of man did that to his daughter? Ryker had walked out of the hotel, ready to get on his bike and head west when Xavier convinced him to stay put. Xavier vowed on his life he would protect Ryker's mate. Xavier had called in several of his Clan to help watch over Rhiannon.

After taking Xavier's call, Ryker returned to the room where the others were waiting, and he explained what was happening with Rhiannon. Collectively, they offered to stay and make sure Elijah was returned to them if Ryker wanted to head back.

"No. Xavier has the situation under control. The poison, or whatever was leached into her system, is gone, and she's going to be fine. I can't keep going back and forth from there to here and accomplish anything. I need to see this through. Then I'll be able to return to both my mate and daughter with good news."

Sultan reminded Ryker they had all ridden their bikes. If John and Paul did bring Elijah to them, they needed a vehicle to take him back to New Troy. Ryker called Judge and asked him to meet them with one of the club's SUVs, and now, there were five Hounds sitting around waiting.

"We have movement," Hawk said from the window. "I don't know what Elijah looks like, but there's a young man with John and Paul."

"Spyder, you and Sultan head downstairs and escort them up here. I don't want the exchange made around humans."

Less than five minutes later, the door opened, and Ryker eyed the young man. He wasn't sure what he had expected, but the tall, lanky kid staring back at him wasn't it. Standing about six foot, the young man was wearing dirty khakis and a plain, white T-shirt. His shoes were worn, and he wasn't wearing a jacket. He looked as though he hadn't slept in days, if the dark circles under his eyes were any indication. The first thing Ryker was going to do was feed him.

"Take John and Paul next door," Ryker said to Spyder. When the humans were safely out of earshot, Ryker approached the kid. "My name is Ryker Lazlo. May I ask your name?"

"Elijah McLean."

"Elijah, my family and I work to make sure people who live in places like Haven want to be there. Are you one of those people?"

"Look, man. I don't know you. You could be a spy for Josiah for all I know."

"I could, but I'm not. Do you know a young woman named McKenzie?"

"Mac?" Elijah's face lit up for just a second before turning dark.

"I'm going to take that as a yes. I want to show you something." Ryker pulled out his phone and opened the photos. He chose the one of him and Mac together sitting on the back deck. "Here."

"She's—"

"My daughter. Mac is my daughter, and when my family and I went in to rescue another woman from Gideon's compound, I found out who Mac is. She came home with me, and she's been waiting for me to find you ever since. Is it okay if I take your picture to send to her?"

"Why the hell would she want a picture of me, and why would she want you to find me? She made her choice even after that bastard raped her."

Ryker was stunned. "Raped?" he managed to whisper. "What are you talking about? Who raped my daughter?"

"Lewis. He forced himself on her, got her pregnant, and she still chose him."

"Mac didn't choose Lewis. Gideon locked Mac up. Kept her isolated the whole time she was pregnant. I'm going to kill that motherfucker!"

Spyder stuck his head through the adjoining door. "Ryot, there are other guests on this floor. Besides, Lewis and Gideon are in jail."

Ryker paced the room. Why hadn't Mac told him about being raped. "Why didn't she tell me?"

Sultan rubbed a hand across his scalp. "Probably because you're her father, and she figured you'd react the way you just did."

"You mentioned Mac, but not the baby. How is it?" Elijah asked.

"Gideon took him and put him up for adoption. After that, Mac tried to run away, and Gideon sent a dog after her. It attacked her. Now I have another reason to kill the motherfucker." Ryker paced the room again, raking his hands through his hair. *Raped. Lewis raped his baby girl.* Ryker did his best to calm down. There was nothing he could do about Lewis now, but somehow, he would find a way to make the human pay. Jail or not. First, he had John and Paul to deal with. When he got back to Mac, he was going to sit down with her and make sure she didn't need therapy.

"The baby was a boy?"

191

"I don't exactly know, but I feel wrong calling him or her an 'it'."

Elijah was quiet for a bit, looking across the room at nothing. When he finally looked back at Ryker, he asked, "Did Mac really send you to find me?"

"Yeah, she did. She loves you, but if you don't feel the same, let me know now. She's been through enough heartache to last three fucking lifetimes. I'm not going to take you to her if you're gonna bail."

"I'm not gonna bail, but..." Elijah walked over to the window and looked out. "I get you think I'm a kid, and at nineteen, I guess I am. But I loved your daughter more than anything. We made plans to get out of the compound and somehow start a life together. It was all I thought about. Then, one day, she comes to me crying, telling me she was pregnant and how Lewis raped her. I wanted to kill him, but look at me. Even before they threw me in the hole, I wasn't much bigger than I am now. Lewis is built like you, so even if I did get my hands on him, he'd have kicked my ass.

"Mac talked me out of going after him, but that didn't stop me from telling anyone who would listen that he raped her. I never saw her after that morning. A week later, I was on my way to Haven with Josiah. Before I was taken, Gideon came to me and told me Mac had made her decision, and my leaving was for the best. I was devastated. I've spent the last few months in a hole with nothing to do but hate Mac for telling me she loved me, then leaving me without a word. At least that's what I thought happened. It's going to take me a second to wrap my head around the truth. I want to see her. If she can look me in the eye and tell me she still loves me, then no, I won't bail on her."

Ryker tried to understand Elijah's reluctance. He had been lied to. Had thought the woman he loved had chosen someone else. "I'd still like to take your picture and send to her." Elijah shrugged and stood still. He didn't smile, but he didn't need to. Ryker snapped the photo and sent it to Mac's phone. He was eager to give his baby girl some good news.

"Are you hungry?" Ryker handed the menu over in case the kid decided he wanted something to eat.

"I'm starving, but I don't have any money."

"Don't worry about that. Choose anything you want, and I'll have it brought up to the room."

Elijah licked his dry lips. "Oh man. I haven't had decent food in so long I wouldn't know what to get. Uh, I guess a burger and fries?"

Ryker placed the order with room service, adding a soda to the order. A little sugar would probably do the kid good. "It'll be up in about twenty minutes."

"Are you really trading me for Anna?"

"No, I'm not. Anna's real name is Rhiannon, and she's very important to me. The same way you are to Mac. I told dumb and dumber in there about the trade so they'd get you out of Haven. We are going to deal with John and Paul, then we'll head back to where we live. New Troy is about three hours from here."

"What's going to happen to Haven?"

"We're going to turn Josiah over to the FBI. My family and I don't have enough firepower to go up against them and win. When we took down Gideon, we didn't have that issue."

Elijah crossed his thin arms over his chest. "For brothers, their leadership style was totally different. I can't wait to hear all about what happened with Gideon."

"I'll tell you all about it on the ride home."

Room service arrived, and Sultan brought the tray to where Elijah had sat at the table. He didn't wait to dig in.

While Elijah ate, Ryker talked. "Do you know if John and Paul brought anything else with them besides you?"

"Yeah. A couple of crates. They made me help load them."

"Excellent. The guns are part of our plan in taking down Josiah."

Elijah swallowed the last of his burger and wiped his fingers on the cloth napkin. "Why are John and Paul cooperating?"

"They think we're making the trade, but we have a little surprise for them." Ryker called out to Spyder. When all the Hounds were listening, Ryker said, "We're ready. Let's get this shit over with so I can get Elijah home to Mac. Spyder, I want you to drive John and Paul's vehicle and follow us to the warehouse. Hawk, go with him." Ryker had called Lucy earlier and had her locate somewhere they could film the two Haven men with the guns. He still disagreed with Sutton about turning Josiah over to the FBI. Ryker wanted his revenge on Juliette's behalf. Revenge that was harsher than being arrested.

When he pulled up at the warehouse, Ryker asked Elijah if he wanted to wait in the SUV or watch from inside. Elijah opted to wait where it was warm. Ryker trusted the kid and left the car running with the heat on.

Hawk pulled Ryker aside before following the others into the warehouse. He looked over Ryker's shoulder where Elijah was waiting in the car. "Poor kid looks like shit."

"I'd say he's malnourished from being kept in solitary and only fed once a day. We'll let Rory feed him when we get home."

"She'll definitely get some meat on his bones, but I was talking about his mental state."

"You heard what he said. His world was turned upside down in more ways than one. We'll get him back to Mac, and hopefully she can convince him she loves him. If he needs to see a therapist, I'll make sure that happens. Hell, all three of them probably need to talk to someone."

When Ryker and Hawk entered the building, Spyder already had the two males standing off to the side next to the crates. Using his phone, Spyder stood back, ready to record their confession. Ryker explained to John what he wanted the male to say, and with a little coercion, John looked into the camera and told who they were, where they were from, and how Josiah Talbert was building an army with stolen guns.

"I've sent the video to your phone. Don't you think this was a little too easy?" Spyder asked once they had John and Paul tied and sitting on the cold, concrete floor. The abandoned warehouse had been the perfect location to video a confession, even if they had to use their Gryphon voices to convince the men to say what Ryker wanted them to.

Elijah was still waiting in the SUV, so Ryker felt he could speak freely. "Probably. But as long as the feds do their job and go after Haven, I don't care. I wanted revenge for what Talbert did to Juliette, but dismantling his compound was our ultimate goal. Sometimes revenge isn't done with claws or talons as much as we want it to be." Those were Sutton's words, not Ryker's, but after a heated discussion, Ryker had agreed with his father's plan.

Ryker pocketed his phone after sending the video to Lucy to forward to the FBI. "I'm ready to be home, so unless you have anything else you want to question me about...?" Ryker wasn't often a dick to the Hounds. Okay, yes, he was, but he was tired. He wanted to see Rhi, and he wanted to get Elijah to Mac.

"Nope. You're the boss," Spyder said. "If you don't need me right now, I'm going to hang around."

"Hot date with a waitress?" Hawk asked.

"You know it. What about it, Ryot?"

"Have fun. We'll see you when we see you."

Ryker joined Elijah in the vehicle while the other Hounds went back to the hotel for their bikes with Judge taking Ryker's. He spent the first part of the drive telling Elijah about taking down Gideon and asking questions about the kid and his life living in a cult. Like a lot of people, Elijah's parents had joined Gideon when Elijah was young. But he remembered what life was like on the

195

outside. He and Mac had that in common, and it was their dream to one day break free and live together in the real world. Ryker liked the kid. For as much as he'd been through at the hands of the Talbert brothers, Elijah seemed to have a level head on his shoulders. It amazed Ryker that someone raised in a cult could retain their values from before the brainwashing began. To him, it took a strong person to endure being subjected to such a primitive lifestyle. A strong person like Rhi.

"You mentioned Anna was important to you. How did you meet her?" Elijah asked.

Ryker frowned, wondering if the young man was being obtuse on purpose. "Her name is Rhiannon. Josiah called her Anna because it sounded less pagan, which she is. She and James were in town for supplies. He took her to lunch, and she ran out the back door of the diner when she told him she was going to the restroom. I was getting gas, and she ran past me and hid in a dumpster. I directed James the other way, then I talked with her and found out a little of what was going on. Something in her story made me realize she was running from the Ministry. We have been looking for Josiah ever since we took down Gideon. Rhi running away the same day I happened to be in town was nothing short of divine intervention."

"You believe in God?" Elijah asked.

"I believe in a god. Not the same one Josiah preached about. Rhiannon worships her goddess. The male who is watching over Rhi and Mac believes in the old gods. Maybe the same one I call mine, maybe not. I think people can worship whichever deity they choose as long as it's done in a respectful manner. Choose your god, but don't dismiss mine just because it isn't the one you were taught to believe in."

Elijah's eyebrows were scrunched in thought. "That makes sense. It's just hard sitting through daily lectures – because that's what they were – about doing God's will

196

when the man speaking didn't live the same life he demanded of others. I was punished because I loved Mac. Sent away because I tried to defend her even though I knew I'd get my ass kicked by men stronger than me. I might not look like much or have anything to offer your daughter, but I promise you I will figure my shit out. I will find a way to make a living and provide for her, if that's something she still wants."

"I appreciate you saying that, Elijah. I don't know all you endured living in a cult, but helping people reacclimate to the outside is what our family does. If you need to finish your education, we can make that happen. If not, we'll help you find a job you're interested in. As for Mac, she wants you in her life. I have to tell you though, with her scar, she's been a little hesitant at going out in public, but the females in our family have been wonderful about getting her out of the house. You'll need to be patient with her."

"Her scar?"

"When the dog attacked her, it bit her face. It's not as bad as Mac thinks it is, but she's self-conscious about it."

"God, I hate that man. I know I'm not supposed to hate anyone, but Gideon and Josiah are the worst kind of people. If I were stronger, I'd return to the compound and take on Josiah myself."

"Well, I'm pretty strong, but even I'm not impervious to bullets, and from what I've heard, Josiah has an arsenal. It's the only reason I'm turning him over to the FBI. If it were up to me, I'd tear him limb from limb with my bare hands." Ryker was white-knuckling the steering wheel. He needed to not think about turning the car around and going after Josiah like he wanted. Not just for Juliette, but for Mac and Elijah as well. "Tell me about your education. I know from Mac and Rhiannon that once you are old enough, you're moved from the classroom to a job. I never asked them, but are you given some type of diploma? Is the school curriculum legitimate?"

"No diploma. As for what we're taught, it was basic math and reading. Most of our studies focused on the Bible. If I need a diploma to get a job, I'm screwed."

"No, you aren't. There are tests you can take to receive what's called a GED. It's as good as if you went through a regular school and received a diploma that way. Depending on some of the courses you weren't taught, you might need to study some subjects, but you, Mac, and Rhiannon can do that together. We have several teachers who work with our family helping people just like you who didn't receive the education you needed. Then you can decide where to go from there. If you want to go to college, you can."

"That would be nice, but I have no money. Hell, I don't have anything. No clothes, nothing. What you see is what I have."

"Don't worry about the money. You mentioned your parents taking you to the compound, but you didn't elaborate on any interaction with them afterwards."

Elijah turned in the seat so he was facing Ryker. "As far as I'm concerned, I have no parents. They turned me over to Gideon and basically forgot about me. I don't even know where they are, not that I care."

"Point taken. You have a new family now. Mac loves you, and we love Mac. That means you're one of us now. I will warn you; our family is large and loud. I have four younger brothers, and they are just as protective of McKenzie as I am. If you treat her with respect, we'll get along fine."

"I will respect her because I love her. She and I have so much in common. It was our love of animals that brought us together. When we worked side-by-side, we would talk about escaping the compound and finding jobs as veterinarians. We knew it was only a dream without having a proper education, but we would talk and make plans for someday."

"Someday is here, Elijah. At least it will be soon. Let's

198

get you back to Mac. She's been putting off moving forward, so I think having you back in her life is going to be good for both of you. Talk to her and see if you're still on the same page with regards to what you want to do with your futures. We'll work with you whenever you're ready."

"Thank you."

They spent the rest of the ride talking about the Lazlos and how they helped others in situations similar to Elijah's. The young man impressed Ryker with the questions he asked and the insight he offered into the inner workings of the cult. Ryker had a good feeling about the kid. Now that Ryker had spent a little time getting to know him, he wasn't hesitant in getting Elijah back with McKenzie. Having Mac on her way to healing would be one less thing to worry about, and Ryker could focus on his own happiness.

The house where Xavier had taken Rhi and Mac wasn't far from Xavier's home. Ryker called when they were about twenty minutes out to make sure it was safe to bring Elijah there. David was still out there, and from what Xavier explained, Rhi's father was not happy. Knowing what the man was capable of, Ryker was more concerned about David than Josiah. David was the one who invested the money for the compound. He had procured the weapons. Kept the compound hidden. David had the capability to manipulate databases. Get people new identities. According to Lucy, he was better with computer manipulation than she was. That was what troubled Ryker the most. How was he going to protect Rhi from her own father?

Rhi was a grown woman in the eyes of the law, so her father couldn't make her go with him unless he kidnapped her. Ryker wouldn't put it past the man. He'd set off the chip in her leg to fill her with poison just so he had access to her in the hospital, only that backfired. Ryker could only imagine how pissed off the human was now that he'd failed. What Ryker couldn't figure out was why he wanted her back so badly. Why turn your daughter over to a cult and ignore her for ten years only to move heaven and earth to get her back?

Those questions would have to wait. Ryker pulled up to the stranger's gate and was met by two males he instinctively knew weren't human. He rolled the window down and introduced himself. The one closest looked off toward the house for a second, then nodded and allowed him to continue toward the house. Xavier was waiting outside for them.

"How's my girl?" Ryker asked as he approached the Gargoyle.

"Which one?" Xavier deadpanned.

The door opened, and a squealing McKenzie burst through and all but tackled Elijah. Ryker smiled at the happy reunion. He was ready for his own reunion.

Chapter Eighteen

Rhiannon

WHEN THE BED shifted, Rhi smiled to herself, thinking it was Ryker who had come to wake her. She opened her eyes to find Mac sitting there, and her smile faded.

"Don't look so happy to see me," Mac joked.

"Sorry."

"No, I get it. You were hoping it was my dad. But good news; he'll be here in about twenty minutes. I thought you might want to freshen up a bit."

"I would, but I don't have my things."

"Manny brought them from Xavier's while you were sleeping. Everything you need is in the bathroom. How are you feeling?"

"Better, at least physically. I can't believe David would poison me."

"Yeah, that's pretty messed up, but if he's in with the cult, it doesn't really surprise me. They'll do anything to keep their compounds a secret."

"I'm sorry for what you went through."

"Yeah, me too. But I'm getting Elijah back, and hopefully we'll be able to have a somewhat normal life together."

"What do you mean?"

"Well…" Mac shifted on the bed. "I think anyone who lives the kind of lives we did inside a cult is going to have

201

issues. None of us come out of there equipped for the real world. We don't have a proper education. We have been brainwashed into believing that way of life is the right way to live. We lived without any type of free will. Now, we all get to make our own decisions. It took me weeks before I felt like I could make a sandwich if I wanted one. I felt guilty for turning on the TV when Dad wasn't home. I would call him for permission to do just about everything. He was patient with me. Still is. But I've been thinking about that, and I believe having me around was getting him ready for you."

"Me? Ryker meeting me was a coincidence. He just happened to be in the right place at the right time."

"Yeah, I don't believe that. He was supposed to have gone out of town the day before, but the woman he was meeting with had to postpone."

"He was meeting another woman?" Rhi sat up against the headboard and rubbed her temple. She was still a little groggy.

"It was a business meeting. But if she hadn't canceled, he never would have found you. If he hadn't rescued me, he wouldn't know what to expect from you. If Kerrigan hadn't been kidnapped, Uncle War wouldn't have been led to the Sanctuary where I was. I think it's all kismet."

"Kismet? What's that?"

"Destiny. Fate. I might not like what I went through to get where I am, but if it meant enduring all the crap so I got to be with my real family and get Elijah back? I'd do it all over again."

"All of it?"

"Yes. What Lewis did to me was horrible, and I probably need therapy to deal with the nightmares, but I would endure it all over again to get to where I am. I just pray Elijah feels the same way."

"If he loves you like you love him, I'm sure he does."

"I hope so. Now, come on. I'm going to wait by the front window. Come find me whenever you're ready."

202

"I will." Rhi crawled out from under the covers and straightened them before heading into the attached bathroom. All her toiletries were waiting on the counter. Was Mac right? Was it kismet that brought her and Ryker together? After taking care of business, she rushed downstairs, wanting to be ready for when Ryker arrived. Joining Mac by the front window, Rhi could feel Mac's excitement. Or maybe it was her own she was feeling.

"I can't believe Eli's on his way here. How do I look?" Mac asked, touching her scar.

"You're beautiful, and Eli's going to think so too."

Rhi wasn't wrong. When Mac ran to meet Elijah, his face lit up like the sun. Rhi held back, watching the two of them together. She wanted nothing but happiness for her new friend.

Ryker

RYKER TURNED TO go find Rhiannon, but she was there, waiting by the door. He studied her, looking for any signs of distress left over from the poison. He must have taken too long to go to her because the smile fell from her face. That wouldn't do. Ryker strode up the stairs with purpose, needing to get to his mate and reassure her nothing had changed. He had to force himself to be gentle. His Gryphon wanted to toss her over their shoulder, take her to the bedroom, and fuck her into the mattress. That wouldn't happen even if they'd been alone. The first time Ryker took Rhi would be gentle and loving.

Ryker cupped Rhi's cheeks and pressed his lips to hers, keeping it chaste considering the audience they had. "How

203

are you feeling?"

"Better now," Rhi whispered, a shy smile spreading across her face.

Ryker took Rhi's hand and pressed it to his chest. "I'm sorry I wasn't here when you were in the hospital."

"I understand. You had business to take care of."

"I did but—" Ryker's phone rang, and he sighed, pressing his forehead to Rhi's. "Sorry." He pulled the phone out and prayed whatever Lucy had to tell him wasn't bad news. "Hey, Luce."

"We have a big problem. Those two men from Haven? They're dead. The feds are looking for you and the other Hounds. What I can gather without getting into trouble myself is David recorded you going into the warehouse. I swear to you, Ryker. I had no idea there were cameras in the area." Lucy choked up, and Ryker's anger at being one step behind David Spencer subsided a fraction. He wasn't mad at his niece. He was pissed that someone like Rhi's father was besting Lucy.

"What about the information you sent to the feds?"

"Honestly? I don't think they received it."

"I need to call Spyder. He stayed behind in New Roseville."

"I've called Julian. He has a new male - Henry - helping out in the lab. Henry is pretty sure he can find David and stop any more interference, but this damage has already been done."

"Can this Henry find David? If he's willing to kill—"

"What? He killed someone?" Rhiannon collapsed to her knees, and Ryker followed her down, wrapping an arm around her.

"Lucy, let me call you back." Ryker disconnected. He held out his phone to Hawk who had been listening in along with the other Hounds, as well as Mac, Elijah, and Xavier. "Call Spyder. Tell him to lay low. John and Paul are dead, and somehow David made it look like we did it. The feds are looking for us." Once Hawk was placing the call, Ryker looked up at Xavier. "I'm sorry we've brought this mess to your Clan. I appreciate all your help, but this is our problem. We'll head back to New Troy."

"Don't be so hasty. You're safer here than you are at home. It's Lucy I'm more concerned about, given her past with the GIA. That and the fact that Tamian is down in New Atlanta with Andrea. The first thing we need to do is get Tamian on his way home. Nobody can protect Lucy better than he can. Until then, she needs to hide. Let Julian and Henry do what they do best." Xavier stepped away and called Tamian, explaining what was going on.

"This is my fault." Rhi's eyes were filling with tears.

"No, Rhi. This is all on your father." Ryker stood, pulling Rhiannon to her feet.

"But he's after me. I won't let anyone else die. I'll go back—"

"No!" Ryker barked out, and Rhi flinched. Softening his voice, he threaded one hand through her hair, cradling her head, while he brushed the tears from her cheek with the other. "You are not going back to him. We'll find a way through this." Ryker was at a loss on how to deal with Rhi's father, but he would not let her feel guilty for David's sins.

A male Ryker had never met was standing just outside the door. He held out his hand to Ryker. "I'm Stefan, and this is my home. Why don't we bring everyone inside? David had drones flying over X's house, and I don't doubt he's already figured out where you are now."

Ryker took the proffered hand and shook. "Ryker Lazlo. Again, I'm sorry for bringing trouble to your family."

The Gargoyle smiled, mischief dancing in his eyes. "Eh. It's been a while since we've had any excitement around here. All I can say is let the human try getting into my home." Ryker prayed it wouldn't come to that, but for the first time in twenty years, true dread filled his gut.

Stefan introduced everyone to his mate, Claudia. She

then welcomed them to their home and told them to make themselves comfortable.

Ryker kept Rhiannon close while he watched Mac and Eli become reacquainted. The love Mac had for Eli was evident in the way she couldn't stop smiling and touching him. Eli was hesitant, but his face was... hopeful. They both looked so young. Too young to have been through so much already, but he vowed to help heal their mental wounds. Theirs as well as Rhi's. He didn't have to be psychic to know she was fretting about David. Learning your father was capable of murder would do a number on anyone, but as someone who had been sheltered for the last ten years of her life, she had to be feeling it deeper. She hadn't been out in the real world where violence and killing wasn't as surprising.

Sitting on the sofa, Rhi sagged against him. He took her hand in his, threading their fingers. "How are you feeling? Really?"

"I'm tired even though I took a long nap."

"Why don't you rest your eyes?" Ryker pulled Rhi closer so she could lay her head on his arm.

"Maybe for a minute." Rhi felt good against him. Ryker was ready for this shitstorm to be over so he could take her home and spend some alone time together. He appreciated Xavier and Stefan opening their homes, but there were too many others around for Ryker's liking. Before Mac came to live with him, Ryker had been a solitary soul. Other than seeing the Hounds at the clubhouse or his family in their homes, he spent most of his time out on his bike, letting the wind hitting his face soothe him. Even when they rode as a group, being on his Harley was a solitary experience.

Xavier stepped into the room with Elizabeth at his side. "Tamian is on his way back. He's threatening to put Lucy on the jet and take her to Italy."

"Does she know that?" Ryker knew his niece was stubborn. She was loyal to her family, and she wouldn't want to leave them while all the shit was going down.

"Yes. Those two are brutally honest with one another. He won't force her to leave, but he'll argue his case."

"It might not be a bad idea. Especially considering her past with the GIA. If David puts the wrong words in the right ears, it might not end well for her."

"That's his argument. Tamian suggested leaving all computer work to Julian and Henry for the time being. Not that David can't manipulate situations to make Lucy look guilty even if she isn't using her computer. According to Tamian, Henry, who is Malakai's nephew from Samoa, is just as good if not better than Julian. The younger male is determined to take down David. Beat him at his own game. Until that happens, we need to make sure Lucy and Rhi are safe. Tamian will take care of Lucy, whether she goes to Italy or not."

"There's something we're not seeing where Rhi's concerned. David ignored her for ten years, so why does he want her back so badly?" Ryker mused aloud.

"It's because of her gift," Eli said.

"How do you know about that?" Ryker asked.

"When you're an outcast, people tend to forget you're around. The barn I was held in wasn't only used as my prison. Josiah used it as a place to talk to David. Getting outsiders to agree to join Haven wasn't about gathering lost souls. It was so they could entice people with certain skillsets or those who had access to money. From what I overheard, they were using Rhi as a healer of sorts. Josiah had James target people who needed medical attention. Those who, say, had cancer or other life-threatening diseases. James promised a 'cure' in return for their money."

Rhi raised her head, but still leaned against Ryker. "I never healed anyone. I wasn't allowed to use my gift because Josiah said it was an abomination."

Elijah's eyebrows dipped low. "What are you talking about? According to Josiah, you used your gift often."

"No, I…" Rhi trailed off, eyes unfocused.

"What is it?" Ryker asked.

"The chip in my leg. What if it isn't just a tracking device?"

"What makes you ask that?"

"What happened yesterday? It wasn't the first time. Whenever I felt the pain in my leg, it would become so unbearable I'd pass out. Then, when I came to, I had lost hours. After coming out of it, I would be dizzy. Disoriented. While I was unconscious, I had dreams. At least I thought they were."

Elizabeth sat down next to Rhi and held her hands. "What were these dreams about?"

Rhi shook her head. "They were never clear, but I had a feeling I had done something I shouldn't have."

Ryker glanced at Xavier. The expression on the Gargoyle's face said he was thinking the same thing Ryker was – the chip in Rhi's leg had been a way to manipulate her.

"Rhi, can you remember anything about the doctor your father took you to before going to Haven? His name? What he looked like?" Xavier asked.

"That was a long time ago. I was a scared teenager. I hated needles, and the ones being used were larger than any I'd ever seen. I passed out. Seems like I do that a lot. Anyway, when I came to, David was arguing with the doctor. He…Wait." Rhi snapped her fingers. "He… he looked like that doctor from the hospital, only younger."

"Dr. Chastain? The Chief of Staff?" Elizabeth clarified.

"Are you sure?" Xavier squatted in front of Rhi. "Think hard. This is important."

"No, I'm not sure they're the same person, but if not, they look similar. I remember the way one of his eyes was green where the other had more brown in it. I tried to focus on his eyes to keep from fainting. It didn't work."

The bad feeling Ryker had earlier got worse. "I need to

call Rev. If this is the same man who was responsible for the implants, I have a feeling he didn't remove the one in her leg. We need to be sure."

"Y-you th-think it's still in m-me?" Rhi was shaking, and her breathing was coming in short pants.

"I'll call Rev," Hawk offered. "You take care of Rhi."

Xavier moved back, giving Rhi some breathing room. "I'm going to call Julian and have him look into Dr. Chastain. We need to know more about him before I barge back in and string him up."

Ryker stood and picked Rhi up, cradling her against his chest. "Is there somewhere I can take her to rest for a bit?"

"I'll show you," Claudia offered and led him to a bedroom on the second floor. "If you need anything, just let us know. Otherwise, we'll give you some alone time."

"Thank you." Ryker placed a quiet Rhi on the bed and removed her boots before taking off his own. He lay down next to her and pulled her against his chest. "Everything is going to be okay. I promise you that."

"I just don't understand why he would fight with my mom about my gift if he was going to turn around and use it."

"I'm not going to pretend to understand how David's mind works, but it's possible he realized he could use your gift for gain. You said your grandmother was against what you and your mom were, so maybe he was playing both sides. Telling his mother one thing while realizing your gift could be used to profit him. Don't worry about it now. Just try to get some rest. Rev will be here soon, and he'll make sure the chip is removed if it hasn't already been."

With Rhi splayed against his side, he cradled her head with one hand while rubbing her arm with the other. Ryker was seething inside. Rhi's gift was special. He had experienced it for himself. When he'd been shot, she had given him her energy. The gift of healing. He just didn't realize it because he was a Gryphon. Ryker knew she took the pain away, but the wound had healed quickly without him shifting. How many others had she shared her ability with? How many times had David or Josiah triggered the chip in her leg to use her while telling her what she was able to do was wrong? Rhi shook beneath his hands. His shirt was becoming damp from her tears. Zeus, he wanted to take her pain from her, but he didn't possess a special gift.

You could kiss her.

She's vulnerable. I won't take advantage of her.

It's not taking advantage. It's making her forget. Taking her mind off her father for a while.

His Gryphon was right, but it would also need to be strong so the kiss didn't lead to more. Ryker gently pushed Rhiannon to her back, rolling with her. He propped on his forearms to keep his weight off her. Ryker didn't ask permission. Instead, he bent his head and pressed their lips together. He tried to keep the kiss innocent, but Rhi had other ideas. She carded her fingers through his hair and tugged. Rhi opened her mouth, silently giving permission. Ryker knew it was a bad idea, but she was his mate. He couldn't deny her this. She was a virgin, but the way she kissed was without hesitation. Like she needed it as much as she needed air. Rhi clung to him tightly as she explored his mouth with her tongue. Ryker had kissed plenty when Juliette was alive. Since then, he kept any physical contact to fucking. To him, kissing was more personal. It had pissed Cassandra off when she tried to latch onto his mouth and he refused. Theirs had been a mutual release. Nothing more. At least that's what it was to him.

But this? This was everything he'd been missing in the last two decades since Juliette was taken from him. Ryker thought he would feel guilty if he ever found someone to share his life with, but he didn't. If Juliette had lived, they would still be together. They would have raised Mac and possibly her siblings. Ryker never would have strayed. He would have loved her until she passed away from old age.

210

But she had been taken from him before they had the opportunity at a long life together. Now, he had a second chance at those things. He wanted that second chance. Ryker wanted love and companionship. Waking up to this amazing woman every morning. Sharing their days together. Making love every night before holding her in his arms while they slept. When he thought of her being a virgin, it no longer felt wrong. He would be her first, and that was a gift.

Rhi was nothing like his Juliette, but she didn't need to be. She was her own person with her own special qualities. Her inner light was just as bright as her outer appearance. Yes, she was young, but that just gave him more time with her.

Rhi wrapped one leg around his hip. Her whimpers started out soft, but the longer they kissed, the louder she became until Ryker realized she was in distress. He jerked back. "I'm sorry. I got carried a—"

"My leg. It's my leg." Rhi hadn't been trying to pull him closer; she'd been trying to rub away the pain.

Ryker rolled off to the side and sat up. "What can I do?"

"Get it out of me, please," she begged. His talons were itching to burst through his skin and do as she asked, but that would cause more harm than good.

"I'm going to call Rev and see where he is. Hang on, Angel." Ryker prayed to Zeus to help Rhi because he was helpless otherwise.

CHAPTER NINETEEN

Rhiannon

RHIANNON WAS READY to cut her leg open. The pain from a knife couldn't be any worse than the burning. How could she have forgotten what it was like every time this happened before? Granted, it had been months since it happened while she was still at Haven. Knowing what it meant, that her father had used her gift without her knowing, was almost worse than the pain. Not that Rhi regretted helping someone, if that's what happened when she blacked out. If her gift helped even one person, she was happy for it, but she would have preferred to be aware of what she was doing. She would have freely helped another. It was how she had been told her gift was wrong, then used anyway. Had it been so Josiah could claim it was somehow divine intervention? Had he taken credit for it when Rhi was able to take away someone's disease? Her grandmother always said Rhi had the devil in her. Rhi didn't believe in the devil. She didn't believe she was going to burn in a fiery pit at the end of her life for having something good inside her.

And why now? Why, when she was under Ryker's body with his mouth on hers, did the pain have to kick in at that moment? Speaking of fires. Ryker lit one deep inside Rhi with nothing more than sensual kisses. Her body was burning up in more ways than one. Her mother always told her Rhi would know who Rhi should give her body to. Now she understood. Ryker was that man. She didn't care that he wasn't fully human. It didn't matter that he was older. She wasn't worried about him having been married before. Knowing he had been married meant he was capable of loving someone enough to make a vow to them. If Juliette had lived, Ryker would still be with her. Rhi knew in her heart he was honorable. If Juliette were still alive, Rhi wouldn't be here with Ryker. Their paths would never have crossed, but to her, that meant someone else would have rescued her. All she knew was things happened for a reason. At least that's what her mother had believed.

The pain she was having to endure was worth it if it was what brought Ryker to her. She gritted her teeth to keep from passing out. Sweat beaded on her forehead, and her breaths were coming quicker. Why was her father or Josiah or whoever controlled the chip hitting the switch? Was it to cause her pain? Were they punishing her for running away? If so, it was working. If she passed out, she couldn't feel. Instead of fighting it, she let the torment wash over her, and Rhi succumbed to the darkness.

"Anna, the woman in the next room has a tumor on her brain. You will go into the room, lay your hands on her head, and you will use your power to heal her. You will not speak. You will do God's will and use the gift He has given you to help this woman."

Rhi padded into the dark room. A candle sitting on a small table was the only light offered. The woman was blindfolded, her body covered with a quilt. Rhi had never healed a tumor before. She didn't know if she could, but she had to try, or she'd be sent to the dark room without food. Doing as Brother Josiah instructed, Rhi placed her small hands on the sides of the woman's head. She closed her eyes, because that's what Momma had taught her to do when she was helping the dying plants. Taught Rhi to close her eyes, ask the goddess for strength and guidance, and push her warmth into whatever it was she was trying to help. In this case, a sick woman. Rhiannon pushed. She imagined her warmth was like

213

the candle. A flame she needed to get inside the woman's head. Rhi collected all the light until it was gathered in her hands and pushed it out. The woman beneath her gasped, and that was when Rhi knew she felt the warmth. Felt Rhi's gift. When Rhi couldn't push any more, she slumped to the ground. Tired. She was so tired. So cold.

"Does she have a fever? Her skin is like ice, and she won't stop shaking." Rhi knew that sweet voice, the one that reminded her of her mother, but she couldn't make her eyes open. A hand to her forehead burned her skin, but she didn't have the energy to say so.

"No. There's no fever. I think she's in shock. Ryot, hold her leg in case she wakes up. I don't want to cut her any more than I need to." That deep voice was familiar as well.

Strong hands held her down, while soft ones touched her face, brushing her hair methodically. The movement was soothing. There was a tug on her leg just above her ankle. It didn't hurt. Nothing hurt at the moment. She was too cold, too numb, to feel any pain.

"I don't understand how we missed this," Rev said.

"We weren't looking for it. Rhi was young when David had the chips implanted, plus she said she had passed out. Rev, I want you to scan her from head to toe. If there were three chips, there could be more. Never again will she be manipulated."

"You got it, Ryot."

"Hang on, Rhi. Just a little longer," Ryker said gently next to Rhi's ear. She wanted to bury herself in his warmth. Her teeth weren't chattering, but she was still cold.

"C-c-cold," Rhi managed to stutter.

"I know you are, but Rev needs to search your body. Hang in there. You're doing so good. I promise I'll get you warmed up when he's done." Ryker kissed her forehead. She would rather he kiss her lips. Her thoughts went back to the way his large body covered hers as they made out earlier. The way her body flamed from the inside out was enough to give her the strength she needed to endure however long it took for Rev to finish searching. Refusing to think about her father, she focused on Ryker's scent. It was a little sweaty, a little leather, and a whole lotta man. She was a twenty-three-year-old virgin, and if she got her way, that title would change before her birthday in a few weeks.

"The good news is Dr. Chastain removed the tracker like he said. The other good news is there was only one more chip imbedded in Rhi's skin. This one didn't leak any type of substance into her bloodstream. I'm thinking the other wasn't supposed to either, since this one caused the same type of reaction with the debilitating pain and subsequent passing out. This is some next level technology."

"Well, he does work for the GIA. There's no telling what type of technology he has available to him."

"Bethany will get her stitched up and then I'll give her something for the pain."

"N-no. D-don't want to b-be groggy." Rhi knew she needed to rest, but she was counting on Ryker taking the pain away with his kisses. Or more.

"Okay, no shot. But I will write a prescription in case you change your mind."

"Th-thank you." Rhi closed her eyes while Bethany once again sutured her. Rhi felt herself being shuffled around on the bed, but she was too drained to figure out why. Warmth surrounded her back, and a strong arm came over her body, the hand threading through her fingers and settling against her chest. She felt safe. She *was* safe.

When Rhi woke, she was alone. She knew Ryker couldn't spend every waking second with her, but she missed his heat. Mentally taking stock, she found she was no longer freezing. What she was, though, was gross. Rhi wanted a shower, so she climbed out of bed and closed herself in the bathroom. The bandages over her stitches were waterproof, so she didn't have to worry about getting them wet. While the water heated, she brushed her teeth.

215

She then stripped out of her clothes and underwear and wrapped the non-bloody pad in toilet paper before disposing of it in the wastebasket. The only good thing about her period was it never lasted long.

The hot water felt like heaven against her aching muscles. Rhi was always sore after one of her episodes. Now that she knew the cause of her blackouts had been removed, she looked forward to not having to endure them anymore. While she washed her hair, Rhi took a moment to think about her father and what she knew about him, which wasn't much. He allowed Josiah to use Rhi's gift to bring people into Haven. She had no idea if her gift had worked the numerous times she had used it without her knowledge or consent. If given the choice, she would never had said no to try and help another human. It pissed her off the preacher railed against her gift, then used it in private. Up until she poured her energy into Ryker after he was shot, Rhi had never knowingly used her gift on a person. After the rabbit incident when she was younger, she had only used her energy to help plants.

David had known about the rabbit. He had exploited her without her knowledge or consent. He had chips inserted to manipulate her into doing his and Josiah's bidding. She hated him. Hated both David and Josiah. *Goddess, forgive me. Please help me find a way to get past my hatred.* Rhi allowed herself a few minutes to find the peace talking with her goddess usually gave her. What she needed was to be outside. That's where her true peace came from. And from Ryker. He was able to calm her with just a touch. Thinking of him putting his hands on her, she took extra care with shaving her legs. Women weren't allowed to shave at Haven unless they were married. It had taken some getting used to, but Rory had brought her a razor to the hotel, and she relished the silkiness of her skin without the hair. She trimmed the pubic hair at the juncture of her inner thighs so it wouldn't escape the sides of her panties, but she left the rest of it natural.

Rhi turned the water off and stepped out onto the plush rug. She enveloped her long hair in a fluffy towel, then used another to dry her body. She watched her movements in the mirror. What would Ryker think of how she looked naked? Would he find her desirable merely for the fact that she was a woman as Josiah had talked about? Or would he find her lacking because she was on the skinny side? Her breasts were pert if smallish. She didn't have curves like other women. If she thought about it, she was built like a boy. There was nothing she could do about it other than eat a lot and put on some weight. Thinking of eating had her stomach rumbling.

Having forgotten to grab clothes, Rhi wrapped the towel around her body and opened the door to the bedroom. Ryker was there, sitting on the side of the bed. His dark hair was damp, indicating he'd taken his own shower. His eyes traveled from the towel on her head to her bare feet, then back up to her face. He wore an expression she couldn't read, but she didn't have a lot of experience when it came to men. *Ha, you have no experience other than going to town with James.*

"I brought you some food," Ryker said, motioning to a tray on the dresser.

"Thank you. I'm starving." Rhi didn't move from the bathroom doorway. She wasn't sure what to do. She wanted to touch him and have him touch her, but she also didn't want to look like an idiot.

Ryker stood and closed the distance between them. He ran a finger along the edge of the towel at her chest. Goosebumps prickled her skin, and heat flooded her stomach, dipping lower. What would he do if she dropped the towel? Would he take her to bed and have his way with her for the first time? Or would he be appalled at her forwardness?

"It's probably a good thing we aren't alone." Ryker

217

loosened the towel around her head, dropping it to the floor. Running his fingers through her hair, he tugged on a strand, lifting it to his nose. "If we were at home, I'd be unable to resist taking you to bed and showing you how desirable I find you. I'm not going to lie, Rhi. I'm a man with certain proclivities when it comes to sex, but for you, I promise to be gentle. I'm going to please you, and I'm going to teach you how to please me. *If* that's something you want. If not, I need to know now before I get in any deeper."

"I want you." Rhi had no idea what possessed her to do it, but she unhooked the end of the towel and dropped it to the floor. Ryker hissed and took a step back. At first, she thought he was appalled at what he saw, but then his eyes turned darker than their normal brown, and he took two steps forward, dragging her body against his. The rasp of his clothes against her bare skin sent delicious waves of heat throughout her body, and the space between her legs ached with want. Rhi had touched herself a few times when alone in the shower. Living in a cabin with two or three other women didn't leave room for privacy. She knew what it felt like to orgasm, but she'd always felt unfulfilled after she came. Ryker's hard bulge pressed against her mound, and she knew that was what had been missing. She wanted his hardness inside her, filling her up.

Ryker's large hands skimmed her back, caressing the top of her butt. His lips were leaving a trail of kisses along her neck, sending more zings to her core and her nipples. Rhi pressed her breasts to his chest, searching for relief to the ache. "Please," she begged against his ear as she clutched his T-shirt.

"Rhi, we can't. As much as I want you, we need to wait until we get home. I don't want our first time to be rushed. I want to make love to you all night."

Rhi was past the point of caring where they were. All she knew was she needed release. "Fine. I'll take care of myself." She let go of his shirt and turned toward the bathroom, but a strong arm banded around her stomach, his large hand splayed across her chest. Ryker cupped one of her breasts and rolled her nipple.

"You've touched yourself before? Made yourself come?"

"Yes," she admitted.

The hand on her stomach slid lower until a calloused finger touched her bud. Ryker rubbed it, and if he hadn't been holding her up, her knees would have given out. Ryker dipped two fingers between her legs, sliding easily through the slickness. "I want you more than I want to breathe, Rhiannon."

"Then have me. I don't need lovemaking. I just need you to fill me up."

"If I take you now, I'm going to hurt you, and I never want to hurt you. What I will do is get you off." Ryker pushed her until she was lying on the mattress. He lifted her legs and said, "Put your feet on the bed." Rhi did, and Ryker spread her knees apart, staring at her vagina. No, her pussy. Ryker was a biker. A virile male who could have any woman he wanted. No way would he call it anything other than pussy. She had heard the men at Haven speak about women and what they wanted to do to them. Just because Haven was supposed to be all about God did mean that it was.

Ryker dropped to his knees, and before she knew what he planned, he buried his face between her thighs. His tongue tortured her nub before dipping inside, lapping at her opening. Within seconds, he had her writhing against the bedding, pushing against his mouth. He licked and bit at her clit while two large fingers explored her passage. He twisted and pumped, never delving far enough to break the barrier. Goddess, she wanted him to break it, but not with his fingers. Rhi's stomach tightened, the sensation of her impending release traveling to all her nerve endings.

"Ryker," she husked. "Ryker, I… oh… I'm…" Her

219

orgasm hit hard as he tormented her clit. Her body quivered and her insides pulsed around his fingers. Rhi leaned up onto her elbows, catching her breath. Ryker licked her release from his fingers before standing. "That was... Yeah. So good." *So good?* "It was amazing." He stared at her a few seconds. The bulge in his pants was still there, but she had no idea what to do about it.

"I'm going to take a leak and wash my hands. Why don't you get dressed and eat a bite?" Ryker disappeared into the bathroom, shutting the door. Rhi blew out a breath. She knew she'd screwed up when she didn't reciprocate, but he really hadn't given her a chance. Wanting to make things right, she pressed her ear to the door. When she didn't hear him peeing, she gently turned the knob and inched the door open. Ryker had his back to her, and his hand... *Oh.*

Ryker

RYKER CLOSED HIMSELF in the bathroom and jerked his hard dick. It only took a few strokes until he was shooting into the toilet. He pressed the hand not holding his cock against the wall and hung his head. Fuck. Rhi was too enticing. Now that he'd had a taste, it was going to take every bit of his willpower not to fuck her. Yes, he promised to make love to her, but she called to his primal instincts, and he would fuck her. One day. Soon. The way she responded to his tongue and fingers, he knew Rhi would be a tiger in bed. Ryker flushed the toilet, then tucked himself back in his jeans before washing his hands and splashing cold water on his face. When he returned to the bedroom, he was pleased to see Rhi was dressed and eating her sandwich.

She wouldn't look at him, and that wasn't good. Fuck,

he'd screwed up going down on her, but she'd enjoyed it. "Rhi—"

"What's the plan?" she asked, cutting him off without looking at him. Her face was flushed. He wanted to know what she was thinking. Was she embarrassed, or did she regret what they'd done?

"Honestly, we don't have one. We're waiting to hear back from Lucy. She's working with Henry Palamo, the Gargoyle in New Atlanta. Henry's sure he can figure out a way to get your father off our trail. Until then, we're just waiting."

"Why not just expose them all?"

"What do you mean?"

"Well, you said you can't go up against Haven because of the guns, so why not tell the cops what they're doing out there? I'll tell them they were holding me against my will. You have the chips my father had implanted. I'll tell the police he had those put in me when I was younger, and Rev can explain what they are and what they did to me. Surely that's considered child abuse. Right?"

"You'd be willing to accuse David?"

"You bet your ass I would. Now that I know what was happening to me when I passed out? It pisses me off. They were using me, Ryker. Using me without my consent. What if that's not all they did to me while I was passed out? I mean, I remember vaguely being sent into dark rooms where I laid my hands on people, but I don't remember anything that happened after. I have no idea how I got back to my cabin or how long I was out of it."

Ryker refused to think of Josiah or one of his men taking advantage of Rhi. He knew she was still a virgin because he'd felt her barrier still intact, but that didn't mean they couldn't have touched her in other ways. If he allowed himself to think about anyone doing something to her in a sexual way, he would tear them apart, guns or not.

"Finish eating, and we'll take this discussion

downstairs."

"I'm full. My stomach is still a little queasy."

Ryker lifted the tray from her lap, and Rhi climbed off the bed. She opened the door for him, and they made their way downstairs. Xavier arched an eyebrow, and Stefan and Claudia were grinning. Fucking shifter hearing. He smirked back at them all, refusing to feel bad about what happened upstairs. Gryphons weren't the only ones who were insatiable around their mates, so they had no room to give him shit. Instead of going into the living room with Ryker, Rhi turned toward the dining room. Shit, he needed to clear the air between them, but now wasn't the right time.

"I'll take that," Claudia said, reaching for the tray.

"Thank you. Has anyone heard from Lucy?"

"No, and she's not answering her phone," Xavier said.

Ryker looked around for Elijah. Not seeing him, he asked, "What about Tamian? Can he reach her mentally?"

Xavier sighed and shook his head. "I haven't been able to reach him either. He should be landing soon, though."

Fuck! Ryker pulled out his phone and called Maveryck. "Mayhem, are Shadow and Ace still sitting on Lucy's house?"

"As far as I know. Why?"

"She's not answering, and Tamian hasn't landed yet. Get on the phone and find out where she is. Call me back."

"Will do."

Ryker paced in front of the fireplace, his mind torn between going to Rhi and waiting to hear back from his brother. When his phone pinged, he expected it to be Maveryck. It wasn't. Instead, it was a text message from an unknown number.

You'll want to see this.

Ryker assumed the message was from David Spencer, and he knew better than to open the attachment, but his curiosity got the better of him. When he saw what it was, his heart stopped.

"Stefan, do you have a printer?"

"Sure, come with me. Is everything okay?"

"No. No it's not." Ryker sent the text to Stefan who in turn printed the document for him. Without looking, the Gargoyle handed it over. Ryker muttered a thanks, then stormed through the house out the back door.

CHAPTER TWENTY

Rhiannon

RHI COULDN'T HELP but notice the tension between Mac and Elijah. Mac had been thrilled to get her boyfriend back, but it was obvious the guy wasn't as happy. Elijah looked like he was ready to run. He had been taken from one compound to another where he didn't know anyone. He had been kept in a cell, and Rhi was well aware of how that solitary existence messed with your mind. It gave you nothing but time to come up with so many different what-if scenarios you didn't know which way was up. Being locked in a room with no windows and only a cot to sleep on and a bucket to pee in had been bad enough.

Rhi hadn't told Ryker about that. She hadn't told him a lot of things, because she didn't want him to think she was crazy. Maybe she was. Maybe the dreams weren't her mind reminding her of her past. Maybe they were her mind trying to confuse her from what she knew with what she wanted to be the truth. And what was that? Rhi wanted to be a normal girl without a special gift her father was willing to exploit. There was nothing normal about her.

When Mac touched Elijah's arm, he jumped up and headed toward the back door. Mac's face fell, and Rhi was torn between comforting her new friend and going after Eli. The call to be outside with nature won out, and she followed after Eli. Rhi found him pacing the edge of the woods. When Rhi was close enough for him to realize he wasn't alone, Eli turned, his face a mask of confusion.

"What do you want?"

Rhi tamped down the urge to run. She knew better than most how men got when they were upset. "Nothing. I just needed some fresh air. To be outside. I know what it's like being held in solitary."

"Bullshit. You and your 'gift' were your golden ticket."

"I don't know what that means."

"Willy Wonka? The golden ticket Charlie won to go see the candy factory?"

"Sorry. Is that a movie?"

"Yeah. It was my favorite as a kid."

"I didn't watch much TV before I was taken to Haven. I spent most of my time outside with my mom. If I was playing with other kids, we were either riding bikes or playing video games."

"I've listened to them" — Elijah motioned toward the house — "complaining about your dad for the last few hours, but they haven't mentioned your mother." Eli crossed his arms over his chest and leaned against a tree. Rhi closed her eyes and asked the tree to offer Eli some comfort. She had never tried that before. Then she focused her own energy on him.

"My mom died right before I turned thirteen. Right before my father moved us to Haven." Rhi didn't know if he wanted to hear about her past, but she offered it up anyway, hoping he would see all her time at Haven hadn't been golden, as he put it.

"All my friends in my neighborhood were boys. We did everything together, so when I got to the compound, I didn't know the rules. I couldn't understand why I wasn't supposed to talk to boys. I argued with Josiah. A lot. I got in trouble for talking. For not believing in God. For talking to plants. I was always in trouble for one thing or another, and my father wasn't around to stick up for me. I was put in a small room with no windows when I wouldn't recite the Bible verses I was supposed to learn.

"As part of my punishment, I was told to read from the Old Testament, but of course I didn't. I read the New Testament, and when Josiah would come to let me out, I'd argue with him about Jesus. That got me more time in isolation. Finally, I stopped arguing and complaining. I stopped talking altogether. That got me even more time in isolation. Then the blackouts started. I was sure I was going crazy from being locked up without ever seeing anyone except the guard who brought my oatmeal."

Eli looked like Rhi had struck him. "You only got oatmeal too?"

"Yep. One bowl a day with a piece of stale bread. Warm water to drink. They let me out after a while. I think it was because I stank so bad. After that, I did what was expected of me because being in a cabin with girls who hated me was better than being alone. That is until James happened. I still don't know why he wanted the pagan girl who wouldn't talk, but for some reason, he wanted me for his wife. It didn't matter that I had no interest in him. I had no interest in any of the men there. My momma said I'd know when I found the man for me because it would hit me in the chest, warming my skin the same way the sun did in the morning. There was no sunshine at Haven." Eli frowned, and she could feel the sadness from several feet away. "There was no sunshine for Mac either. Not after they separated the two of you."

Eli stared off into the distance, his shoulders hunched. "Elijah, Mac didn't want Lewis. You have to know that deep down. She loves you. You are all she talked about. Well, you and her uncle Maveryck's twins. I haven't met them yet, but from what she says, her little cousins are funny. But talking about them also makes her sad. I think they remind her of her baby."

Elijah stepped away, but Rhi didn't miss the tears.

226

"How can she still love me? I'm the reason for her scar."

"No. Gideon is the reason for her scar. It's a crime to hold someone against their will. When Mac ran, it was Gideon who sent the dog after her. With you gone, there was no sunshine for her."

"I don't know how to do this. At The Sanctuary, I knew my place. I had a job. A purpose. Now? I have nothing. No formal education. No skills. No money. Nothing. I have nothing to offer Mac other than a painful reminder of what happened and why. At least there I knew what to expect. Out here?" Elijah shook his head. "Out here, I'm nobody."

"Am I nobody?"

"What? No. Of course not."

"And why's that? I'm in the same boat you are. I had the same education. I have no money or skills either. But the difference between you and me? I'm a freak whose father is killing people. He's killing people because of me. All the people in that house? Their lives have been disrupted because I ran. They're in danger because I didn't want to marry James. I don't have anything to offer anyone either. But Ryker found me and introduced me to his family. They made me feel something I haven't felt since my mom died, and that's hope. But is hope a good enough reason for me to risk their lives? My selfishness has already killed two men. How many more have to die because I want a different life?"

Rhi took a couple steps toward him and placed a hand on his cheek. She pushed her energy into his skin while she talked. "You have a chance at something good with Mac. Her family will help you. They'll see to it you find the path that's right for you. I know they will because Mac loves you and her family loves Mac. Please, give it a chance. Be her sunshine."

Elijah shuddered. Rhi released his cheek and stepped back. She knelt to rub her hands over the grass, drawing power from the ground to replenish that which she'd shared

227

with Eli. The back door opened, drawing Rhi's eyes toward the house. McKenzie stood on the patio with her arms crossed over her chest.

"Be her sunshine," Rhi urged, and Elijah took off jogging toward Mac. She smiled as Elijah took McKenzie in his arms, but it was short lived. Whatever Mac said had Eli frowning and them both looking Rhi's way. The back door opened again behind them, and Ryker strode out. His stormy gaze landed on her, and she braced for whatever bad news he was bringing. Rhi shivered. Not from being cold, but because the Ryker walking toward her was the same one she first encountered. The cold, closed-off one.

When he reached her, Rhi took a step back. Not because she was scared, but she didn't want to be tempted to use her gift to alter his mood. If she stood a chance at having Ryker in her life, she had to accept the male he was, as he was. Whether he was being broody or sexy or attentive or pissed off, she would have to learn to love all versions of the biker.

Ryker

When Rhi stepped back, Ryker did his best to tamp down his anger. He never wanted her to be afraid of him, but this shit was out of hand. "You lied to me."

"What?"

"You. Lied. To. Me. You told me James wasn't your husband."

"He's not. I think I would know if I got married, Ryker."

"Then how do you explain this?" Ryker shoved the paper he'd printed off at her. He watched her face as she looked at the marriage certificate. One dated just a week prior.

"I've never seen this before." Rhi looked up, tears in her eyes. "I swear to you, I am not married."

"That's not your signature?"

"No... I..." Rhi frowned. "I didn't sign this. You have to believe me."

Ryker did believe her. At least he wanted to, but he'd been fooled by the last woman he let himself get close to, and that had been when his heart wasn't on the line. Someone he wasn't thinking about spending the rest of his life with. If he found out Rhi was lying, he didn't think he'd recover.

"It's been five years since I picked up a pencil or pen. Besides, this" — she waved the paper in Ryker's face — "is written in cursive. I never learned cursive. I always wanted to because my mom had the prettiest handwriting. In school, we were only taught to print, so someone else, probably someone older, had to have signed this. That or David used a program on his computer to do it."

"How do you know this came from your father?"

Rhi took a deep breath. "Because James isn't smart enough. At least I don't think he is. I don't know that much about him."

Ryker stared at the crumpled paper in her fist. He wanted to believe she was telling the truth. He wanted to pull her into his arms and apologize, but he couldn't make his feet move. What if he was wrong?

What if you're not? Do you want to lose her? Look deep. She's not a liar or manipulator.

"If David can create a fake marriage certificate, maybe we can create one of our own. Or maybe not a marriage certificate, but something like it. Lucy can do that, can't she? And I'll sign it for real. That way there will be proof that I didn't sign the fake one my father sent you."

Ryker slid his fingers through his hair. "I'm sure she

229

could if we could find her. Lucy's not answering, and the Hounds who were watching her are both in the hospital. They were shot."

Rhi gasped. "This has to stop! Too many people have been hurt because of me. Do you have a way to contact him?"

Ryker did, but he didn't want her to know that. Not until he knew what she was thinking. "Why?"

"I think I should call him. Agree to go with him."

"No. Rhi, that's not—"

Rhi placed her fingers against his lips. "Let me finish. I will agree to go with him and then you can swoop in and take care of him. How many more humans and Gryphons have to get caught in the crossfire? All because of me? I'm tired. Tired of running. Tired of worrying about you, your family, and your friends. Tired of having all my choices taken away from me. I want my life back, and I don't mean the one at Haven. I mean the one I had before it was stolen from me by my father."

"I won't risk putting you in danger."

"But you'll risk everyone else? That's not right. My life isn't more important than anyone else's. It's probably less important than most."

Ryker bristled. "I don't ever want to hear you say that again. You're important to me." Ryker gave in and cupped Rhi's neck, pressing his forehead to hers. "You have given me my life back. Given me purpose beyond the club and my family."

"Then let me do this. Unless you have a better plan to bring him out of hiding, you know it's the right thing to do."

Ryker did know, but that didn't mean he agreed with it. It was his duty to protect Rhi. Even if it was a charade to bring David out of hiding, there was always the chance something would go wrong. David Spencer was a man with means. A man not afraid to kill to get what he wanted.

"Let's go inside. I want to talk with Xavier before we make the call."

"Thank you."

"Don't thank me yet." Instead of taking her hand, Ryker gestured for Rhi to walk ahead of him. "I won't agree to a meeting without a solid plan in place."

Ryker could feel Rhi's trepidation. How could he not? Her father was killing people and she felt it was her fault. How did he convince her it wasn't? Was it the gods' fault humans waged wars in their names? Innocent people often were caught in the crossfire, but in this case, he wasn't convinced John and Paul were innocent. He still hadn't heard back from Spyder, but hopefully that was a good thing. He'd told the Hound to lay low. With David having access to their phones, it wasn't safe to be calling or texting.

It was quiet when they returned inside. The mood was somber. Rhi bypassed the living room, and Ryker followed her until she closed herself in the bathroom. Wanting to give her a few minutes to herself, he retreated to where the others were waiting.

Xavier was on the phone, his face a mask of anger. Elizabeth was rubbing her mate's arm, but it was clear she was just as upset. Most of the others were standing around the room, silently waiting. Ryker's phone vibrated with an incoming call. He stepped out of the room to answer his father.

"Pop? Tell me you have good news."

"It's not as bad as it could have been. They were shot with tranquilizers, but it metabolized fairly quickly. If this shit keeps up, I'm going to invest in guns for all of us. We can't fight this level of enemy with our… bare hands. I have contacted a mutual friend to help. I'm not going to say anymore since I doubt this line is secure." Ryker understood who Sutton was referring to, and taking out a contract of their own wasn't a bad idea. "Let me know if you hear from Lucy, and I'll do the same. Stay safe, Son."

"You too, Pop." Ryker disconnected and rubbed the back of his neck. It had been a long time since tension gripped his body as tightly as it was then. They were Gryphons. Stronger than humans. But they weren't stronger than bullets. When he walked into the living room, he searched for Rhi. She hadn't returned, but before he could go check on her, Xavier growled low in his chest, causing the hair on Ryker's arms to stand up.

"That was Julian. Henry hacked into Lucy's cameras. Four armed men came onto the property, shot your males, and then took Lucy at gunpoint."

"Was it the same men as before?"

"One of them was."

"That doesn't make sense. My males told them Rhi wasn't there."

"Explain to me how your Gryphon voice works." Xavier wasn't judging. At least Ryker didn't think he was.

"Usually, we only use our voice to keep our Gryphon side from being exposed to humans. Sometimes, in cases like this, we manipulate a mind into forgetting what someone has seen. Since I wasn't there when the humans came into Lucy's house looking for Rhi, I don't know what she told them. But with David having access to Lucy's cameras, I don't think it matters. He would have seen Rhiannon in the house and told Josiah she had been there even though his men hadn't located her the first time they looked."

"Tamian is going to rip them to shreds, and I'm going to help. I know you can't go up against guns, but we can. Give me the location of the compound. I'll take some of my males, meet Tamian at the airport, and we'll go get Lucy back."

"This isn't your fight."

Xavier's anger filled the room, making it hard to breathe. Ryker hadn't experienced a pissed-off Gargoyle, and he never wanted to again. Xavier's fangs were digging into his bottom lip. Ryker's Gryphon was trying to break through, but he knew better than to let it out.

"It is now. Lucy is ours just as much as she's yours if not more since she is Tamian's mate and the future queen."

"You're right. I didn't mean to insinuate Lucy isn't important to you, but we brought this to your family. We've never been in a position where we couldn't fight our own battles."

"Asking for help isn't a weakness, Ryker. Especially where family is concerned. Our two Clans are connected through her, so think of us as an extension. Lucy would be the first one to tell you we're one big family now."

Ryker knew Xavier was right, so he gave him the location of the compound. It didn't sit well with him that someone else was going to take down Josiah, but in the end, having it finished was more important than who was doing it.

"Let's find Stefan. I want you to explain to us how your family normally goes about taking care of a compound as a whole."

Ryker needed his father for that conversation. Sutton was the diplomat where Ryker was more of the muscle. When he remembered his dad had called in reinforcements of his own, he knew he needed to call Sutton and have him on speaker so he was aware of what the plan was. Ryker wanted to check on Rhi, but she was somewhere in the house, safe for the moment. Right then, his priority was Lucy. Ryker, Xavier, and Stefan closed themselves in Stefan's office for privacy. Elijah wasn't aware of shifters, and they didn't need him to overhear anything they would have to wipe from his mind.

"I'm going to call my dad. Since David might be able to listen in, I'm going to be vague about everything, but he'll know what we're talking about.

"Did you find Lucy?" Sutton asked when he answered the phone.

"Pop, you're on speaker. I have Xavier and Stefan in the room. No, we didn't find her, but Xavier and some of his males are willing to step in."

"That's... I need to make a call."

Ryker took a chance on telling Stefan the truth. With Lucy being Xavier's daughter-in-law, chances were good he already knew of the Hounds mercenary business. "Pop, I think this is our best bet in getting Lucy back and taking care of the other problem at the same time. The phone call you made earlier would be one against many."

"You're right. I was thinking with my heart and not my head."

Xavier propped against the side of the desk and crossed his arms over his chest. "Sutton, I need to know how you handle those in the compound who are innocent."

"We've never gone up against a group this armed. Normally, we go in, take down the head of the snake, and have a talk with the members. Those who wish to leave, we take them to a secure location. We don't force anyone to leave against their will. If a crime has been committed, we call the police to come in once we have the target secure. In this case, we would have to tell them about the men coming after Rhiannon and Lucy being taken. What I don't understand is why she went with them. Why didn't she use her voice on them?"

"Do you think she went willingly to get inside?" Stefan asked.

"Anything's possible, but I doubt it. Not with Tamian out of town," Xavier replied. "They're a team."

"Unless whoever broke in had something that guaranteed she complied," Ryker added. "Pop, is everyone in the family accounted for?"

"As far as I know. Nobody's called with an alert."

"Fuck. This doesn't make sense." Ryker blew out a breath.

234

Xavier pushed away from the desk and clapped Ryker on the shoulder. "Lucy's smart. I have no doubt she has a plan. We will find her. The first place we're going to look is at the compound."

"I'll head that direction. Ryker, give Xavier my phone number. Xavier, you call me as soon as you have Josiah in custody and the compound locked down."

Ryker's phone beeped, indicating an incoming call. "Pop, that's Lucy. I'll call you back." Ryker immediately switched over. "Lucy?"

"Lucy can't come to the phone right now, but if you want to see her again, you'll bring Anna to us," a male voice responded.

"Don't do it!" Lucy shouted from the background, then and "Oomph" sounded.

"I swear to —"

"No need for threats. I'll text you the address. And if you don't come alone with only Anna, Lucy here dies." The phone disconnected.

"So much for no threats," Stefan said. "Now what?"

Xavier flashed his fangs. "Now, we go get my daughter-in-law."

"Are you really going to hand Rhiannon over to them?" Stefan asked.

"Yes, he is," Rhi said from the doorway.

Ryker turned, surprised. He had been so focused on the phone call he hadn't heard Rhi sneaking up behind him.

"Eavesdropping is rude, Angel."

"So is making decisions for me." Rhi stepped farther in the room and sat down in one of the armchairs. Turning to Xavier, she said, "Tell me your plan."

235

Chapter Twenty-One

Rhiannon

RHI KNEW SHE shouldn't eavesdrop, but the conversation was about her in a roundabout way. Her father or Josiah had taken Lucy to get Rhi, and that wouldn't do. Lucy was much more important than Rhi.

"There is no plan. We are not trading you," Ryker said.

"Yes, you are. This is my decision. Everything that's going on is because I ran away from Haven. Lucy is too important for you not to make the trade."

"You're important too. We'll figure something else out," Ryker argued.

"There's no need. If you do what they ask, you get Lucy back."

"But I lose you in the process." Ryker's dark eyes burned with something Rhi didn't recognize. Wait, he would lose her? Did he want to keep her?

"Ryker's right. We'll figure something else out," Xavier added.

Rhi felt like she was back at Haven where her opinion didn't matter. She had thought things would be different with Ryker. When he kissed her and especially when he gave her an orgasm, she'd thought he saw something in her worth keeping. *But I lose you in the process.* Obviously, him wanting to keep her came with rules. Ones she didn't want to abide. She escaped Haven to get away from controlling men. With a nod at Xavier, Rhi left the office, ignoring the biker she thought she had a future with.

"Rhi, wait," Ryker called after her, but she kept going until she was back outside with the trees. She stopped at the one where she and Elijah had talked. Pressing her hands to the rough bark, she closed her eyes and inhaled, centering herself. She wanted this – the future Rory talked about where Rhi got a job with a florist or working in a garden somewhere. If she traded herself for Lucy, she wouldn't get that opportunity, but it was the right thing to do.

Lucy was important to her family. Both sides. She was going to be a queen for goodness' sake. Rhi was a nobody with a gift she no longer wanted. It did nothing but cause heartache. Elijah said Josiah used Rhi to heal people, but she didn't even know if that was true or not. She couldn't remember more than the snippets she saw in her dreams. If what Elijah said was true, she knew they were memories instead. Josiah wanted her back so he could continue using her to bring new people into Haven. She was his golden ticket, as Elijah called it.

Buzzing came from overhead, and Rhi opened her eyes to look for the source of the noise. A small white box was floating in the air a few feet above her head.

"Rhiannon, you aren't safe. I need you to listen to me," a voice said from the box. A voice that sounded like David's.

"You want to talk to me now? After ten years of silence? I don't think so," she said to the floating device.

"I did what I thought was best to protect you, but I screwed up. Please, Rhi. You have to trust me."

"Rhi?" Ryker called out, and the box flew off.

Rhi stepped into the trees and walked deeper into the woods. She didn't want to talk to Ryker.

"Rhi, I know you're out here. I heard you talking." Leaves and twigs crunched under his booted feet. "Please, Rhiannon. Just hear me out."

Rhi peaked around the large oak she was hiding behind. Ryker was searching for her, worry etched on his gorgeous face. She hated being the cause of his distress. Rhi wanted to be Ryker's comfort. A source of happiness for him. Never sadness. Sighing, she returned to the edge of the woods. When Ryker saw her, his shoulders relaxed, and he quickly closed the distance between them, pulling her into his chest. Rhi wanted so badly to wrap her arms around him. To feel the safety of his embrace. But she couldn't. She couldn't allow herself to wish for what she would never have.

"Rhi, talk to me. Please."

"There's nothing to talk about. You've made your decision, and in turn, made my decision for me. I ran from Haven to get away from having my choices taken from me."

Ryker pulled back, keeping his hands on her upper arms. "That's not what I'm doing."

"That's exactly what you're doing. Tell me your plan. How do you propose getting Lucy back without trading me?"

"The Gargoyles are going to Haven. They are impervious to bullets."

"But Lucy isn't. What happens if she gets caught in the crossfire?"

"You aren't any safer than she is."

"Sure, I am. Josiah needs me to help bring more people and money into Haven. He's going to use me, not kill me."

"And you're ready to go back to that? The kind of life where you don't have any say what you do or you're made to do?"

"No, I never want to go back, but I will for Lucy. Besides, I don't have any say over what's happening now." Rhi fisted her hands at her side, fingernails digging into her palms.

"I'm trying to keep you safe. I'm sorry if you feel like I'm not giving you a say in what happens, but this is what we do. I promise I'm not like Josiah or James or your father. I don't want to make all your decisions for you. Just this one."

Rhi wanted to believe him. "What about a compromise?"

"What's your suggestion?" Ryker pushed her hair behind her ear, and Rhi couldn't help but lean into his touch.

"Trade me for Lucy, then come rescue me." Ryker started to argue, she could see it in his eyes, so she placed her fingers against his lips. "They're not going to hurt me, but we can't say the same for Lucy. They've already killed two of their own men."

"You're something else, Rhiannon Spencer. Your mother would be proud. I know I am." Ryker touched his forehead to hers, his breath warm against her face when he exhaled. If he agreed to her plan, she didn't know when she would see him again, if ever, so Rhi tipped her face up and kissed him. Ryker palmed her cheeks, tilting her head the way he wanted, and drove his tongue into her mouth. She had intended the kiss to be sweet, but it quickly turned heated. She memorized his flavor, savoring it. Her heart beat wildly, passion igniting her core. Rhi gripped the back of his tee, pulling him closer, until a faint buzzing reminded her of her father's voice.

"We're being watched," she whispered against Ryker's lips.

"What?" Ryker looked back toward the house.

"No. Up there." Rhi pointed to where the noise came from. "It's a flying box."

"What? A flying box? Do you mean a drone?"

"I don't know what it's called, but right before you came out, it was buzzing around my head."

"Shit." Ryker released her and looked around. He took several slow, measured steps, his feet not making any noise. He bent his knees and launched into the air, catching the

239

drone. Ryker smashed the plastic against a tree, shattering it into hundreds of pieces. He then stomped it several times for good measure. "Let's go," he said, grabbing her hand and pulling her toward the house.

As soon as they were inside, Ryker located Xavier. "We have a problem. There was a drone flying around outside."

"It was David's," Rhi added.

Ryker frowned. "How do you know it was his?"

"He spoke to me. Or the box did. But it was his voice." Rhi shrugged.

Ryker dropped her hand and turned her to face him, grabbing her arms tightly. "He what? What did he say to you? Why didn't you tell me that part?"

"I didn't get a chance before you went all Hulk Smash on it."

Ryker released her and crossed his arms over his chest. She didn't know if he got the reference, so she continued. "Never mind. He said he needed to talk to me, that I was in danger."

"Yeah, from *him*." Ryker released her arms and ran a hand through his already messy hair.

"Well, he knows where I am, so it's probably a safe bet he's going to show up at some point."

"Shit. He's always one step ahead of us. Even if we move somewhere else, he's going to find you."

"Then let me go back to Haven like we talked about. You get Lucy back, I'll be back where he wants me, he leaves both your families alone, and you figure out a way to rescue me after you figure out a way to take him down."

"That's not a bad idea," Xavier said.

Ryker bowed up, and Rhi took a step back. "It's a terrible fucking idea. Would you send Elizabeth to the wolves knowing they wanted to eat her alive?"

Xavier didn't flinch at Ryker's outburst. "No. But I don't think Josiah wants to hurt Rhi."

240

"No, he just wants to use her. When he figures out he can't because we removed the chip in her leg, he's going to be pissed that he can no longer control her."

"I'll take that chance. My choice, remember?" Rhi placed her hand on Ryker's forearm and squeezed. "Please. Let me do this for Lucy. I trust you. I trust all of you. Now, I'm asking you to trust me."

"Fuck." Ryker studied the ceiling before turning to Xavier. "Do you think you and your Clan can get Rhi out of there?"

"Yes, or I wouldn't suggest it. But if we're going to do this, we need to get a move on. We need to get to the airport and intercept Tamian before he goes Hulk Smash." Xavier winked at Rhi, and she grinned at him. Ryker tensed beneath her hand, so she slid it down to entwine their fingers.

"I'm going on record to say I don't like it, but I'm putting my trust in you."

Xavier inclined his head. "I won't let you down. I need to make some calls, so if you'll excuse me."

"Since David knows where we are, should we find somewhere else to take all the mates?" Ryker asked Stefan.

"No. I'm remaining here. I don't think it will be necessary once Rhiannon is back at Haven, but I've already called in more males to help guard my home."

"How did you know I would agree to trading?"

"You aren't the only one with a stubborn mate. We do what we can to protect them, but they have their own minds. Even though we might not agree with their choices, ultimately, it's their right to make those choices."

Claudia chose that moment to join them. She stood in front of Stefan and leaned her head back against his chest. "You're damn right it is." Claudia looked at Rhi and smiled. "I'm proud of you, Rhiannon. It takes a strong woman with a good heart to willingly go back into a shitty situation. But I know these males, and they will rescue you. I want you to go into this situation believing that. And you," she turned her gaze to Ryker. "Know that we will keep Mac and Elijah safe while you're gone."

Ryker's phone pinged. Rhi released his hand so he could read the message. "It's the location for the swap. It says I'm to come alone."

"Yeah. That's not happening," Sultan said. The large, bald male had been scarce for the last few hours. "We'll put some distance between ourselves and you, but you aren't going into this situation without backup. Guns or not."

"You should take my SUV. It'll be easier to blend in than your bikes will," Stefan offered.

"I'd appreciate that." Sultan gripped Ryker's shoulder. "Ready to riot?" he asked, playing on Ryker's biker name.

"As I'll ever be." Ryker turned to Rhi. "Are you sure about this?"

"I'm sure. I would never forgive myself if something happened to Lucy."

Ryker pressed a kiss to her forehead. "Okay. Let's do this."

Rhi was putting on a brave front, when inside, she was silently screaming. She had no doubt it wasn't going to be as easy as waltzing back into Haven and being forgiven for running, but she wasn't about to tell Ryker that. She prayed to the goddess the Gargoyles were as fierce as they thought they were.

They stopped off in the living room to tell the others what was going on. Mac grabbed Rhi in a tight hug while Elijah looked like he was going to be sick. "Promise you'll be safe," Mac whispered.

"I promise." Rhi gave her new friend a smile she didn't feel. She glanced at Elijah and nodded. He was the only one who knew what she was really facing. Elizabeth and Claudia offered their own hugs, and Rhi let their warmth and caring wash over her. Since she didn't have her mother, she accepted the love these two females were offering.

Ryker

RYKER WAS TORN. He loved Lucy. She was family. He didn't want to admit he loved Rhi, no matter how strongly his heart beat when she was near. How his breath hitched when she smiled at him. How he wanted to wrap her in his arms and never let her go. He knew love at first sight wasn't a myth because of his parents. The pull to Rhi was like nothing he'd ever encountered. Not even with Juliette. When he finally let down the twenty-year-old guard he'd kept on his heart, he was able to see her for who she was and what she could mean to him. What she already meant. Ryker wanted Rhi in his life. He wanted to love her. To protect her. Build a life together. Yet here he was, sending her back to a prison she'd only just escaped.

It was Rhi's choice to go back. To do this for Lucy. Ryker sighed, admitting her selflessness made him fall a little more in love with her. She was young in years but old at heart. Ryker didn't know what all she had endured over the last ten years. Rhi had only touched the surface of her life. What he did know was his female was strong. She had to be to escape. To willingly go back to save someone else. Someone she'd only recently met. Rhi had no loyalty to Lucy, but she was doing it because she saw Lucy's value to the family. A value she failed to see in herself.

They drove in silence. Ryker had so much he wanted to say but didn't know where to start. Sultan was somewhere behind, keeping his distance in case David was watching.

243

He was glad for the backup, but he didn't want to do anything to screw up Lucy's chance. Ryker's phone rang through the Bluetooth in the SUV. He hit the button on the steering wheel to answer. "Go ahead."

"Pull over. Pull over now." Ryker had never heard his sergeant-at-arms panic, but there was no other word to describe Sultan's tone.

Ryker flipped his blinker and merged into the slow lane so he could pull off to the shoulder "What's going on?"

"Someone took control of the car. Moved us over to the shoulder, then all the electronics went out."

"What the fuck?" Ryker's vehicle picked up speed as though someone else were controlling the car. "Call Mayhem. Tell him what's going on."

"What *is* going on?"

"Someone else is in control of my car, and there's not a fucking thing I can do about it. Give him the address of where we're supposed to make the swap. I have a bad feeling about all this."

"I'm on it."

Ryker looked over to Rhi. Her knuckles were white where she was clinging to the "oh shit" handle above her. His own knuckles matched hers where he gripped the steering wheel. Whoever was in charge of the vehicle expertly maneuvered it through traffic, taking a ramp twenty miles before the one that led to where Lucy was supposedly waiting. When they stopped at a red light, Ryker tried to open the door, but the locks were engaged. When he tried to unlock the door, nothing happened. The voice from the GPS was recalculating based on their unexpected departure from the highway.

"Unfuckingbelievable!" Ryker slammed his hands on the steering wheel, and Rhi jumped. Ryker tapped the brake, but nothing happened. He pulled the emergency brake, and the SUV slowed some, but not enough for Ryker to get them out of the vehicle. If he could break the glass, he could shift and… Fuck! "Call 911," Ryker barked into the cab, but the Bluetooth didn't engage. He punched the button on the steering wheel, and nothing happened. Handing Rhi his phone, he instructed her to use the emergency button on the home screen.

"Nine-one-one, what's your—?" The phone went dead.

When it immediately rang, Ryker answered it, "You have to help us. Some—"

"That someone would be me. You might as well sit back and relax. Help isn't coming." The line disconnected before Ryker could curse the man on the other end.

"Fuck!" Ryker pushed the seat back as far as it would go and reached under the dash, pulling at any wires he could grab. His phone rang, and he answered without looking, thinking it would be emergency services. "We need help."

"If you touch another wire under the dash, I will wreck your vehicle."

"You son of a bitch!" Ryker sat back in the driver's seat and grabbed his hair with both hands.

"I'm sorry," Rhi whispered.

"Why are you sorry? No. This isn't on you, Angel." Ryker reached over and took Rhi's hand. "Look at me." Rhi's eyes were filled with tears. "I'm the one who's sorry. I'm supposed to protect you, and I'm not doing a very good job of it."

"Why does he care now? After ten years, why is David all of a sudden worried about what happens to me?"

"You think he's worried?"

"You don't?"

"I think he's trying to get you back so he can take you to Haven."

"Then why not take us to where Lucy is?" Rhi looked around as the vehicle started rolling again. "According to the GPS, we have twenty miles to go."

"Maybe that was to throw us off? So we wouldn't send

someone ahead? Who the fuck knows? I sure as hell don't. I've seen some crazy shit in my time, but this takes the cake."

The SUV continued until it pulled into the parking lot of what looked like an abandoned warehouse. It was steered around the back of the building and through a large, roll-up aluminum door. There was just enough light coming through the opening to show the building was empty. When the car stopped, Ryker tried the door again, but it wouldn't budge. He unbuckled, ready to climb into the backseat and kick out the windows. An industrial-sized flood lamp turned on, momentarily blinding Ryker. The locks clicked, and Rhi's door was slung open. Ryker turned to grab her, but a large rifle was pointed at him. David Spencer pulled his daughter out of the car.

"Stop! Dad, what are you doing? Let me go!" Rhi fought her father, but he was too strong for her to get away.

"Stop fighting me, or I'll put a bullet between his eyes," David said. Rhi immediately quit struggling. She looked at Ryker, her eyes wide with fear. "Thanks for keeping my daughter safe, but I'll take it from here." David released the rifle and replaced it with a handgun. He aimed and pulled the trigger. The sting against Ryker's neck was immediate as was the dizziness. He slapped at his neck, finding a tranquilizer dart.

"Rhi!" Ryker was able to push the door open, but he fell to his knees as soon as his feet hit the cracked concrete. "Rhiannon!" Ryker struggled to stand, using the door as leverage. His vision blurred, and he was unable to remain upright.

"Let's get you home," David said.

"Stop! Dad, let me go! Ryk—" Rhiannon's shouts were cut off after a car door slammed shut. A few seconds later, another door closed. Squealing tires were the last thing Ryker heard before he passed out.

246

CHAPTER TWENTY-TWO

Rhiannon

"PUT YOUR SEATBELT on," David said. Rhi tried the handle, but the door wouldn't open. "Don't make me sedate you, Rhi. Put your seatbelt on. Now."

"Why are you doing this?" Rhi grabbed the buckle and fastened it when her father barreled out of the parking lot, gravel flying behind them.

"To keep you safe, of course. I'm sorry, Rhi. It wasn't supposed to be like this."

"Like what? Like kidnapping? Harassment? Murder? How could you kill those men?"

David snapped his head toward hers. "I haven't killed anyone. How could you think that?"

"Maybe because I don't know you? You're not my dad."

"What are you talking about? Of course I'm your dad."

"No. My dad died the second he took me to Haven. You abandoned me. Left me with Josiah for ten years. Do you even know what he did to me?"

"Did he hurt you? I swear if he touched you—"

"Stop. Just stop it!" Rhi hit her fist against the window, trying to break it. When that didn't work, she kicked both feet against the windshield.

"For God's sake, stop!" David yelled. The car swerved when he reached over to grab at her leg. Rhi turned in the seat, trying to kick his hand. "Jesus Christ, Rhi. You're going to make me wreck!" Now, there was an idea. Rhi released the seatbelt and lunged for the steering wheel. A sharp pain hit her chest, and she dropped back against the door. David was holding the same pistol he'd used to shoot Ryker with.

"You shot me," she whimpered.

"You left me no choice." David pulled the car over, but before it stopped, Rhi's vision blurred. The passenger door opened, and David grabbed her under her arms, dragging her from the vehicle. She couldn't fight. Couldn't move. Couldn't...

Rhiannon's head was pounding. That was the first thing she noticed when she awoke. The second thing was the soft mattress against her back. The third was a hand brushing her hair back off her forehead. The movement wasn't helping the pain. She groaned against her will, and the hand stopped. The bed she was lying on dipped then rose, and a soft click sounded with the closing of a door. Rhi squinted her eyes, but the room, or wherever she was, was blessedly dark save for a light shining through a cracked-open door, presumably a closet, on the other side of the room.

Gritting against the pain, Rhi opened her eyes and took in her surroundings. She had to be dreaming. Falling back in time, Rhi was surrounded by all the things from her childhood bedroom. The jewelry box her mom gave her for her twelfth birthday sat atop the white dresser. Next to it was a photo of her and her mom, smiling at each other, their faces smudged with dirt. Rhi was young in the picture. Back when everything was right in her world. Before the incident with the bunny. Before her parents argued. Before her mother died, and her father dragged her off to Haven. The poster of her favorite pop star was just as she remembered. Time hadn't faded the color or curled the edges.

Across the room, the small TV sat atop the chest of drawers, her video console and controllers stacked just the way she left them after she and her friends played for hours

248

before her mom fed them pizza for supper. The lilac curtains were tied back with the darker purple sashes. The window was cracked in the bottom left corner from when Jimmy Turner hit it with a rock trying to get her attention late one night after she'd gone to bed. Jimmy had been her best friend. The one she sat with on the bus. The one she helped with his math homework when he didn't understand algebra in the seventh grade. The one who held her hand after her mom died. The one whose mother held her as she cried after the funeral.

Rhi rubbed her chest where her father had shot her with the dart. Whatever was in the tranquilizer had done a number on her head. Was Ryker also lost to the past the way she was? Was he remembering something that was no longer there? Had he been whisked away to a happier time? Or was he lost to the days after his wife and unborn child had been stolen from him? *Ryker.* Rhi blinked back the tears as she prayed to her goddess. Prayed that Ryker was okay. That whoever was holding Lucy hadn't harmed her. That when Rhi woke from this fog, she wouldn't be back at Haven.

Curling up on her side under the soft blanket, Rhi noticed the stuffed rabbit with the long, floppy ears. Jimmy had won it for her at the fair. She had told him the story of the baby bunny she nursed back to health, leaving out the part about her gift. Daisy had made her promise to never speak to anyone, even her best friend, about her ability to heal things. Rhi had kept that promise until she set her hands on Ryker. Rhi didn't count what happened at Haven, because she had never uttered a word about what she could do. Whether her father had told Josiah or the preacher had seen it with his own eyes, she never mentioned her gift. She'd been found out anyway, and Josiah had used Rhi for his own gains.

Tugging the bunny to her chest, Rhi closed her eyes and prayed for peaceful sleep. She also prayed that when she woke next, she would be back with Ryker and this all would be a sordid dream.

Ryker

RYKER'S GRYPHON WAS pissed if the roaring in his head was any indication. He pushed himself to sitting and looked around. "Fuck. Fuck!" He climbed to his feet and leaned inside the driver's door in search of his phone. He didn't have to look hard because it was ringing. "H-hello?"

"What the hell, Ryot? I've been calling for an hour." Sultan was pissed.

"After Spencer took control of the SUV, he drove it to a warehouse, shot me with a tranq, and took Rhi. I just came to."

"Godsdamnit. Do you know where you are?"

"Yes, but don't worry about me. You need to get to the meeting spot and see if Lucy's still there."

"Lucy's fine. She used her voice on the men holding her."

"Why didn't she do that in the first place before they could take her?"

"I'll let her explain that part to you." Sultan sounded proud of Lucy.

"Did she get any information out of them?" Ryker pulled himself up into the driver's seat and leaned his head back.

"Yes. They were working under Josiah's orders, not David's. They said Josiah is losing his mind because David has gone AWOL."

"Where are you?" Ryker transferred the call to Bluetooth after starting the engine.

"We're still at the meeting point. I didn't know what you wanted to do with Josiah's men."

"If your car wouldn't start—"

"Yeah, about that. After about twenty minutes, everything came back online. It's working fine now."

"That doesn't make any fucking sense."

"I guess Spencer wanted us out of the way so we wouldn't interfere in his plans for getting Rhi."

"But why didn't he kill me? He had a rifle, but he chose to tranq me instead."

"Maybe he knows you're important to Rhi? Fuck, Ryot. Who knows? I'm glad he didn't."

"Yeah, me too. I'm headed your way. I'll be there in about twenty."

"We'll be here."

Ryker's mind was swirling. He was happy to know Lucy was okay, but now he was worried about Rhiannon. David was missing from Haven, but what did that mean for Rhi? Ryker would like to think the male wouldn't hurt his daughter, but he had ignored her for ten years. That didn't incite warm and fuzzies. Not all fathers were as good and kind as Sutton. Some were pricks, and some were sadistic bastards.

He rolled up to the meeting spot, where Lucy was pacing alongside the SUV Sultan had been driving. She turned, and when she saw him getting out of his own vehicle, she ran straight at him. He braced himself for impact, spreading his arms, catching her.

"Oh, Little Dove. I'm so glad you're okay."

"I'm sorry, Uncle. I promise I'll find Rhi."

"Hey, none of that. You've done nothing wrong." Ryker kissed her temple, then set her on her feet. Sultan was there, relief shining in his green eyes. His job in the MC was to protect Ryker.

"But I've done nothing right, either. I thought David was the one who sent these guys after me. I went with them

251

knowing I could use my Gryphon voice at any time things started going sideways. I didn't expect David to intercept you. That man is pissing me the hell off."

"You and me both. At least the fucker tranqed me instead of shooting me. What I can't figure out is why. Sultan said Josiah sent these men after you."

"Yes. It seems David has gone missing from Haven. Not only does Josiah not have Rhi to do her thing with the sick people he's been bringing in, he doesn't have David either. According to the driver, David has been instrumental in the success of Haven. Josiah might recruit new members, but David's the one who was controlling the money and bringing in the guns. You and I both know with a couple of keystrokes, David could wipe them out."

"But why? Is someone at the GIA getting too close to the truth?"

"I've been thinking about that. My job was to track government movement and what relationships they'd formed with the Ministry, if any. It's possible whoever took my job found something relating to David and his work with Haven, but given his skill level with a computer, I doubt that's the case. He's too good at covering his tracks and wiping out anyone else's."

"Back at Stefan's, David used a drone to speak with Rhi. He told her he had to get her 'out of there because she wasn't safe.' But we're trying to protect her."

Lucy kicked a rock and watched it tumble across the ground. "We are, but maybe he doesn't know that. What do you want to do with these bastards?" Lucy jerked her thumb toward the car where Josiah's men were unmoving.

Ryker thought about it for a moment. If he sent them to the FBI, that wasn't a guarantee Haven would be taken down quickly with all the bureaucratic red tape. "Have you called Xavier and told him you're safe?"

"Yes. He had just arrived at the airport when I called. He, Tamian, and the others are headed to Haven now.

252

Tamian wants a piece of Josiah for kidnapping me."

Ryker knew how the male felt. He also wanted a piece of Josiah, but he would have to be okay with Tamian doing the dirty work for him. He walked over to the car and opened the door, speaking to the four men. "Go back to Haven. If Josiah's there, tell him David showed up with several men, overpowered you, and took Lucy. Tell him Anna willingly went with her father." The driver nodded, and Ryker closed the car door and waited until he could no longer see the taillights before he turned to the others.

Sultan ran a hand over his scalp. "This is some next-level shit. I knew the technology was out there, but him taking over driving your vehicle? I'll stick to my bike." Hawk and Judge mumbled their agreements.

"You're not wrong. That was one of the most disturbing encounters of my life." Ryker didn't miss the way Lucy flinched, so he went to her and grabbed her hand.

Lucy's eyes were filled with fire. "We need to get back home so I can talk to Henry. See if he can figure out where David would be holding Rhi. We also need to find a way to clear your name with the feds."

"Shit. In all the excitement, I forgot about them. The last thing I need is to be locked up."

"Why don't you guys head back to Stefan's? If David contacts the feds and they show up there, you can voice them. I'll go home and get busy," Lucy suggested.

"You're not driving back by yourself. What if David decides to sabotage the car while you're driving?"

"I'll ride with her," Judge offered.

Lucy smiled at the Hound. "I appreciate that, and if you don't mind, I'd like you to drive."

"Lucy, if you would, call Henry while you're on the road. I'd rather stay in the area in case he can get a location for David. I don't want to get to Stefan's just to have to turn around and head back this way. It seems all I've been doing these last few days is running in circles."

"I'll do that. Hang in there, Ry. I know this shit is upsetting. Hell, I'm frustrated. When we find David, and we will, I want a shot at the bastard."

Ryker doubted Lucy was more frustrated than he was. Rhi was his mate. They were off to a rocky beginning, but he had to believe he'd been put in her path for a reason. If Quinn hadn't rescheduled their meeting, he never would have been in the area when Rhi escaped from James.

"I'll do what I can. Keep your eyes open, and if you run into any trouble on the way home, call me."

Lucy kissed him on the cheek, then got into the SUV with Judge. He watched them drive away, lost as to where to go from there. Ryker gripped his hair tightly, pulling until the pain registered.

"Talk to me, Ryot." Sultan stood just off to the side, not getting in his way.

"I haven't felt this useless since Juliette was taken. Fuck, man." Ryker released his hair, flexing his fingers.

"We'll get her back."

"Yeah? David has been two steps ahead of us this whole time. He has mad computer skills with technology available to him we haven't seen before. Hell, they could be out of the country by now for all we know."

"They could be, but give your mate some credit. Rhi's smart, and she's determined. If anyone can get away from David, it's her."

"Not if he keeps her drugged or tied up or... Fuck!" Ryker's lion tried to break free. He crouched down, but Sultan stepped into his space.

"Not here. We're too exposed."

Ryker took several calming breaths, his beast retreating. When he stood, he closed his eyes. "I pushed her away. When I first met Rhi, I pushed her away even though I felt the pull. My Gryphon claimed her within minutes of meeting her."

"Come on. Let's take a walk." Sultan took off toward

the interior of the park, and Ryker followed. When they were hidden by trees on the walking path, Sultan asked, "Why did you push her away?"

"She's young. Rhi has been through a lot in ten years, but she has no real-world experience. Hell, she's a virgin, and I'm not exactly the gentlest of lovers. That's why my arrangement with Cassandra was perfect. She was an assassin. She gave as good as she got."

"Cassandra wasn't mate material. If she had been, you would have met up with her more than once a month. Besides, just because Rhi is a virgin doesn't mean she won't be feisty. That much repressed need is going to need to be sated."

Ryker thought about the way Rhi came apart when he went down on her. She held nothing back.

"What else?" Sultan asked.

"What else what?"

"What were the other reasons you pushed her away?"

"For reasons Sutton showed me were bullshit. I thought I needed to focus on being Pres and making sure our merc work was steady again. I didn't need the distraction of a female."

"And Sutton did all those things with Rory by his side."

"Right. But Rory's one of us. How do I explain to Rhi that I go out and kill people for a living?"

"You aren't giving her enough credit. That girl has lived with monsters for ten years. You seriously believe she hadn't thought about putting a stop to them at some point?"

Ryker thought back to when they had James tied up in Lucy's basement. She had said she wanted to kill the man. "You're right; Rhi is tough. And yes, I pushed her away in the beginning. But I also got my head out of my ass. After I was shot and she used her gift on me? It was like she shared her soul with me. I never thought I'd get a second chance after Juliette, but when Rhi's energy combined with mine, I knew I would never let her go. All the reasons I had for pushing her away evaporated like smoke from a cigarette. I've watched War and Mav get their second chance, and now I want mine."

Sultan stopped walking and turned to Ryker. "Did I ever tell you about my mate?"

"You have a mate?" Ryker searched his memory and couldn't remember hearing Sultan talk about any one particular female.

"Had. My situation was like Mayhem's only without having my kid returned to me. Crystal and I were together for ten years. She wanted the house and kids and dogs. Everything that comes with being in a long-term relationship. But she also wanted me to give up the club, so maybe War's situation is mixed in there too. She wanted me to park my bike and get a nine-to-five job. In the ten years we were together, I never told her the truth about us. About what I am. I kept telling myself I should come clean and claim her, but something – namely my Gryphon – held me back. Deep down, I knew she wouldn't accept it. She gave me an ultimatum, and I let her walk away. What I didn't know was she was pregnant with my kid. I saw her one day a few months later, her stomach round with a baby. Unless she cheated on me, it had to be mine because we hadn't been broken up that long.

"I was torn, man. I wanted my kid in my life, but at what expense? I wasn't happy with Crystal. She was miserable with me. I knew having a baby together wouldn't change that because I wasn't going to change who I was. Couldn't change. But fuck, I wanted to be a father. I sat on the knowledge I had a baby on the way while trying to figure out how to approach her. I wanted to be in my kid's life, that much I knew. It took a couple weeks to make up my mind to approach her with a plan to co-parent without getting back together. By the time I had figured out what I wanted, she had gotten into a wreck. It was bad. Her folks were the ones who called me. They didn't understand why

256

the hospital had called them and not me. Crystal must have taken my name off her contact list. I had been on a three-day job, and by the time I got back, her parents had agreed to putting Crystal on life support, keeping her alive trying to save the baby. Crystal wasn't far enough along for the doctors to take the baby. Long story short, Crystal deteriorated quickly, and the baby was suffering. Even though I didn't have the right to make a decision on her behalf, her parents told me the decision was mine since it was my child. They didn't know we weren't together. I didn't tell them any different. In the end, I made the decision to pull the plug."

Sultan didn't try to hide the tears. "That's been fifteen years. Crystal might not have been the perfect female for me, but I loved her. Loved that little baby. The child who never had a chance because I was a selfish bastard. Then again, if I had given in to her and parked my bike, gave up the club, got a different job, it would have slowly killed me. I would have resented her, and the kid would have suffered for it. But I remember how good things were in the beginning, and fuck if I don't want that. I want a female to come home to. The kids and dogs. I want someone to look at me the way Rhi looks at you. Someone strong who knows I'm a Gryphon and doesn't care. Someone who gets excited when the bikes start up and the rumble hits their chest. You have a shot at a second chance, and I'd give anything to be in your shoes."

"I'm sorry you went through that, Brother. And I pray you find your perfect female."

"Me too, but first we have to rescue yours. With the feds on our asses, we're going to have to lay low 'til Lucy and this Henry find a way to help, and I know just the place to do it." Ryker trusted Sultan with his life, so he followed the Hound back to the SUV. Sultan opened the back and pulled out their packs. "I don't trust David not to fuck with the car again, so we need to fly."

"What if Lucy gets a lock on Rhi's location?"

"I've got that covered too." Sultan led Ryker back down the same path until they came to the thickest part of the woods. He made his own trail through the trees. They both scanned the area, and when they were certain no humans were around, they stripped, putting their clothes and phones in their packs, and shifted to their eagles. Ryker's blue wings stretched out alongside Sultan's white ones, and they flew west.

After about an hour, a small cabin nestled in a forest came into view, and Sultan guided them to the ground. They shifted back, and Sultan spread his arms. "Welcome to my home."

CHAPTER TWENTY-THREE

Rhiannon

RHI SAT UP and looked around. She was still in her childhood bedroom. "So not a dream," she muttered. Her stomach rumbled, but she ignored the hunger pains. She had to find a way out. Rhi stood and shuffled to the door, twisting the knob as silently as possible. Everything was as she remembered. Her photos still hung on the wall of the hallway, showing her age progression from a tiny baby to an awkward thirteen-year-old. She stepped into the bathroom to pee. Hygiene took a back seat to stealth. Forgoing washing her hands, Rhi took stock of herself in the mirror. She seriously needed to do something with her eyebrows. Hers were bushy where all the other females she'd met in the last few days had sleek brows instead of caterpillars. Rhi headed downstairs, subconsciously keeping to the right to avoid the squeak of the third and fifth steps. The first place she went was toward David's office.

Not finding him there, she searched the rest of the first floor. She called out to her captor, "David?" When he didn't answer, Rhi rushed toward the front door. She didn't know where he was or when he'd be back, but if she could slip out now… Rhi tried the knob but the door wouldn't budge. She next went to the window, only to find black wires crisscrossed over them. "What the…?" Rhi didn't know if the wires were an alarm of some sort or a bomb. She wouldn't put it past David to set the place to blow. The door leading into the garage opened, but there was no remote to open the rolling metal door. The back door had the same black wires running around it as did the windows. She didn't bother going upstairs.

Since she didn't want to take a chance on setting off an explosion, Rhi decided to look around, starting in the kitchen. The fridge was stocked with plenty of food and all her favorite sodas from when she was a teen. Rhi grabbed a grape drink. Since she couldn't cook, she searched through the pantry. If she was going to be a prisoner, at least she wouldn't be a hungry one. She chose a cup of instant mac and cheese and tossed it in the microwave after reminding herself how to prepare it.

While she waited the three and a half minutes for it to nuke, she walked over to the back door and looked out over the yard. Her breath caught at where the garden should have been. Weeds and tall grass had overtaken the area, and that hurt her heart. It should have been preserved in her mother's honor instead of being forgotten. That was another reason to hate her father. The microwave dinged, pulling Rhi away from the window. She tore open the pouch of fake cheese and squeezed the gooey mess into the noodles. After stirring it with a spoon, she blew on the first spoonful before taking a bite. She swallowed a moan at the memory of her favorite food. Her mom had once made a dish of homemade macaroni and cheese, but Rhi preferred the fake stuff. At least she had as a kid.

Rhi ate in silence, save the ticking of the grandfather clock in the living room, contemplating how screwed up her life was. She stood with the spoon in her mouth, her eyes unfocused, when the garage door groaned as it opened. Rhi briefly considered running upstairs, but too soon, the door leading into the kitchen from the garage opened and David walked in carrying a pizza.

"Oh, good. You're awake. I brought your favorite –

pepperoni and extra cheese, although I see you've already found something." He placed the box on the counter and opened the cabinet beside the microwave, grabbing some paper plates. "Help yourself if you're still hungry." The longer he spoke, acting as though he hadn't drugged her and kidnapped her, the madder she got.

Rhi tossed the empty cup in the trash and threw the spoon in the sink where it clattered loudly. David turned, a slice of pizza hanging in midair. "There's no need to pitch a fit, Rhi. Why don't you have a seat so we can talk?"

Rhi crossed her arms over her chest, scowling. "You want to talk? Fine. Start by telling me why you abandoned me at Haven. Tell me why you put tracking chips in my body. Tell me why one of those chips was used to manipulate me. Tell me why this house looks the same as it did ten years ago. Tell me why you think it's okay to drug me and kidnap me. Why it's okay to work for someone evil like Josiah Talbert. Helping him keep people at Haven against their will. Promising them cures for all their money. Tell me, David, how you think it's okay to kill two men and blame it on someone who's innocent."

"Rhi, I didn't kill anyone. As for those men being innocent, they were holding you captive. I had to get you away from them."

"Captive? They rescued me from James. *You're* the one holding me captive."

"I brought you home. I thought you'd appreciate the gesture. You can pick up in the garden where you and Daisy left off. As for the chips, I needed a way to track you in case Josiah moved you. It was for your own good."

"My own good? How is zapping me into a semi-conscious state for my own good? How is manipulating me into using my gift without my knowledge for my own good? A gift I was told was of the devil? Do you even hear yourself? What happened to you? When did you become this monster?"

"There are things you don't know. Things you couldn't possibly understand. If the wrong people found out about your powers… Rhi, everything I did was to protect you."

"The only person I need protecting from is you! I've seen how real fathers treat their kids. They don't use them, hide them for ten years in a cult. They don't kidnap them while tormenting the people who are actually doing the protecting!" Rhi sucked in a breath. "I'm not thirteen; I'm an adult. I am plenty old enough to make my own decisions. Decide who I want to live with and where. I don't know what you have against the Lazlos, but they're the good guys. The ones who help people like me get away from people like you."

"You know nothing about them. Tell me, Rhiannon, did you know the man you're so set on defending is a cold-blooded killer? His whole family is a group of vigilante mercenaries who kill people for money. And you call me a monster. I won't have my daughter living with that kind of people."

Rhi didn't let her father see she was shocked by his words. He could be telling the truth, and if he was, she would decide later how she felt about that. "As opposed to living with someone like Josiah who lies about who he is and what he stands for? Someone who kidnaps innocent victims and puts them in solitary cells? He stole a married woman, a woman who was pregnant, and gave her to his brother as a gift. Then that man turns around, takes the baby, and gives it to someone else to raise so his followers wouldn't know the truth. A man who allowed one of his guards to rape a young girl then sold her baby. Yes, David. The man you're working for is *sooo* freaking good all because he claims he's doing God's work. You disgust me. I'm glad Mom died because it would break her heart to see the kind of man you really are. The Lazlos might be mercenaries, but they've shown me more love in a week than you have in a lifetime."

262

David dropped the pizza slice on the plate, glaring at her. "You know nothing about me, and your mother would understand why I've done the things I needed to. You think you're an adult, but until you're faced with life-altering situations, having to make decisions for the greater good, you won't understand the pressure I've been under."

"Oh no? Being forced to try and cure someone of cancer by laying hands on them isn't life-altering? Being forced to live in a community nothing like the way I grew up isn't life-altering? Being told the deity you believe in is wrong isn't life-altering? Having a grandmother who—"

"Okay, I get it. You think what you've been through was rough. You don't know the meaning of the word." David ran a hand down his face. "I'm not trying to make light of what you've endured, but believe me, it's nothing compared to what I've been faced with. Maybe one day you'll understand, but for now, you're just going to have to trust me."

"Trust you? I will never trust you. I can't stand to be in the same room with you. I want nothing to do with you, and I'm leaving. With or without your permission."

"I'm afraid I can't let you go, Rhi. You don't understand the danger you're in."

"The only one dangerous to me is you." Rhi took off running back to her bedroom, slamming the door behind her. She leaned against it, closing her eyes, trying to get her breathing under control. Her father – no, David – was mental if he thought she was staying there with him. But he was smart with all sorts of things she didn't understand at his command. She would need to bide her time. Get him to let his guard down. Then, just as she had with James, she'd make her move.

Rhi walked over to the window and looked out. The house next door hadn't changed much over the last ten years. She wondered if Jimmy's parents still lived there. If they did and she saw them outside, maybe she could get them to help her. Rhi was looking for any type of movement outside when her bedroom door opened. David had a plateful of pizza in one hand and her grape soda in the other. He placed them on the dresser.

"Just in case you get hungry." He didn't say anything else before leaving her alone again.

She *was* hungry, but did she trust him not to poison her? He said he was protecting her, so that had to count for something. But it didn't mean he wouldn't drug her. He'd already proven that when he knocked her out. Rhi had already decided to bide her time, so if he did drug her and she passed out, that would make her time there in her old home go by quicker without her having to interact with her father. Rhi picked up a slice of pizza and sniffed it. It didn't smell funny, and there didn't appear to be any type of powder sprinkled on it. She shrugged, then took a bite. Rhi moaned around a mouthful of extra cheese. God, how she'd missed pizza. She devoured the three slices and downed the soda. Never again would she take greasy food for granted. She wiped her hands on the paper towel David had brought, then resumed staring out the window.

Movement next door on the second floor caught her eye. Was that... Jimmy? It was! Rhi reached for the lock when she felt her body getting numb. "Son of a bitch."

Ryker

"I THOUGHT YOU lived over on Beecher Street." Ryker took in the cabin as they both got dressed. It didn't look like much on the outside. The surrounding woods were what captivated Ryker. "You can shift here without worrying about someone seeing you."

"I can. There isn't a neighbor for miles. While I do have a house on Beecher, it's not home. This place? It's where I come when I need to clear my head. When I need a little downtime after a contract. I don't come here as often as I'd like since it's three hours from the clubhouse. Come on. I'll show you the inside."

Ryker was much more impressed with the interior. One large room housed the living room, kitchen, and dining area. There were two doors other than the one they had entered. Ryker assumed one led out back while the other was for the bathroom. It had a homey feel with bright-colored pillows scattered across the tan sofa, while a worn quilt rested on the back of a matching recliner. There was a ladder leading to a loft bedroom.

"No TV?"

"No. I like the quiet so I can think. If I want noise, I go outside and listen to nature."

"This is a great place."

"It's been in our family for hundreds of years. For whatever reason, each male in our family only has one offspring, and it has always been a male. Each father passes the cabin down to his son and so on. My father gave it to me about forty years ago. I updated the bathroom and made minor repairs, but for the most part, it hasn't changed. There's a well about twenty yards out the back door that supplies the water, and there's a propane tank on the west side of the house that runs the water heater and stove, but there's no electricity. Another reason for not having a television. There is a cellar with an ice box, but usually when I come here, I bring a cooler to keep beer in. There's a firepit out back where I cook whatever I catch if I don't want to heat the house by using the stove."

"I'm impressed. I can see why you'd want to stay here."

Sultan went around opening windows, letting the crisp air flow through.

Ryker walked over to one of the windows and looked out. "I didn't see a driveway as we flew over."

"That's because there isn't one. There's a break in the trees on the back side of the property large enough to drive through. I park in a small clearing, then I hike the rest of the way in. I don't want outsiders knowing about this place, and a driveway would tempt someone to check it out."

"Makes sense. What about cell phone coverage?"

"It's spotty at best here at the cabin, but if we walk toward the clearing, there's a small area where the signal is strong. Since we're waiting on Lucy to call, I'd say we need to head that way. I have a satellite phone, and I'll give her the number so she can reach us when we're at the cabin."

The path Sultan took was worn, but not enough to be detected from above. If Ryker owned the place, he'd be hard pressed to leave. Then again, he had a club to run and their merc business to oversee. That would be hard to do out in the middle of nowhere. When they reached the clearing, Sultan called Lucy from the sat phone. She and Judge were almost to her home, and she was still waiting on Henry to get back in touch with her. She promised to call as soon as she knew anything. Ryker borrowed the phone to call Sutton and ask about how things were going at Haven. His dad didn't answer, so he left him a message with the number. He relayed how David had gotten the jump on him and had managed to take off with Rhi.

With nothing else to do but wait, Sultan offered to hunt for their supper while Ryker took the phone back to the cabin. He was glad for the chance to be alone for a bit. As he walked, he let his thoughts drift to Rhi. He wondered how she was faring, wherever she was with her father.

The satellite phone buzzed, and Ryker answered it. "Go ahead."

"Hey, Son."

"Pop? Tell me you got them."

"I wish I could. When Xavier and his men arrived,

Josiah and most of his guards were gone. The ones who remained were more than welcoming when Xavier asked to look around. There are no guns anywhere on the property. I went in and asked everyone to meet me in the church. When I explained what was going on, I was met with a lot of disbelief. There was a handful of people who decided to leave now that Josiah had abandoned them, but most decided to remain where they were. David Spencer's wife was the most vocal out of all of them. She said, and I quote, that I was a messenger from Satan, sent to deceive the good people of Haven. She defended both her husband and Josiah. She didn't have anything good to say about Rhi, either. It was all I could do not to backhand her."

"Did you use your Gryphon voice on them?"

"I did. Not even the guards could tell me where Josiah had gotten off to or where David might be. I'm glad Xavier was here, though. I thought Tamian was going to burn the place down."

"I know how he feels. If I wasn't sure there were innocent people in the prison, I'd burn it down around Gideon and Lewis."

"Their day's coming."

Yes, it is. Ryker wasn't going to let either one of the males get away with what they did to Juliette and Mac, but he wasn't going to tell his dad that. Ryker had a plan. One he would carry out alone, once he got Rhi away from her father and back where she belonged – home with him.

"I'll let you get back to it then. I hope I'll see you soon."

"Keep the faith, Son. Rhi is your mate. She's your second chance. I don't think Zeus would take her away from you so soon."

"I hope you're right." They said their goodbyes, and Ryker sent up a prayer. It was rare he prayed, and when he did, it wasn't for himself. This time, he was selfish and asked for Rhi to be kept safe and brought home to him. When he reached the cabin, he gathered some firewood and stacked it in the pit. He went inside and searched until he found a box of matches. Once he had the fire going, he sat down on a stump and waited for Sultan to return. Ryker set his forearms on his thighs and let his hands dangle between his legs. He stared into the fire, mesmerized by the dancing flames.

Sometime later, the snapping of twigs caught his attention. Ryker looked over his shoulder. Sultan had both hands full of dangling rabbits.

"It's not steak, but…"

"They'll fill our bellies." Ryker rose to help the Hound skin the animals. Sultan disappeared inside for a few minutes. When he returned, he was carrying a bowl of spices. After washing the blood off the meat, Sultan skewered each rabbit onto the metal spit before applying a layer of spice to each one. He then placed the rod into the vees of the stand.

Sultan went to wash his hands, and when he came back, he had a bottle of whiskey. He offered the bottle to Ryker who took a long swig before passing it back. "This reminds me of the camping trip."

Sultan grinned. "Yes, but without the twins entertaining everyone."

Ryker couldn't help but smile thinking of Mayhem's boys. He and Sultan passed the bottle back and forth, with Sultan turning the spit while Ryker told him about Sutton's phone call.

Once the rabbits were done, they removed them from the fire and chowed down. Ryker had eaten plenty of small animals in both his lion and eagle forms, but he preferred his meat cooked. Whatever spices Sultan used covered the gamey taste, and Ryker picked the bones clean, washing it down with more whiskey.

Sultan added wood to keep the fire going, then sat on the ground, leaning against a stump. Ryker wasn't one to get into anyone's personal business, but something Sultan said earlier had him curious. "Can I ask you a personal question?"

Sultan took a drink before handing the bottle back to Ryker. "Of course."

"You said everyone in your family only has one son. Since Crystal died before your child was born, does that mean you still have a chance at another child? Sorry if that's insensitive."

Sultan rubbed the back of his neck. "It's not, and honestly, I don't know. I'd like to think if I ever found another mate, Zeus would allow me to have my one child. Even if the baby turned out to be a girl and broke the cycle, I'd really like to know what it's like to raise a child. I'm not getting any younger."

"I hear you. I lost out on so much time with Mac. Don't get me wrong; I love that girl to pieces, but I would love to have a baby with Rhiannon. I want to make a home with her." Something niggled at the back of his brain. Something David had said before Ryker passed out. *"Let's get you home."*

"Shit, that's it." Ryker grabbed the satellite phone and dialed Lucy's number. "Luce, I think I know where David took Rhi. Before he shoved her in the car, he said, 'Let's get you home.' Have Henry check their old residence and see if it's still in his name."

"I'm on it." Lucy hung up on him, but Ryker didn't take offense. The situation was dire, so manners took a back seat to urgency.

"You think he would take her somewhere so obvious?" Sultan asked.

"Well, they haven't lived there for ten years, and Spencer has an apartment he stays in when he's working. We know he didn't take her back to Haven, so it's the only thing that makes sense."

"I hope you're right, Ryot. I pray you're right and one step closer to getting Rhi back where she belongs."

CHAPTER TWENTY-FOUR

Rhiannon

RHIANNON'S BACK ACHED. When she opened her eyes, she realized why. She had fallen asleep on the floor. No, she had passed out from being drugged. Again. Stretching her legs out, she noticed something wrapped around her ankle. It was a piece of black plastic attached to a band. She pulled on it, but it wasn't coming off. *What have you done to me now?*

Pissed at the man, Rhi stormed out of the bedroom and down the steps. "David!"

"You don't have to yell," he said, walking out of his office.

"What is this?" Rhi stuck her leg out, pointing at the thing around her ankle.

"That is a monitor. Since I have things I need to take care of away from here, it assures me you won't run away. You see, not only is it a monitor, it also contains an electric current. If you try to step foot outside the house, it will send enough shockwaves through you to hurt immensely. Should you be so stubborn as to push through that pain, once you are more than fifteen feet outside the door, it will zap you with enough juice to stop your heart."

"Why would you do that to me?"

"Because I can't risk you getting into the wrong hands again. Do you have any idea what would happen if everyone knew what you were capable of? It's bad enough

Josiah found out."

"How did he find out?"

"I'm afraid that was my mother's doing. Instead of bragging about your abilities, she told him as a warning of your pagan nature. Of course, he didn't believe her until he saw you in the garden, bringing a dead plant back to life. When he confined you to the indoors, I had no idea how he was going to use you."

"But you're the one who put that zapper chip thing in my leg. That's how he controlled me when it was time for me to perform my magic."

"Yes, well, I didn't realize when he took control of the remote he would use it in such a way. He said he would only use it if you became belligerent and needed to calm you down."

"What about going outside and working in the garden? Now I don't even have that to look forward to."

"It's autumn. You will need to wait until spring to plant anything, so it's really not a hardship."

"Maybe not for you." Rhi glared at the man, her heart filling with even more loathing. He had practically placed a bomb around her ankle.

"If I thought I could trust you, it wouldn't be necessary. I'm sorry, Rhi. I truly am."

Rhi rolled her eyes. "Yeah, I'm sorry too. Sorry my mother ever met you." Rhi ran out of the room so he wouldn't see her tears. Wouldn't see how broken and defeated she felt. If what he said was true, she couldn't ever leave the house again. Rhi went straight to the window and looked toward Jimmy's house. The lights were out, so she couldn't tell if he was home or not. Leaning her forehead against the cold glass, Rhi let the tears fall. She looked past her reflection into the dark of night. The quarter moon was barely visible through the clouds, but it was enough. The moon had always called to her, and Daisy had said it was the goddess's beacon. Rhi rubbed her inner forearm,

271

wishing she had the same tattoo her mother had. It was a triple moon goddess inside a circle of lavender.

Ryker was out there somewhere. Was he looking at the moon, thinking about Rhi, the way she was dreaming about him? She spent the rest of the day staring out her bedroom window, silently begging Jimmy to come back upstairs. To look out his window and see her. The longer she stood there, the more she lost all hope. When her eyelids started getting heavy, Rhi crashed on her childhood bed. It wasn't as comfortable as she remembered. Sure, it was better than the cot she had at Haven, but it didn't compare to the bed at Claudia and Stefan's home where Ryker had made her feel like a woman for the first time in her life. The way he'd made her come apart had her wishing for so much more. If she ever found her way back to him, Rhi was going to jump the male. Give herself over to him fully. She would make it her life's mission making him happy in whatever way he needed.

When she finally succumbed to sleep, her night was filled with dreams of his kisses both on her lips and elsewhere. It was as though her subconscious was replaying their stolen moments. She woke with a smile on her face until she remembered where she was. When her father knocked on her door, her smile faded.

"I made your favorite." David pushed open the door, carrying a tray of fluffy pancakes and bacon. That had been her favorite breakfast when she was younger, but it was more from cooking alongside her mom than the food itself. He set the tray on the dresser. "I have to leave for a while. There are things I need to take care of at work, but I shouldn't be too long."

Rhi did her best to remove the scowl from her face. She had a plan, and it wouldn't work if she didn't get David to let his guard down. "Thank you. It looks delicious." He puffed up, smiling like he used to whenever he looked at her mom. "Uh, if I take a shower, is this thing going to electrocute me?" She wiggled the ankle with the black box.

"No. It's waterproof. I bought your favorite shampoo and conditioner along with a few other items I thought you might need. They might not be what you prefer, but I figured anything was better than the shit they had at Haven."

That comment surprised Rhi. For the last ten years, David had done Josiah's bidding. He'd married one of the women who bowed down to the cult's leader. "What about Marion?"

David frowned. "What about her?"

"Where is she? I mean she is your wife."

David scrubbed a hand over his face, and when he turned to Rhi, she noticed how tired he looked. He glanced at his watch. "I suppose she's sitting in the chapel like a good sheep." David snarled his lip. "I don't love her, Rhi. Nobody could ever replace your mother. But I needed a wife to make it look like I was following the path."

"I don't understand."

"I know, and I promise I'll explain everything soon. But right now, I have to get to the office. There's plenty of food, and I subscribed to the biggest package available through the cable company. You should be able to find plenty of movies to keep you occupied while I'm gone."

"Thanks. I'm sure I'll be fine," she lied. Rhi wouldn't be fine until she was back with Ryker.

David stared at her a few seconds before walking out and shutting the door behind him. Rhi blew out a breath. This acting like she was giving in was for the birds. Rhi stood from the bed and picked up a piece of bacon, staring at it. She took a tentative bite, wondering if he had drugged her food. When she didn't feel weird after a few minutes, she finished off the slice. Rhi opened her door, listening for him to leave the house. The whirl of the garage door opening then closing seconds later let her know it was safe to move about the house. She carried the tray downstairs and set it on the dining room table. Instead of sitting, she took a bite of pancakes and walked around the downstairs while she chewed. While most everything looked the same as it had before they moved to Haven, some things were different. There were no photos anywhere.

She padded to David's office hoping to find a phone. There wasn't one. Nor was there a computer. Not that she would have known how to contact anyone other than the police using either. She opened every desk drawer, not knowing what she hoped to find. They were empty. She then searched all the closets expecting to see everything that had been there before they left. They too were empty. She left her parents' bedroom to search last, knowing it would be hard to see her mom's things scattered around. What she saw didn't make sense. Instead of being thrown back into the past, the room was empty. There was no bed, no clothes in the closet. There were no toiletries in the attached bathroom. She had expected to feel sad from seeing her mom's things, but this hurt worse. And if there wasn't a bed, where had David slept?

Rhi returned to her bedroom and took a good look at everything. The curtains were lilac, but the fringe at the bottom was missing. The furniture was white, but the knobs were brass instead of being the purple ones her mom had bought especially for her tenth birthday. There were no scuffs. No markings of wear. The comforter was white. Plain white without the lavender floral print. Everything was new. It was all a ruse. David hadn't kept the house and its belongings the way Rhi first thought. But why? Why go to the trouble of making her think everything was the same?

She made her way back downstairs, her breakfast now cold. Rhi couldn't eat it anyway. Her stomach was in knots. Rhi needed the solace of nature, so she headed for the back door expecting to see more black wires. There were none, but she assumed it was because of the shackle around her ankle. Her ankle monitor beeped, reminding her of David's words. Rhi wasn't sure how excruciating it would be, but at this point, she would risk it. She stuck the foot with the monitor out the door, and a pain went through her leg akin to what happened when the chip had been activated. Rhi grabbed onto the doorframe for support, gulping down air to keep from vomiting.

Would the pulsing continue if she crossed the threshold? Or would it be one zap and that was it? *Only one way to find out.* Rhi jumped through the door, landing in a crouch. The pain zinged through her body again, but it was just the one jolt. That she could handle. She took a few minutes to garner the strength to get up and keep going. When she felt as though she wasn't going to pass out, Rhi stood and walked down the steps until she was standing on the grass. Kneeling, Rhi placed her palms against the cold ground. Shivers ran up her arms, more from the energy pulsing through her than the cool morning air. Closing her eyes, Rhi dug her fingers through the grass until she reached the dirt below. Why had she been given a gift if she wasn't allowed to use it for good? Not that trying to heal a disease wasn't good, but the reason behind the healing hadn't been to help the person, but for Josiah to gain more money.

Rhi grabbed handfuls of grass, pulling it up by the roots, then flinging it into the air. The more she pulled, the worse she felt. This yard had been her haven before being stolen away to the one where her life turned to crap. "Oh, Momma. Why did you have to leave me?" Tears streamed down Rhi's cheeks, her grief finally catching up with her. After the funeral, instead of finding solace in the garden, Rhi had hidden away in her room. Now, looking back, she berated herself for not coming to the spot she spent so much time laughing and joking with the one person who never let her down. Daisy had softly imparted her wisdom out here when they were on their knees, planting, nurturing, growing life in each and every plant and flower.

275

It wasn't her mom's fault she got sick. Rhi couldn't blame Daisy for the way her life turned out. That was all on David. In that moment, Rhi wished her gift was one of doling out pain instead of healing. "Forgive me, goddess." Rhi had taken her mother's words to heart about putting only positivity out into the universe less the negative came back to her threefold. She had been good. She had done what was asked of her. So where was the reward? Why was she a prisoner again?

Rhi curled up on her side, carding her fingers through the blades of grass under her hand. Sobs wracked her body as she let herself fully mourn all she'd lost.

"You are strong, my little flower."

Her mom's voice was a whisper, but Rhi heard it, nonetheless.

"You are powerful, my Rhiannon."

"But I'm not," Rhi cried, her throat tight.

"You are powerful. Use your gift."

"I have nothing to use it on."

"Use your gift, Rhi. Call on the energy of the earth and use it."

"Mom?" A soft breeze blew across Rhi's skin even though there was no wind moving the trees. "Mom," Rhi whispered. The monitor's beeping drew her gaze to her ankle.

"You are powerful, Rhi. Believe in yourself the way I have always believed in you."

"I am powerful." Rhi took a deep breath, held it, then exhaled. She removed her shoes and socks, letting the feel of the earth beneath her feet ground her. Rhi closed her eyes, holding her arms out to her sides. Inhaling deeply, she drew in the scents of nature, the goddess's reminder of her gifts to her children. Rhi let her mind wander back to when she was a child and her mother taught her prayers and chants. She grasped the one she needed, but after repeating it in her head, she knew she had to change the last line if this was to work. Rhi centered herself and spoke aloud.

"Mother Earth, hear me calling
I'm your daughter, you're my home
Sister moon, hear me calling
In the night, we are not alone
Father Sun, hear me calling
Let your strong light shine in me
All my ancestors, stand by me
Give me strength to be set free."

Rhi repeated the chant three times, her voice rising in volume each time. The power from the earth flowed through her, and with the last "free" she spoke, Rhi felt electric. She opened her eyes, focused on the monitor, and pushed the energy from her body through her hands. The plastic cracked and popped. Rhi pushed harder with her mind, gritting her teeth, growling with exertion. The plastic case exploded, and Rhi crossed her arms over her face to shield it from the shrapnel.

Giggles escaped her throat, and she pumped her fist in the air. "Thank you, goddess. Thank you, Mom." The strap was still attached to her leg, but she could deal with that. Now, Rhi had to figure out where to go and how to get hold of Ryker. First thing was getting away from the house in case David decided to return.

Rhi slipped on her socks and shoes, then went inside to grab her jacket. She didn't bother looking around. This house was no longer her home and hadn't been since her mom died. Instead of heading out the front, Rhi slipped out the back door and headed through the woods. The path was overgrown, but she knew it like she knew her own name. She, Jimmy, and their other friends had worn it down, trampling through the trees when they wanted to take a shortcut to Mikey's house. He lived on the next street over, and whenever they needed to get home quickly, they took the path instead of the streets.

Rhi stopped at the edge of the woods, trying to get her bearings. She knew Stefan's house was an hour away from Xavier's whose was almost that far from New Troy where Ryker lived. She just didn't know how far it was to Stefan's from where she was. Rhi decided the best place to research would be the library. Surely, they had maps. She never visited the local library when she was younger because she didn't like to read. It was something she did because school required it, but they had their own library. The building was quite a ways from her old house, but she didn't have an option except to walk since she didn't have any money or identification. By the time she got there, she had removed her jacket.

It didn't take long to find a map, but that didn't help her situation much. She had no way of getting in touch with Ryker, and she was a good four hours away. Rhi looked up to think, and that's when she saw the directional signs, one of which pointed her to the computers. Rhi headed that direction, but when she sat down, she had no idea what to key in. She opened an internet browser and typed in Ryker's name. When that didn't give her anything, she typed in Lucy's name. Still nothing. She searched for all his brothers, his mother, the Hounds of Zeus, which populated some photos of the bikers at a couple charity events, but the articles had no contact information.

Frustrated didn't come close to how Rhi felt. She leaned back in the chair and blew out a breath. As she stared at the screen trying to think of what else to search, the monitor went black. Rhi thought she might have somehow broken it, but then a message box popped up. Rhi leaned closer as words began to appear. *"This is Henry. Help is on the way. Stay put."*

Henry? Rhi had heard that name. He was some friend of a friend of Tamian and Lucy, but how did she know it was really him? Her dad was the computer expert. He could be playing a trick on her.

Rhi rolled her bottom lip between her finger and thumb. How did whoever this was know where she was? Rhi looked around for a camera. She spotted several along the walls next to the ceiling. She wanted to trust this to be real, but she couldn't. Not with her father out there.

"How do I know you are who you say you are?"

Another screen opened toward the bottom of the monitor, and a cute guy's face appeared. He was super tanned and reminded her of a movie star. The camera moved around the room, and another face appeared. Whoever the guy was waved, even though he was frowning.

The picture disappeared, and Henry was typing again. *"That was Julian. We're both trying to keep your father occupied so your Hound can come get you."*

"Please hurry. I don't know how long the library stays open. I have no money and nowhere else to go."

"The library stays open until seven, so that gives Ryker plenty of time to get there, provided your father doesn't find you first. Log off the computer, and don't do any more searches. That's how I found you."

"Okay, but tell him to hurry."

The screen went blank, then returned to the internet browser. Rhi logged off as best as she could. She remembered from middle school how the teacher told them nothing was ever truly deleted. Since she didn't know how long she had to wait, Rhi decided to find a book to occupy her time. Now that she could choose the book instead of being forced to study the Bible, she was kind of excited. She wound her way to the romance section and started pulling books out and looking at the covers. When she found one with a man who looked a lot like Ryker, she took it over to a table and opened it. Maybe she could learn a little about sex so she'd know what to expect when she was alone next with her Gryphon.

279

David

"NO, NO, NO!" When David's computer alerted him to the back door opening at the house, he had expected it. What he didn't expect was for Rhiannon to be brave enough to push through the pain. He should have, though. His daughter was extraordinary. It was why he had inserted chips into her. To always be able to find her if she was in trouble. Working for the GIA, David knew how people with special skills were treated. Studied. Analyzed to see how their abilities could be used as weapons. His daughter would never have to go through that. Not if he could help it.

David thought by taking Rhi to Haven she would be safe. He spent his days with the GIA tracking down the very people he lived with. Leading a double life was exhausting but necessary. He had done it for Rhi. To keep a promise he made Daisy on her deathbed. To ensure no one ever found out what Rhi could do. He failed. Josiah had used his baby girl, but she'd been strong enough to escape. Now, he had to find her. Again.

He had created an algorithm to alert him when various terms were searched on the internet. Names of those who had taken Rhi, claiming to protect her. When his computer pinged again, he typed in a few commands and watched the scene play out. Henry Palamo was getting on his last nerve because the man was good. When David got a look at the man, he shook his head. The man was barely more than a kid, but his skills were on par with David's. It had been a long time since he'd come across anyone nearly as good as he was.

He wouldn't curse the kid too much, since Henry had led him right to his daughter. Now, he just had to get to the library before Ryker Lazlo did. David wanted his baby girl to grow up and find love the way he had with Daisy, but he didn't want her to fall for a mercenary biker. David rushed out of his office and headed toward the small town he and Daisy had raised Rhi in.

When he arrived, he didn't see any SUVs or bikes, so David was sure he had gotten there in time to get Rhi out. He strolled into the building like any other person entering a library. He nodded at the young man behind the desk and turned toward the computers. Rhi wasn't there, but it didn't take him long to find her sitting in a chair, engrossed in a book. David came around behind Rhi and clamped his hand over her mouth.

"I should have known you'd find a way to get out of your monitor. You're more powerful than even I knew," he whispered against her ear. "Don't fight me, Rhiannon. I just want to talk." Rhi stopped struggling and nodded behind his hand. "Good girl. Let's head out the back door. There's a small park across the street where we can chat."

Rhi went with him willingly. When he got her across the street, she turned on him. "I will never go with you. I have a new life now. A new family."

"Those bikers are not your family. I am."

"Are you even my father?"

"Of course I am. Why would you ask that?"

"I overheard you and Mom arguing before she died." Rhi crossed her arms over her chest, looking more like her mother in that moment than she ever had.

"Whenever you acted out, Daisy would joke that you were my child in those instances. I will take you right now to have a DNA test done. But we need to get you out of here. The Lazlos don't understand what's at stake. If the GIA finds out about you—"

"No. I don't care about the GIA, or Haven, or you. Like I said, I've found my family."

"Rhiannon, I forbid you to take up with a bunch of mercenaries. You're coming with me."

"I said no!" Rhiannon shouted and flung her hands toward him. David was caught in a web of energy. Rhiannon drove him to his knees, and there was nothing he could do about it.

CHAPTER TWENTY-FIVE

Ryker

DURING THE NIGHT, Ryker couldn't find sleep, so he had shifted to both his lion and eagle. The Gryphon wanted to come out too, but Ryker held it at bay. Sleep wasn't an option with his worry for Rhiannon swirling through his brain. At least in animal form, the worry lessened as they focused on their surroundings. Eagles could be explained away, but lions in the middle of the woods in Upstate New York? Not so much. They had just finished breakfast when the satellite phone rang. Ryker swallowed down his anxiety. After spending all night worried about Rhi, he prayed it was good news.

"Morning, Luce."

"You were right. David took Rhi back to New Smithville. She's at the public library, and you need to hurry before David figures out where she is."

Ryker jumped to his feet. "I'm on my way. But what about the feds?"

"We're working on that. Just get to Rhi, and hopefully by the time you get there, we'll have that sorted."

"Thanks, Little Dove." Ryker disconnected and relayed the call to Sultan.

"That's great news. Let me close up the cabin right quick."

Ryker stripped while waiting, storing his clothes and phones in his bag. Sultan walked out of the cabin naked and shifted into his eagle midstride, clutching his own bag in his talons. Ryker pushed his bird faster with each mile they flew. When they reached the woods where they'd left the SUV after what felt like days instead of hours, they shifted back and dressed quickly. His cell phone had pinged midflight, and when he checked the message, he let out a huge sigh. "Henry discovered the digital trail leading from David's computer to the manipulated video, matching the IP address for it and coding signature. He sent that with the original video including their timestamps and IP addresses to the feds." Ryker climbed into the passenger side, letting Sultan drive so Ryker could text Lucy. "I don't understand some of this, but the feds are now looking for both Josiah and David. Maybe this will give us some breathing room."

Ryker searched the address for the library, then plugged it into the GPS. They were an hour away, and it was the longest sixty minutes of his life. He prayed Rhi was still there and unharmed.

"Breathe, Ryot. It's going to be okay." Sultan squeezed Ryker's knee, and some of the tension melted away. Some, but not all. He wouldn't relax until he had Rhiannon safely in his arms.

When the library came into view, it was all Ryker could do not to jump out before Sultan parked. There were a couple of cars in front of the small building. He scanned their surroundings, keeping his eyes peeled for David. He entered the library with Sultan on his heels. It was quiet inside with a young guy manning the information desk. Ryker didn't see Rhi.

"Can I help you?" the librarian asked.

"I'm looking for my girlfriend. Tall blonde. Really pretty."

"Only woman fitting that description was back in the reading nook earlier. I didn't see her when I went to restock

284

some books just now."

"Which direction is the reading nook?"

"Back there." The man pointed toward the right side of the room.

"I'll go this way," Sultan said, indicating the left side of the building. Ryker took off toward the right. When he got to the seating area, Rhi wasn't there. A book was lying on the floor, and Ryker's heart sped up. If Rhi had been reading it, she would have either put it back or set it on the table. Something was wrong. He scanned every aisle until circling back to the front door. Sultan shook his head.

"Was there anyone else in here?" Ryker asked.

"Yes. A man came in about twenty minutes ago." The librarian tapped his finger to his chin. "Come to think of it, I don't remember seeing him leave. What's going on? Do I need to call the cops?"

"Where's the back door?" The guy pointed toward the back corner, and Ryker took off running as Sultan asked if there were security cameras. There was another parking lot behind the building with only one car parked in it. Ryker assumed the little hybrid belonged to the librarian.

"No!" Birds scattered from the sound of a woman shouting.

Ryker turned toward the voice. He'd know it anywhere, and his Rhi wasn't panicking. She was pissed. There was a small park across the side street, and Ryker kicked it in, not using all his shifter speed lest he draw attention to himself. When he found his mate facing off with her father, she was drawing a crowd.

"I said no!" Rhi had her hands out in front of her body, like she was holding off an attacker. But David wasn't coming after her. He was on his knees, his face screwed up in pain. To the humans looking on, it probably appeared as though David had proposed and Rhi was turning him down. But Ryker had been on the receiving end of her hands. Rhi must have tapped into her powers, but these weren't ones of healing. Ryker's hair stood on end when the energy Rhi was forcing into David hit Ryker as he neared.

Rhi was so focused on her father she wasn't aware of Ryker or the handful of humans standing around with their cellphones out. Sultan ran up beside him, taking it all in.

"What the fuck?" Sultan shivered, getting a blast of energy.

"That's my girl," Ryker whispered.

"Don't move!"

Ryker had been so fixated on Rhi he hadn't noticed a couple of suits entering the park, guns drawn. Ryker and Sultan raised their hands slowly. Lucy said Henry was trying to fix things with the feds, but he didn't know if that had happened or they were about to be arrested for murder.

"David Spencer, you're under arrest. Put your hands up."

When David didn't move, Ryker said, "Rhi, it's okay."

Rhi turned to look at him. "Ryker?"

"I'm here, Angel. It's okay. You can put your hands down." He didn't mention anything about her powers. That was a subject the feds didn't need to overhear. Ryker lowered his arms, keeping them open. Rhi released the energy holding her father, and David slumped to the ground. The feds were on him, placing cuffs around his wrists. Rhiannon faltered, and Ryker caught her before she hit the ground.

"Is she okay?" one of the agents asked.

"She will be. It's not every day your father kidnaps you."

"We're going to need a statement from both of you."

The other agent pulled David to his feet. David tried to pull away, twisting and yelling, "No! Rhi, it's not safe. I need to get you somewhere I can protect you."

"The only one I need protection from is you."

David continued to struggle, but the agent was stronger. He carted a still-shouting David off to the waiting vehicle. The remaining agent's face softened when he turned back to Rhi. "I have no idea what you've been through, but it would be better to get your statement now while everything is fresh on your mind."

"I'm okay." Rhi looked up at Ryker. "You're really here."

"I am, and I'm never letting you out of my sight again." Ryker cupped her cheek as he kissed the opposite temple.

The agent told the crowd to disburse before leading the three of them over to a picnic table. It took almost two hours before Agent McCauley was satisfied, both with Ryker recounting what happened at the warehouse and Rhi telling how David drugged her not once but twice. Ryker knew there were things Rhi omitted from her statement, but he was glad she had. The world didn't need to know about her power. It was bad enough Josiah was aware of some of what she was capable of, and with the cult leader in the wind, Ryker wouldn't rest easy until he was found. The agent assured Ryker they were searching for Josiah, but that only made him feel marginally better. Agent McCauley assured them the evidence the FBI received along with their statements were enough to put David away for many years to come. They exchanged phone numbers, and he said he'd be in touch.

Still seated at the picnic table, Ryker took Rhi's hand in his. "Tell me what happened."

Rhi blew out a deep sigh, then proceeded to recount what she encountered from the time David kidnapped her to when Ryker found her in the park. "I guess my powers are getting stronger the more I use them. When I was in the backyard, I didn't think I'd be able to get out of the ankle monitor, but I did. Something shifted. It's hard to explain, but it was as if my whole body came alive with electricity. And when David was demanding I go with him because he *forbade* me to be with you, something snapped inside me. I know I'm supposed to use my gift for healing, but I couldn't bear the thought of being away from you any longer than I already had been. I pushed all my energy toward David, not to hurt him, but to keep him from hurting me. From taking me again."

"That's amazing, Angel. And I doubt your goddess will hold that against you. Like you said, you weren't harming David."

"I guess." Her shoulders were slumped.

"What's wrong?" Ryker pushed her hair behind her ear, then traced her lobe with his fingertip.

"I just thought... It's stupid, but I thought there might be some good explanation for why he was working for the Ministry. Why he ignored me for ten years. But there isn't other than he's selfish. When I woke up in my old bedroom, I went back in time, wishing I would walk downstairs and see my mom out in the garden. Wishing David would be the loving man he'd been before..." Rhi choked up, and Ryker pulled her to his chest.

"Let it out, Angel." Ryker whispered loving words against her hair. He held her as she cried. As she once again mourned the loss of her father.

When the tears subsided, Ryker gripped her chin so she was looking at him. "I'm sorry I couldn't stop David from taking you."

"It's not your fault. He lost his mind somewhere along the way, claiming it was all to protect me."

"I can't fault him for wanting you safe, but what he did for the Ministry had to be about more than that. He embezzled money, and he armed them with weapons. That isn't something a GIA agent would do. Not without ulterior motives. If he had been undercover, it would be one thing, but once your mom passed away, I think he probably used Haven as an excuse to hide you while he worked with them for his own gain." Ryker took Rhi's hand in his and kissed her knuckles. He wanted to shield her from the pain her father had caused. Ryker didn't admit he thought David was using Rhi to make the Ministry money. Her father was going to jail, and she'd been through enough heartache for one lifetime. "You are an amazing woman, and I am proud of you. However, I think it's best if we don't broadcast what you're capable of. It's bad enough Josiah is aware of a portion of it."

"He's not the only one. When I was at Xavier's, I had a dream. I'm pretty sure it was my mind's way of making me remember something from my past. After the incident with the rabbit, I overheard my parents arguing. David said he saw me heal the rabbit and that my grandmother knew too. Grandmother fought with my mom, and after Momma ran out of the room, Grandmother said something about someone named Abraham getting impatient. I still don't know what that means."

"That means you're still on the Ministry's radar. Now that David is in custody, I'm not as worried. He was the one able to track you down."

"But they still know where you live." Rhi twisted her hands in her lap. "I've already brought enough trouble to you and your family."

"*You* are my family. Both Mac and Kerrigan were targeted by Josiah and his brother. We're not going to stop until every single leader of the Ministry is brought down for what they've done to you, Mac, and Kerrigan. Now, let's go get Mac and Eli so we can go home."

"Home?" Rhi whispered.

"Yes. Your home is with me. Are you okay with that?"

Rhi nodded, and Ryker wiped her tears with his thumbs before placing a kiss to her lips. Instead of going straight to New Troy, the three of them headed to Stefan's home to pick up Mac and Eli. Ryker sat in the back seat with Rhi while Sultan drove. He was ready to get Rhi home, but he wasn't so selfish as to rush out of Stefan's without staying to eat the meal Claudia had cooked. It had been a long, trying day for his mate, and he would do anything to help her feel better. Claudia and Elizabeth did that. Neither one looked much older than Rhi, but their maternal sides were ever present. Rhi lapped up the affection. He needed to make sure Rhi got to spend time with Rory once they were back home.

Before hitting the road, Ryker asked Mac to follow him outside. He had been watching her and Eli interact. There had been tension between the two before he left, but they seemed to have worked through their issues. Eli was attentive, smiling at every move Mac made, every word she spoke. There was a lightness in his daughter that hadn't been there before. Ryker had worried how Eli would treat Mac knowing she had been raped, but the love Eli had for Mac shone through his eyes and the gentle way he stroked her scarred cheek.

"What's up?" Mac asked as soon as they were outside.

"Just making sure everything is okay with you and Eli. Before I left, he seemed, I don't know, hesitant."

"He was, but after I explained everything that happened, he understood I didn't have a chance to talk to him before Josiah took him away."

"And he's okay with… everything that happened?" Mac bit her bottom lip and turned away. "McKenzie, look at me." When she did, he placed his hand on the back of her neck. "I'm here for you, honey. Whatever you need. I won't pressure you, but I think you would do well seeing a therapist. You've been through a fuck-ton of trauma. All three of you have."

"Maybe we can get a family discount," Mac joked.

Ryker huffed out a laugh. "Maybe. So you think Eli's going to be okay with everything?"

"Yes. We've talked. A lot. I know it won't always be easy, because we both have things to work through, but I figured we could work through them together. All of us."

Ryker leaned forward and kissed his daughter on the forehead. "You can include me in that scenario. I promise

I'll help anyway I can."

"Thanks, Dad." Mac hugged Ryker with a strength born of Gryphons, even if she didn't get that particular gene.

As soon as they finished eating, Ryker approached Stefan and Xavier. "I can't thank you both enough for all your help."

"No thanks needed. We might not be related by blood, but we are family." Xavier stretched out his hand, and Ryker shook it, then did the same with Stefan, thanking him anyway for his hospitality.

Rev and Bethany had remained at Stefan's just in case they were needed, so Sultan hitched a ride home with them. Ryker and Rhi rode up front while Mac and Eli sat close together in the back seat. When Eli asked what was going to happen to him, Ryker was honest.

"You're coming to stay with us, if that's what you and Mac want."

Ryker watched in the rearview mirror as the two kids exchanged a silent conversation. It was Mac who answered.

"It is. We have three bedrooms, so there's plenty of room." Mac rested her head on Eli's shoulder. Ryker appreciated his daughter suggesting Eli sleep in his own room, but they were adults. Adults who were in love.

"Yes, there is. With Rhi in our room and you and Eli sharing, that will leave a spare for when the twins come to visit." Ryker caught Mac's eye in the mirror and winked. His daughter blushed, but the smile she gave him was worth everything. "We'll give you time to get settled, and whenever you're ready, we'll see about getting your GEDs. Lucy can help with any documentation and identifications you'll need. The way I see it, the future is wide open for the three of you. If the two of you are still interested in working with animals, I'll see to it you have the education to make your dreams happen. If you've changed your minds, I'll help any way I can. For now, though, we need to get Eli some clothes."

"I don't have any money," Eli reminded Ryker.

"Don't worry about that. We have a special account set up for anyone we rescue from the Ministry. This is what our family does. Don't think of it as charity. Think of it as help getting you started on your new life." Ryker never liked shopping, always leaving it to his mom, but he wasn't taking Elijah home emptyhanded. They stopped at the mall, and after a couple arguments, Ryker convinced Eli to get what he wanted, not the cheapest options on clearance. While he waited on Eli to make his choices, Ryker called Spyder, letting the male know it was safe to come out of hiding. The Hound had sounded way too happy about that, but Ryker didn't ask what happened with the waitress. It was none of his business.

Three hours later, Ryker pulled the SUV into the driveway at his house. Their house. He had gone from living alone to now having three others in his space, and he couldn't be happier. Ryker carried the females' luggage inside while Eli grabbed his shopping bags. Elijah stopped just inside the front door, taking it all in. The young man's eyes were wet, and Ryker gripped him gently on the shoulder. "Welcome home, Son." Ryker ignored the tears, not wanting to embarrass Eli. "Mac, why don't you and Eli put his clothes in the washer, then you can show him around. Rhi and I are going to unpack her things and rest a while." Ryker didn't wait for anyone to disagree with his plan. He turned to Rhi and took her hand, leading her toward the stairs.

When they were alone in their bedroom, he closed the door. "Why don't you put your toiletries in the bathroom while I put your clothes away?" The tall chest was full of Ryker's underwear and T-shirts, but the dresser was practically empty. He sorted Rhi's things, and they both finished at the same time.

"You can rearrange things once we get you more clothes. I would have bought you more new ones today, but

292

I wanted the focus to be on Eli."

"You don't have to buy me stuff." Rhi stood with her arms hugging her body, so Ryker took the few steps to close the distance between them. Pulling her snug against his chest, he wrapped his arms around her.

"I'm going to spoil you, so you might as well not argue."

"But what can I do for you? I have nothing to give in return."

"Oh, but you do. You already shared your gift with me when you healed me. I want more of that. More of you. Just love me, Rhiannon. Just love me and let me love you in return. I want your happiness. That's all I need from you."

"That I can do." Rhi tilted her head back, offering her mouth, and Ryker took it. No more words were needed. Rhi tugged Ryker's tee from his jeans and slipped her hands between the material and his skin. His Gryphon and he were on the same page. They wanted to mark Rhi. Mark her as theirs. Between kisses, they took turns removing the other's clothes until they were both naked. Rhi rubbed her hands over his chest, trailing her fingers over the ink on his right pec before placing an openmouthed kiss on the ink.

His cock was hard and throbbing. When Rhi encircled his erection with her smaller hand, he almost came at the first touch. He wanted to bury himself balls-deep in his mate, but he wanted her to be comfortable touching him too, so he let her explore. Mac's voice just outside the door had Rhi jumping back. With the four of them living together, there would be times when things got loud and possibly awkward, but Ryker never wanted Rhi to shy away from sex, even if someone else was in the house.

"Don't worry about them, Angel. I have a feeling they'll be too busy getting reacquainted to care what we're doing."

"Does that bother you? That they're, you know."

"No. They're adults who love each other. Having sex is a natural part of their relationship. Just like it will be ours.

But if them being this close to us bothers you, I'll build us a house with bedrooms on opposite ends."

"You'd do that?"

"I'd do anything to make you happy."

Rhi bit her lip, and it was killing Ryker. He wanted her more than he'd wanted anything in a long time, but he wouldn't take her if it meant she was uncomfortable. After a few seconds, Rhi took his cock in her hand again, and Ryker both sighed in relief and burned with need.

"I want you, but I don't know what to do," Rhi admitted.

"Do you want to get me off with your hand or your body?"

"Yes." She grinned at him, and Ryker's heart skipped a beat.

"Why not both then? You make me come with your hand to take the edge off, then we can make love."

Rhi nodded. "Show me."

Ryker did just that. He fisted his hand around hers, showing her how he liked to be stroked with a firm grip. His mate caught on quickly. She even twisted her fist over the tip, using his precum to help with the glide. Rhi's eyes were focused on what her hand was doing, but when Ryker reached out and teased her nipples, twisting each one until they were hard peaks, Rhi gasped and looked up. Her pretty, blue eyes darkened with lust and need. He already knew how she tasted, but now he wanted to know how she felt when he was buried inside her pussy. When her strokes halted, he placed his hand back over hers and urged her to continue. It didn't take long for his orgasm to hit. Ryker leaned his head back and closed his eyes, doing his best not to shout the house down. His release spilled over her hand. Before he could pick his T-shirt off the floor to clean his jizz off, she lifted her fingers to her mouth and took a tentative lick. Ryker almost came again right then and there.

CHAPTER TWENTY-SIX

Rhiannon

RYKER LIFTED RHI'S hand, cleaned it off with his T-shirt, then tossed the shirt to the floor. Rhi was ready for more. She had wondered what sex would be like, but before Ryker, she had dreaded it. Mostly because she had been worried it would be with someone like James. It was the main reason she'd been determined to escape Haven. Having to live somewhere she wasn't accepted was one thing, but to be given to a man she didn't like? That had been the worst scenario she could imagine. Rhi remembered the way his parents had stolen kisses, not caring who was watching. Now, she could have that with Ryker. That and so much more. Josiah had preached about sex being wrong unless it was between a married couple. She disagreed.

Still, Rhi was nervous and excited at the same time. She had no idea where her boldness was coming from, but she wanted to give Ryker the only thing she had to give besides her love. He already had that. How could she not love the male who had rescued her from her previous life? He could have left her in that dumpster. Could have walked away at any time after taking her to the hotel and his parents showing up. Could have gotten mad at her for bringing trouble to his home and family. But he hadn't. Ryker had done everything in his power to keep her safe. He had given her a home – a real home – and a large family she hadn't yet

295

met most of. She wanted to give him something in return. Rhi remembered him hinting at the way he liked sex. When he promised to be gentle, she figured that meant he preferred it rough.

"Don't hold back. I want to see the real you. I want to give you what you need, how you need it."

Ryker shook his head. "I won't hurt you."

"I know you won't. Even if you're rough, you won't hurt me. I trust you, but I want you to trust me."

That must have been what he needed to hear. Ryker picked Rhi up and placed her in the middle of the bed, lying down on top of her. He propped himself on his forearms and bent his head to kiss her. What started off as gentle exploration quickly turned heated. Rhi's body ached with need. She ran her nails down his back, and his muscles rippled beneath her fingertips.

Ryker pulled away and stretched to open the nightstand drawer. After rummaging around he sat up. "I don't have any condoms. There's no chance you're on birth control is there?"

Rhi shook her head. "No reason to be before now."

"Fuck." Ryker scrubbed his face with both hands. "How do you feel about babies?"

"I love them, but I understand if you don't want them." Ryker was older with a grown daughter. Rhi had always dreamed of being a mother herself, but she would give up that dream to be with this amazing male.

"Honestly, I thought that ship had sailed, but I would love to have a child with you. Granted, I'd like to have more time for just the two of us before we start a family... Fuck it. If it happens, then so be it. Are you okay with that? If not, we'll wait until we can get protection."

"I'm more than okay with it. I don't want to wait." Rhi reached out and stroked him, bringing his erection back to life. "I want everything with you."

Ryker moved between her legs, his now-hard cock

nestled against her core. He rocked his hips back and forth, letting the tip tease her hole. Her body thrummed in anticipation, her nipples aching to be touched. Rhi, still feeling bold, teased her stomach with her fingers, inching them up toward her breasts. Ryker's eyes tracked their movement, his Adam's apple bobbing as he swallowed hard. *He likes that.* Keeping her gaze on Ryker's face, Rhi remembered how he had twisted the nubs, so she did it to herself. Fire spread from her chest, down her stomach, to where she was still empty.

"You gonna watch? Or are you gonna take me?"

Ryker's eyes snapped to hers, and he grinned. "When did you get so bold?"

"When you decided to tease me and not give me what we both want."

The smirk fell from Ryker's face as he thrust into her, not stopping until he was fully seated. Rhi cried out, forgetting about the barrier.

"Shit, Angel. I'm so sorry." Ryker started to pull away, but she grabbed his arms.

"No. I'm fine. Please, make it feel better."

Ryker closed his eyes for a couple seconds, but when he opened them, there was something else behind them. Something akin to what she felt for him. It was too soon to be in love, wasn't it? Ryker pushed back in, and the pain was soon replaced with a pleasure Rhi had never known. It was more than sex; it was two bodies connected, making them into one being.

"Okay?" he asked.

"More than. It's perfect." Rhi hadn't tried using her energy from the inside since the first time she figured out she couldn't heal herself, but now she was stronger. Digging deep, Rhi imagined pushing her essence into Ryker through their connection.

"Holy shit. Are you…?"

"Did you feel it?"

"It's unbelievable. You're unbelievable." Ryker lowered his head and took her mouth with his, tangling their tongues. Rhi wrapped her legs around his hips, digging her heels into the globes of his butt. "Harder," she urged. Sliding her arms under his, Rhi gripped his shoulder blades. The power in Ryker's body was impressive. She couldn't wait until she could get a good look at all of him. She wanted to explore every inch of the male with her hands and her mouth.

Ryker changed the angle of his thrusts, hitting her clit just right. She knew her body. Knew the signs of her impending release, but she wasn't ready. "No, no, no," she chanted, and he stopped moving.

"What's wrong?"

"I'm too close. I don't want this to be over already."

Ryker smiled and began moving again. "Don't worry. We'll have all night to do it again. And again." He held back, though. Rhi encouraged Ryker to take her hard like she knew he wanted, but he didn't. He was gentle. Too gentle, and it drove her crazy. He took her to the edge over and over.

"Ryker, please."

"Shh, Angel. Let me make love to you."

Rhi nodded, reaching up to run her fingers through his beard. Who was she to argue if he wanted to make love? Using her feet, she pulled him tighter, urging him to go faster, but he didn't. Ryker grabbed her legs under her knees, raising her butt off the bed, changing the angle in which he thrust into her. The cords in his neck tightened, and his face was bathed in concentration. Too soon, Rhi was coming. She gripped his biceps and pressed her head against the pillow as her walls clamped down around his cock, gasping through the pleasure.

"Aw, fuck!" Ryker groaned, his erection buried deep inside. He rotated his hips, grinding against her mound, and the pressure built again.

"Don't stop. Oh, goddess, please don't stop," she begged.

Ryker kept pressing against her clit, and a second but no less powerful orgasm rocked her. Rhi slapped his bicep when the last spasm subsided. "Stop. Gotta... too sensitive..."

Ryker brushed her hair back from her face, kissing her forehead, her cheeks, her chin, then finally, her lips.

"You are perfect, Rhiannon Spencer. I'm so glad for that rainstorm."

"Yeah? Why's that?"

"If it hadn't started pouring, I'd never have pulled off the interstate. I'd never have found the adorable, sopping-wet woman in the dumpster. I'd never have found the other half of me."

Rhi kissed Ryker, smiling against his mouth. She thanked her goddess for sending the rain.

Ryker eased out of her body and went into the bathroom, wetting a washcloth to clean the mixture of blood and semen from her legs. He stretched out next to her, pulling her onto his chest. Ryker stroked his fingertips over her skin, lulling her to sleep. When they woke, it was early morning. They headed downstairs to get breakfast started. Mac and Eli were already busy in the kitchen. Rhi expected things to be awkward, but they weren't. If Mac and Eli had heard Rhi and Ryker having sex, they didn't let on. The four of them sat down at the dining room table, eating together as a family. Rhi didn't mind sharing Ryker with his daughter. She was glad Mac was there. The two had bonded over their ordeals living within the Ministry, and she wanted them to continue getting closer. It had been too long since Rhi had a friend, and she wanted that in Mac.

"Eli and I were talking," Mac said once they were all seated. "Once I explained how the family has plenty of money to send us both to college, we've decided we'd like to go."

"That's wonderful. I'll call Lucy after supper and have her get busy on Elijah's identification. Tomorrow we can look into you all getting your GEDs," Ryker said. He turned to Rhi. "What about you, Angel? Are you interested in college?"

"Not really. I'd like to do what Rory said and maybe work in a florist or somewhere with a greenhouse."

"We'll look into that too. Whenever you're ready." Ryker brushed his fingers across her hand before going back to eating. Rhi glanced up to see if Mac was watching, but her attention was on her boyfriend.

"Rhi and I were talking," Ryker started after he had cleaned his plate. Mac snorted, and Ryker glared at her which made her laugh harder. "That right there" — he pointed at his daughter — "is why we were having this particular conversation. What would you think about me building a bigger house? Maybe one with two suites on opposite ends of the house? I was thinking somewhere with a little bit of land where Rhi could plant a big garden. Maybe have a greenhouse for the colder months."

"Ooh, can we get a dog?" Mac asked. Rhi was surprised Mac would want one after what happened to her face.

Ryker crossed his arms over his chest, but he was smiling. "And who's going to take care of it while you're off at school?"

"Well, I thought I'd take some online classes first. You know, to get me used to school before I attempt going to a campus. I'd rather figure out I'm not smart enough from the comfort of home than in front of a group of people."

"Honey, you are smart enough. And if you need help, Lucy can help you."

"Lucy has her hands full without having to tutor me."

"I'll take care of the dog," Rhi offered, batting her eyelashes. She'd always wanted a pet. "Uh, if that's okay."

"Oh, I see how it's going to be. Eli, you and I have our work cut out for us with these two."

300

Elijah had been mostly silent up until that point. "Yeah, but I'd give Mac anything in the world if it makes her happy."

"Good answer, Son." The corner of Eli's mouth turned up in a hint of a smile at Ryker's words. "How about this. Let's talk about getting a new house first. That way when you do get a dog, it'll have plenty of room to run. You two can work on your education, get into your new routines. Get yourselves settled a bit."

Mac tilted her head to the side. "You really want us all to live together?"

"I don't see why not. At least at first. There's no reason for you and Eli to have to worry about anything other than school. Not when I have the means to support us all. I think the three of you have been through enough for one lifetime, and if I can make it better, I will. If you don't want to live with me and Rhi, I'll help you find your own place. Whatever is best for you and Eli."

Mac got up, walked around the table, and draped her arms around Ryker's shoulders. She leaned her head against his and whispered, "Thank you."

Ryker patted Mac's arm. "No need to thank me. I missed out on so much of your life, so I'm being a little selfish wanting you around as long as I can have you."

Rhi sighed as she stood and began gathering dirty plates. She tried not to think about her own father, but it was almost impossible not to. The man had given his reasons for what he did to Rhi, but she would never forgive him for taking her to Haven and leaving her in Josiah's care. As she began filling the sink with soapy water, Mac joined her.

"You want me to wash while you rinse?" Mac asked.

"Works for me." Rhi changed places with the other woman. "If I get a vote, I'd like for you and Eli to stay with us. At least for a while. I spent the last ten years being ignored by everyone, and it's nice having a friend around."

301

"A friend who's going to be my stepmom," Mac said, grinning.

Only if Ryker and I were to get married. Rhi wasn't getting her hopes up. "Is that going to be weird for you?"

"Nope. You make my dad smile. I've not known him long, but before he met you, it was rare he smiled about anything other than the twins. Those two can make anyone laugh. I can't wait for you to— Ow!" Mac pulled her hands out of the water, holding her finger. "Damn knife."

Rhi grabbed Mac's hand and held it under the running water. She called on her gift and pushed it into the cut on Mac's finger. The bleeding stopped, and the cut sealed itself.

"What...? Did you do that?" Mac was looking between Rhi and her now-healed finger.

Rhi shrugged. "What good is having a gift if I don't share it?"

"That's amazing."

"What's amazing?" Ryker asked as he and Eli entered the kitchen.

"I cut myself." Mac held up her finger to show her dad.

"I don't see anything."

"I know. That's why it's amazing. Rhi healed the cut." Mac grinned proudly.

"Mac, why don't you go sit with Eli? I'll help Rhi with the dishes." Ryker hip-checked his daughter out of the way, and Mac's face lit up again. It was a beautiful thing to see. The scar didn't detract from Mac's beauty. Speaking of faces...

"Hey, Mac? I need a makeover. My eyebrows are out of control, and I want to get my hair trimmed. Would you be willing to go with me?"

"Sure. If you want, I can call the same girl who did my hair. She does Lucy's too."

"I'd appreciate that." Rhi turned and put all the dishes back in the soapy water from where Mac's blood had dripped on them.

"I'm glad you said a trim." Ryker nudged Rhi's shoulder with his own. "I know it's your hair, but I really like it long."

"Me too, but it needs some TLC. In Haven, I had to cut it myself, and let me tell you, it's not easy." While Rhi washed the dishes, she kept the mood light by talking about her mom. When they were finished cleaning the kitchen, Ryker led her upstairs. Mac and Eli were watching television in the living room, and as much as Rhi liked the couple, she was ready for more alone time with her male.

Ryker sat down on the bed and leaned against the headboard. "Come sit with me. There's something I want to talk about."

"Did I do something wrong?"

"No, Angel. You've done everything right, and that's what brought us to this conversation." Rhi settled next to him, and Ryker slid his arm around her shoulder. "Remember when we talked about Gryphons claiming their mate?" Rhi nodded. "It's the human equivalent of getting married. I'd be honored if you would let me claim you."

Rhi climbed onto Ryker's lap, straddling his legs so she could see his eyes. "Really? You want something permanent with me?"

Ryker pushed her hair behind her ear. "I do. I want us to build a new house and fill it with kids. Don't get me wrong. I love Mac with all my heart, but I missed out on watching her grow up. I want that. I want to watch my child grow from a tiny seed inside your stomach into a tiny human. I want to teach him or her to ride while you teach them all about nature. I want that with you. I want you to make our house a home. And I want you to be mine forever."

"Yes." Rhi leaned forward and kissed Ryker with all the unexperienced passion she had.

Ryker groaned against her lips. He gently pushed against her shoulders, and Rhi sat back and wiggled her butt over his erection.

"You're killing me, Angel. I need to tell you something." Ryker gripped her hips, halting her squirming. "To claim you, I have to bite you. My lion comes forth—" Rhi gasped, and Ryker grinned. "Not like that. Just the teeth." Ryker's teeth elongated, but that wasn't much better than the thought of him letting the whole animal loose on her.

"Won't that hurt?" Rhi shivered thinking about those sharp fangs piercing her skin.

"No. I'll bite you when we're having sex, right as we're ready to orgasm. The bite heightens the experience."

"You mean it's more intense than usual? I don't know if I can handle that. I mean, you giving me an orgasm is already like an out-of-body moment. I might pass out."

Ryker caressed her cheek. "You're precious. And if you pass out, I'll have to think of a way to revive you." He winked at her, and she squirmed against his hard cock. She couldn't help herself. Now that she knew how good sex could be? It was all she could think about. Well, not all. He was talking about building a new home with property where she could have gardens and a dog and kids and—

"Angel? Did I break you?"

Rhi slapped his shoulder. "No, you didn't break me. I was thinking about… Never mind. Let's get to this claiming. I need you inside me, like ten minutes ago."

Before she knew what was happening, Rhi was naked and on her back. She propped up on her elbows while Ryker removed his own clothes. She bit her bottom lip as all his glorious skin was revealed. "Turn around," she commanded, and Ryker did as she asked. Before Ryker, Rhi had never seen a naked man, but she had a feeling he wasn't the norm. His back was broad, and his butt was firm and round. She wanted to sink her own teeth into the globes and nibble. Just as she leaned forward to do so, Ryker turned, and his erection was in her face. *Hmm, I could nibble on that*

304

instead. Rhi sat on the side of the bed and took his erection in her hand, then leaned over and licked the tip.

Ryker gripped her hair and twisted it around his fists. His eyes were darker than she'd ever seen. "Not this time. Right now, my beast is barely hanging on, and if you put your mouth on me, I won't be able to hold it back." He released her hair and motioned for her to scoot back toward the pillows. When she was lying in the middle of the bed, Ryker set a knee to the mattress and crawled on top of her.

"I need you, Rhiannon. Need to claim you. Please tell me you still want this."

"Yes, more than anything."

Ryker's erection teased her opening as he leaned over and kissed her. Unlike the first time, he didn't ease his way in. He thrust in, and before he was fully seated, he began moving in and out with purpose. All Rhi could do was hold on for the ride. And what a ride it was. Ryker making love to her was a beautiful thing, but Ryker taking her hard? It was passionate, possessive, breathtaking. Rhi dug her nails into his shoulders. If she hadn't been watching his face, she would have missed seeing his eyes change to those of his lion's. Ryker's sharp teeth elongated, and when Rhi nodded, Ryker sank them into her flesh.

Her orgasm was instantaneous. The brief pain of his teeth was overpowered by the euphoria that flowed through her body. Rhi's energy flowed through her, meeting with the mating call, answering in a claiming of her own. Ryker roared with his release, rattling the windows. In that moment, Rhi knew she was where she belonged. *Home.*

CHAPTER TWENTY-SEVEN

Ryker

RYKER HAD HIS second chance, and it was magnificent. He never expected the young, virgin runaway he found in the dumpster to turn his world upside down and then put it back to rights, but she had. Rhi was nothing like he expected his mate to be, but she was everything he needed and so much more. She never shied away from when he needed things a little rough in the bedroom. She met him thrust for thrust with a passion he'd never known.

After the morning of their claiming – because Rhi had claimed Ryker in her own way – they had to explain to Elijah there wasn't a wild animal in the house. Ryker had sat the young man down and told him about Gryphons. He had shifted into both his eagle and lion, letting Eli get used to seeing a shifter. It wasn't until they had gone to Lucy's for a family gathering that he'd let the Gryphon loose. He owed it to Rhi to see what he was, and the awe in her eyes was humbling. Rhi loved his lion best though. Loved for him to shift into the large cat so she could run her hands through his long mane.

Ryker had found eight acres not too far away to build a house on, and after going through plans, he and Rhi had decided on the perfect design. The house was exactly as he envisioned it, with two master bedrooms and plenty of other rooms for any children they had together. He couldn't wait for it to be finished so they could all move into it together.

"Uncle Right!" Major yelled, running into the game room where Ryker was shooting a game of pool against Hayden. Ryker grinned at the way Major said his biker name.

Hayden tried to correct him. "It's Ri-yut."

"That's what I said. Right."

Ryker shook his head. "What's up, Little Dude?"

"Look!" Major held up his pointer finger, and Ryker leaned over to inspect it.

"It's a finger," Ryker deadpanned.

Major giggled, but he was turning his finger back and forth. "It's not bleeding." When Ryker saw movement out the corner of his eye, he looked toward the door where Rhi was standing, holding Marshall's hand. Ah, now he got it; Rhi had worked her magic. In more ways than one. Marshall's love for Natalia was matched only by his love for Rhiannon. The two of them spent many hours outside playing in the dirt, talking to plants, and Rhi teaching the younger twin about gardening. Ryker didn't realize there were plenty of things that could be planted in the colder months.

"Can we ride now?" Major asked, bringing Ryker's attention back to the older, more rambunctious brother. Major had taken to motorcycles like Ryker had when he was that age. The kid didn't care how cold it was. He put on layers and settled into the sidecar Hayden had designed for Mayhem's bike.

"You have to bundle up first." Ryker tussled Major's hair, and the boy took off running through the house yelling, "Lolly! Bundle me up!"

"Are you coming with us?" Marshall asked Rhi.

"You don't think I'm going to let you boys have all the fun without me, do you?" Rhi swung their joined hands, and Marshall gave his own giggle. "Go get your coat and gloves, and I'll be right behind you." When Marshall ran off after Major, Rhi strode over to Ryker and raised her lips to him. Kissing was one of Rhi's favorite things to do, and she didn't care who was around to watch. Ryker obliged, keeping it chaste. Riding his bike with a hard-on wasn't fun, and with Rhi snuggled against his back with her arms around his waist, her fingers stroking his abs, it was how he found himself riding more often than not. Rhi had taken to the bike so well she had asked him to teach her how to ride by herself.

Josiah was still in the wind, but Ryker knew with Henry and Julian helping Lucy, they would find the man. Gideon and Lewis had their day in court. Kerrigan and Mac had testified against them both, and the guilty verdict along with long sentences had been enough for the women. For Ryker and Warryck? Not so much. With several Hounds at his back, Ryker had intercepted their transport van when the men were being moved from the courthouse to the prison. Sultan had used his Gryphon voice on the officers so none of them were harmed, but he couldn't say the same for Gideon and Lewis. By the time his and War's lions were finished with the men, they were barely breathing. Ryker and his brother left their bloody, broken bodies in the woods for any scavengers to find. As Gryphons, they were supposed to protect humans. As mates and fathers, they had taken out revenge for the females the two men had dared harm. Ryker went to bed that night with Rhi in his arms and slept better than he had in a long time.

The mercenary work was going well with Quinn being their handler. One night while they were getting ready for bed, Rhi stopped singing mid-song and asked Ryker about being a mercenary. When he asked how she found out, she admitted David had told her about the family's business. Ryker explained everything about their profession, and his Angel just nodded and made him promise to be safe before she went back to singing softly.

With Lucy's help, Rhi, Mac, and Eli had studied hard and passed their GEDs. Mac still wasn't comfortable going to a college campus, so she and Eli had enrolled in online classes. Ryker could see the positive changes in his daughter the longer she and Eli were together, and the more time she spent with the other mates. He had offered for all three of them to see a counselor, and so far, they were all doing well with a professional's help. They were also experiencing the Lazlo family's brand of love, and it was helping to ease the pain for their pasts.

When Lucy wasn't helping the family by using her computer skills, she was holed up with Lucius's journals. She wouldn't tell anyone whether or not she was able to come up with a way to prolong the human mates' lives. She confided in Ryker she didn't want to get their hopes up until she was one-hundred-percent sure it would work. Ryker already had his hopes up. He wanted as many years with his Angel as he could get.

Kerrigan, Lucy, and Natalia had taken Rhi and Mac out for a girls' day of pampering. When Rhi returned home, she looked like a different woman. Her eyebrows had been shaped perfectly, and her long hair had been trimmed and highlights had been added. His mate was simply stunning. Rhi loved getting out of the house. Not to get away from Ryker, but as she explained it, she had been kept away from the real world for far too long, and she had so much to see.

Elizabeth invited her back to visit, and Rhi took her up on her invitation. She got another mother's doting, and she also got to spend time with Manny giving her driving lessons, and after, she and Lawrence spent time in the gardens. His Angel was adapting and growing, and it was beautiful. Another beautiful thing about her was the triple moon goddess she had inked on her arm in honor of her mother. Rhi kept Daisy close with the tattoo in honor of the woman who not only brought her into the world but also taught her some important life lessons that Rhi kept alive in her memory.

When the twins returned to the game room, both were bundled up, ready to ride. "Come on, Rhi Rhi!" Major yelled. When Rhi didn't immediately move to follow, Ryker took a good look at his mate. She had been quiet the last few days, but he hadn't thought anything about it. Now, though, he could tell something was on her mind.

"What's wrong, Angel?"

Rhi turned to Ryker with tears in her eyes, but her smile let him know they were happy tears. "I was going to wait to tell you, but we might need our own sidecar soon."

"Why would we...? Rhi, are you...? Are we...?" Ryker couldn't make the words come. His own eyes were wet as he lifted his beautiful pagan off her feet.

"Yes, we are," she whispered against his mouth.

Ryker spun Rhi around and shouted, "We're having a baby!"

Those in the family who weren't outside getting ready to ride ran into the game room. Hugs and congratulations took a while, but eventually, Ryker was straddling his Harley with Rhi snug against his back. When everyone was ready, he called out, "Hounds, let's ride."

As he led the pack, Ryker couldn't stop smiling. Rhi's stomach would soon get round, and he couldn't wait to feel his little one kicking his back as they rolled down the highway. Gryphon or pagan, Ryker didn't care which the child turned out to be. He couldn't wait to be part of their life together with their momma. Ryker thanked Zeus for putting Rhi in his path, and he thanked her goddess for the rainstorm that made him take the exit that led to finding her. It had been a long time coming – twenty years long – but Ryker Lazlo was no longer a lonely, bitter Hound.

The End

A NOTE FROM THE AUTHOR

This was probably the hardest book for me to write since I started on my journey. Not because of the storyline, but because of all that is happening around the world. I poured a lot of my frustrations and empathy into this book, and I hope the love shined through. I've known from day one it would take a special kind of woman to pull Ryker from his mind, and Rhiannon was just the one to do it.

ABOUT THE AUTHOR

Multi-genre author Faith Gibson began writing in high school, and through the years, penned many stories and poems. As her dreams continued getting crazier than the one before, she decided to keep a dream journal. Many of these nighttime escapades have led to a line, a chapter, or even a complete story.

"Love is love, and there's not enough love in the world." This belief she holds strongly, and it's the prevailing theme in her works, all of which come with a happy ending.

Faith believes her purpose in life is to entertain the masses, even if it's one person at a time. Living just outside of Nashville, Tennessee, with the love of her life and her pit bull pup, when she's not hard at work writing her next adventure, she can often be found playing trivia while enjoying craft beer, listening to live music, or off on an adventure of her own.

Connect with Faith via the following social media sites:

Facebook: https://www.facebook.com/FaithGibsonauthor/

Instagram: https://www.instagram.com/authorfaithgibson

Sign up for her newsletter:

www.faithgibsonauthor.com/Newsletter

www.ingramcontent.com/pod-product-compliance
Lightning Source LLC
Chambersburg PA
CBHW072344020726
47506CB00004B/1000